W9-BEC-865

FOREVER IN MY HEART

FOREVER IN MY HEART

Jo Goodman

KENSINGTON BOOKS

KENSINGTON BOOKS are published by

Kensington Publishing Corp.
850 Third Avenue
New York, NY 10022

ISBN 1-57566-069-5

First Zebra Paperback Printing: July, 1994
First Kensington Hardcover Printing: January, 1996

Printed in the United States of America

For Joseph Allen Dobrzanski—
he'll be a good man someday.

Chapter One

New York City, March 1879

"I don't want a chatterbox."

Lisa Antonia Hall gave the speaker a sidelong glance, her mouth pursed to one side as she considered the request. Patrons of her establishment generally made their preferences known along physical lines. It was not unusual for someone to ask for a brunette with a wasp-like waist and wide hips or a buxom redhead with a trim ankle. The request for a quiet partner was a bit out of the ordinary, yet did not entirely surprise Mrs. Hall. Of necessity she was quick to assess the character of her customers and she had learned to trust her own judgments. The man standing beside her looked as if he had little patience for the niceties.

He had already loosened his black silk tie and let the wrinkled tails drape haphazardly against the snowy whiteness of his shirt. One of his large hands rubbed the back of his neck, lean fingers kneading the corded muscles at his nape. His swallowtail coat was unbuttoned and revealed a dove-gray satin vest beneath. The silver embroidery shimmered as he took a deep breath and slowly exhaled.

It was clear to Lisa that he was attempting to control his impatience. She smiled approvingly, raising her eyes from the flat of his belly to his face. It was an interesting face, one she was sure she would have remembered if she had seen it before. Tension marred his handsome features, a certain grimness pulled his mouth flat and etched tiny lines at the corners, lending him an intensity of expression that was at odds with such male beauty. A muscle worked in his jaw, momentarily filling out the hollows just beneath his cheekbones.

Mrs. Hall's gaze narrowed briefly as she studied the cast of his complexion. His skin was bronzed, touched by gold and copper tones. It occurred to her briefly that he might have some Indian heritage, in which case she would have to ask Samuel to show him the door. It didn't come to that. She decided the bronze had been beaten into him by the sun and wind and she was relieved by her observation. She didn't think Samuel *could* have ejected him.

Lisa Antonia Hall was unembarrassed as her patron returned her steady gaze. His dark eyes, only a shade short of black, were unamused. The arch of his brows, raised the merest fraction, hinted at an air of superiority that might have intimidated someone less brazen. Undeterred, her gaze shifted to his hair. It was thick and lustrous, overlong at the back, and where it brushed his collar it looked like a spill of ink against a clean sheet of paper. She almost reached to brush it back. Instead she fiddled with her bracelets, lining up the clasps while she determined what she was going to do.

Her eyes dropped to the black leather bag at his feet. She wondered what it held. A change of clothes? Medical supplies? Liquor samples? She realized she would be sorely disappointed to discover he was a whiskey drummer. When she looked at him questioningly she was glad he merely stared back and offered no enlightenment.

"I have a girl in mind who will give you a quiet encounter," Mrs. Hall said finally, smiling engagingly. "She's upstairs now. Will you trust my judgment or would you like me to introduce you down here? If she's not what you had in mind we'll find someone who is."

In a fluid motion he picked up the leather bag. "If she's not taken with the sound of her own voice then she's the one I want," he said dryly. He glanced at the wide, carpeted staircase. "Which way at the top of the stairs?"

Mrs. Hall hesitated. The bracelets on her left wrist jangled as she raised her hand slightly. "Left," she said. "Then two doors down on the right. Her name is Mmm—." She stopped as a finger was pressed lightly to her lips.

He shook his head and smiled for the first time. Had it reached his eyes it would have transformed his face. "I don't want to know," he said. "It's just not that personal."

The madam thought she was immune to a man's touch yet she felt the imprint of his finger on her mouth long after he withdrew it. She watched him mount the stairs and knew a surge of hunger. Her heart hammered in her breast. She barely noticed which way he turned when he reached the landing.

He turned the brass handle and swung open the door. Except for an oil lamp flickering on the bedside table the room was dark. Light from the gas jets in the hallway behind him made a silhouette of his imposing figure. He stood on the threshold a moment and surveyed the room, letting his eyes adjust. A movement in the center of the bed caught his eye as the whore sat up and stared back at him. She didn't say a word.

He liked her already.

He stepped inside and dropped his bag on a table just inside the doorway, nudging the door closed with the heel of his shoe. Taking off his evening jacket, he hung it carelessly over the wing of a chair and surveyed the room, giving little more than a cursory glance to the whore or the wide spindle bed.

Several braided area rugs covered the hardwood floor. French doors opened onto a small balcony with a stone balustrade. The mantel held a variety of photographs and figurines, none worthy of a second look. The grate was cold and ashes were scattered across the apron. A scuttle of coals and kindling had been set nearby.

Milk-glass globes covered the unlighted gas jets. The wallpaper was nearly as dark as the woodwork, setting a gloomy tone. On the far side of the bed was a dressing screen. He walked over to it and moved one panel aside, revealing a wardrobe and a hip bath filled with water. He dipped his finger in—the water was not hot any longer but a few degrees better than tepid.

"I've interrupted your bath," he said, turning toward the bed.

She didn't look at him but when she shrugged the wide strap of her nightshift slipped over her shoulder. She lifted it immediately only to have it fall again. This time she let it be, bowing her head slightly so her hair fell forward, shielding her.

His smile was small, his eyes cynical. "Your display of modesty is duly noted. Affecting, but quite unnecessary." He turned away again and pointed to the bath. "Don't let me stop you. I have time." When he didn't sense her moving behind him he added more firmly, "Go on. It won't do you any harm and it may even relax you."

The bed creaked as she crawled across its wide expanse on all fours. He moved to the other side of the room and sat down in the wing chair, stretching his long legs. Leaning his head back, he closed his eyes, missing her furtive, over-the-shoulder glance but sensing it nonetheless.

"I'm not going to join you," he said tiredly. He heard her move quickly, her bare feet padding lightly on the area rug. She bumped into the screen before she moved behind it. His eyelids raised a fraction and he watched her shadowed movements through thick, dark lashes. Her nightshift was placed over the top of the dressing screen. The wardrobe opened and he heard her sifting through the drawers. He wondered what she was looking for then he saw her pause and pin up her hair. A moment later water lapped gently against the sides of the hip bath as she stepped inside. He closed his eyes again and wished that he had not drunk quite so much.

"I was told you wouldn't talk much," he said, "but I didn't expect complete silence." No comment was forthcoming. "Suits me." He unbuttoned his vest and checked his pocket watch. The realization that it was a few minutes shy of midnight gave rise to a soft groan. It was not his usual manner to drink before dinner or during dinner or to have more than a shot sometime after dinner. He could only guess how badly he was going to feel in the morning and yet he acknowledged that he was not numb enough now.

Behind the screen the water stirred again. He noticed the towel at the foot of the bed. Sighing, he pushed himself out of the wing chair and scooped it up. Skirting the screen, he dangled it in front of the whore.

"Fetching," he drawled. His bored tone gave lie to the single word. His eyes were flat, almost uninterested, as they skimmed her. Splashing had dampened the curling ends of her hair and tendrils clung flatly against her neck and temples. Droplets beaded on her naked shoulders and her fine-boned and fragile features were shiny with mist. He was blocking his own light from the oil lamp and he stepped aside, watching her sink a little lower in the bath. Only the line of her collarbones was visible above its dark, mirror-like surface.

"There's no reason to act like a shy maiden in front of me," he said. "This is professional, not personal." He paused, watching her closely. "Isn't it?"

She blinked, returned his stare, then nodded slowly.

He dropped the towel, which she managed to catch in one hand before it hit the water.

"Red," he said.

"Hmmm?" Grimacing, she touched her throat lightly with her fingertips. "Pardon?" she said. This time she felt the vibration of her voice against the pads of her fingers.

"Your hair's red. There's not much light in here. I wasn't sure." He wasn't a man given to impulse but it was exactly what moved him now. He hunkered down beside the bath. He thought for a moment that she might flinch, then wondered why the notion would even cross his mind. Still, he found himself asking, "May I?"

She looked at his raised hand, the fingertips just inches from her ear, and nodded.

The back of his fingers touched her cheek and rested there briefly. He lifted a tendril. It was soft and silky and slightly damp. He frowned as he noticed faint bruises along her throat. He touched one lightly. "You've been treated roughly this evening."

She nodded.

"Good thing I'm here then. We'll see what we can do about that." Her skin was flushed. "You're warm," he said. "Out of the bath— now." He stood and turned away. There was hurried movement behind him, water splashing, and the sounds of the towel being drawn briskly against her skin. He slipped off his vest and laid it next to his evening jacket. When she came into his line of vision again she was wearing her white cotton nightshift. He looked down at her bare feet and the trim ankles. "You'd better get back into bed. Even on the rug, the floor's cold. Do you want me to light a fire?"

Crawling back into bed, she shook her head.

His low laughter was deep and faintly dangerous as she pulled the thick down comforter around her shoulders. "Just the same," he said, "I think I'll do it." He had already decided he didn't want a quick poke under the covers. He fully intended to enjoy himself and that meant enjoying the whore's body with his eyes as well as his hands. His decision vaguely surprised him. Thirty minutes ago a quick poke was all he had in mind. He could even admit that he wanted to hear her voice again. Her husky timbre was like a shot of good whiskey, something to be savored.

It took him a few minutes to get a fire started. Standing, he brushed his hands on his trousers. The streaks of gray ash on his black evening wear made him go to the porcelain basin by the bed and wash his hands. "It wouldn't do to leave fingerprints, would it?"

Her smile was tentative.

"I think you could use a drink."

The smile faded as her lips parted in surprise.

"Medicinal purposes only," he said encouragingly. He saw her immediate acceptance in the relaxation of her shoulders. Another quick look around the room convinced him he hadn't missed a liquor cabinet on his earlier survey. He shrugged. "Good thing I've come prepared." He crossed the room to his black bag. Opening it up, he retrieved a quarter-full bottle of Scotch nestled among stacks of bound bills. He turned, showing her the bottle. "Glasses?"

She shook her head.

"Then you'll have to tipple right out of the bottle." He shut the bag, left it on the table, and carried the bottle to the bed. Sitting down on the edge, he handed it to her. When she hesitated he said, "It will make you feel better, I promise." He could have added that it had already done wonders for him.

She uncapped the bottle and raised it slowly to her lips. When she didn't drink immediately he put his fingertips under the bottom and tipped it. She took a large swallow, paused, and noting the amused challenge in his eyes, took another.

"That's better," he said. He found himself grinning as she made a face. "Obviously you have no appreciation for good Scotch."

The liquor eased the tightness in her throat but she still spoke in a husky whisper. "I don't drink much."

"I don't either—much." He offered her another swallow which she accepted with hardly any prompting. He watched her for another reaction and when none came he raised both brows. "It seems to agree with you rather quickly." He took the bottle, put it on the bedside table, and touched her face again with the back of his fingers. His thumb traced the arch of her cheekbone. "But then that's what it's supposed to do. You're not so flushed." She was still warm to the touch, almost unnaturally so, but the color in her face was no longer mottled. The hint of rose spread evenly over her skin, highlighted by the light from the oil lamp. The shape of the face was oval, the eyes wide, just a fraction too large for the elfin face. She wasn't a classic beauty by any means but she was something more than he had expected to find in any New York brothel, even an expensive one like Mrs. Hall's. He nearly spoke his mind but thought better of it. It would have been the worst kind of compliment, one she wouldn't have appreciated.

He let his hand drift over her cheek. His knuckle touched her mouth. Her lips were full. His light touch made them part. The Scotch had made them moist. His darkening eyes were fastened on her mouth. "Show me your tongue," he said lowly.

She opened her mouth and stuck out her tongue a full inch and a half. "Aaaaahhhh."

He was so surprised that he burst out laughing. His hand dropped away from her face. "That wasn't quite what I had in mind but it's a very pretty tongue. Very pink. Nice teeth, too. And you've kept your tonsils." He nudged her jaw. "You can close now. I've seen quite enough. Another drink is definitely in order." He took a long pull on the bottle himself and saw out of the corner of his eye that she had expected him to give the bottle back to her. He obliged and let her finish it. "For someone who doesn't drink much, you've developed quite a taste for it."

She offered him a crooked, somewhat sleepy smile. "I think I like good Scotch," she said. "As medicine, of course."

"Of course," he agreed dryly. He made himself more comfortable, swinging his legs onto the mattress and leaning back against the walnut headboard. He took one of the loose pillows and stuffed it behind the small of his back. "Much better," he said, satisfied. He looked askance at her. During his adjustments she had edged from the center to the far side of the bed. "There was no need for you to move. I'm not going to attack you, but I can hardly reach you if you remain over there." He saw her hesitate, mulling his words. Finally she seemed to see the sense of what he was saying and scooted toward him. He fluffed a goosedown pillow and slipped it behind her back. When she turned on her side toward him her knees bumped his. The strap of her nightshift slid over her left shoulder again.

He noticed that when she attempted to pull it up her movements were slow and awkward, almost disjointed. The liquor had swiftly taken its toll. He hadn't considered that she may have been drinking earlier as he had. Watching her now it seemed likely. Under his breath he said, "We're a fine pair."

She frowned, looking at him oddly, but made no comment.

He leaned back, exposing the strong line of his throat, and closed his eyes. "I can't remember when I've had a longer day," he said, sighing.

She looked at the gilded clock on the mantel. "New day."

"I suppose it is. And it's starting just the same way." In bed with a whore. His mouth curled to one side as he considered this turn of events in a new light. At least *this* whore wasn't a relation. He should be thankful for that. "God, I'm tired."

"Rest," she said softly.

He shook his head but his eyes didn't open. "It's a nice offer," he said, "but not the reason I came here. I should see to you. You've obviously been waiting."

"I didn't mind," she said with effort. "Mrs. Hall made me comfortable."

He heard the faint slur in her words, the singsong cadence that hinted at the effects of the liquor. He wondered at her comfort. The room was relatively spartan compared to others he had seen. "This isn't much," he observed.

She paused, then said with quiet conviction. "My experience says it's better than the streets."

He opened his eyes and looked at her. "I suppose it is."

She held his gaze for a long moment before breaking away.

"You're flushed again," he said. He laid his hand lightly on her bare shoulder. His thumb brushed the pulse in her throat. "Your heart's racing."

She nodded guilelessly.

"Why don't you drop that cover a little and let me have a look."

She hesitated.

He nudged the blanket a fraction lower with the heel of his hand. "How am I supposed to examine you if I can't see you?"

She considered this.

He added, "You have some expectations, I assume."

"Not many."

It was said so matter-of-factly, he gave a shout of laughter. "Oh, you *have* been treated poorly! That doesn't speak well for men like myself." Brooking no argument, he pushed the comforter aside. His fingers slid along the deeply-cut neckline of her nightshift and rested lightly on the uppermost button. He raised his dark brows in a silent question.

She laid a hand over his and shook her head. "I'll do it."

The husky catch in her voice intrigued him. He let the sound of it wash over him as he watched her fingers fiddle with the top button. "You're not a chatterbox."

She wasn't looking at him. Her concentration on the button was complete. "No," she said quietly. "I'm not."

"Another," he said.

She glanced at him, her eyes shaded by thick lashes.

He pointed to her hand. "Another button, please."

Her fingers were clumsy but she managed to slip the button through its hole. The neckline of her nightshift parted as her hands dropped away, revealing the curves of her breasts.

Her skin looked very smooth, he thought, and soft. The back of his fingers touched her breast. "That flush of yours starts about here," he said.

She said nothing, simply watched his hand.

Her heart was thudding against his fingertips. He smiled. "There's nothing wrong with your heart." He cupped the underside of her breast and her heartbeat, rather than her flesh, seemed to fill the palm of his hand. He opened another button. "Come closer," he said. When she didn't move immediately his hands slipped around her rib cage to urge her nearer. The other strap of her nightshift fell. No matter where he touched her he could feel her heart thudding.

He laid one hand on her back near her shoulder blade. Her breathing was light and shallow. He leaned forward, his mouth near her ear. "Take a deep breath," he said. "That's it. Hold it." His hand rubbed her back. "Let it out slowly." Her heart steadied; her breathing slowed. "Better," he said. "For a moment there I thought you might faint."

"So did I," she said gravely. "I'm a little dizzy."

He released her. "Why don't you lie down?"

She didn't hesitate. "All right." Shifting on the bed, she brought the pillow under her head. She started to close her nightdress but he stopped her. Except for the exposed outer curves of her breasts she was still modestly covered. The glimpse of her skin was tantalizing.

He savored the thought of pushing aside the material and taking her nipple in his mouth.

"I don't have much success when it comes to patience," he said, touching her cheek again. Her dark green eyes were searching his face, her smile gentle and encouraging.

"I think you're doing fine," she said.

She was possibly the most artlessly provocative woman he had ever encountered. He surprised himself again by not merely enjoying it, but savoring it. "Why, thank you," he said. "It's good of you to encourage me."

Her smile deepened as her eyelashes lowered sleepily. "I hope to do so fine one day."

"So you admit you have something to learn?"

Her short, emphatic nod was interrupted by an abrupt yawn. She stretched a little, slipping one arm under the pillow as she turned on her side.

He couldn't help notice her movement had completely uncovered one breast. Her nipple was puckered, the coral tip a hard bud. He was amazed to find himself swallowing hard, like a schoolboy confronted with his first naughty French postcard. "So you're willing to learn a thing or two from me?"

"I'd like that very much."

Once again her grave sincerity made him chuckle. "You're something of a surprise," he said. "Not what I expected when I walked in here this evening."

She snuggled deeper into the pillow. "Hmmm."

One of his brows kicked up. "Are you going to fall asleep?" The languid shake of her head was not encouraging. He was regretting sharing his liquor with her. In a fluid motion he slid out of bed and began stripping off his clothes. His pristine white shirt joined the jacket and vest on the wing chair. He pushed his shoes near the apron of the fireplace and tossed his stockings next to them. His trousers and drawers were carelessly thrown over the arm of the chair. In spite of his haste, when he reached the bed he realized he hadn't been fast enough.

His lady of the evening was as unaroused as he was aroused. He was tired enough to be philosophical about it. He'd remember this the next time he asked for a whore who didn't talk much. Apparently she was not prepared to use her mouth for anything else either.

He raised the comforter and sheet and slipped in beside her, turning her on her side away from him so her sleek back and bottom was nestled against his chest and groin. His hand sought out the opening of her nightshift and he laid his palm in the valley of her breasts. His chin rested close to the crown of her head and the damp fragrance of her hair teased his senses.

He slept.

When he awoke she was all over him. The pins in her hair had disappeared and the long fall of dark red spilled over his shoulder and chest. Her mouth was tasting his skin just above his nipple. The damp edge of her tongue licked at the sweet and salty flesh. He drew in a shaky breath as one of her hands slid down his abdomen. Lower. Lower still. And cupped his arousal.

He groaned. Her hand stilled. He laid his fingers over hers and encouraged her exploration, her stroking. It wasn't long before it wasn't enough.

Her legs tangled with his as he twisted and rolled her onto her back. His knee separated her thighs. He felt the vibration of her whimper against his skin, then the full outline of her lips on his. Her mouth was hard and hungry. The edge of her tongue teased him. She moved restlessly, searching, stretching. He could feel the outline of her breasts, the exquisite, tender abrading of her nipples on his flesh as she pressed the length of her body to him.

One of her hands slid along the back of his neck. Her fingers sifted through the thick, dark strands at his nape. A shiver tore along his spine as her nail lightly curved along the outer edge of his ear. He raised his head and saw the faint outline of her smile, the sleepy cat-green eyes, and recognized the reflection of his own lust.

She arched, turning her head at the exact moment his mouth would have fused with hers. His lips scraped her cheek, her jaw line, then finally the curve of her neck. Her hands stroked his back and learned the ridges of hard, bunched muscle as he moved over her.

His skin retracted in anticipation of her touch. He wanted her hands everywhere, doing everything; he told her so, whispering against her ear in a voice so husky in its need that he hardly knew it as his own. The palms of her hands slid along his shoulders, down his arms, passing over his ribs and around to the small of his back.

She paused at the base of his spine, teasing him with touches that chased sensation all the way to his toes. She clutched his buttocks, pressing his rock-hard need solidly to her. She ground against him, delivering the same message with her mouth, her tongue circling his, pushing, probing.

He didn't know if anyone had ever wanted him the way this woman did.

Then he remembered he was paying her.

She was a whore.

Suddenly, surprisingly, he wished it were different.

He moved himself away from her, adjusting his position, smiling when she reached for him blindly. He brushed her hand aside as he knelt between her legs. He pushed back her raised knees and raised her buttocks and when she reached for him again he plunged into her.

She cried out.

The sound of it made him want something else. He wished it were his name he heard and not just a wild, animal cry. He withdrew, thrust again. She was tight. And hot. She surrounded him, held him. She reached for his forearms, grasped him, ran her palms over his muscles. She arched. He was deep inside her. Her nails made crescents on his skin. His fingertips pressed whitely against her flesh.

He felt her accept his rhythm, the force of his thrusts, and knew she was caught in the same spiral of passion as he. He watched her head move from side to side, her mouth parted, her throat exposed. There was a flush to her breasts and a sheen of perspiration that made her skin glow in the lamplight.

There was a catch in her voice as she sipped the air. His own breathing was harsh. He felt tension as a hot, licking flame just beneath the surface of his skin. His muscles were pulled taut, need driving him into her again and again.

It was a fierce, selfish pleasure that overtook him in the end. He strained against her as he climaxed. Tension unfolded, dissolved. He spilled into her, unable to call back his moan as he collapsed against her.

Almost immediately he was asleep.

* * *

Lisa Antonia Hall fingered the string of pearls at her neck like worry beads. "I had no idea it would take you this long to get here," she told the man in front of her. "What's the good of keeping you on retainer if I can't depend on you?"

Morrison James dropped his black leather bag on the carpet and shrugged out of his coat. He draped it over the back of a chair in Mrs. Hall's private apartment and rubbed the back of his neck wearily. His thick black hair, liberally threaded with silver at the temples, was ruffled in some places, flat in others. His broad face still bore the imprint of a pillow wrinkle on one cheek and his complexion was ruddy from sleep. His spectacles were slightly askew on the bridge of his nose.

"A retainer is what you pay your lawyer, Lisa," he said. "And protection money is what you pay the cops. I can't recall the last time you paid for my services."

She stopped playing with her pearls and tapped his chest with her index finger. Her smile was spun sugar. "That's because you take it out in trade."

The doctor gently removed her hand and smoothed the front of his nightshirt which was haphazardly tucked into his trousers. He straightened his suspenders before he thrust his hands in his pockets and rocked forward on the balls of his feet. "Be glad I do. I'd make you pay me the earth otherwise."

Since he usually kept one of her most expensive girls busy for most of the night, Mrs. Hall thought his price was already too high. But good medical care was hard to come by so she was generally philo-sophical about the trade-off. "Well, you can have your pick tonight."

"Slow evening?"

"For most of the girls. Not for me. I've had my hands full."

He didn't want to hear the story. He yawned and readjusted his glasses. "Why did you send someone around to my house?" he asked. "It's not Beth again?"

She waved her hand impatiently. Her bracelets jangled. "No, not Beth. Not any of my girls actually, though come to think of it, you could take a look at Jane while you're here. I think she's sickening for something."

"Lisa," he said, drawing out her name in bored accents. His eyes fell on the decanter of whiskey on her sideboard. "May I?"

"Help yourself."

Morrison poured himself a drink, tossed it back, and poured another. He leaned against the sideboard and rolled the shot glass between his palms. "It's long gone midnight, Lisa, and I'd only just climbed into bed when your man came around."

She frowned. "I sent him out hours ago."

"I was in surgery at the hospital. He missed me there." He sipped his drink. "I've had a busy night myself, so what can I do for you?"

Lisa dropped into an overstuffed chair. "You've heard me speak of Harlan Porter?"

"The pimp?"

She nodded. "The very same."

Morrison James was interested in spite of himself. In the dozen years he had been coming to Mrs. Hall's he couldn't remember ever finding it dull. He sighed. Obviously it wasn't for an emergency that he had been summoned this evening. Whatever her need, she was also hiring his discretion. "You'd better tell me the whole of it," he said, resigned and curious.

She smiled warmly. "Of course I will . . ."

He felt himself swell and grow hard. She was curved against his body. His arm was around her waist, his palm cupping the underside of her breast. He eased himself into her. She pushed at him and accommodated his entry. Her bottom slapped his groin. He buried his mouth against her neck, in her hair. He tasted her skin, let the fragrance of her flesh fill his nostrils. Her breasts filled his hands. Her thighs were warm. She turned her head and sought his lips. Her mouth was hot.

She was burning from the inside out.

"That's it," he whispered with husky urgency. "Move with me." When she did he felt as if he owned the fire. "God, you're sweet . . . so sweet." She was taking all of him and the sensation was almost unbearably intense, pleasure running the border with pain.

His hand slipped between her thighs and his fingers probed. He stroked, teased. He heard the sleepy cadence of her breathing give way to something more rapid, more frenzied. Hardly knowing the words he was saying he encouraged her, holding himself back until he felt the rise of pleasure in her.

"Please," she said. Only that, just *please*. But she said it again. And again.

When she shuddered and melted against him there was no longer a reason to keep any part of himself from her. He gave her back the heat and fire and shared the strength of his passion. This time when they were spent she turned in his arms and promptly fell asleep.

The oil lamp was a mere thread of light now. It edged her profile. He studied her face, the delicate features that were not strictly beautiful but commanded attention nonetheless, the strands of red hair gilded with copper and gold, the smooth complexion that absorbed the wash of lamplight. He wondered that he bothered looking at all, wondered that he seemed intent on making a memory when he had first thought of using her only to forget.

He should go, he thought. He hadn't planned on spending the night in the brothel. But she was fastened to him like a burr on a blanket and detaching her didn't appeal to him at the moment. He'd leave something generous for her and slip away before morning. At thirty years of age he didn't relish sneaking into his father's home in the middle of the night. This way he could join everyone at the breakfast table.

He fell asleep, a cynic's smile curving his mouth as he thought what they would think of him carrying in the morning paper in his evening clothes.

"So what happened to Harlan?" Dr. James asked as Lisa drew her story to a close.

"Beth chased him off, waving a broom."

"Good for Beth," he said approvingly. "And the girl?"

"She's upstairs. I put her in a room across the hall from Beth. She could barely talk, of course, though whether from fright, illness, or some harm Harlan did to her I can't say. That's why I sent Huggins around for you. She was warm to the touch and I didn't think some laudanum would come amiss."

"How much?"

She shrugged. "The usual amount, I suppose. You know I don't measure the stuff."

"I know you tend to use a heavy hand spooning it out."

"At least I had the sense to remove the liquor from the room." She chuckled. "Remember how wild-eyed Beth was from mixing the two?"

"I remember she complained about a sore head for three days." He set down his drink. "I think I better see your orphan in the storm now," he said. "Is she someone you might want for the house?"

"I'd want her, but I don't think she's interested. She could have done herself well enough by staying with Harlan and she made it clear she wanted no part of him." Lisa shook her head, fingering her pearls again. "I'm more than a little afraid she's wandered into these streets by mistake."

"So," he said slowly, "you've finally come to the point of my visit. You're concerned that taking her in could have repercussions."

"Exactly so. But credit my conscience a little. I was more concerned about *not* taking her in."

He nodded. "You know you don't have to worry that I'll say anything about tonight . . . to anyone." He patted Lisa's shoulder. "She may not be anybody anyway."

Lisa looked up at him and smiled uneasily. "You don't know how much I hope that's true."

Morrison James picked up his leather bag. "You said you put her in Beth's room?"

"No. Across the hall." She paused, watching him frown as he tried to place the bedchamber. "Up the stairs. Turn . . ." She stopped, looked at the bracelets on her left wrist. "Turn left." The madam's grin was self-depreciating. "Honestly, one would think at my age I'd know right from left. Left at the landing," she repeated. "Then the second door on your right." Her grin faded slowly. Her eyes were thoughtful a moment, then worried, then frantic. She stood suddenly and clutched her necklace in lieu of clutching her heart.

"What is it?" the doctor asked. "Lisa? What's wrong? You look nearly apoplectic."

"I think I may have told him the wrong room!"

"Who?"

"I meant for him to have Megan." Her eyes darted around the room as she considered the implications of her mistake. "Oh God, what if—"

"Who?" Morrison James asked again. "Lisa, you really must explain yourself if I'm to be of any help."

Mrs. Hall headed toward the door, certain she would be followed.

She twisted the handle and stepped into the hallway, turning immediately for the private back stairs leading to the second floor. "I don't know his name, not that it really matters," she said as she hurried along. "I think he's been here before but I didn't deal with him. He was a cold son of a bitch. I wondered if we should even accommodate him." She raised her skirts and quickly took the steps, pausing just a moment at the top to catch her breath before she charged down the hall. "I should have shown him to the room," she said, fretting. "What if he found the girl and . . ." She couldn't finish her sentence. She looked helplessly at her long-time friend. "What if there's trouble?"

Morrison James set his hand on the madam's shoulder, stopping her in her tracks. "Listen to me, Lisa, you're working yourself up for no good reason. You may not have given the wrong directions. He may have found Megan. And if the worst has happened, how bad is it really? It's quite possible that the girl has no one to come to her defense should the incident become public. You've weathered greater storms than this."

Mrs. Hall ducked away from the doctor's shoulder and hammered on Megan's door. "I just have a feeling," she said. "And it's the kind of feeling I've learned to trust." She stepped back as the door was opened by a young woman with rumpled, honey-blond hair and a sleepy, disgruntled smile.

"Is he in there with you?" Lisa asked. She had to know the worst before she went into the other room. She had to be prepared.

Megan blinked in surprise. "No one's with me." Her round face screwed up comically as she tried to stifle a yawn. When she gave in to it her jaw cracked. "Excuse me, but I've been sleeping hard. My last customer put me through the paces."

"A tall man?" asked Lisa. "Dark hair? Black eyes?"

Megan shook her head, leaning against the door jamb. "Don't you remember? You set me up with Billy Davis."

Morrison James put his hand to his forehead and rubbed his temple. "You had the mayor's right-hand man in here this evening?" he asked. "The same Billy Davis who is threatening to close down every brothel in the city?"

Mrs. Hall and Megan both looked at him as if they couldn't understand his amazement. "A man with his particular needs has to go somewhere," said Lisa philosophically. To Megan she added,

"He was in here hours ago. Well before midnight. You haven't had anyone else?"

"No."

The madam's heart sank. Still, she had the presence of mind to show concern for one of her favorite girls. "Billy didn't hurt you, did he?"

She shrugged. "No more than usual. Nothing I can't handle."

Mrs. Hall frowned. "Morrison will see you as soon as he's finished with our unexpected guest."

"You mean Harlan's victim?"

The madam nodded. "Come on, Morrison, we may as well go in there now. I think my worst fears have been realized."

"Now, Lisa," he said trying to calm her. "You don't know—" He stopped when she shot him a warning glance. They hurried down the hall. This time when they reached the door Mrs. Hall didn't bother knocking. She turned the handle and stepped into the room. Morrison followed while Megan hovered on the threshold.

The room was too dark to see much of anything at first glance. The gaslight from the hallway helped a little. It was the only reason Lisa didn't shut Megan out.

The madam marched over to the bed and began plucking at the rumpled mound of blankets, tossing them on the floor until she uncovered a tousled head of black hair. "Where is she?" she demanded by way of a wake-up call.

He opened one eye and groaned. His head throbbed. He shut the eye, hoping it would help. It didn't. A strident voice was repeating: *Where is she? Where is she? Where is she?*

Morrison James pointed to the empty bottle of Scotch lying on its side on the floor. "I thought you removed the liquor."

"I did," Lisa said. She followed the line of his pointing finger. "I *did*," she repeated, picking up the bottle. "He must have had this." She held it over the man in the bed, shaking it threateningly. "Did you give her any of this?"

Any of this? Any of this? He could no longer determine if the questions were being repeated or if he was hearing echoes. He opened a single eye again and managed to grab the sheet that was about to be torn from his naked back. "Do you mind?" he asked coldly.

Lisa dropped the sheet. She also put the bottle back. "What happened to her?"

He supposed the question was being put to him. It was difficult to tell, what with the madam's eyes darting nervously around the room and the fact that there was an audience. He sat up slowly, pulling the sheet over his lap, and leaned against the headboard. He cast a bleary eye in the direction of the clock on the mantel. It looked to be nearly three-thirty. He rubbed his eyes with a thumb and forefinger. "What is it you want to know?" he asked tiredly.

"The girl who was in here, what's become of her?"

He stopped rubbing and greeted the madam with a caustic glance. "How would I know?" He lifted one corner of the sheet and made a pretense of searching under it. "No, not there. Have you checked the privy? The kitchen? What about another room? Surely I'm not the only man she's entertained tonight."

Lisa reached in the drawer on the bedside table and found a match. She struck it and lighted the oil lamp, turning up the wick for a fuller flame. Replacing the glass globe, she held up the lamp and pointed to the dark stain he had uncovered when he rearranged the top sheet. "The young lady you were with this evening isn't entertaining anyone else," she said in icy tones that were every bit a match for his. "More to the point, she's *never* entertained anyone else. And it's unlikely she found much in the way of entertainment with you!"

The words were as effective as a cold shower or a pot of black coffee. He was wide awake. He stared at the dried blood spotting the bottom sheet and felt himself paling. "What the hell's going on here?" he asked, pushing himself out of bed. He dragged the sheet with him, hitched it around his waist, and cinched it. He glared at the madam, then at the man at the foot of the bed, then finally at the woman in the doorway. "I didn't ask for a damned virgin!"

"Oh, I believe you, honey," Megan said. "And if you'd come to the right room, you wouldn't have gotten one."

"Right room? What do you mean?" His brows drew together as he glowered at Lisa Hall. "What does she mean? You told me this was the room. Left at the top of the stairs. Second door on the right."

Lisa's fingers were working nervously on her pearls. She sat down heavily on the bed. "This is awful! Horrible! Do you have any idea what you've done?"

His dark brows rose. "Any idea what I've done?" He paused, his upper lip curling cynically. His black eyes were cold. "If this is a scam, then you've picked the wrong john. I didn't ask to initiate one of your angels and I'm not going to pay just because she's fallen hard."

Morrison set his bag on the bed and spoke up in Lisa's defense. "No one is trying to take your money. There's been a mistake, that's all. Megan, check the wardrobe. Perhaps she hasn't left." As Megan went to do his bidding, Morrison's eyes alighted on the bottle of Scotch. "I'm Dr. James. Mrs. Hall asked me to come by to see the girl you were with. She . . . umm, she wasn't well. You didn't answer Lisa's question. Did the girl drink some of that?"

"Most of it."

Lisa's soft groan was smothered by Megan's announcement that the wardrobe was empty.

"What's going on here?" he demanded, taking the offensive. His eyes fell on the doctor's bag and he remembered his own black leather satchel. He looked around for it, first on the table just inside the door, and when it wasn't there, he scanned other parts of the room. "Where is it?" he demanded. When the others merely looked at him blankly, he repeated the question more harshly. "I had a bag with me. Almost exactly like the doctor's. What the hell have you done with it?"

"I haven't touched it," Mrs. Hall said. "None of us has."

"What did you tell the girl to do with it?"

"You're mistaken," Morrison said. "If the bag's gone, Lisa didn't have anything to do with it. This is a respectable house."

"It's a *brothel.*"

"It's an honest one," Megan said, offended by the stranger's arrogance.

"Find my bag and I'll apologize," he said with dry sarcasm. Unconcerned with modesty, he dropped the sheet and pulled on his drawers and trousers.

Megan sighed. "I wish you *had* found the right room."

He merely grunted, unmoved by the flattery. He slipped on his evening shirt and tucked in the tails, snapping his suspenders in place. Sitting in the wing chair he put on his stockings and shoes.

Morrison James was eyeing the cut and style of the clothes. Expensive. Perhaps he could be reasoned with. "Look, it's not what you think it is. Even so, you don't want your name in the papers, do you? Be reasonable and let us handle it."

He stopped in the middle of fastening his cufflinks and gave the doctor the edge of his hard, penetrating stare. "That's how it works, doesn't it? The whores steal from their customers and you count on us being too scared or embarrassed to report it." He finished with the cufflink and smoothed the pristine sleeve over his forearm, then adjusted it at the wrist. "Do I appear to be frightened?" he asked. "Embarrassed?" Neither of his questions garnered a reply. He noted his audience was looking distinctly uncomfortable. "Your whore—and you'll understand if I doubt she was the innocent she's being made out to be—was unexpectedly good, but she was not worth twelve thousand dollars."

Mrs. Hall's necklace snapped and pearls skittered across the floor.

Morrison James dropped onto the bed in surprise.

Megan's lower jaw simply fell open.

"You shouldn't be working here," he told them. "There's a play at Wallack's Theatre right now that would benefit from your talents." He slipped on his jacket, ran a hand through his hair, and turned on his heel. At the door he stopped. "I don't care if you find the girl, but you damn well better find my bag."

Mrs. Hall gathered her wits as he was stepping into the hallway. "Wait! I don't know where to reach you."

"I know how to find you."

"But your name . . . it would . . . that is . . ."

His narrow smile was dangerous. "Holiday. Connor Holiday." He was satisfied to see it had an impact. As he was closing the door he heard the doctor sigh, "You've stepped into it this time, Lisa."

Chapter Two

The same evening, a different view

She was lost. If someone had told her to accomplish just that task she would have said it was impossible. She had grown up in the city and considered herself more than passingly acquainted with Manhattan's particular maze of avenues and alleys, boulevards and backyards. It was true that she didn't walk everywhere but she believed herself to be observant, and she had often noted buildings and businesses as landmarks when she traveled in a hansom cab or in the family carriage. It was her nature to pay attention to things and she took some pride in it.

Which was why it was so difficult to accept that she was lost. Nothing was familiar. The houses were clapboarded, built nearly on top of one another, leaning in, without any yard or greenery or fence to distinguish them. Any single row, she noticed, seemed to sag in the middle. At night it was difficult to know their state of repair but she suspected there were roofs in need of shingles and windows in need of glazing. A number of houses had signs at the front door announcing rooms for rent; others were actually saloons or dance halls. Several, she saw, had red glass globes covering their window lamps. She was not so naive that she didn't know what they signified.

It was a source of some amazement to her that an evening that had begun innocently at the library was coming to a close in Manhattan's seediest red light district.

Looking around, trying to gauge the distance of the waterfront and get her bearings, she acknowledged that she wasn't prepared to take full responsibility for her predicament. She had been cajoled, harassed, and finally dared to take part in a scavenger hunt and then abandoned when her partner found favor with another. Her sister had a lot to answer for.

She stepped back into the shadows as a door to one of the dance halls was flung open and a boisterous group of sailors staggered arm in arm into the street. Their ribald humor brought a blush to her cheeks. She was pressed flatly against the darkened porch alcove of a rooming house with no retreat available. She closed her eyes and prayed they would pass without noticing her, or if they noticed, without accosting her.

She dared to peek as their voices faded . . . and found herself staring into a pair of lightly colored, curious eyes. The lopsided smile spread and widened and then he called to his friends, "Come see what I've found!"

She tried to duck out of the way but the sailor's reflexes were not as slowed by drink as she hoped they might be. He thrust out his arms, one on either side of her shoulders, and braced himself comfortably against the alcove.

He glanced over his shoulder, looking for his friends, then back at his captive, a simple grin still plastered on his face. "It appears they didn't hear or they're not interested," he said. He blinked widely, paused, then looked her over from head to toe. "Must be they didn't hear. They couldn't *not* be interested. You're something to look at. Not the usual sort for Canal Street."

She sighed. At least she knew where she was now, but it was not as promising a sign as she hoped. She was not likely to be mistaken for a woman of gentle upbringing on Canal Street, not with all those red lights winking at her from the porch stoops and windows. She realized she should not be so accepting of her circumstances, certainly not with the drunken sailor leering stupidly in her direction, but her options were strictly limited. She wasn't strong enough to fight him off and only just on the mend after three miserable days in bed with a sore throat and laryngitis, she could hardly raise a whisper, let alone a scream. That left brazening it out.

She, a young woman of twenty-three years, well known for not having a brazen bone in her body, stared boldly back at the sailor.

"You have a place near here?" asked the sailor, raising his eyebrows hopefully.

She shook her head.

The brows lowered as he frowned. "Can't take you back to the ship."

She was relieved. It seemed they were without alternatives. He would have to let her go. She started to push his restraining arm aside.

"Not so fast." He was still frowning, thinking furiously. "There's the alley."

That was a horrifying thought. "No," she said. Her voice was not much above a whisper, husky with the last remnants of her cold, and more invitation than refusal. "Not the alley."

"Then right here."

Equally horrifying. Her eyes widened as the sailor's calloused hands dropped inside her coat to grab her waist. Before she could move he was taking a step toward her and lifting her against the wall of the alcove. She pushed at his shoulders but it was a futile gesture. Her feet were no longer touching the stoop. "It's not free, you know," she said.

She was gratified to see that gave the sailor pause. He dropped her. The moment he thrust his hands into his pockets to find his money she tore past him. Raising her skirts, she ran down the sidewalk and into the street, dodging two draft horses and a beer wagon that had just turned the corner. Running blindly, her sense of direction deserting her again, she darted in a narrow passageway between two houses to catch her breath.

Her chest hurt as she gulped air. She remembered her mother's voice just that morning telling her she should spend another day indoors, that even a trip to the library was not advisable. But she had to study. She may not have been particularly brazen, but she, like every other member of her family, was headstrong. Her mother's words went unheeded at the breakfast table only to echo mockingly now.

Her heart was pounding so loudly that she didn't hear the sailor's approach until the second before she was caught in his embrace.

"Why'd you run?" he asked.

She recoiled from the sour beer smell of her assailant. She turned her head aside and her stomach turned over as she felt his mouth on her neck. Having no real faith that it would work now any better than it had earlier, she pushed hard at the sailor's shoulders. She imagined the surprise on his face mirrored hers as he was flung aside.

She only had eyes for her rescuer while the sailor dropped to his knees, groaned, then scrambled awkwardly away.

The stranger doffed his hat and made a sweeping bow. "Your servant," he said.

The gesture was grand, unnecessary but appreciated. She wondered where he had come from. "Thank you," she said softly.

"May I?" he asked, offering his elbow and an escort out of the alley.

She hesitated, watching him warily.

Her rescuer understood. "It's natural that your experience has made you cautious, but I assure you, we're not all as loutish as your sailor."

"He wasn't my sailor," she said. She swallowed with difficulty; the back of her throat felt raw.

"You're not feeling well."

She was pleasantly surprised by his observation. Really, she thought, there was nothing particularly threatening about her rescuer's countenance or demeanor. He was a tall man with a narrow face and easy smile. His manner demonstrated concern as he bent solicitously toward her. His dark eyes watched her closely, a certain appeal for her trust in them. "I have a sore throat," she said.

He nodded. "I thought it must be something like that. When you didn't scream . . ."

"I couldn't."

"Then what we need to do is get you somewhere warm *and* safe."

She made her decision; she gave him her arm.

They stepped out of the alley and onto the street. Gaslight laid a muted yellow circle around them. When a trio of men spilled out of a nearby saloon she edged closer to her rescuer.

Her action did not go unnoticed. "Harlan Porter," he said, introducing himself.

"Thank you, Mr. Porter." She did not return the introduction. Sometimes it seemed that scandal was synonymous with her last name, but thus far she had managed not to be at the center of it.

There was no desire on her part to have that change now. She would not have herself or her family embarrassed if any of this night's adventures came to light. "Will you hail me a cab?"

"I'd be happy to, but we'll have to walk a bit from here. Hansoms don't generally come this way. Perhaps it's obvious to you now, but this is not the most savory section of the city."

She fell into step beside Harlan Porter, grateful for his protection. The thoroughfare did not seem quite so sinister in the presence of her companion; the music and laughter from the dance halls was less raucous. They walked for several blocks and she noticed a gradual improvement in the area. Structurally the houses went from clapboard to brownstone, the street was less rutted, the signs indicating businesses were in good repair, and the pedestrians were no longer staggering. Red lights still dotted the occasional window but the establishments appeared to cater to the uptown crowd.

"Cabs frequent the street just beyond here," Harlan Porter told her. "If you want to wait, I can go ahead and get one to come here."

Not wanting to be left alone, she shook her head furiously.

"Very well, but you're tiring. May I suggest a shortcut through here?" He pointed to a passage between two homes similar to the one where she had been accosted by the sailor.

Her first instinct was to run. When rational thought asserted itself she realized it was better to face her fear. After all, she couldn't avoid dark, narrow passages the rest of her life. That described most of the aisles in the library that she loved to frequent. Besides, she reasoned, it had been the sailor who had posed the threat, not the space, and it was small of her to generalize his behavior to all men. Harlan Porter had extended himself to her generously.

"Or perhaps you'd rather walk around," he suggested.

She shook her head, touching her throat to indicate the ache. "I'm tired," she said.

"Don't try talking. I understand. We'll take the shortcut."

She smiled, thankful for her guardian angel. Linking arms again, she allowed Harlan Porter to lead her into the darkest shadows between the buildings.

"As far as I can tell," he said casually as they walked, "the only thing wrong with you is that you're a tad too trusting."

With no more warning than that he pushed her hard against the brick wall of one of the houses and pressed his forearm equally hard against her throat. She slumped almost immediately.

Consciousness seemed to come slowly. First there was the sweet sensation of breathing, then the sting of something cold and wet on her face. She heard voices next, and moments later light began to sift through the veil of her heavy, dark lashes. It was as if her senses were coming alive in layers. She groaned softly and brushed ineffectually at the wetness on her face.

Harlan Porter wiped her cheeks and brows once more with the damp handkerchief. He considered her efforts to push him away as a good sign. She was of no value to him if she was out cold.

They were no longer in the passageway. It was the first thing that registered when she opened her eyes. Neither were they alone. Harlan Porter was holding her steady with one arm and using the other to gesture wildly as he spoke to the man who had joined them. They were standing at the servants' entrance at the rear of a large brownstone and it appeared to her that the stranger had come outside because he didn't want Harlan Porter in the home.

"I'm telling you, Wicken," Harlan said again, "he's going to want to see what I've got here. She's a near perfect match to what he described to me."

She saw Mr. Wicken's square jaw harden and his eyes narrow as he assessed her skeptically from head to toe. She doubted her efforts to return the stare were nearly as threatening.

"It may be as you say, Porter, but you have to get past me first, don't you?"

Harlan frowned. "You want to use her first, is that it?" When his question was met with stony silence he finally shrugged. "It's your neck," he said. "As for myself, I don't care, and it makes no difference to her, but if he ever finds out that you're sampling his goods, he'll put you out in the street."

"Is that a threat?" Wicken asked.

"He won't find out from me," Harlan said. "I can't speak for the lady."

Wicken's eyes returned to her. Without warning his hand shot out and encircled her neck. His fingers squeezed hard enough to bruise her skin while his eyes slid insolently over her face. "Well?" he asked. "Will you be saying anything?"

The pressure and pain in her throat was so great that she thought she would simply faint with it. She clawed at Wicken's forearm but he didn't remove his hand. She closed her eyes and only Harlan Porter's arm at her waist kept her upright.

"Let her go, Wicken," Porter said.

Wicken released his hand slowly, smiling as she sucked in air. "I think I can count on her keeping quiet."

Porter propped her against the wall and put out his hand, palm up, to Wicken. "I'll take my finder's fee now, thank you."

"Not until I've had my sample. She may not be worth anything; then Mr. Beale won't pay."

"He's always paid because I've always found him what he's wanted."

She seized her opportunity as Porter and Wicken argued. She pushed away from the wall and hurtled herself over the porch rail, sprinting across the backyard and into the alley behind the house. Ignoring Wicken's shout and Porter's demand that she stop, she skirted the edge of a picket fence until she found the gate. She fumbled with the closure, forced it open, and ran into the yard of another brownstone. Heading straight for the back porch, she took both steps in a single leap and threw herself against the screen door, pounding on the frame with the last of her strength.

Harlan caught up to her just as the door was flung open. She was pushed into the dark corner of the porch where she doubled over, catching her breath.

The proprietress of the house stepped outside. Lisa Antonia Hall's voice was strident and her tone no-nonsense. "What's going on out here?" she demanded. She peered into the darkness. "Harlan? Is that you?"

For a moment Porter hovered on the lip of the first step before he backed down onto the flagstone walk.

"It *is* you," Mrs. Hall said, disgust rife in her tone. "I can't say I like you skulking around my tulip bed." She glanced over her shoulder and called to one of the woman standing in the kitchen. "Beth, bring a broom. We've got vermin."

Harlan held up his hands. "Now, Mrs. Hall, there's no need for name calling."

The madam came to the edge of the porch and looked down on Harlan. "I'm not name calling," she said, hands on her hips. She smiled sweetly. "If I recall my Shakespeare . . . a rat by any other name."

The sound of choked laughter in the corner of the porch drew Mrs. Hall's attention. She looked over the cowering figure of the young woman and shook her finger at Harlan.

"I suppose you have an explanation?"

"She's part of my stable," he said.

Mrs. Hall snorted, revolted by his comment. "That's the problem with you, Harlan, you keep confusing horses and women."

Harlan looked past Mrs. Hall's shoulder to where Beth stood militantly holding her broom. "Both of you need to stay out of this. It's between me and the girl."

"It doesn't seem to me that she wants any part of you," Mrs. Hall said. "Is that right, honey?" Her question received a quick, emphatic nod. "That's enough for me, Harlan. Now get off my property or I'll send Samuel for the police."

Harlan didn't move as he weighed his choices. "That's going to take a while."

"About two minutes," she snapped. "Our local cop is taking his leisure upstairs and he's not going to feel kindly toward you for disturbing his rest." Her smile hardened as she saw the impact her statement had on Harlan. "Remove yourself now."

He took another step backward but it was too tentative for Beth. She came rushing past Mrs. Hall, broom raised, and went tearing after Harlan, poking and flailing until he was through the gate and on the other side of the picket fence.

In short order Mrs. Hall hustled her guest into the house and seated her at the kitchen table. Beth came in shortly and put down the broom and began boiling water for tea.

"What has she got to say for herself?" Beth asked, reaching for mugs out of the cupboard. Her short stature prevented her from getting them the first time. She gave a little hop and nudged two mugs toward the edge of the shelf. When she turned around she saw the young woman was smiling weakly at her antics. Beth's plain, round face was animated by her own encouraging smile. "Well, at least you haven't lost your sense of humor."

Mrs. Hall rubbed her temple with one hand, wondering what she had come upon this time. "I believe, Beth, that our guest has lost her voice."

"Really?" Beth looked at her, her brows raised questioningly.

She touched her throat self-consciously and nodded.

Mrs. Hall pointed to her neck above the collar of her gown and coat. "She has bruises."

Beth looked more closely. "So she does. I should have used a gun on him, not a broom." She sighed. "I suppose there's no way of knowing how she got mixed up with the likes of him."

"Not now," Mrs. Hall said dispiritedly. It seemed her role in tonight's disturbance would not be ended quickly. "I can't let her just leave, not in her condition, and not with Harlan likely to be lurking around the corner. I think I better send for Morrison." She turned to her guest. "That's a doctor friend of mine. I think it would be best for him to see you."

She protested by shaking her head violently. The motion made her dizzy and undermined her purpose.

Mrs. Hall rapped out her orders briskly. "Beth, tell Samuel I want him to find Dr. James and bring him here, then finish making the tea and bring it to the room across from Megan's. I'll put this young lady in there and find her some dry clothes. I don't think a hot bath would be amiss. Get Jane to help you make one ready." Feeling like something less than the Good Samaritan, she helped her guest to her feet. "I think there's some laudanum in the medicine cupboard in my apartment. Bring the bottle when you bring the tea."

Beth saluted smartly which brought a glimmer of a smile from the madam. Mrs. Hall linked arms with her patient, supporting her. "This way, dear heart, we're going to take care of you."

She was given no choice but to follow and was actually very relieved that decisions were completely taken out of her hands. She could barely put one foot in front of the other. Clear thinking was quite simply beyond her.

Mrs. Hall chatted the entire time she hovered, helping her out of her damp clothes and into a clean nightshift, turning down the bed, then brushing out her hair. She commented on her appearance, the quality of her clothes, the fine stitching of her gown, and the tailored cut of her coat. She remarked on the oddity of her being in the company of Harlan Porter—she called him a procurer of young women in deference to what she thought were her guest's finer sensibilities—then chastised her roundly for being where she had no business being in the first place.

There was neither denial nor confirmation of any of Mrs. Hall's suspicions, leaving the madam to wonder if she had correctly surmised anything about her guest. When Mrs. Hall held up the laudanum to be taken it was accepted without demur. Lassitude was like a comfortably warm blanket and it was accepted, even reveled in. She understood the nature of Mrs. Hall's business, understood the position of Mrs. Hall within the house, but none of it mattered. The coddling was reassuring. It was only a matter of time before she would be strong enough to go home. She would rest for a few hours and then leave, and think of a way to reward Mrs. Hall for her kindness. It was her last thought before she drifted off to sleep.

Mrs. Hall ordered Beth and Jane to leave the bath they had drawn. She tucked the covers around her patient and tiptoed out of the room. As an afterthought she returned long enough to remove all the liquor from the sideboard cabinet, then went to see to her other guests while she waited for Morrison.

She woke suddenly, frightened and disoriented. The single lamp on the bedside table didn't afford much light. She squinted at the clock on the mantel and made it out to be just past midnight. Her heartbeat slowed as she recalled the events of the evening and recognized the strange surroundings as a safe haven. She pulled the comforter around her shoulders and snuggled more deeply into the soft mattress.

The door handle turned. She sat up suddenly and stared at the imposing figure silhouetted in the doorway. Her immediate thought was to run as he stepped inside, then she saw him drop a leather bag on the table just inside the door and her breathing came easier. The doctor! It was all she could do not to laugh hysterically with relief.

She watched him look around the room and finally walk over to the dressing screen. He moved a panel aside and dipped his finger in the bath Beth and Jane had prepared. As soon as he turned his attention toward her she looked away.

"I've interrupted your bath," he said.

She wanted to tell him it didn't matter, that the sleep had done her as well, but the aching tightness in her throat was still there. She shrugged instead. The wide strap of her nightshift slipped over her shoulder and she hurriedly put it back in place. To her embarrassment it fell again. This time she let it go. Feeling unaccountably shy in front of the physician, she lowered her head so her hair fell forward, shielding her.

"Your display of modesty is duly noted," he said. "Affecting, but quite unnecessary."

She wanted to crawl under the covers at his dry, cynical observation. He must be aware of his own good looks, she thought, and probably just as aware of his female patients assuming, or hoping, his interest in them might be personal, not professional. She vowed to do better.

"Don't let me stop you," he said, pointing to the bath. "I have time."

In spite of her vow, she hesitated. If he had been on the wrong side of fifty with kind eyes and a gentle smile, she knew her response would have been different. It would have helped if he had a slight paunch or spindle legs. He had none of those things.

The man who had walked into her room was straight and tall, slender-hipped with a way of moving that reminded her of a sleek black cat staking out its territory. His eyes were very nearly black, reserved and watchful as they took in everything about his surroundings. Though it seemed he had paid her scant attention, she felt as if it were otherwise.

He was still in his evening clothes which supported her first impression that anger was simmering just below the surface of his bored and weary look. There was a tightness to his mouth that did not invite a smile and the hollows just beneath his cheekbones were pronounced. Obviously, she thought, he had been called away from some social function to tend her and was taking little trouble to hide how he felt about the inconvenience.

There was nothing about this man that made her comfortable.

"Go on," he said more firmly, indicating the bath. "It won't do you any harm and it may even relax you."

He *was* the doctor. She crawled across the bed while he sat down in the wing chair on the opposite side of the room. Apparently she wasn't moving quickly enough for his purposes because he added in a weary tone, "I'm not going to join you." She moved so quickly then that she bumped the dressing screen as she slipped behind it.

She was miserably disappointed in herself. It was not like her to be skittish. She blamed it on the laudanum that Mrs. Hall had given her, the lateness of the hour, and the doctor's less-than-encouraging bedside manner. She got rid of her nightshift and found pins in a drawer in the wardrobe. Once she pinned her hair so it wouldn't get wet, she eased herself into the tub. She had just closed her eyes, enjoying the warmth, when she heard him call to her.

"I was told you wouldn't talk much," he said, "but I didn't expect complete silence."

She swallowed and tried to say something, but nothing came out.

"Suits me."

She thought it was an odd thing for him to say. She hoped he had something in that black bag of his that would give her back her voice. She had a few things she wanted to tell him about how he dealt with his patients. She slipped lower in the tub and let the mist touch her face and throat. She remained that way for several minutes, liking the experience too much to rush it.

"Fetching," he drawled.

She was so astonished by his intrusion that she sank even lower. He was holding a towel above her, an indication, she supposed, that it was time to get out.

"There's no reason to act like a shy maiden in front of me," he said. "This is professional, not personal." He paused, watching her closely. "Isn't it?"

She blinked, returned his stare, then nodded shortly. She was thoroughly humiliated that he may have sensed some personal interest on her part. It was probably the very reason he affected such remoteness. Caught in her thoughts, she barely managed to catch the towel when he dropped it.

"Red," he said.

She couldn't imagine that she had heard him correctly. "Hmmm?" Grimacing, she touched her throat lightly with her fingertips. She forced herself to speak no matter the pain. "Pardon?"

"Your hair's red. There's not much light in here. I wasn't sure." He paused. "May I?"

She looked at his raised hand, the fingertips just inches from her ear, and nodded. His hand brushed her cheek and she knew he must be getting a sense of her temperature. He did not miss the bruises on her neck either. He touched one of them lightly and said, "You've been treated roughly this evening."

She nodded, wondering how much Mrs. Hall had been able to tell him.

"Good thing I'm here then. We'll see what we can do about that. You're warm. Out of the bath—now."

She was happy to see that he stood and turned away. She got out of the tub quickly, dried off, and put on the nightshift. When she came around the screen she noted he had removed his vest and tossed it next to his evening jacket. He was looking at her bare feet.

"You'd better get back in bed. Even on the rug, the floor's cold. Do you want me to light a fire?"

She did, but she didn't want to put him to the trouble. He seemed to sense that because he laughed softly as she crawled back into bed and pulled the comforter around her shoulders.

"Just the same," he said. "I think I'll do it."

She watched him work silently and efficiently. When he was done his hands were gray with ash. He went to the porcelain basin and washed them.

"It wouldn't do to leave fingerprints, would it?"

Her smile was tentative. She appreciated his small attempt at humor to set her at ease.

"I think you could use a drink."

She felt her smile fading, her lips parting in surprise.

"Medicinal purposes only."

She relaxed. She knew a number of physicians who swore by the efficacy of warm whiskey and lemon for a sore throat, though it was not something she had ever tried. She saw him look around, then shrug.

"Good thing I've come prepared." He crossed the room to where he had placed his black bag and retrieved a quarter-full bottle of Scotch. He turned, showing her the bottle. "Glasses?"

She had no idea where they might be. She shook her head.

"Then you'll have to tipple it right out of the bottle." He brought the bottle to the bed, sat down on the edge, and handed it to her. "It will make you feel better, I promise."

It wasn't warm, it didn't have lemon in it, but she trusted him nonetheless. She uncapped the bottle and raised it slowly to her lips.

He gave it a nudge and she took a large swallow. He urged her again, this time challenging her with an amused look.

"That's better," he said, grinning when she made a face. "Obviously you have no appreciation for good Scotch."

The liquor eased the tightness in her throat. "I don't drink much." That was very close to the truth. A glass of sherry made her woozy. Two glasses and she could barely recall drinking the first. Since she prided herself on having control she had never tested what damage could be done at three glasses.

"I don't either—much."

Without much prompting, she took another swallow. Perhaps Scotch had a different effect than sherry. At least it didn't taste nearly so bad this time.

"It seems to agree with you rather quickly," he said, taking the bottle from her. He touched her cheek again with the back of his fingers. "But then that's what it's supposed to do. You're not so flushed." His hand slipped over her face. His knuckle touched her lips. "Show me your tongue."

She opened her mouth wide and stuck out her tongue. "Aaaaahhhh." She was surprised when he laughed.

"That wasn't quite what I had in mind but it's a very pretty tongue. Very pink. Nice teeth, too. And you've kept your tonsils." He nudged her jaw. "You can close now. I've seen quite enough. Another drink is definitely in order."

Expecting him to pass her the bottle, she gave a little start when he took a long pull on it himself.

He handed it to her and let her finish. "For someone who doesn't drink much, you've developed quite a taste for it."

She offered him a crooked, somewhat sleepy smile. "I think I like good Scotch," she said. She certainly would never scoff at its value for easing a sore throat. "As medicine, of course."

"Of course," he agreed dryly. He put the bottle over the side of the bed and made himself more comfortable. He leaned back against the walnut headboard and stuffed a loose pillow behind the small of his back. "Much better."

A little wary of his efforts to stretch out beside her, she moved to the far side of the bed. Her action did not go unnoticed and brought his derision.

"There was no need for you to move. I'm not going to attack you, but I can hardly reach you if you remain over there."

There was sense in what he was saying, she reminded herself. He had already helped ease some of her pain. He could hardly conduct an examination if he couldn't touch her. She scooted toward him. He fluffed a pillow and put it behind her. Her knees bumped his and the strap of her nightshift slid over her left shoulder again. She tried to push it up but her movements were awkward. The liquor and laudanum were having an effect on more than just her throat.

"We're a fine pair," he said.

She frowned, looking at him oddly, not understanding.

He leaned his head back, exposing the strong line of his throat, and closed his eyes. "I can't remember when I've had a longer day," he said, sighing.

Looking at the gilded clock on the mantel, she saw it was past midnight. "New day."

"I suppose it is. And it's starting just the same way. God, I'm tired."

She had a tender heart and it went out to him. "Rest," she said softly.

"It's a nice offer, but not the reason I came here. I should see to you. You've obviously been waiting."

"I didn't mind." It was an effort to talk, but not precisely for the same reasons it had been earlier. Even to her own ears her words sounded slurred. "Mrs. Hall made me comfortable."

"This isn't much," he said.

She was as aware of the spartan conditions of the room as he, yet she said with quiet conviction, "My experience says it's better than the streets."

He opened his eyes and looked at her now. "I suppose it is."

She held his gaze for a long time before breaking away. Her own forthrightness embarrassed her.

"You're flushed again."

She realized that she was, though not for the reasons he thought— at least she hoped he would assume it was because of her illness. She let him take the pulse in her throat.

"Your heart's racing."

She nodded.

"Why don't you drop that cover and let me have a look."

She called herself all manner of fool for hesitating when he was being nothing but matter-of-fact. She felt him nudge the blanket with the heel of his hand. She was being so stupid, she thought.

"How am I supposed to examine you if I can't see you?"

Of course he was right, yet she couldn't seem to move. Those dark eyes of his were searching hers.

He added, "You have some expectations, I assume."

She was no longer certain what she expected from him. "Not many." As if to prove her point he gave a shout of laughter.

"Oh, you *have* been treated poorly! That doesn't speak well for men like myself."

She supposed he was referring to physicians in general but she didn't ask for clarification. He was pushing aside the comforter. His fingers slid along the neckline of her shift and rested lightly on the uppermost button. She put a hand over his and shook her head. "I'll do it." It was easier to talk now but the husky quality of her voice had not improved. Again she hoped it was not mistaken for anything but a symptom of her illness.

"You're not a chatterbox."

His observation was one that had been made before. It was her experience that it bothered most people. "No," she said quietly. "I'm not." She finished undoing the top button.

"Another," he said.

She glanced at him, not understanding.

He pointed to her hand. "Another button, please."

She undid it with fingers made clumsy by the liquor and laudanum. She stared down at his hand as it hovered near her heart.

"That flush of yours starts about here," he said. His fingertips touched her skin just above her heartbeat. "There's nothing wrong with your heart." He opened another button of her gown. "Come closer," he said. When she didn't move immediately his hands slipped around her rib cage to urge her nearer. He laid one hand on her back near her shoulder blade.

His confident, impersonal touch relieved her but her heart was hammering and her head was muzzy.

"Take a deep breath," he said. "That's it. Hold it." His hand rubbed her back. "Let it out slowly."

She did. Her heart steadied and her breathing slowed.

"Better," he said. "There for a moment I thought you might faint."

"So did I," she said with grave honesty. "I'm a little dizzy."

He released her. "Why don't you lie down?"

It was his best suggestion, she thought. "All right." She stretched out on her side, bringing the pillow under her head.

"I don't have much success with patients," he said, touching her cheek again.

She wondered at his admission until she remembered his comment on the kind of day it had been. Perhaps he was not so arrogant after all; perhaps he had been humbled by an earlier failure. She felt as if their positions were suddenly reversed and she was being called upon to be the healer. Her smile was gentle. "I think you're doing fine," she said.

He blinked, his eyes darkening. "Why, thank you," he said. "It's good of you to encourage me."

Her smile deepened as her eyelashes lowered sleepily. It was her most heartfelt desire to be part of his profession. She decided to tell him. "I hope to do so one fine day."

"So you admit you have something to learn?"

She nodded emphatically. How could he think otherwise? She yawned widely and stretched, slipping one arm under the pillow as she turned on her side.

"So you're willing to learn a thing or two from me?"

"I'd like that very much." And she meant it. His manner not withstanding, she was impressed with his dedication. He may not have appreciated the interruption of his social evening, but he had come nonetheless.

"You're something of a surprise," he said. "Not what I expected when I walked in here this evening."

It seemed everyone, except Harlan Porter perhaps, realized she didn't belong in a brothel. Too tired to think why that might be, or if it were a good or bad thing, she snuggled deeper into the pillow. "Hmmm."

"Are you going to fall asleep?"

She shook her head slowly, feeling the frayed edges of sleep curl around her thoughts. She felt him move off the bed. She slept.

* * *

The heat of his body woke her. She was astonished to discover she was touching him everywhere . . . then more astonished that she wasn't drawing back. He was pressed against her, his hands in her hair, his mouth at the curve of her ear. His breath was hot and sweet. He was whispering and the vibration of it against her skin sent a shiver down her spine. Delicious sensation rocked her body. Her hands slid over his rib cage. Her hair spilled over her shoulders and across his chest, anchoring her against him. She laid her head in the curve of his shoulder. Her mouth brushed his skin.

His warmth enveloped her. She snuggled against him, liking the strength and heat of him. His fingers brushed the soft underside of her elbow. It was the most natural thing in the world to press a smile against his skin. She felt his nipple harden as her mouth grazed him. Her breasts swelled and she drew a shaky breath. He drew out unfamiliar responses when he touched her, whereever he touched her.

At first it wasn't enough, then it was too much. Almost, she amended as she curled against him, almost too much.

He was moving against her, groaning. His hands slid between their bodies and over hers.

She wondered how to touch him, then he showed her, moving her hand for her, moving it over him. Her legs tangled with his as he twisted and rolled her onto her back. His knee separated her thighs. She whimpered, partly in wanting, partly in surprise. He covered her mouth with his. It was hard and hungry across hers. She could feel the edge of his tongue. She moved restlessly, pushing, arching, but the weight of him secured her. His chest was a wall against her tender breasts. His legs were pressed against the length of hers.

For a moment she was frightened by what she felt and what he was making her feel. She meant to grab his hair but her fingers curled in the dark strands at his nape. She tried to scratch him and caught the outer edge of his ear instead. When he reared back she smiled uncertainly.

His gaze darkened and he lowered his head. Mesmerized by those eyes, it was only then that she arched, turning her head at the exact moment his mouth would have fused with hers. His lips scraped her cheek, her jaw line, then finally the curve of her neck. She pushed at his back, pressing the heels of her hands against the bunched muscles as he moved over her.

He whispered in her ear. She heard the words and barely comprehended their meaning. His hands were massaging her, teasing her with sensation that flitted over her skin. She couldn't think. His mouth was on hers, his tongue circling hers, pushing, probing, doing all things that his hips were doing at the cradle of her thighs.

Suddenly he pulled away from her. The loss of him took her breath, made her shake. She reached out to steady herself and he smiled as if he understood her need. He brushed aside her hand as he knelt between her thighs. He pushed back her raised knees and raised her buttocks and plunged into her.

She cried out. The pain was unexpected. Before she could catch her breath he withdrew and thrust again. This time she grasped his forearms and held on. She arched and felt him deep inside her. Pleasure stirred again at the urging of his body. She was filled by him and a certain empty aching was gone.

She accepted the force of his thrusts, the rhythm of the joining. Her head moved from side to side and no sound emerged from her parted lips. He left her nothing to do but feel. As the sweep of sensation demanded her surrender, her struggle ceased. His breathing was harsh. She could only take in air in small sips. She felt his taut muscles as need drove him into her again and again.

Her pleasure shattered as he cried out.

He collapsed against her and slept almost immediately. In spite of her desire to do otherwise, she followed him, nesting in the curve of his body.

There was no pain the second time.

It was much later that she eased out of bed, wobbly on her feet at first. She steadied herself by holding onto the post at the end of the bed, studiously avoiding looking at the bed itself or the man lying across it. When she could trust herself to move without stumbling she went to the dressing screen. The water in the bath was cool but she used it to tend to the ache between her thighs. She went through the motions, unable to think clearly about what she was doing or why she was doing it. Her movements were clumsy and awkward and that fact registered with more clarity than any other.

She found her clothes in the wardrobe. Stripping out of her shift, she tossed it over the screen and dressed slowly, making certain she did nothing to attract any unwanted attention from the bed. When she was finished she sat at the vanity and brushed out her hair. Her strokes were deliberate, long, and almost punishing. She did not watch herself in the mirror. Instead her eyes were fixed on the nightshift she had worn and the stain of blood near its hem.

It had ridden up near her thighs when he . . .

She blinked and pulled herself back to the present. Moving by rote, with barely any conscious thought of her intent, she picked up the nightshift and rolled it into a ball. She wanted no trace of herself left in the room. Once she was gone it would be as if nothing had happened. Nothing.

She did not want to carry the nightgown where anyone could see it. She slipped on her coat and tried hiding it there. It was too lumpy. That was when her eyes alighted on the black leather bag just inside the door. Hesitating only a moment she picked it up, opened it a crack, and stuffed her nightshift inside.

She glanced around the room to make certain she hadn't forgotten anything. Odd, she thought, how that expression came to mind when what she wanted to do was forget everything.

She opened the door carefully and listened for sounds in the hallway. It was quiet abovestairs. Music drifted up from below. Without a backward glance she stepped into the hall and headed for the back stairs. Her flight was uneventful. No one met her on the stairs. The kitchen was empty.

She paused again at the back door. Thoughts of what she might face outside were as frightening as what she would face upstairs. Her hand trembled on the handle. She gripped it tightly.

Sucking in her breath, she twisted the handle and pushed open the door. Then she ran, knowing everything about who she was and what she wanted to be depended upon never looking back.

A hansom cab took her the entire way up Broadway to 48th Street. Even at night the thoroughfare was busy. Peddlers were setting out their wares for the early-morning crowd and the last of the late-night revelers. Milk wagons were making deliveries to the boardinghouses while restaurants were ejecting their most stubborn customers. Not interested in the noise or the activity, she curled in one corner of the cab, her head turned away from the window. She paid the driver quickly, her head bowed so she would not be recognized, and walked the last two blocks alone once the cab was out of sight.

The house at the intersection of Broadway and 50th Street was only slightly smaller than the palatial French country home on which it was modeled. Rose bushes edged the foundation of smooth gray stone and morning glories climbed a trellis on the southern side. She entered the yard at the front, pushing aside the iron rail gate, then went around back to the delivery entrance. There was a key above the door jamb. She stood on tiptoe to get it.

The house was quiet. It surprised her. She had expected that someone would be waiting up for her but apparently no one had lost any sleep worrying. That could only mean her sister had fabricated a story that credibly explained her absence.

She took off her shoes and carried them. It wasn't necessary to light a lamp—she knew the way to her room in the dark. She slipped inside her bedchamber and put down the shoes and the black leather bag. She started a fire in the grate and stripped off her clothes and threw them on the fire, stoking it so it wouldn't be smothered by the material. She added the nightshift, then shoved the doctor's bag under her bed. After scrubbing at the basin she crawled into her bed.

It was astonishingly easy to fall asleep.

A rough hand on her shoulder nudged her awake. At the windows the curtains had been pulled back and morning spilled into the room. Even with her eyes closed she could feel the press of light and heat from the sunshine. She opened her eyes slowly and found herself staring into the strained and worried face of her younger sister.

"Do you have any idea how frightened I've been since you disappeared?" she demanded in a harsh whisper. "What time did you get in? I was in and out of the house most of the night looking for you! And it was no easy feat with Mother and Jay Mac playing cards in the parlor until midnight. I know it wasn't fair of me to leave with Daniel but it was a poorer trick you played me." She frowned, tears gathering in her eyes. "It was a trick, wasn't it? Oh, Maggie, I'm so sorry, but I've got to know that you're all right. Please tell me where you've been all this time."

Mary Margaret Dennehy blinked once. She sat up slowly and felt her sister's hand drop away. "Do you know, Skye," she said carefully. "I haven't the faintest idea."

Chapter Three

Six weeks later

The door opened softly. Connor didn't look up because he knew who it was and because it would irritate his uninvited and unwanted guest; he continued to fiddle with his cufflink. "What is it, Beryl?" he asked indifferently.

She had hardly made a sound. She closed the door behind her and leaned against it, watching him deliberately ignore her. It annoyed her but it also gave her an opportunity to simply stare at him. Knowing it would irritate him in turn, Beryl took her fill. "Is it my perfume?" she asked quietly.

Connor turned suddenly. He caught her off guard. Beryl's pale blue eyes, a starting contrast to the dark chestnut color of her hair, were fastened on the breadth of his shoulders. Since she had recommended the tailor, she was probably congratulating herself on the fit of his evening coat, he thought cynically. Making no effort to conceal his impatience he asked, "Is *what* your perfume?"

"The reason you noticed me before I said anything."

Beryl Walker Holiday was easily the most beautiful woman he had ever known. "It was any number of things," he said. "Your step in the hallway. That breathy little sigh. The rustle of your gown. *And* your perfume. Is that what you wanted to hear?"

Her smile transformed a beautiful face into a radiant one. She pushed away from the door and took a step into the room.

Connor went on. "Men always notice you before you say anything," he told her. "It's when you open your mouth that they turn away." Suiting his actions to his words, Connor turned and began adjusting the gold stud on his left sleeve.

Beryl rocked slightly on her heels as if feeling the blow physically. "I think you take a certain amount of delight in being cruel to me," she said. "Have I hurt you so badly that you must punish me at every turn?"

"Save it, Beryl. I've heard this speech before."

She was thoughtful, touching the tip of her index finger to her lips. She could not make him look at her so the calculated innocence of the gesture was wasted. Beryl dropped her hand to her side. Changing tactics, she said, "You're looking quite handsome this evening. The cut of that jacket suits you."

He gave no indication that he had even heard her.

Beryl approached him, walking behind Connor to critically assess the man while pretending interest in his evening wear. "You should always dress that way," she said. "It becomes you." He was quite magnificent, she thought, with his lean strength contained in tailored trappings. True, his dark hair brushed his collar unfashionably and the fingers that fiddled with the cufflinks were calloused, but Beryl found even these things appealing. The idea that Connor's restless energy could be leashed in a black swallowtail coat and trousers was an intriguing one. The idea of unleashing that energy was exciting, almost as exciting as the prospect of being caught in it. When Beryl looked past Connor's shoulder into her reflection in the mirror she saw her eyes had darkened.

Connor caught the sultry cast of Beryl's glance and his own eyes narrowed. Barely able to conceal his impatience, he asked, "Was there something specific you wanted or have you only come to gloat?"

She patted his shoulder lightly and stepped the rest of the way around him. Although she pretended not to understand, one corner of her mouth rose in a sly, knowing smile. "Gloat? Aren't you being absurd? Why would I be gloating?"

He shrugged away from her touch and straightened the tails of his jacket. "Enough, Beryl. I'm not answering your questions. If you have something to say, say it."

Her smile faded. Her hand dropped slowly to her side. "All right, then," she said. "I find it quite interesting that you've decided to put yourself up for sale." Her eyes followed him in the mirror as he left her side. She watched him go to the wardrobe and root through one of the drawers until he came away with a silver flask. He unscrewed the cap and raised it to his lips. "You may want to go easy with that," she said. "You're not at your best when you've been drinking."

Ignoring her, Connor took a long swallow. He capped the flask and slipped it inside his vest pocket.

Beryl's taffeta gown rustled and the iridescent shades of purple shimmered as she moved toward him. She put one hand on his forearm in an imploring gesture, but there was no hiding the edge of anger in her tone. "You're being ridiculous, Connor. You don't seriously mean to go through with this. That land can't be so damned important that you'd sell yourself for it."

"I think I'm proving that it is," he said quietly. He removed her hand from his forearm.

"But so cheaply?"

His short laugh held no humor. "We all have our price, Beryl. Just because you held out for more . . ." He shrugged.

She slapped him hard.

Connor didn't retaliate. He pinned her with his stare, letting the heat and color of the imprint fade from his cheek before he spoke. "I trust you have that out of your system," he said calmly. "The next time you even think about hitting me I'll lay you out."

Beryl had held her ground. At his icy, controlled words she took a step backward. "You good as called me a whore," she said.

"So?"

Beryl's beautiful features contorted with fury. "You *bastard!*"

Knowing that his calm was all the more infuriating to her, one of Connor's dark brows kicked up. "Bastard? I don't think so. God knows, though, had I been one I probably wouldn't have these problems. That land would have been mine free and clear when my mother died, instead of ending up in my father's hands."

"If she had wanted you to have it she should have made a will," Beryl snapped. "Perhaps she meant for Rushton to have it. It forced you back to New York, didn't it? It forced you to acknowledge that you have a father. Perhaps Edie knew exactly what she was doing all along."

The fact that Beryl could be right did nothing for Connor's temperament. He had dwelled on the same idea himself, but it was another thing entirely to hear it from her. He had never thought of himself as unreasonable yet he was being forced to reconsider that opinion. "Leave it alone, Beryl. My mother's wishes had nothing whatsoever to do with you."

The strain of anger dissolved in Beryl's features. High color receded from her complexion, leaving it milk-white and smooth. Her full mouth settled in serene composition. The pale blue of her eyes was emphasized by the dark centers and the glistening wash of unshed tears. "Do you really hate me so much, Connor, that you can't even contemplate that I might be right? Is it so intolerable to give me my due?"

Yes, he thought, it *was* intolerable. He said nothing and turned away. Did he hate her? he wondered. Or did he hate himself? It wasn't easy to admit that, against all reason, he could still find himself attracted to her. That was the power she held over him, that in spite of everything he could not quite manage to feel the indifference he feigned. To feel nothing at all would be liberating; hatred bound him. It didn't matter that it was unfair—he resented her all the more for that. He found some small comfort in the fact that he didn't love her, had probably never loved her. That would have been unendurable.

"We should be going," he said. "That is, if you're still planning to accompany Father and me. I assure you it isn't necessary."

"I'm well aware of that, but the invitation included me." She walked to the full-length mirror again and smoothed the crown of her deep chestnut hair. She curled a tendril at her ear with her index finger. "And I'm insatiably curious," she said. "I want to meet the man who thinks he can buy you for his daughter." Her smile was wickedly beautiful. "And I want to meet the daughter."

A muscle worked in Connor's jaw. He had to force himself to relax. "Don't ruin this for me, Beryl."

"What if she turns out to be mud-fence ugly? Or worse, a shrew? What do you really know about that family except that scandal touches almost everything they do. I've heard stories since I came to

New York. John MacKenzie Worth's money quiets rumor but doesn't silence it. Have you thought of that, Connor?"

"Shut up, Beryl," he said with menace.

"Are ten thousand acres of Colorado so damned critical that you have to marry a bastard to keep it?"

Connor let a moment tick by. Into the expectant silence he said quietly, "I'd still marry you if I thought it would help me keep that land, and God knows how much I despise you. So you see, Beryl, it doesn't matter who or what she is or isn't. My mind's made up." He started walking toward the door.

"You must regret losing that twelve thousand dollars," she said as he opened the door to leave.

He glanced at her over his shoulder. "You can't imagine how much."

Connor had no time to dwell on the stolen money and opportunities lost. He met his father in the hallway.

"Have you seen Beryl?" Rushton Holiday asked.

People often remarked on the striking resemblance between father and son. Separated by only twenty years, they had finally reached that age where it was not unreasonable or surprising for strangers to mistake them for brothers. It could have been a flattering observation to both men but neither Connor nor Rushton saw it that way. Of course, there were the obvious similarities that they could accept: thick, ink-black hair that was only just graying at the temples in Rushton; shoulders that were set at an equal breadth; height that favored Connor by a mere half-inch; and a jaw line squared off aggressively. It ended there. Connor thought his father had a cold, intolerant manner. Rushton saw cynicism in his son's expression. The patrician features of the father appeared aloof to the son, and the same handsomely molded lines on the face of the son appeared arrogant to the father. Their dark eyes were mirrors, yielding little of any thought or emotion they did not intend to be known.

They were so much alike they could barely be civil.

"She's in my bedchamber," Connor said. "I just left her."

Rushton searched his son's face with a hard, penetrating stare. "She has no business being in your room."

"Have this conversation with Beryl, Father. I didn't invite her in. My conscience is clear."

"Damn you, Connor," he said under his breath. "I want you to stay away from her."

"That's awkward, don't you think? We're both living under your roof. Granted, it's an enormous roof, but there are limits to what I can do." He looked at his father expectantly, a half-smile playing on his mouth, his eyebrows raised slightly.

Rushton sucked in his breath. It was Edie staring back at him. The impression came and went with startling speed and equal clarity and then Rushton was left staring into a face that was a younger reflection of his own. In spite of the resemblance Rushton thought of Connor as Edie's son, not his own. "I'll get Beryl," he said tightly. "And then we'll leave. Hickes is out front with the carriage."

Connor wondered what had given his father that briefly haunted expression. "Very well," he said. "I'll be waiting."

The atmosphere inside the carriage was tense. Connor had one of the upholstered bench seats to himself while Rushton and Beryl sat opposite him. Gaslight from the street filtered in the window at regular intervals as the carriage skirted the edge of Central Park. Rushton's countenance was brooding, Connor's resigned, and Beryl's anxious.

She drew her cape more securely about her shoulders, warding off the chill seeping under the door and under her skin. "Rushton, can't you talk some sense into him?"

It was Connor who responded. "Be serious, Beryl. It was his idea. Anyway, do you think I would be in this position if *he* didn't need the money? You should be delighted I'm willing to do this. Money in his coffers means money in yours, or hadn't you thought that far ahead?"

"But your father can have the money by selling the land."

"Save your breath, Beryl," Rushton said. "Connor knows that. It's only because he is stubbornly insisting on buying the land that there's a problem."

Connor couldn't help himself. "It's my *home,*" he shouted. The echo of his words seemed to slam against the walls of the carriage. Beryl recoiled in response. Rushton's mouth thinned and his jaw tightened. Swearing under his breath, Connor drew back the communicating panel and rapped out an order for Hickes. The carriage stopped almost immediately and Connor opened the door. "I'll walk the rest of the way."

Beryl leaned forward to try to stop him but Rushton put out his arm, blocking her. "Leave him," he said.

"But we'll arrive before he does. What will we say?"

"We'll circle the block until he gets there."

Unhappy but mollified, Beryl leaned back in her seat as the carriage began to roll again. "Must you sell the land, Rush?"

"Yes. The fall in the market makes it absolutely necessary. No matter what Connor thinks, I'm not doing this to spite him." He looked sideways at Beryl. "And I'm not doing it to satisfy your social aspirations or to keep you in a style to which you've only recently become accustomed."

Beryl's arm looped inside Rushton's and she snuggled closer to him. "Do you think I care a fig for social aspirations or indecent wealth?"

Rushton looked down at her upturned face. A banner of light briefly illuminated her pained expression as she made no attempt to hide her hurt. He patted her arm gently, his smile and tone only faintly mocking. "I think you care very much, my dear, else why would you have married the father when you could have had the son?"

The brisk pace that Connor set only partially curbed his anger. He wanted to hit something or, better yet, someone. He had never been one to spoil for a fight but tonight he found himself hoping there would be one. He didn't even care if he was the one laid out on the sidewalk as long as he got a few licks in first.

Perhaps it was the aura of anger that kept others at bay, but no fellow pedestrians along Seventh Avenue or Broadway came within three feet of him. A stray dog followed briefly but stayed well outside of kicking range. A trio of children mimicked his glowering expression as he passed them but thought twice about asking him for money. Connor noticed none of it.

In his mind's eye he was seeing the fine-boned and fragile features of a scheming harlot, the red hair of a temptress, and the wide, clear, green eyes of a jade. *She* was the one he wanted to meet, the one he wanted to hurt. With the money she had stolen he had intended to buy the Colorado ranch from his father. Never again would he have had to worry that the land could be taken away. His father was selling his heritage out from under him and Connor, as hurt and frustrated as he was by this further evidence of betrayal, still reserved the largest fraction of his anger for the whore who had beguiled him rather than the father who had birthed him.

Connor halted in front of the spiked iron gate at the corner of Broadway and 50th. He leaned against the rails, catching his breath and clearing his head. Behind him the mansion beckoned invitingly with lighted lamps in each of the front windows. On the upper story a drape that had been drawn back was abruptly dropped in place. His attention on the approaching carriage, Connor didn't sense he had been observed. He straightened, ran his fingers through his hair in an absent, nervous gesture, and waited for his father and Beryl to alight.

By the time he reached the front door of the palatial gray stone house his breathing had calmed and his uncertainty was hidden behind the cool and distant reflection of his darkly mirrored eyes.

From inside the receiving parlor John MacKenzie Worth heard the housekeeper open the front door and greet his guests. His normally impassive features were anything but as he alternately stared at his wife and youngest daughter. His mouth gaped in his broad face and his dark blond hair seemed to grow a little grayer as his authority was called into question. "What do you mean she's not joining us for dinner?" he demanded. "Why didn't you tell me this earlier?"

Moira Dennehy Worth merely shook her head, a genuine smile on her sweetly bowed mouth. "I suspect, dearest, it's because we knew you'd take it badly. And you are, so there you have it."

Jay Mac speared his daughter with a glance that had been known to make a business colleague's brow bead with sweat. Mary Schyler was not only not cowed, she stared back and gave as good as she got. "That's your story, I suppose," he said, at once admiring and aggravated.

Skye nodded, dimpling as she gave her father a placating smile.

"The very same," she said. "Did you really think Maggie wouldn't see through your machinations?"

He frowned and straightened the stems of his spectacles. "Your sister rarely sees past the pages of a book, how was I to know she'd . . . wait a minute here, Skye . . . what machinations are you referring to? Moira? What is your daughter talking about?"

"I think it's too late to play the innocent, darling," Moira said. She glanced in the mirror above the mantelpiece and smoothed her dark red hair. "Our guests will be upon us any moment." She stopped fiddling with her hair and came to stand in front of Jay Mac. She smoothed the shoulders of his evening jacket while her loving expression revealed how much she adored him. "Over dinner I hope you will refrain from referring to Skye only as *my* daughter or Mary Margaret as *her* sister. You have a terrible habit of disclaiming fatherhood when you're aggrieved."

Skye giggled. "Poor Jay Mac. He's been so poorly abused by his five daughters that it's a wonder he claimed us at all."

Jay Mac shot Skye another withering glance but he spoke to Moira. "Do you see what I have to put up with in return? I'm only called Papa or Father when it suits them. I'd like to know which one of them started calling me Jay Mac and why you allowed it all these years."

Moira's eyes were dancing as the parlor door was opened. "I'm certain it was Mary," she said in a low voice.

"I'm not amused," he replied sternly. As the father of five girls, now women, all with the first name of Mary, it was not a very satisfactory answer. He supposed he deserved it, though. Even he could admit that he was being a trifle pompous and overbearing. There had been so many years that he had only been able to claim his daughters with his heart and not his name that it wasn't entirely surprising that one of them had hit upon calling him Jay Mac and it had stuck. To all the world he was Jay Mac Worth, he thought, so why should it be different in his own home?

A casual acquaintance might mistake the unusual familiarity and strong-willed conflicts between Jay Mac and his daughters as showing a lack of respect, but no observation could have been farther from the mark. Nor did Jay Mac always deal good-humoredly with his five Marys, though there had been demonstration recently of a lighter touch. John MacKenzie Worth could be scheming, ruthless, and tyrannical when it came to business, and securing the futures of his daughters was his most important business.

Tonight was no exception as he set his sights on Mary Margaret's happiness.

Moira moved from Jay Mac's side to greet her guests. Introductions were accomplished smoothly and there was no mention made of Maggie's absence. Indeed, none of the Holidays knew that another daughter had been expected to join them. The extra place setting was whisked aside before they entered the dining room. Connor was seated beside Skye and opposite Beryl and Rushton. Moira and Jay Mac presided at the head and foot of the table.

She was too young, Connor thought, listening to Skye chatter about some skating party she had recently attended with her friends. She was silly and empty-headed, and perhaps, as he watched her toss her flame-red curls over her shoulder yet again, even more vain about her appearance than Beryl. How could he live with that for the rest of his life? Then he wondered if he'd have to. If she were willing to stay in New York, he would be quite willing to stay in Colorado. It would be the reverse of the arrangement his own parents had made years ago—it might even be satisfactory. Then she grinned at him disarmingly, a strand of spinach from the soup lodged between her front teeth, and he knew he couldn't marry anyone so childish that she thought spinach teeth was a good joke.

Jay Mac's eyes narrowed on Mary Schyler, indicating that she had done quite enough to dissuade Connor Holiday from showing her any flattering attention. Moira managed to muffle her laughter with a cough behind her napkin. Beryl hoped the young woman would keep smiling her great green grin. It was a certainty that Connor was no longer contemplating marriage as a way of securing the land—not that anyone had expected him to make a proposal this very evening. Beryl relaxed as she realized that even courting the Dennehy bastard was going to be out of the question.

Rushton was disappointed though he was as careful as his son not to show it. He had hoped for something better. Now there was no choice but to sell. It wasn't a subject to be discussed now, with the women present. The business was better settled after dinner over whiskey and cigars.

Jay Mac speared a tender bit of roast and held it up a moment, hoping to salvage something from the evening. "Is your beef this good, Connor? I understand you have several hundred head of cattle on your ranch."

"At the risk of offending your cook, my beef is better."

"Is that so?"

"You can't ship it this far east without it losing some of its texture and flavor. My beef goes to market at St. Louis but I think it tastes different at Denver. If you want a good steak then you should spend time at the Double H."

"Double H?" asked Moira. "Your ranch has a name?"

"It comes from the brand we use," Connor explained. "H for Hart—my mother's maiden name—and H for Holiday. We brand the cattle to discourage rustling. Markets know my brand. If my cattle shows up without me or my men attached in some way they know the animals have been stolen."

"Does it happen often?" Skye asked, interested in spite of herself. She took a moment to remove the spinach she had strategically placed between her front teeth.

"More often than I'd like."

"Do you catch them?"

"Sometimes."

Skye's eyes widened slightly. "And then what?"

Rushton cleared his throat. "I don't think you really want to know, at least not here, not now."

"Oh, but my constitution's quite strong," she said. "I can talk about most anything and still manage to eat."

"I'm sure," Beryl said with quiet sarcasm.

"Well, I'm certain I don't want to hear," said Moira, "though I find it very interesting that your ranch is in Colorado. Is it possible you've met either of my daughters who live there?"

Jay Mac smiled indulgently and said quickly, "Colorado is rather larger than you think, Moira. It's unlikely that Connor knows either Michael or Rennie."

"Michael?" Beryl asked. "I thought you only had daughters."

"Mary Michael," Moira said.

"And Mary Renee," Schyler added. "We're all Marys. Mary Francis. Mary Margaret." She dimpled, pointing to herself. "Mary Schyler. I suppose you might think of it as *our* brand."

"How charming," Beryl said, her tone conveying just the opposite.

Skye pretended to be oblivious to the undercurrent of ridicule in

Beryl's remark. "Oh, it's very Catholic," she said blithely, smoothing her napkin in her lap. "Mother is, you know. Irish Catholic. Though I imagine you heard that in her accent. The Irish part, I mean. I don't think being Catholic gives one a particular accent." She smiled guilelessly at Connor. "Do you?"

"No," he said, careful not to choke.

"I didn't think so," she went on. "Father, on the other hand, is quite the Protestant. Presbyterian, specifically. But then you probably knew that. Catholics do not get nearly so far in business as my father has, though why religion should play such a role has never been satisfactorily explained to me. I think it also helps that his family was here before the revolution."

Jay Mac's complexion has taken on a mottled cast that could not be completely hidden by either his ample side whiskers or his thick mustache. "That's quite enough, Mary Schyler."

When Skye heard the particular tone and inflection in her father's voice, coupled with her full name, she bent her head, suitably chastened.

"Oh, it sounds terribly fascinating," Beryl said, deliberating provoking Skye to further conversational indiscretions. She ignored her husband's warning glance and Connor's angry one, smiling serenely and continuing to eat without missing a beat. Jay Mac, she thought happily, would never find a husband for his daughter unless he gagged her.

"Mary Michael lives in Denver," Moira said with a touch of urgency, eager to have something else to discuss.

Connor rescued her immediately. "Denver's a booming town. Have you visited her there?"

"Only once, and I confess to having enjoyed myself immensely. It was lovely to be with Michael and Ethan, of course, and my granddaughter, but the town had a charm I found very exciting."

Connor grinned. "I've never heard anyone from the east refer to Denver as charming."

Moira blinked, stunned momentarily by her guest's rare and roguish smile. It didn't matter that she was in love with her husband or that she had five daughters or that she was Connor Holiday's senior by a quarter of a century; she felt the full force of his boyish grin all the way to her toes. She was quite afraid she was blushing. "Well," she said somewhat defiantly, "I found it charming. It's loud and boisterous and colorful."

"So's the Bowery," Jay Mac said, "and you don't have to leave New York to get there."

Moira dismissed her husband's comment out of hand. "You love Denver, so it's no good pretending you don't." She turned back to Connor. "Michael's husband is a federal marshal assigned to the Denver area."

"You said Ethan," Connor said. "Do you mean Ethan Stone?"

"Why, yes," she said, pleased. "So you see, Jay Mac, Connor knows Ethan. It wasn't so silly to suppose that he might."

Connor shook his head before his hostess got carried away. "I know Marshal Stone by reputation. I've never had cause to seek him out."

Skye broke a dinner roll in half and began buttering it. "Not even about the cattle thieves?"

"Most especially not about them." He turned to Moira. "And your other daughter who lives in Colorado?"

"That would be Rennie. It's Rennie Sullivan now. She and Jarret—he's her husband—move around quite a bit. Rennie and Jarret work for Jay Mac's company, Northeast Rail. Our daughter is an engineer; she designs trestles and bridges and rail right of ways. Jarret builds them."

The last traces of Connor's smile vanished. His expression had become remote again, polite but cold. "I didn't realize that Mr. and Mrs. Sullivan were more than employees with Northeast."

"My," Beryl said, "Colorado does seem to be shrinking. Do you know everybody, Connor?"

"It's beginning to appear that way, isn't it?" And with his cool, distant tone he managed to convey that further mention of Rennie and Jarret Sullivan would be unwelcome.

Jay Mac picked at his dessert. Normally Mrs. Cavanaugh's cherry pie would have brought a request for seconds, but tonight his appetite had abandoned him somewhere between the soup and salad. Nothing he had planned for this evening was unfolding in quite the way he had envisioned.

Mary Margaret had led the mutiny by refusing to attend. Skye charged in where her sister feared to tread. Rushton seemed eager to have the business put behind him while Connor appeared not to want to discuss it at all. Moira's graciousness had been taxed by Beryl's thinly disguised contempt for Skye and her outrageous behavior. Had Jay Mac been forced to choose the person who was finding the dinner party the most entertaining, he would have picked Mrs. Cavanaugh. If her facial expressions were any indication, then she found most of what she heard while serving and removing courses to be vastly amusing.

Moira motioned to Beryl and Skye. "Why don't we leave the gentlemen to their after-dinner drinks?" she said. "We'll have coffee in the parlor."

In her eagerness to quit the room, Skye nearly toppled her chair as she leapt to her feet. She apologized clumsily, flushing to the roots of her flame-red hair, and left the table quickly. Moira and Beryl followed at a more sedate pace.

Connor waited until the door to the dining room closed before he rounded on Jay Mac and his father. "You've both blind-sided me," he said.

John MacKenzie Worth rose from the table and went to the sideboard. He was not as tall as either Holiday but he wore power and authority like a mantle. His carriage was straight with his shoulders set as firmly as his mouth. He began pouring drinks. "How is that?" he asked. "Since you and I have never met before today I fail to understand how I was able to . . . how did you put it? . . . blind-side you."

"Oh, you didn't do it alone." His gaze fell hard on his father. "You were helped immensely."

Jay Mac set a tumbler of whiskey in front of Connor. "Would you like a cigar?"

"I don't smoke," he said tersely.

"Neither do I," Jay Mac said. "At least not any longer. Gave it up when Michael was brought back to me alive and well." He offered Rushton the cigars and was pleased when one was taken. He might not smoke himself but enjoyed the peculiar pungent fragrance. "But I don't suppose you want to hear about that now," he said, lighting Rushton's cigar.

"No," Connor said dryly, "at the risk of being impolite, I can't say that I do." He knocked back his drink and without waiting to be offered more he went to the sideboard and poured his own refill.

Watching Connor, Jay Mac returned to his seat. "You don't drink to excess, do you?" he asked. "Your father never mentioned that might be a problem."

"My father doesn't know me well enough to say one way or the other," Connor said. It was difficult to keep bitterness out of his voice. "But it's never been a problem, at least not until I arrived in New York two months ago." He leaned back against the sideboard and crossed his long legs at the ankles. "I didn't know that Mrs. Sullivan was your daughter."

"I can't think how that matters."

"It matters. It's the reason you tried to stop your wife from talking about your family in Colorado. You knew very well that I had more than a passing acquaintance with both your daughter and son-in-law."

"Rennie and Jarret are both valued employees of Northeast Rail. It's incidental that they're related to me."

Connor doubted that Jay Mac really thought that way. John MacKenzie Worth was one of the richest and most powerful men in the country. Nothing about his influence was incidental. Connor directed his next question to his father. "You knew about Mr. and Mrs. Sullivan, didn't you?"

Rushton nodded. "Of course. But I agree with Jay Mac. It hardly matters. If they hadn't come across the land and seen its value someone else would have."

"It's enough that I know the value of that land. I don't need railroad surveyors and engineers to tell me what I have."

"You could hardly expect to keep your valley a secret forever."

The tips of Connor's fingers pressed whitely against the tumbler. "But it isn't my valley, is it?"

"That's true," Rushton said. "It's mine."

Jay Mac rolled his tumbler between his hands thoughtfully. "When my daughter telegraphed that she had found an excellent location for the line from Cannon Mills to Denver I was interested. Cannon Mills has untapped resources in silver and gold because until now there's been no way to ship out the ore. Northeast Rail has made a name for itself in the territory by giving rail access to miners and mining consortiums at fair cost. We did it first at Queen's Point and later in Madison. The people in Cannon Mills want the rail line."

"I told your daughter when she and the others came to do the survey that no part of the land was for sale. She asked to complete her survey anyway and I let her."

"Rennie's very persuasive."

Connor recalled the heated discussion that had swayed his judgment. "A gross understatement." He took a short swallow of his drink. "When she left with her team from Northeast I thought that was the end of it. Mrs. Sullivan, it seems, is not only persuasive, but persistent as well. She went to the land office in Denver and discovered that I didn't hold the deed. I suppose that changed everything in her mind. She recognized my father's name and had you call on him. I don't know when the conversation turned from land to heirs, or even who first broached the idea, but somewhere along the way the two of you stopped talking about railroad accesses and started talking dynasties."

Connor put down his drink. "Frankly, gentlemen, I'm just not interested." Not waiting for any response, he left the room.

Rushton and Jay Mac both listened for the sound of the front door being opened and closed. It never came.

"Where would he go?" Rushton asked.

"He's probably cooling his heels in the library. It's just down the hallway and I remember seeing the door was open earlier."

A cloud of blue-gray smoke circled Rushton's head as he exhaled slowly. "That didn't go well at all."

"No, it didn't," Jay Mac conceded. "I like your son though. He's not easily intimidated."

"He was insolent and insulting."

Jay Mac shrugged. "His back's to the wall and he knows it. I admire him for wanting to hold onto the land." He sipped his drink. "I apologize for my daughter's behavior this evening. I had hoped things would proceed along a different course."

"I confess that I thought your daughter would be older. I'm not certain that she and Connor would suit at all."

"Older?" Jay Mac frowned. "She's twenty-three. Surely that's old enough. Your son's what? . . . thirty? They're of an age where they would suit admirably."

"Twenty-three?" mused Rushton. "I wouldn't have guessed more than sixteen."

"How would you have guessed at all? She wasn't even here this evening."

Rushton looked at Jay Mac in some confusion. "Not here? But—"

"Oh, you thought Schyler was . . . heavens no . . . of course *they* wouldn't suit." He chuckled with genuine amusement. "Skye's nineteen though, not sixteen. I'm afraid she put on quite a show for your son tonight. It was really meant as a warning to me."

"A warning?"

"Yes, indeed," Jay Mac said. "She was telling me to . . ."

"Stay out of my life, thank you very much," Skye said, plopping down on the overstuffed chair in her sister's bedchamber.

"Did you actually say that?" Maggie asked, suspicious of her sister's bravado.

"I may as well have. Oh, Mag, you should have seen me! You would have been so proud!"

Maggie was also proud that she had had the courage to defy her father and not show up at all. Now, next to her younger sister's resourcefulness, it didn't seem so very much. "Proud or embarrassed?" she asked.

"Oh, both, I'm sure," Skye went on happily. Complaining that she didn't feel well, she had asked to be excused from the after-dinner conversation and her mother had barely been able to contain her relief. "No one knew quite what to do with me. I almost felt sorry for poor Mr. Holiday."

"Father or son?"

Skye shrugged. Her bright hair spilled over her shoulders. "Both, I suppose. Does it matter?"

"I think it's harder to feel sorry for the father. He's in this up to his neck with Jay Mac." She sighed and closed the book she'd been reading, keeping her finger in place to mark her page. "What's got into Jay Mac? I mean, why now? He's never mentioned marriage for me. He knows I want to be a doctor. I have an excellent chance of being accepted by that women's college in Philadelphia."

"Who knows why Jay Mac does the things he does? Besides the fact that he loves us and thinks he knows very well what's best for us. Michael stood up to him and so did Rennie."

"Rennie ended up marrying the man he picked out for her."

"True, but it was her choice. And Mary Francis did what she wanted."

"Mary Francis became a nun," Maggie said dryly. "Even Jay Mac has to realize there are limits to his influence."

Skye laughed. "Well, my point is that she did what she wanted. You'll have to do the same, Mag."

Maggie's lower lip was sucked in under her teeth. She worried it gently, her wide, green eyes uncertain. "I don't know. I'm not like the rest of you. It's not so easy for me."

"Easy? Who said it was easy? Do you think my heart wasn't thumping near out of my chest? I pushed that spinach between my teeth and smiled for all I was worth and prayed I had the courage to keep it there. I simpered and chatted and pretended I'd never completed a sentence, let alone a complete thought, in my entire life. Jay Mac was glaring at me, especially when I went on about religion, and Mama looked as if she wished herself anywhere but where she was. Rushton Holiday felt sorry for me, sorrier for Jay Mac and Mama. Beryl Holiday—who I do not like one bit, I can tell you, though she's astonishingly beautiful—was looking rather pleased because I was so clearly unsuitable for her stepson."

"And Connor?"

"He, my dear sister, shows the measure of just how difficult this was. Connor Holiday is a very handsome man. Very handsome. He was considerate, too. And polite. A trifle cool perhaps, reserved really, but that was to be expected. Playing the fool in front of him was rather like cutting off my nose to spite my face. Teaching Father a lesson about interference has never been so painfully humiliating."

"If you've taken a liking to Mr. Holiday then perhaps you should . . ."

Skye held up her hand, cutting off her sister. "Oh no, I worked too hard making my point to do an about-face. Besides that, I don't think Connor would have me as a gift."

Since her sister was a beautiful, and an often-sought-after companion, Maggie knew Skye must have made a horrible impression. "Then neither of us is going to have him."

"You'll have to make a stand. Jay Mac and Rushton are still plotting."

"How do you know that?"

Skye shook her head in disbelief. "Maggie?" she asked impatiently. "How can you *not* know that?"

* * *

Rushton Holiday stubbed out his cigar. "Where do we go from here?"

Jay Mac had long since finished his drink. He contemplated another one then decided against it. A clear head was called for. "Do you still want to sell the land?"

"I've never wanted to sell it, but you know the market. I need the funds."

Jay Mac nodded. He had been lucky to have sold some stocks early, anticipating the most recent downturn by only days. "Rennie says the tract of land leading from the mountain ridge through the valley is all she needs."

"It's the best grazing area. That's why Connor is so opposed. It cuts across the waterway and splits the property. Granted, it's a small strip when held against the entire acreage, but it's the most valuable—to your railroad *and* my son."

"Rennie has found another route that would be acceptable."

"Acceptable, but not ideal."

"True, but if you weren't willing to sell I'd have to take what I could get."

Rushton rubbed the bridge of his nose with his thumb and forefinger. "We've done business before, Jay Mac. We've been fair and honest traders and I'd like to think I know you a little better than most of our colleagues. You're not certain you want the land any longer. I can hear it in your voice."

"If you'll recall, Rush, I was never certain I wanted that strip. It was what Rennie wrote about Connor that intrigued me. She was impressed by his commitment to the land and more than a little impressed that the money she offered didn't turn his head. Connor thinks Rennie went to the deed office on her own, but I sent her there. I recalled you once saying something about property in Colorado; it seemed unlikely that the name Holiday was strictly coincidence.

"I continue to be more interested in Connor as a husband for my Maggie than in the ranch. If he were to marry her I'd settle the deed on him and we would forget all about using any part of the ranch for the line."

Rushton poured himself another drink. His jaw was set hard. A small furrow had appeared between his dark brows. "I'm not so desperate for money that I haven't thought all this through. I explained it all to Connor. He knew what was expected of him."

"But he didn't agree right away."

Rushton's mouth lifted in a half-smile, remembering. "No. He's my son, after all. Would you have respected him if he had?"

Jay Mac knew that he would not have. "You never told me what changed his mind."

"I suppose I didn't think it mattered." He tipped back a third of his drink. "After I talked to him he was angry. I think you can imagine how the interview went. You've seen how my son and I are together. There's no love lost between us." He shook his head, clearing it. "Afterward he went out and tied one on. He'd brought enough money east with him to stake himself in a poker game somewhere in the city. Don't ask me how he did it but he swears he won an entire twelve thousand that evening."

"He swears it? You've never seen the money?"

"I've never seen it. He was feeling a little full of himself, or perhaps he was still angry, I don't really know. He went to a brothel. He says the woman he was with that night stole his money." Rushton watched Jay Mac carefully to see what reaction he had to the story. Jay Mac's expression was contemplative, not judgmental. "He agreed to meet your daughter later, after it was clear to him that his money wasn't going to turn up."

"I see. Then he came here tonight feeling as if there was no other choice."

"Very much so. You neglected to tell me the name of the daughter you had in mind for him. We've never done business on such a personal level before. I'm afraid I assumed you meant Schyler. I'm certain Connor must think the same."

Jay Mac nodded wearily. Children should not be so difficult, he thought. "Before we agree to make this strictly a business transaction, let's see if we can't think of a way to bring Connor and Maggie together."

Beryl was finding Moira pleasant company, not as silly or frivolous as her youngest daughter. "Really," she said, laughing lightly over the rim of her coffee cup. "It's beyond me why anyone thought

Rush's son and your daughter would be a good match. She's terribly young for him."

Moira took no offense in the remark though she found it interesting that Beryl Holiday would cast her stone in that direction. Moira didn't think she was too far off the mark by putting the difference in Beryl and her husband's age at two dozen years. She was certain Beryl was younger than Rushton's son. "I doubt either Jay Mac or Rushton thought it through," she said easily. "It's very much like Jay Mac to do so in personal matters, though I can't say about your husband."

"And I don't think I can say about Rush. We've not been married all that long."

"I'd forgotten, though you're obviously well suited. One would never suspect that it's been less than a year."

"Just under eight months, actually."

"Under eight months? Why that's quite hard to believe." Moira added a dollop of cream to her coffee. "How did you and Rushton meet?"

Beryl realized the question was asked in all innocence but it still caught her off guard. "Didn't you know?" she asked in an attempt to recover her composure. "I thought everyone knew. I met Rushton when he came to visit Connor a year ago."

Moira didn't understand why that would have caused Beryl the slightest discomfort, yet it was clear her guest was flustered by the question. "I'm sorry," Moira said. "Have I put my foot in it somehow?"

"Oh no," Beryl said, forcing a smile. "I'm so used to people knowing . . . I just assumed . . ."

"Dear, you don't have to explain yourself—I'm sure I don't need to know."

"No, it's quite all right. You're bound to learn it and it's nothing I'm ashamed of. You see, I was Connor's fiancée when I met Rushton."

"I see," Moira said slowly. And she did see. A lot more than Beryl Holiday thought she had revealed.

"I don't want to hear any more, Skye," Maggie said. "You did wonderfully well and I'm envious and grateful, but it doesn't change the fact that I don't know what I can do." She ignored Skye's pouting lower lip. "I think I'll go to the library. I have more reading to do." She raised her book which still held her index finger captive. "You're welcome to join me as long as you'll be quiet."

"I don't think so. Jay Mac says you spend all your time in books and for once I'm inclined to agree with him."

Maggie smiled. "Careful, Skye. I could use that against you." Her sister's musical laughter followed her into the hallway.

Taking the back stairs to avoid the company, Maggie slipped into the library quietly. A feeling of calm overtook her almost immediately. The smell of the leather bound volumes, the stillness in the air, the expectancy of adventure and knowledge to be pried free of the pages—Maggie sensed it all. This was the room that signified home for her and she would miss it most of all.

She found a bookmark and laid aside her reading on the table inside the door. The fire in the hearth was a welcome surprise. She had expected to have to light one herself. Intent on stoking the flames, Maggie skirted the pair of large wing chairs facing the fireplace. She picked up the poker and tapped it against the marble apron. The voice that came from behind her caught her completely off guard.

"I swear to God I should beat you with that."

Chapter Four

She was precisely as he remembered her. There was some small satisfaction in knowing that his memory hadn't betrayed him. There *had* been a whore, just as there had been twelve thousand dollars.

He waited for surprise to give way to recognition as his dark eyes took her in. The fire behind her cast her delicate features in shadow and created a penumbra about her head, streaking her hair with gold and copper. She wore it pulled back, loosely caught with a grosgrain ribbon. He could see that her full mouth was parted, that her cat-green eyes were widened a fraction larger than usual. She gripped the poker like a weapon, holding it up near her shoulder to get a full swing.

Her dress was plain navy blue, more for service than fashion. The high neckline was buttoned modestly to her throat, the sleeves rolled up to her elbows, and an apron tucked neatly about her waist. When she moved suddenly, intending to dart out of the way, he noticed that the toes of her shoes were scuffed. Whatever she had done with his money, it hadn't been spent on herself. Yet.

He leaned forward and grabbed a handful of her skirt as she attempted to dash past him. Connor yanked her hard, sending her off balance. She dropped the poker harmlessly on the floor and came crashing over the arm of Connor's chair to land squarely in his lap.

Maggie pushed at his chest but he held her fast, locking his arms about her waist and pinning her wrists with his hands. She quieted only when she recognized the futility of struggling and Connor was patient enough and strong enough to wait her out.

Summoning the threads of her dignity, Maggie said, "Please let me go, sir."

"In time."

Maggie frowned, turning her head to look at him fully. His voice was soft and rough and somehow dangerous. It was also vaguely familiar. She didn't understand how that could be. Uncertainty caused a shiver.

He felt her tremor. "The fire's warm enough," he said. "I doubt you're cold. That leaves scared. Have I frightened you?"

Though she didn't understand it, it seemed to Maggie that he would have been satisfied by her fear. She merely blinked at him.

"What are you doing here?" he asked.

"I . . . I came for a book."

Connor gave her a little shake. "Don't be stupid."

"I don't know what you mean." She pulled impatiently, trying to free her wrists. "Please let me go. You're hurting me."

"I'm not," he said. "But I should. I should beat you within an inch of your life and unless you answer my questions I just may do it."

"I'll scream."

He laughed at her threat. "That's not the sort of thing you generally announce. You simply do it. Anyway, try it. See what happens."

Maggie looked down at her captured hands. To stop her from screaming he would have to let her go. Hadn't he realized that?

He had, of course. As soon as Maggie opened her mouth to scream Connor jerked her lower in his lap and covered her mouth with his own. She was too surprised to clamp her teeth closed against his intrusion. His tongue pushed, his lips moved across hers. He deepened the kiss even when there was no response from her. He drew it out until he felt her sag against him, not submissive, merely resigned.

Connor pulled back and studied her. Except for the swollen ripeness of her lips her face was devoid of color. Her eyes were awash with unshed tears. Her breathing was shallow and light and where once he had thought she was only frightened, he now saw she was terrified. Connor released her completely and gave her a push off his lap.

Maggie scrambled to her feet and out of Connor's reach. She

stared at him mutely, her vision blurred by the tears that would not fall.

"You're not going to faint, are you?" he asked.

Was she? She didn't know. She'd never done it before. "I don't . . . I don't think so." Why was it so difficult to catch her breath? She could barely hear for the slamming of her own heart. "You're not going to do that again, are you?"

"Are you going to try to scream?"

She shook her head.

"Well then, I won't do *that* again," he said roughly. He pointed to the wing chair at an angle beside him. She dropped in the seat like a stone. Connor nodded approvingly and yanked the chair closer, turning it so she was facing him directly. "Tell me what you're doing here. And not that nonsense about getting a book. I want to know what you're doing in this house."

"I live here."

"Do your employers know about your other profession?"

"My employers?" Maggie's head began to pound. The ache behind her eyes was nearly blinding her. "You're confusing me. I don't think I want to—"

"Where's my money?" Connor demanded tersely.

Maggie bowed her head and began to rub her temples with trembling fingers. Tears finally slid over her pale cheeks.

Connor was unmoved. "My money," he repeated harshly.

Maggie looked at him helplessly. She started to get up but he grabbed her by the wrists again and jerked her back into her chair.

Leaning forward, Connor rested his forearms on his knees. His eyes were intent on hers, his features coldly set and unsympathetic. "You can call out for anyone you wish," he said, "but are you prepared for what I'm going to say when they get here?"

She frowned. "What . . . what would you say?"

"That you're a thief and a whore."

Maggie sank back into the chair, revolted. "I think you're a horrible man, Mr. Holiday."

Connor had a long way to go before he felt any shame for anything he'd done since Maggie entered the room. He actually smiled at her pathetic pronouncement about his character. "So you *do* know who I am."

Maggie impatiently brushed away her tears. "Of course I know who you are. Everyone's been expecting you and I saw you arrive earlier tonight. You didn't come in the carriage with your father and stepmother."

His eyes narrowed, pinning her back with the force of his stare. "If you hope to avoid another nasty confrontation, then don't refer to my father's wife as my stepmother. Her name is Beryl."

"All right."

"You're very compliant," he said, watching her closely.

"I don't know what else to do." There was a ball of nausea in the pit of her stomach. She folded her arms across her middle as if she could keep it in place. The back of her throat stung with rising bile that she forced back. "Are you going to hurt me?"

"Not if I get my money."

She felt tears creeping back into her eyes. She shook her head, biting on her lower lip. "I don't know about any money."

"Liar."

"I don't." She swiped at her eyes. "Please, I want to go upstairs now."

Connor had no difficulty ignoring her plea. "I suppose you don't know about Mrs. Hall's house either."

Maggie stared at him blankly.

"And you never prostituted yourself there."

She blanched.

"You never spread your thighs for me, never crawled all over my body, never took me in your mouth, and never left with my bag filled with more money than you could make in four lifetimes."

When Maggie stood this time he didn't stop her. She held one hand over her mouth, certain she was going to be sick. It wasn't until darkness was upon her that she realized she was fainting.

Connor caught her before her head hit the floor. She slumped against him, a dead weight in his arms as he lifted her. There was a chaise on the far side of the library and he took her there and laid her down. He tapped her cheeks lightly with the back of his fingers. She didn't stir and the only color in her face was the hue he forced there.

Shaking his head, disgusted, Connor stepped into the hallway and strode toward the dining room. He poked his head in the door. Jay Mac and his father were still deep in discussion and didn't notice him until he had been standing there a full ten seconds.

Jay Mac saw him first. "Connor, come in. I'm glad you've decided to join us. Your father and I were just—"

Connor held up his hand, interrupting his host. "I need your assistance in the library. One of your hired help has fainted."

Jay Mac was on his feet instantly. Rushton followed. Connor preceded them back to the library, ushering them in. He was closing the double doors and was unaware that Jay Mac had stopped in his tracks only a few feet inside the room.

"I thought you said it was a servant," Jay Mac said, his eyes fixed on his daughter's pale face.

Connor turned. "She is, isn't she?"

Jay Mac shook his head and went to Maggie's side. "Rushton, will you find Mrs. Cavanaugh, our housekeeper? Ask her for smelling salts, but don't alarm her. She'll alert Moira and there's no reason for that yet."

Rushton left the library, a sinking feeling in his chest as to the identity of the unconscious girl. He gave his son a hard, accusing stare in passing.

"What the hell happened?" Jay Mac demanded. He sat on the chaise at the level of his daughter's waist and took her hand in his, rubbing it. "Maggie's always been delicate but she's not prone to fainting."

Maggie. Connor had wondered about her name. "I believe I frightened her, sir. She wasn't expecting to see me in the library." It was the truth as far as it went and Connor had no qualms about saying it.

"That doesn't sound like Maggie." He tapped her cheeks the same way Connor had earlier. "But then she hasn't been quite herself these past six weeks. I don't know what's been wrong." He was hardly aware he was speaking aloud. "She insists it's nothing, but I wonder."

Connor stepped closer to the chaise. He could just make out Jay Mac's whispered and strained voice and each word was another nail in his coffin.

"A father can't help worrying."

That last nail slammed home. Connor looked past Jay Mac's shoulder to Maggie's composed and still features. His thief, his whore, was the daughter of John MacKenzie Worth.

Rushton appeared at that moment with the smelling salts. Connor took them from his father and knelt beside the chaise. He took the stopper from the ammonium salts and waved it slowly beneath Maggie's nose. She responded almost immediately, wrinkling her nose and trying to get away from the sharp, pungent odor. Connor pulled back his hand and waited. Her long lashes fluttered and when she saw Connor leaning over her she said the first thing that came to her fuzzy mind: "I don't need a doctor."

Jay Mac patted her hand a little harder, laughing with relief. "Of course you don't. I'm not going to send for one."

"But . . ." She looked at Connor in some confusion, an elusive memory, a certain uneasiness, playing at the back of her mind. He simply returned her stare. She could see her own reflection in his dark eyes. Then she remembered other things, the terrible accusations he had hurled at her, and she cringed from the blankness of his expression now.

"I'm sorry I frightened you," Connor said.

He wasn't sincere, she thought. Didn't Jay Mac know? Couldn't his father hear it? She tore her eyes away and looked at her father. "I'd like to go to my room now," she said a trifle breathlessly. "I'm feeling rather silly." She squeezed her father's hand. "Mama doesn't know, does she?"

Jay Mac shook his head and helped Maggie up. Connor sat back on his haunches and put the stopper back in the bottle of salts. Rushton stepped aside as Maggie came to her feet. She blushed, embarrassed to have made his acquaintance under these circumstances.

"If you'll excuse me," she said, her eyes dropping to the floor. "I . . . I can make my own way to my room." She lifted the hem of her gown a few inches and hurried from the library.

"So that's Mary Margaret," Rushton said once she was out of earshot. "You never mentioned that she was sickly."

"She's not." Jay Mac and Connor spoke at the same time.

"She's not," Connor repeated more softly. "I frightened her."

Rushton ignored his son and looked questioningly at Jay Mac. "What have you been keeping from me, Jay Mac? I thought we had put all our cards on the table but I'm not so certain any longer. Is there something about your daughter that makes it imperative she make a marriage soon?"

Jay Mac stiffened. "I don't think I like what you're getting at,

Rushton. Perhaps you'd better make yourself entirely clear or drop the subject altogether."

"I didn't think I minced my words," he said stiffly. "But if you need it said differently, then I'm asking you: Is Mary Margaret pr—"

Connor did not allow his father to finish the sentence that would good as finish a business relationship that had survived the better part of a decade. "I'd like to ask for Maggie's hand in marriage, sir," he said to Jay Mac.

"Connor!" His father spoke his name sharply, forgetting momentarily that he had never exerted any influence in his son's life, and if he had, the time had long since past where it could be influenced by a single utterance of Connor's name.

Connor continued to address Jay Mac. "I'm quite serious about this, sir. I would like permission to call on your daughter."

Jay Mac's ash-blond brows were pulled together in a single line above his eyes. He took off his spectacles, folded the stems, and tucked them into his vest pocket. It gave him time to think. There were things here he did not understand. Of that much he was certain. He and Rushton both had what they wanted, yet he didn't feel entirely satisfied and it was clear that Rushton didn't, either.

"I'd like to speak with Maggie privately first," Jay Mac said.

It was not what Connor wanted but he had no choice. "Of course."

"But not tonight. I don't think she's up to it tonight."

"I understand."

"Come and see me in two days. At the Worth Building. Do you know where it is?"

"I can find it." Connor looked at his father. "I'm ready to leave. If you and Beryl want to stay longer I'll walk."

"That won't be necessary," Rushton said. "We'll go with you."

It was much later that night when Jay Mac and Moira had retired to their bedchamber that he told her about Maggie's fainting spell and Connor Holiday's offer. Moira stopped plaiting her hair and turned on her vanity stool to seek out Jay Mac's assurances. It was one of the few times she saw nothing in his face to ease her worry.

One of them had to say it and Moira could see that Jay Mac couldn't bring himself to do it. "Do you think Maggie's pregnant?"

"No!" He sat down slowly on the edge of their bed. "That is, I don't know. Who could be the father? She hasn't been anywhere, seen anyone . . . she knows her books and medicine, nothing . . . no one else."

Moira could see that it was time to return the strength he usually showered on her. She left her vanity and sat beside him on the bed. "It's not the end of the world if she is," she said softly, taking his hand. "We had five daughters out of wedlock. We raised five children without benefit of a church vow between us."

Jay Mac barely heard her. "She's been so secretive."

"Maggie's always kept to herself."

"Yes, but if she's pregnant . . ."

"What's bothering you, Jay Mac?"

"The father's married. I know it. That's what it is. It's why we've never seen her with anyone or heard her talk about him."

"You were married," Moira reminded him gently. "I was your mistress for twenty-eight years and I still would be if Nina hadn't died."

"That was different," he said stubbornly.

She smiled. "And someday I shall make you tell me how. Right now, however, I'm going to see our daughter and ask her myself if we have reason to be concerned on that count. And if I haven't insulted her beyond all reason, you can tell her later about Connor Holiday's offer."

Maggie was sitting up in bed, an unopened book in her lap, when her mother entered her room. She had been holding the book for the better part of an hour, never finding the energy or interest to read any part of it. She put it aside and shifted her legs to make room for Moira.

"I thought you'd be sleeping by now," Maggie said.

"I could say the same thing to you."

"Is anything wrong?"

"And ask you the same question."

Maggie's smile faltered; her green eyes darkened. "Jay Mac told you what happened downstairs." She saw in her mother's careworn expression that she had guessed correctly. "He shouldn't have.

There was no need. I'm fine, really. It was the silliest thing. I don't know why it happened."

Moira searched her daughter's fine-boned features. Of all her daughters it was Maggie who most emphatically bore the Dennehy stamp. Her character, in turn, was also more like Moira's than Jay Mac's. Moira wondered if Maggie ever regretted that she was not more like her father or her sisters. Perhaps it was that very reason that Moira herself felt closer to Maggie. They shared a quiet strength. Moira had tapped hers many times over the years; Maggie, she knew, did not yet suspect what she was capable of.

"Perhaps we should ask Dr. Turner to examine you," Moira said. She pulled her hair over her shoulder and began to plait it. "When people faint there's usually a reason."

"I think it's just been nerves, Mama. You know how it is when Jay Mac sets his sights on one of his own. I suppose it's my turn now and I don't know if I'm up to it. I want to go to medical school. Why is he trying to stop me?"

"Is that what he's doing?"

Maggie leaned forward and took the braid out of her mother's hands and began to plait Moira's hair herself. She had always found it easier to talk if her hands were occupied. "What would you call this . . . this *obsession* with Connor Holiday?"

"I don't think your father believes that medicine is a fitting profession for a woman."

"That's not fair. Michael's a newspaper reporter. Rennie's an engineer. Are those fitting professions for women? Must I become a nun like Mary Francis?"

"If you recall, your father wasn't very pleased with her decision, either." Moira laid her hand over Maggie's busy fingers. "You've had your education, dear. Four years and a degree just like your sisters. That's more than most men in your father's position allow for their daughters. If you want still more then you should be prepared to take it on your own and not look to Jay Mac for help."

"I have money saved. What I don't have I'll work for. I'm not afraid of that. But, Mama, I want to do it with your blessing. Yours and Jay Mac's. Do you think I can't do it? Is that it?"

Moira shook her head. Her hand squeezed Maggie's. "Your father and I have talked about this for a long time, for as long as you've made your wishes known. Neither one of us doubts your ability.

Don't ever think that. What we doubt is that you can support yourself. No, hear me out. You must have considered it. Who will come to see you? Who will have you as part of their practice? You'll always be frustrated by what you can do for others and will never be given the chance. *That's* what worries your father, and if I'm honest, it worries me as well."

None of this was what Maggie wanted to hear. The knot that had never left her stomach tightened. "So I should get married."

"Not if you don't want to." Moira took a calming breath. Her hand dropped away and she turned so she could see her daughter fully. "There's no reason that you think you have to, is there?"

Maggie's brows furrowed. She tilted her head, emphasizing the slant of her eyes. "You mean other than Jay Mac's insistence that I should."

"Other than that."

"I'm not sure I understand. Why would you . . ." Her voice trailed off as her frown cleared and her mouth gaped slightly. "Because I fainted? Oh, Mama! How could you? Is that what you and Jay Mac think? That I'm carrying a child?"

"It occurred to us," Moira said honestly. She didn't look away, feeling that she owed her daughter that much. "You've been so quiet recently. I'm not even certain when we first noticed it—perhaps as long as a month and a half ago. We've been worried, Maggie, you can't expect that we wouldn't be. You'd tell us, wouldn't you, if you were pregnant?"

Something kept Maggie from answering that question. She answered another. "I'm not pregnant," she said.

"Could you be?"

"Immaculate Conception?"

"Don't be blasphemous."

"I'm sorry."

Moira sighed. "And I'm sorry, too, Maggie. Sorry that I had to ask. Deeply sorry that I didn't have more faith in your judgment." She leaned toward Maggie and kissed her daughter's forehead. "Go to sleep now. Let's put tonight behind us."

Maggie caught her mother's sleeve before she could move away. "Do you ever regret raising all of us alone?"

"Is that what you think? That I raised you alone? It's not true, Maggie. Your father was always with me, even when he was with his wife. He probably saw more of you than if we had lived under the same roof all those years. Every spare moment he had he spent with us. Don't ever forget that. Know this, Mary Margaret: I have no regrets about my life with your father. None."

"Do you think your parents were disappointed in you?"

"They were dead by the time I met Jay Mac, but yes, I suppose they would have been deeply disappointed with the choices I made."

Maggie merely nodded, thoughtful. She dropped her mother's sleeve. "Good night."

Moira smiled. She stood there for a moment longer, watching Maggie as she turned on her side and drew the comforter about her shoulders. Moira turned back the bedside lamp, then she left the room, only a little less troubled than when she had entered it.

It was a long time before Maggie drifted off to sleep. In the back of her mind were the things that Connor Holiday had called her. Thief. Whore. The things he had said she'd done: spread her thighs, crawled all over his body, took him in her mouth. He was an evil man. A disturbed, deranged man.

But Mary Margaret Dennehy would have slept easier if she could have accounted for eight hours on the night of March 24.

Connor Holiday leaned against the granite blocks in an alcove of the Worth Building. His stance was casual, ankles crossed, arms folded in front of him. He looked as if he were watching the pedestrian traffic on Broadway, taking in the hurried single-mindedness of New Yorkers going about their business. At another time he would have found all the activity entertaining in its own fashion. Now, on a street crowded with people, for all intents and purposes, Connor Holiday was alone.

She didn't want to marry him. The words played again in his mind. Sometimes in Jay Mac's voice, sometimes as if he were hearing Maggie's husky, melodious tone. She didn't want to see him. She didn't want to have anything to do with him.

The outcome of the interview with Jay Mac wasn't entirely surprising. Connor had expected Maggie Dennehy to have objections. What he wasn't prepared for was that Jay Mac, who had initiated everything, who had plotted and prodded and prompted toward a very different end, was actually going to honor them. It made Connor wonder if Maggie had told her father the content of their conversation in the library—or the circumstances of their first meeting.

He shook his head. He couldn't quite imagine Maggie repeating his actions or his accusations to Jay Mac. Connor couldn't quite imagine still being alive if she had. Yet there wasn't a thing he had said that he would take back. All of it was true. He remembered the evening at Mrs. Hall's establishment very well even if Maggie Dennehy pretended not to, and there wasn't much that had happened there that he would take back, either.

Connor pushed away from the granite wall and thrust his hands in his pockets. He needed to know more. If he was going to collect on what Jay Mac's daughter owed him, he needed to know something more than he did now.

When he jogged down the steps outside the Worth Building, when he turned the corner onto Ann Street, Connor had no clear destination in mind. He thought he was still uncertain about where and how he might have his questions answered. He would have said his walking was aimless, without purpose or direction, yet twenty minutes after leaving the Worth Building Connor found himself in the middle of the red light district.

Lisa Antonia Hall didn't usually see visitors before noon. The girls were still abed and she never felt as if she were at her best. She made an exception when Samuel told her who was waiting in the foyer. Connor Holiday was trouble. It had been too much to expect that she had seen the last of him.

She patted down her hair, arranged the string of pearls around her neck, and smoothed the skirt of her gown over her hips. Papers cluttering her mahogany desk were quickly stuffed inside the middle drawer. She eyed her palm-sized pistol, wondering if she should keep it handy, then decided against it. It was pushed to the back of the drawer as her business ledger was shoved in.

Mrs. Hall stood behind her desk while Connor was shown into her office. She smiled in greeting, hoping she was more gracious and cool and in charge than she felt.

"What can I do for you, Mr. Holiday?" she asked, indicating to Connor that he should take a seat in front of the desk. "Would you like a cup of coffee? I can ask Samuel to bring some for us." The

bouncer, and sometimes butler, was hovering near the door waiting
for his orders. When Connor declined the offer Mrs. Hall dismissed
him. "I imagine that you being here means you haven't recovered
your money."

Connor realized it was a rather large concession on the madam's
part to make that statement. "Then you do believe I had the money
with me."

"When cooler heads prevailed that day the doctor and I both
believed you." She leaned back in her chair, tilting her head to one
side. "I would hope by now that you realize your accusation in my
direction was unfounded."

"I don't know that with certainty, but I'm willing to listen. I'd like
to hear more about the girl you put me with that night."

Mrs. Hall held up one beringed hand and shook her head slowly.
"I did not put you with that young lady, not on purpose. It was your
misfortune, and certainly hers, that I have the most difficult time with
directions of a left and right nature. I admit to not noticing which
way you turned at the top of the stairs, but I thought I was sending
you to Megan's room, nowhere else."

Connor was reserving judgment, his gaze fixed on the madam.
"Why do you say it was *her* misfortune? I'm the one who had twelve
thousand dollars stolen."

"That young woman came into this house a virgin. The evidence
on those sheets says she wasn't one when she left."

Connor blinked, not quite believing what he was hearing. "Surely
that's not a circumstance unknown here."

"My girls all have experience before they work for me."

"She didn't."

"She wasn't one of my girls."

He forced himself to relax. "I think I'll have that coffee after all,"
he said.

Lisa nodded and rang for Samuel. After giving her man the order
she turned back to her guest. "After you left here six weeks ago I had
this house searched from top to bottom. I supervised every aspect of
it personally. We went through the attic and the root cellar. We
turned over beds and tore apart wardrobes. Your bag and your
money aren't here. When you didn't return I assumed you had come
to that conclusion yourself or that you had found it." The bracelets
on her left wrist jangled musically as she made a sweeping gesture

with her hand. "I invite you to look anywhere you wish. You may inspect my ledgers, my personal bank books, or the finances of any of my employees until you're satisfied that we don't have your money."

Lisa reached inside the middle drawer and pulled out her expense ledger. She slid it across the desk toward Connor. "You can start with this one though they're all at your disposal. Running an establishment such as mine requires a certain amount of discretion, confidentiality, and practices that are above reproach. That includes trust. The clientele entertained here expects it." She nudged the ledger again, challenging him to pick it up. "I'm very aware you haven't made any slanderous remarks concerning my business. I would have felt the effect of them by now if you had. My clientele is only loyal to a point. They would have abandoned me if they thought I couldn't be trusted."

She waved Samuel in as he returned with the coffee. When her cup was served, creamed, and sugared just the way she liked it, she picked up the thread of her conversation again. "Which leads me to believe, Mr. Holiday, that in spite of your words to the contrary, I think you know that I'm innocent of any wrongdoing."

Connor drank his coffee black. Playing his cards close to the vest, he resisted the temptation to tell the madam she was right. "Tell me what you know about the girl," he said. "She's the only lead I have."

Lisa replaced her cup in its saucer and folded her hands on the desktop. "I know very little, though you can be sure I made some inquiries of my own. My sources in this case aren't entirely reliable."

"Tell me anyway."

"The best I can piece it together is that she somehow wandered into the district on her own. Not even this end of the district. She was lost along Canal Street before she got this far. Apparently she was accosted by a group of sailors looking for some entertainment. They were probably too drunk to take note of her clothing or her manner and see that she didn't belong where they found her." Lisa heated her coffee with a little more from the pot. "Harlan Porter, a pimp of the worst sort, rescued her."

"Rescued?" asked Connor.

"A relative term, to be sure," she replied dryly. "It seems he led her along, promising to get her home, then ended up drugging her and trying to sell her to Horace Beale. Beale, by the way, is an old man with a taste for young flesh."

The surface of Connor's remote calm rippled a little. His fingers whitened a fraction on the delicate china cup.

Mrs. Hall had seen the infinitesimal change in her guest's features but she didn't comment. It satisfied her to imagine that he was remembering the girl in that moment. "My man Samuel, who managed to get these details from Harlan with very little in the way of physical persuasion, tells me that she escaped Harlan at that point. He chased her and caught up with her in my back yard. One of my young women sent him running and we took in the girl.

"I'm no fool, Mr. Holiday. I knew that girl wasn't part of the life and it certainly wasn't my intention to help her take it up. The poor thing was ill. She had bruises on her neck where Harlan or the sailors had choked her and between that and her sickness and the drugs she couldn't get a word past her throat that anyone could understand.

"We set her up in a spare room, drew a hot bath for her, gave her some laudanum, and sent for the doctor."

Connor jerked. Coffee sloshed over the rim of his cup and trickled down his fingers. Lisa was there immediately with a linen napkin, mopping his hand and fawning over him. He took the napkin from her and set his cup aside. "It's nothing," he said.

"Did you burn yourself?"

"It's nothing," he repeated curtly. He didn't know himself why it had happened, not with any certainty. It was something Lisa had said, something that caught his attention, his memory, in a particular way and then was gone before he could grasp its implication. "You were saying . . ." he said as she returned to her chair.

"Actually I was finished. You know better than I what happened next."

Connor had recovered his calm. He dropped the napkin on the serving tray. "I was sent to the wrong room."

"Not intentionally," she said quickly.

"Perhaps," he conceded after a moment's pause. "I'm not a fool either, Mrs. Hall. When I arrived in that room I had no reason to believe your guest wasn't precisely what she seemed to be. She was compliant and she wasn't a chatterbox."

"She was feeling the effects of the drugs and she was ill."

Connor's dark eyes narrowed. "What are you saying? That I forced her?"

"I wasn't in the room. Did you?"

He stood and leaned forward at the desk, bracing himself stiffly against it, towering over Mrs. Hall. "You don't know anything about it."

Lisa Antonia Hall was not cowed. She stared up at him calmly. "If you ever find the young woman perhaps you'll ask her what she thinks. Perhaps she feels she was perfectly entitled to your money after what you took from her."

Something flickered in Connor's eyes before they became reflective again. He straightened, turned on his heel, and left without a word in reply.

Skye rounded the corner in the upstairs hallway and came to a halt on the landing. Looking down the wide staircase to the foyer below, she saw her sister adjusting her yellow straw bonnet in the mirror. "Where are you going?" she called. "It's barely daybreak."

Maggie almost stuck herself with her hat pin as she jumped. The wild strawberries decorating the brim bobbled.

"I didn't mean to frighten you," Skye said, hurrying down the stairs.

"It's all right." That was because it was guilt that had made Maggie jump, not fear. She adjusted the bonnet again. "I was woolgathering."

"Oh?" Skye asked hopefully.

"None of your business."

Skye pulled a face, disappointed. "Oh."

Satisfied with the arrangement of her bonnet, Maggie stepped away from the mirror. "I'll be home in time for luncheon." She placed one hand on the door knob.

"Where are you going?"

Maggie's hand tightened on the knob but she answered easily. "To the library."

Skye nodded. Then she noticed her sister didn't have any books or papers or pens. And it was absurdly early for such a visit. Her brows knitted. "Maggie," she began earnestly, "if there's something that—"

"Not you, too!" Maggie said. It was not hard to appear betrayed. It was exactly what she felt. "Please, Skye, don't do this. Mama and Jay Mac are so certain there's something wrong that they watch me all the time. I'm feeling smothered in my own home. I can't go anywhere without being interrogated."

"You haven't gone anywhere," Skye pointed out. "Not in weeks you haven't. Not since you told Jay Mac you weren't going to marry Connor Holiday. One would think you're afraid you'll run into him."

"Don't be ridiculous. He's probably back at his ranch by now."

"Well, if he is, it won't be for long. Jay Mac is getting ready to close the deal with Rushton. The Double H won't be Connor's after that."

Maggie closed her eyes momentarily as she felt uncertain guilt wash over her again. Weeks ago she had accepted the fact that somehow she was at fault for Connor losing the land, yet she had no clear idea why that should be so. "It was never Connor's," she told her sister sharply. "It was his father's."

Skye frowned. "You're different, Maggie. Something's not—"

"I'm going to the library." She slipped outside and closed the door firmly behind her.

There was the scent of early summer in the air. The day was warm, slightly humid, and the air was redolent with the fragrances from flower gardens in full bloom. Maggie's light shawl was more of a wrap than she needed but she drew it around her shoulders protectively, chilled from within. It made no difference that she was out of the house. She was still smothered. It was her own company that she wished to escape, her own thoughts, the terrible sense of dread that seemed to weigh her down so she was alternately sluggish or numb.

She didn't want to think about where she was going or what awaited her there, but she found she had almost no choice in the matter. She couldn't call up the numbness to serve her when she needed it most.

Maggie Dennehy lowered her head and hunched her shoulders as she approached the large brownstone on the northeast corner of 52nd Street and Fifth Avenue. The residence of Madame Restell was a pretentious one, built long before the wealth of the city began moving uptown. It was a quiet scandal that the denizens of Fifth Avenue could now count the most notorious and expensive abortionist in the city as one of their own. She was excluded from public social circles, but she had intimate knowledge of the private ones. After more than thirty years of practice she was feared, and therefore protected.

Maggie hurried up the front steps, glad it was still very early and the normally busy thoroughfare had only a little traffic. She rang the bell and was shown in almost immediately.

Maggie waited nervously in a sumptuously appointed parlor furnished in royal purple and gold. Thirty long minutes ticked by before Madame Restell joined her.

"You shouldn't have come here," she said haughtily. She was a slender woman who carried herself with a stately air that lent her height and consequence. The pale skin of her face was engraved with fine lines, especially around her mouth where they underscored an unfaltering and sour expression. The clear, sharp eyes were frankly assessing, wise, and shrewd. "This is my home. I have offices on Chambers and Greenwich Streets. I advertise them."

Maggie had come to her feet upon Madame Restell's entrance. Her fingers fidgeted nervously in the folds of her gown. "I . . . I didn't know," she said uneasily. "I only knew that you lived here."

"Then this is a social visit?" she asked coldly.

"No."

"No. Of course it's not. It couldn't be, could it? We've never met before." She waited expectantly, wanting a name to put to the delicately featured face in front of her.

"Must you know my name?"

"*Naturellement.* You know my name. Knowing yours is my best protection."

It didn't even occur to Maggie to try to lie, she was so bad at it. "Mary Margaret Dennehy."

Madame Restell didn't blink. With typical directness she said, "One of Jay Mac Worth's bastard daughters." When she saw Maggie's surprise at her instant recognition she added, "I find it amusing to know the skeletons in other people's closets."

Maggie bristled and her wide green eyes fired brightly. "My sisters and I are hardly skeletons since Jay Mac has never tried to hide our existence."

"Nor tried to get rid of it either, it seems," Madame said bluntly. "It's a certainty you weren't referred here by your mother."

At the mention of her mother Maggie blanched. Her legs felt unsteady beneath her.

"Sit down before you drop." Madame Restell rang for tea. When it was brought she served some to Maggie but took none for herself. "Drink it all," she ordered. "It will put color back in your cheeks. Have you lost weight recently?"

"A few pounds, I think."

"Judging by the fit of your gown I'd say it was closer to ten. And you have none to spare. Have you been trying to lose it?"

Maggie shook her head. She saw Madame's shrewd eyes drop to her tea cup and Maggie quickly took a sip.

"That's better," Madame said approvingly. "Then you weren't trying to hide the fact that you're pregnant?"

"Am I?"

"Don't you know?"

"That's why I came here." She took a large swallow of her tea, burning the inside of her mouth this time.

"You came here to find out if you're pregnant?" Madame asked slowly, scarcely believing it.

"Shouldn't I have?"

"Most women go to a doctor first or wait until they know with absolute certainty."

"But I can't go to my doctor. He's a family friend and I don't want anyone to know."

"So you came here."

"That's right." She set aside her cup and saucer. "Will you help me?"

Madame Restell looked hard at her guest. John MacKenzie Worth's daughter. It was a lovely irony. The man had been trying to buy her property and move her off Fifth Avenue for the better part of a decade. He had fathered five bastard daughters and carried on an open affair with his mistress for years, and he was not only accepted by society, he was one of its leaders. She welcomed the opportunity to make him beholden to her. Mary Margaret Dennehy. It was too delicious to pass. "Come with me, child, and bring your tea."

Maggie left by a side entrance less than an hour later. She was too dazed to bow her head or hunch her shoulders, too insensible to comprehend the risk she was taking by allowing herself to be seen.

She could only think of the packet that Madame Restell had slipped into her hand at the end of the examination. Infallible French pills. Maggie didn't know if she was afraid enough to use them or more afraid not to.

Beryl Holiday opened the front door because the knock came while she was passing. It bothered her that with five servants in the house none of them ever seemed available for the little duties she thought were so intrinsically their province. She vowed to speak to Rushton about it again. It was intentional, she thought, not mere coincidence. The servants didn't respect their new mistress.

"Yes?" she asked. "Is there something I can do for you?"

"You must be Mrs. Holiday."

At least the woman hadn't mistaken her for a servant. "That's correct."

"I'm Maggie Dennehy."

Beryl stared at Maggie blankly. It took her a moment to recognize and place the name. When she did, she blinked widely, shocked that Connor had made an offer for her. Mary Margaret Dennehy was thin and curveless. Her cheekbones were too prominent, her eyes too large, her mouth too full. Beryl supposed her hair was a nice feature but the humidity had curled it haphazardly around the bonnet she wore.

"Of course, Miss Dennehy. Won't you come in?" Beryl, feeling more in control of things by the second, opened the door wider.

Maggie hesitated. "Is Mr. Holiday at home?" she asked. "Connor, I mean. I've come to see Connor."

Beryl's inclination was to lie but she wasn't given the opportunity. Connor stepped out of his father's study and into the hallway. "I'm right here, Beryl," he said. "Please show Miss Dennehy in."

There was no choice but to comply. She ushered Maggie in. "May I take your shawl?" she asked politely.

In response Maggie drew it around her like armor. Her grip relaxed only when she caught the amused, almost superior glance that Beryl tossed off in Connor's direction. Maggie raised her head a notch, straightened her spine, and walked boldly toward Connor. He stepped aside to let her precede him into the study and blocked Beryl from following.

"Don't even think it, Beryl," he murmured. "You heard Miss Dennehy. She came to see *me.*" He started to shut the door and paused to caution his former fiancée. "And no eavesdropping."

Beryl stamped her foot. "You're hateful, Connor Holiday."

"I know." He shut the door in her face.

Maggie was hovering near the chair where he had been sitting and reading. Her eyes had strayed to the book that curved open over the arm of the chair. She was tilting her head, trying to read the gold leaf lettering on the spine.

"Don't twist your neck," he said. "It's Jules Verne's *Twenty Thousand Leagues Under The Sea.*"

Maggie didn't attempt to hide her surprise. "I don't know what to make of that," she said honestly. "Are you enjoying it?"

"Very much so." He watched her consider that, finding it odd that she could amuse him with her seriousness.

"I wouldn't have expected it."

"You don't know me very well."

It was like a wash of cold water slipping over the surface of her skin. She felt her skin go alternately hot and cold but she managed to say steadily, "I wasn't sure that you would be here."

"You came anyway."

"I took a chance. I thought perhaps you'd have returned to Colorado by now."

"I'm leaving in a few days."

"I see." She found it easier to look anywhere but at Connor. "My sister told me this morning that my father and yours are getting ready to close the deal on the land."

"That's right." He watched her expressive eyes fix on a point beyond his shoulder. She was worrying her lower lip. "Is that why you've come?"

She looked at him. "What?" Her eyes darted away again. "No, that's not it."

"So you don't have my twelve thousand dollars." He was almost sorry he said it, she looked so pained.

Maggie shook her head. "No, I don't . . . I can't . . ." Her soft voice trailed away. A film of tears formed in her eyes and she blinked quickly to force them back.

"Maggie?"

She turned away. "Those other things you said to me that night in my home," she began before she lost her courage, "were they true?"

Connor surprised himself by hesitating. Finally he said, "Yes. They were all true."

Even though she had been expecting nothing less, her shoulders sagged slightly. She drew in a deep breath and turned to face him again. She raised her chin and this time she found the courage to look directly in his cool and remote eyes. "A few hours ago I found out I was carrying a child. I wondered if you might be the father."

Chapter Five

Connor Holiday had had his gut twisted by double-fisted punches that were less numbing than the blow Maggie had just dealt him. He knew he had heard her correctly and he didn't insult her by asking her to repeat it. "Why don't you sit down, Maggie?" That way he could do the same. He felt he had to.

She looked around and chose the short sofa opposite Connor's chair. She perched on the edge like a fledgling bird, hands folded neatly in her lap, her face raised expectantly.

Connor went to the door, opening and closing it softly to make certain Beryl wasn't on the other side. He returned to his chair, put his book aside, and sat. "Don't you know who the father is?" he asked quietly.

Maggie's face flushed with color but she managed to keep looking at Connor. "There's been no one . . . that is, no one I know of. I only thought of you because of those things you said."

He leaned forward in his chair and rested his forearms on his knees. His hands pressed together, forming a steeple with his fingers. "Isn't it time you stop pretending?"

"Pretending? Oh, I see. You think I'm making it up." She shook her head. "Perhaps I don't want to remember, Mr. Holiday, but it's still true that I *can't* remember."

Connor thought that over, then responded to the only thing that made sense to him. "It's *Connor*, Maggie. You may as well call me that. Then there's no confusing me with my father."

A terribly gruesome thought occurred to Maggie. Her expressive eyes relayed her panic. "Did I . . . you know . . . with your father?"

Something flickered in Connor's eyes. His voice was colder than he intended. "No. That's not something *you* have to answer for."

Relieved, still a little confused, Maggie released the death grip she had on the folds of her gown. "But I did with you," she said.

"Yes."

She shook her head wonderingly. "It's hard for me to believe," she said, not much above a whisper. "It's as if it happened to someone I don't even know." She stilled and stared steadily at Connor, trying to imagine herself touching him. It was difficult to get past the granite remoteness of his face, the coldness that seemed powerful enough to burn her with its intensity. Had her fingers threaded in his inky-black hair? Sifted through the thickness at the nape of his neck? Had she touched the hollows just beneath his cheekbones or felt the warmth of his bronzed skin?

Had she kissed him? She remembered the kiss in the library of her own home when he had wanted to stop her from screaming. She was wondering, though, about a different sort of kiss, one that was without force or anger, just for pleasure's sake. Had she kissed him like that?

Maggie's eyes had dropped to Connor's mouth, her expression intent on the shape of his lips, until she realized the hint of the smile she saw there was at her expense. Embarrassed, she dropped her gaze to her lap. "I don't see how I could have done what you say."

"You did."

"But I don't know how."

"You learned."

"But—"

"Maggie," he said, his tone approaching gentleness. "You're carrying a child. How much more proof do you require?"

Her knuckles whitened as her fingers knotted in her lap. "Can it be anyone else's child?"

Connor's faint smile vanished. "That would make it more palatable, is that it? It's easier to believe as long as I'm not the one who had his calloused ranch hands on you."

She knew she had angered him but had no clear sense about why.

"Yes . . . no . . . that's not what I meant." Maggie stood and crossed her arms about her middle. She went to the study's single arched window and stood in front of it, looking out. "I don't know what *you're* talking about now. You must know this isn't easy. None of it. I walked for hours before I gathered the courage to come here and maybe it's only fear that's keeping me rooted in this room, but I'm still here and I came for answers. I need you to fill in gaps, not create them." She turned toward him again and asked frankly, "Are you the father of my child?"

He could have said he wasn't certain, that he couldn't account for the hours after she left him or the days and weeks that followed, but he declined to muddy the waters or perpetuate the notion, in his own mind or hers, that she was a whore when he knew it was no part of the truth. "The child's mine," he said.

Maggie was silent for a time, just thinking. She didn't even feel Connor's steady regard. "It was March 24th, wasn't it?"

"Yes. You remember that?"

"Not the way you think. It's the only day in my adult life that I can't entirely account for." She glanced at him. "Where did we meet?"

Connor stood. He pointed to the sofa while he reached to ring for a servant. "I think you'd better sit down, Maggie. I'll have some lunch brought to us. This could take a while."

They didn't speak at all while lunch was being prepared. Maggie browsed through Rushton's collection of books while Connor pretended to do something other than watch her. She caught his attention without any guile on her part and that puzzled him. She was outside the realm of his experience. It was easier to deal with her when he thought she was a jade. Then he remembered there was still the matter of twelve thousand dollars. For some reason that made him relax.

Maggie wasn't hungry and under Connor's watchful eye it was even more difficult to eat, but somehow she managed to do credit to the luncheon that had been prepared.

"Tell me what you remember about the 24th," Connor said. He buttered a roll and gave Maggie half.

"I was at the library most of the day. Skye came in with her friends and wanted me to join them on a scavenger hunt." She took a small bite of the roll. "I didn't really want to go but my sister can be very persistent. It was easier to give in. We broke into teams and went looking for the items on our list. Skye's main reason for wanting me along was so she could be with her friend Daniel. No one else would have let her disappear alone with him, but she didn't give me any choice in the matter."

"So she was with Daniel and you were by yourself."

Maggie nodded. She smiled slightly, unaware her eyes had clouded. "I didn't mind," she said. "I wasn't afraid or anything like that. I continued to collect things on our list. My problems began with a pair of white gloves."

"I don't understand," he said. What he did understand was that she had hated being left to carry on alone and it seemed a betrayal of her sister to say so. "What about the white gloves?"

"I needed to find some. I saw a man coming out of Delmonico's who was wearing a pair and I thought I would simply ask him for them." She sighed. "Only I'm not so brazen as all that and I followed on foot a long way before I realized I could *never* ask him to give me his gloves for a silly game. I let him go on and that's when I think I realized I was lost." Maggie looked down at her plate, pushing a bit of cold roast beef to the side, then raised uncertain eyes to Connor. "I don't know anything else. The next thing I clearly remember is Skye waking me up in my own bed the following morning."

Connor held her gaze for a long time before her eyes finally dropped away. "Do you want to hear this, Maggie?" he asked. "Have you really considered whether you want to know what happened?"

"I can't *not* know," she said quietly.

Connor saw that she wasn't going to eat any more so he put aside the serving table that had been placed between them. She declined his offer of tea. He poured a small tumbler of whiskey for himself. "I don't know all the details of that evening, not about the things that happened before I met you, or after you left me, but I think I know enough to fill in some of those hours."

"I'm ready," she said.

Connor doubted it. "You followed the man with the white gloves from Delmonico's to the red light district." He saw by the embarrassed color in her cheeks that he didn't have to explain what that meant. "While you were there, perhaps while you were trying to find your way out again, you were accosted by some sailors."

Maggie stared at him, fascinated as he went on. She heard the words he was saying but there was no connection to herself or anything that she had ever done. This time it *was* as if these events had happened to someone else. It was impossible to imagine that she had ever encountered a man like Harlan Porter or escaped him only to find herself a guest of a brothel . . . and to be mistaken for a whore? . . . it was the most incredible stuff and nonsense Maggie had ever heard.

She held up her hand, cutting Connor off. "This is ridiculous," she said bluntly. "I can't listen to any more of it. Now I know why you like *Twenty Thousand Leagues*. It's not a fantasy to you. Not if you think what you're telling me is true." She started to rise.

"Sit down, Maggie," he ordered.

"You can't—"

"Sit down."

She did. Her green eyes were angry now.

"I have no reason to lie about these things."

"You have twelve thousand reasons," she pointed out. "And you're trying to lay the blame at my feet."

"You have a baby in your belly," he said roughly. "And you came here looking for someone to blame."

"I came looking for answers."

"It's a sure thing you didn't come looking for the truth." This time it was Connor who stood up. The fact that Maggie shrank back when his shadow fell across her infuriated him. "How did you think it happened, Maggie? How did you imagine we met?"

"I don't know. I didn't think about it . . . I couldn't."

"Liar. I'll bet you thought we met in Central Park, that we walked along the promenade or around the pond. You probably imagined we were overcome by a moment and couldn't help ourselves. Is that how your romantic head and heart got you with child?"

She simply gaped at him, speechless.

"We *were* overcome by a moment," he said brutally. "But it was *animal,* not romantic. I thought you were there for me and I believed *you* thought you were there for me. It didn't happen once. It happened twice and the second time was better than the first. It happened in Mrs. Hall's brothel, not on a bed of grass in Central Park.

It happened with me, not one of your whey-faced city suitors. And that's the truth, Miss Dennehy. You can rail against it all you want but it doesn't change what happened. It certainly doesn't change the fact that you're pregnant."

Maggie stood. "No, but maybe Madame Restell can do that." She brushed past him on her way to the door.

Connor grabbed her wrist and stopped her in her tracks. He felt her shudder but he held her fast and gave no quarter even when she turned to face him defiantly. "What did you say?" he asked sharply.

His eyes should have been the color of ice chips, she thought. Eyes that were so deeply brown that they were almost black should have been warmer. Perhaps it was because she couldn't see into them that they were so cold. Even his anger was cold. Only his palm around her wrist was warm and there he held her so tightly she couldn't move her fingers. "I said," she repeated slowly, enunciating each word so there would be no mistaking it, "that perhaps Madame Restell could do that." His grip didn't ease. "Now let me go. You're hurting me."

His fingers relaxed but he didn't let her go. "Who's Madame Restell?"

Maggie had forgotten that Connor hadn't been raised in New York. "She's one of your neighbors."

"That's no answer."

"It's the only one you're getting from me. Now, let me go." She was sick with fear and it made her brave. The thought of humiliating herself by losing her last meal in front of him gave her courage she hadn't known she possessed. He was looking at her as if she were a particularly fascinating insect. Any moment she was afraid he might pluck off her wings.

Instead he set her free.

Maggie rubbed her wrist, returning circulation to her fingers. She watched him warily. "I want to leave now."

"I'm not going to stop you."

She nodded. "Thank you for that at least."

He went to the study door with her. "When I call on you at your home I expect to be able to see you."

She had no idea why he expected that but she managed a short nod. She was biting her lower lip again.

He opened the door for her. "I'm leaving for Denver in a few days. We should settle things between us before then."

Maggie bit her lip harder and nodded more emphatically this time. "Settle things," she said. "Yes, we should do that."

Moira caught her daughter as she was slipping through the front door. "Skye said you'd be home for luncheon. You didn't make it."

Maggie removed her hat and placed it on a table inside the entrance hall. She ran her fingers through the crown of her hair. "I apologize, Mama. I thought I would be. I hope you didn't worry."

Moira didn't respond directly to that statement. "Your sister's waiting to see you in the parlor."

"Skye? Why is she waiting . . ." Her voice trailed off as another thought occurred to her. She tried to inject some enthusiasm into her tone though the return of dread and panic was what she was feeling. "Mary Francis is here?"

"Hmm-mmm. She came late this morning and stayed for lunch. She didn't want to go back to the convent without seeing you."

"That was sweet of her." There was no doubt in Maggie's mind that her father and mother had arranged this. Mary Francis rarely arrived unannounced; her responsibilities with Little Sisters of the Poor were too enormous to give her the freedom to come and go as she pleased. Mary preferred to stay where she was most of the time. Her presence at home meant that Moira and Jay Mac had called for the big gun.

Maggie was thinking just that as she entered the parlor. Nothing about her sister's appearance supported Maggie's thoughts. It was a matter of agreement among the four younger sisters that Mary Francis was the real beauty of the family. The perfect symmetry of her features set her face at rest, giving her a serenity of expression that seemed otherworldly at times. That her face was framed by the cornet of her habit only emphasized the impression. She was tall, slender, graceful in her movements, even inside the bulky and figure-hiding habit. It wasn't Mary's appearance that made Maggie think of a big gun. It was firsthand knowledge that Mary Francis never minced her words, that she was rarely reticent, and that she packed the punch of a cannonball. Maggie never particularly thought Mary was suited to the sisterhood. She should have been a general.

"It's good to see you," Maggie said, reaching out to hug her sister. She felt herself enveloped in her sister's arms and Maggie wondered if she hadn't been mistaken. She felt such peace in Mary's embrace. She realized she meant it; it *was* good to see Mary Francis again. "No one mentioned you were going to be here today."

With typical frankness Mary said, "I think that was the plan. Jay Mac was concerned you'd run scared."

Maggie laughed. It sounded strange to her ears and she realized then how long it had been since she found anything amusing. "I well may have." She sat down on the sofa and Mary Francis joined her. "Are you here to pry certain secrets out of my head?"

Mary grinned. "Something like that. No one seems quite certain what's going on with you, Mag. The only thing everyone agrees on is that you're unhappy."

It bothered Maggie that she was the subject of so much discussion behind her back. She managed to force a smile. "Do I seem so unhappy to you?"

"Yes. That smile doesn't particularly support your efforts."

Trust Mary to see right through her. "I suppose you have a theory. Mama and Jay Mac thought there was a man." She was amazed she could say these things so matter-of-factly. If she worked at it she would be able to lie, even to Mary Francis. "Skye thinks I'm still mad at her for a trick she played on me weeks ago."

"Any truth to either one of those?"

"No."

Mary's calm, forest-green eyes were unwavering as she studied Maggie's face. "What's your explanation?"

"Nothing's wrong."

Mary Francis shook her head. One slender hand rested on her rosary beads. They slipped through her fingers in an unconscious gesture. "That's where you're making your mistake. To say that nothing's wrong when something so obviously is commands everyone's attention. Do you understand what I'm saying?"

Maggie wasn't certain. Was Mary Francis teaching her to prevaricate or helping her protect her privacy? Or was it a little of both? "I think I do."

"You don't, but it's sweet of you to pretend." Mary Francis released her beads and took Maggie's hand in hers. "I know you'll tell us the truth when you're able," she said. "In the meantime, know that you're in my prayers."

It was the stinging ache of unshed tears at the back of Maggie's throat that kept her from blurting out Madame Restell's name. It was difficult to swallow, impossible to speak.

Mary's hand squeezed Maggie's. "Tell me about medical school," she said. "Have you heard anything?"

Somehow she managed to get the words out. "I expect to hear something soon. I've been studying a lot in case I'm accepted."

"Mama says you spend a great deal of time at the library."

She nodded. "I like it there. It's quiet and peaceful. Rather like the convent, I imagine."

Mary's beautiful smile animated her face and brightened her eyes. "Oh, Maggie, not at all like the convent. Except for prayers it fairly echoes with joyful noise. If I want to be contemplative, *I* go to the library."

"Mama would wring her hands if she heard you talking like that," Maggie said.

"Poor Mama. I think she's afraid if I'm not more respectful I won't be able to atone for her sins. I try to tell her that Our Lord did that already but she sees me as her sacrificial lamb."

"Mary Francis! That's practically blasphemous!"

"I think it *is* blasphemous." She shrugged. "And then I think it anyway. And say it. I can't seem to help myself. Sometimes I wonder if Mama promised her firstborn to the church so everyone else might do as they wish."

Maggie's eyes widened. She'd never had an inkling that Mary Francis felt that way.

Mary patted her sister's hand. "Now, don't go thinking I'm saying something I'm not," she cautioned. "And whatever you do, don't point Jay Mac and Mama in my direction. Perhaps I'm a little more sensitive to your dilemma, whatever it is, because I'm in the middle of my own. You should be thankful. It wouldn't have taken me but two minutes to pry your secrets loose otherwise."

Maggie knew that was true. "What will you say to Mama?"

"That she should get involved in charity work like other *grande dames.*"

"You won't!"

Mary Francis gave her younger sister a sidelong glance almost begging to be dared. "Oh, all right," she said, giving in, "but it would have kept her from worrying about you for a while."

"I can take care of myself, Mary," Maggie said softly.

"I know," came the gentle reply. "That's what I'm going to tell her."

Connor did not try to see Maggie that evening, for which she was grateful. She spent most of the night in her room staring at her supply of Infallible French Pills. At bedtime she tried a dozen hiding places before she decided to sleep with them under her pillow.

The next morning it was the breeze just above her face that woke her. She blinked, her eyes crossing as she tried to focus on the thing Skye was waving in front of her nose. "What is that?" she asked, batting it away.

"A letter," Skye said excitedly. She was dancing in place and looking every bit as young as Beryl Holiday had first thought her. *"The* letter! C'mon! Wake up!"

Maggie pushed herself upright and managed to relieve Skye of the bobbing letter with one swipe.

"It's from the Philadelphia Medical College," Schyler said helpfully.

"I can see that." She examined the seal on the envelope and ran her index finger around the edge slowly.

"Well? Aren't you going to open it?"

It felt too light to be an acceptance. It was probably a rejection. An acceptance would have some instructions in it, wouldn't it? Maggie started to wedge her nail under the seal. She stopped.

"What is it?" Skye demanded. "Aren't you excited?" Then with sudden insight she understood the problem. Her face fell. "Oh, no. You don't want me here. That's it, isn't it?"

"I'm sorry, Skye. I need to do this alone. It's not you, it's anybody. I suppose I'm a little afraid." It seemed these days she was afraid of everything. "You understand, don't you? I'll tell everyone at breakfast. No matter what the news, I'll need that much time to myself."

Skye leaned forward and kissed her sister on the cheek. "I hope it's wonderful news," she said. "The very best." Then she dashed out of the room, fingers crossed on both hands.

Maggie had to wait for her slamming heart to quiet. She cracked the seal, pulled out the letter, and unfolded it very carefully. Taking a deep breath, she read silently.

At the end there were tears in her eyes. She let them fall. They dripped on the back of her hand; they smudged the ink. She came to a decision then. She knew what she had to do. It was the same thing she couldn't have done yesterday even with a gun held to her head. It seemed incredible that a single letter could exert so much influence.

Maggie reached under her pillow and found the packet of Madame Restell's pills. She rose from the bed slowly and padded on silent, bare feet to her bathing room.

Three expectant faces were turned in her direction as she entered the breakfast room. Jay Mac had delayed his trip to the office to hear Maggie's news. She gave them a half-hearted smile and saw they understood immediately.

"It's not the end of the world," she said brightly, a shade too brightly perhaps, she thought. "I can reapply next spring for the fall term."

"But you did so well on your exams," Schyler said. "And you were a straight-A student."

"That's not the only thing they care about. I wasn't a very popular student. I didn't join any clubs or take any leadership positions." She shrugged. "Anyway, there are only twenty-two openings in the school and my letter says they had more than a hundred applications."

Jay Mac shook his head in patent disbelief. "A hundred women who want to be doctors? It defies common sense."

"Jay Mac," Moira said severely. "This is not the time or the place." She rose from the table and poured orange juice for everyone.

John MacKenzie Worth was properly abashed. "I'm sorry, Maggie. It doesn't matter what I think. I know your heart was set on this."

"It's all right, Papa." Everyone at the table except Maggie noticed that she called Jay Mac "Papa." It was the clearest evidence they had of how horribly sad she was feeling. "I've been thinking that this is the way it would be. I wasn't really very hopeful. Maybe that's what everyone's been noticing about me these last months. I suppose I've been expecting rejection all along."

Skye's elbows spread across the table as she leaned forward, her expression pained and earnest. "I'm sorry, Mag. I know how much you wanted it to be otherwise. I wish . . ." She trailed off, blinking back tears. Her sister's hurt and disappointment was very real to her; she absorbed it as her own.

"It's all right," Maggie said gently, becoming the comforter. "I was prepared a little bit more than you. I've been thinking of other things I can do."

Jay Mac nodded. "That's right. There's no sense waving the white flag in every direction. Why, you could—"

Moira interrupted her husband before he enumerated all the things *he* thought Maggie could do. She looked significantly at Jay Mac. "I'd like to hear Maggie's thoughts."

Maggie glanced at her father. He was chafing a little at Moira's interruption but showed no signs of overriding her suggestion. Maggie picked up the jam and began spreading it on a slice of bread. "I've been thinking I should be getting some practical experience," she said. "I don't know if it would have occurred to me if Rennie hadn't mentioned it in a letter not so long ago, but she did and it has."

Jay Mac stopped eating. A strip of bacon dangled in his fingers at a midpoint between his plate and his mouth. He was very interested in what Rennie may have suggested. He was also very worried. When his daughters began putting thoughts in one another's heads they were a force to be reckoned with. "I don't suppose her recommendation had anything to do with Connor Holiday and you and marriage."

Maggie put down her knife and looked squarely at her father. "Papa, *everyone* knows that was your idea and the less said about it, the better."

Moira hid her smile behind a napkin as the crisp bacon strip snapped in Jay Mac's fingers. Skye grinned openly at Maggie's courageous confrontation.

"What I want to do," she went on, "is study with Dancer Tubbs."

Now Jay Mac's brows shot nearly to his hairline. Moira lowered her napkin slowly. There was no smile to hide any longer. Skye's face reflected her confusion. All three of them, with nearly identical inflections of incredulity, said simultaneously, *"Dancer Tubbs?"*

Maggie continued as if there had been no amazed reaction by any member of her family. "I don't know, of course, if Mr. Tubbs will have anything to do with me, but I know how he feels about you, Jay Mac, and I thought that may count for something."

"But Dancer Tubbs lives in Colorado," Moira said.

"Yes, I know. But so do Rennie and Michael. It's not as if there'd be no family there."

"I thought Dancer Tubbs lived alone in the middle of nowhere in Colorado," Skye said.

"He does," said Maggie. "But that doesn't bother me. Rennie would always know where to find me."

"The conditions would be very primitive," Moira said.

"I could adjust," Maggie replied. "Anyway, you have to think of what I'd be learning. Jay Mac's said himself that Mr. Tubbs knows a great deal about healing. He saved Jay Mac's life after the train wreck at Juggler's Jump; set his broken legs and brought him back to good health. Rennie thinks the world of him. He healed Jarret's shoulder when no physician anywhere could. Rennie says Jarret has full use of his arm and hand now and she credits Mr. Tubbs."

"I don't think it would be safe," Moira said.

"How couldn't it be?" asked Maggie. "No one bothers Mr. Tubbs. He keeps to himself. I'm certain I'd be quite safe."

Still disbelieving what she was hearing, Skye shook her head slowly. "Are you quite certain you read Rennie's letter correctly?" she asked. "Was she seriously suggesting you do this?"

"I didn't mean that it was her idea exactly. She wrote something that put the idea in my head."

"Well," Jay Mac said firmly, "you can put the idea out again. You're not going."

Silence blanketed the breakfast room. Skye stared at her plate. Moira studied the napkin in her lap. Maggie felt heat and color rise in her cheeks as she looked steadily at her father. Jay Mac began eating, the matter settled in his mind.

"Excuse me," Maggie said softly. She stood, dropped her napkin on her chair, and left the room before anyone saw her tears.

* * *

"Where are you going?" Beryl asked as she slipped into Connor's bedroom.

"None of your business." He shrugged into his jacket.

Beryl closed the door behind her and leaned against it. "What did that Dennehy girl want yesterday?"

"I'm surprised it's taken you this long to ask," he said.

Beryl's eyes narrowed and her mouth tightened. He knew perfectly well why she'd had to wait to ask the question. Connor had managed to make himself inaccessible. "So?" she asked. "What did she want?"

"None of your business." He walked to the door and was forced to stop when Beryl refused to step aside. "Get out of my way, Beryl."

She didn't move. "Are you going to see her?"

"It's really none of your concern. You're my father's wife, not mine." He waited a beat. "Move, Beryl."

She shook her head. "Why do you keep pretending you don't want me, Connor?"

He managed to hold his temper. "It's not a pretense," he said.

"Rushton knows you still want me."

"That's something you'd like him to believe. There's no truth in it."

Beryl reached out boldly and laid the flat of her hand against Connor's groin. "Oh no?" she asked. Under the practiced manipulation of her hand she felt him respond. "It seems you're lying."

A muscle worked in Connor's taut jaw. He took Beryl's wrist in his hand and very deliberately removed it from his groin. "Get out of my way, Beryl."

The hardness in his opaque eyes thrilled and frightened her. She moved this time.

Connor stepped into the hallway and nearly ran into his father. "She's in there," he said, jerking his chin toward his room and making no attempt to hide his disgust. "You know, you probably saved my life by marrying Beryl Walker. It's a damn sure thing you saved hers." He kept on walking.

Once outside Connor didn't bother to hail a hansom. He hated the confines of carriages, even the open ones, and itched to be riding his own mount again. None of the horses in his father's stable were bred for the hard free-range work that Connor's animals performed on the ranch. Rushton's mounts were beautifully matched high steppers, purchased for show. They had speed. Connor's mounts were sure-footed mountain climbers and hard-driving herders. They had endurance.

It was just seven o'clock when Connor arrived at the Worth home. The housekeeper opened the door to him. "Connor Holiday to see Mary Margaret."

"Sure, and I know who you are, young man," Mrs. Cavanaugh said. "It's a real pleasure, I can tell you that, though I don't speak for anyone but myself. Always a pleasure to cast these eyes on a handsome devil like yourself."

Completely disarmed, Connor hesitated on the threshold.

"Well, step inside. She's not going to entertain you on the stoop." Mrs. Cavanaugh shut the door behind him. "Truth is, she may not entertain you at all. She's in the library. I'll announce you."

Sensing an ally, Connor touched the housekeeper's arm, stopping her. "I know where the library is. Perhaps it would be better if I just went ahead alone."

Mrs. Cavanaugh considered it, her mouth puckered to one side thoughtfully. "She'll be fit to be tied," she said, "but it's nothing I've not seen before. Go on with you." She waggled a finger at him sternly. "I'll be close by."

Maggie was sitting in one corner of the sofa, her stockinged feet curled under her, her gaze unfocused and vague. There was an unopened book on the rug beside her shoes. The drapes were drawn, keeping out late spring's twilight. Except for a single oil lamp on the table beside the sofa, the room was dark.

She looked up when she heard the door click shut. "I didn't think it would be you," was all she said. She went back to staring at the shelves of books on the opposite wall.

"May I?" he asked, indicating the chair in her line of vision.

She shrugged.

Connor sat down. She was staring right past his shoulder and he didn't try to gain her full attention. It gave him a moment to study her. She was sitting at the edge of the circle of light, her features partly obscured by shadow. Half of her hair was a dark blend of browns, the other half shot through with threads of copper and gold. Her eyelids were faintly swollen, the rims just hinting of red. As deep as he could see into her eyes he could only see sadness.

"Your housekeeper let me in," he said quietly.

Still not looking at him, she nodded. "There's no one else here."

"I hadn't expected that."

"Jay Mac's still at his office. He . . . he got a late start today. Mama's gone to see Mary Francis at the convent and Skye's with friends. Would you like some refreshment? Mrs. Cavanaugh could—"

"No, nothing for me." He watched her withdraw again. The change was almost imperceptible, just a small movement of her head and a slight hunching of her shoulders, but he was coming to know what it meant. "After you came to visit me yesterday I asked a few questions," he said. "I know about Madame Restell."

Maggie wasn't surprised, merely resigned. "I shouldn't have told you."

"But you did."

"I was angry."

He nodded. "And frightened, I think."

She shrugged again.

"Have you done anything about your threat?" he asked.

Now she looked at him. "You mean, am I still carrying your child?"

He was silent a moment. "Yes," he said, "that's what I mean."

She watched him carefully. "No. Madame Restell's pills are as advertised: infallible." What was it she saw there in the darkly remote eyes? Pain? Relief? It was gone so quickly that Maggie wondered that she had seen anything at all. Indifference was his practiced expression. She wished that it might be hers.

"I see," he said. "I believe I will have something to drink now."

Was he celebrating or mourning? Maggie rose gracefully from the sofa and went to the sideboard. She pointed to the various crystal decanters and stopped when he indicated the whiskey. She poured three generous fingers in a tumbler and handed it to him.

"Nothing for you?" he asked as she returned to the sofa.

"No." She had never been able to drink. Alcohol went right to her feet and emptied her head of every sensible thought she'd ever had. She almost told him but she suspected he already knew that about her. "Nothing for me."

He warmed the whiskey by rolling the tumbler between his opened palms. "When are you going to marry me?" he asked.

She blinked, stared at him, and blinked again.

Connor repeated the question.

"I heard you," she said. "But I wonder if you heard me. I told you Madame Restell's pills worked. I'm not pregnant. There's no reason for you to marry me."

"If you recall, I asked you to marry me before I knew there was a baby."

"If you recall, I said no."

"Why?"

"Why!" She was surprised to hear the passion in her voice. "I don't love you!"

Connor was fascinated by the brightness that had come into her eyes. "So?" he asked reasonably.

"I don't even like you."

"I know. It's mutual." He paused, watching her. A cold half-smile played at one corner of his mouth. "Or did you suspect I might feel differently about the woman who calmly tells me she's aborted my child?"

Maggie shivered at what she saw in his eyes this time. He didn't merely dislike her, she realized. He despised her. An idea, one that would have been impossible to imagine minutes earlier, began to form in her mind. "You want the land, don't you?"

His gaze didn't waver and he didn't lie. "Yes."

"I don't believe I took your money that night."

"And I don't believe it was anyone else."

"It's not like me," she said. "I've never stolen anything."

It was Connor's turn to shrug indifferently. "The way I remember it, you did a number of things that night you've never done before."

Something tugged at the edge of her memory and Maggie was awash with a physical sensation she couldn't understand or explain. Pleasure rushed through the center of her. Her breasts swelled and her nipples hardened. A hand was on her skin. A mouth. A tongue wet her lips, pressed against her teeth. Please, she heard a voice say. Please. It was her own voice. She closed her eyes.

Maggie jumped to her feet and pressed her knuckles against her mouth. Pleasure shattered as the memory disintegrated and Maggie was left with a burning sense of shame. She wrapped her arms around her middle and stepped away from the light.

"Maggie? Are you all right?"

She nodded. It was all she could do. It was difficult to catch her breath but how could she tell him that? How could she tell him what had happened when she hardly knew herself?

"Do you want me to ring for the housekeeper?" he asked.

"No." She sat down slowly and resumed her curled position, tucking her feet under the skirt of her coral gown. "It's nothing."

Connor wasn't so sure. He raised his glass, drank a little, then watched her over the rim.

"I don't suppose I can convince you about the money," she said.

"No, I don't suppose you can."

"But you know I don't remember."

"I'm still skeptical about that," he said. "But I'm willing to be convinced."

Of course, she thought, when there was no way she could offer proof he was willing to hear the evidence. "If I agreed to marry you," she said, "you would get the land."

"That was the arrangement suggested by your father. My father sells the land to Jay Mac and it becomes your dowry."

"And therefore yours."

"That's right."

"And what do I get?"

Connor didn't hesitate. "Satisfaction that your debt has been paid in full."

"Only one of us agrees there *is* a debt," she said. "I only have your word that there ever was any money."

Connor stretched his legs out in front of him. "There was money," he said.

"Even if I agree there was, it's still not enough to make me marry you."

If Connor had ever had any doubt he was dealing with Jay Mac's daughter, Maggie was making certain he knew it now. He wondered if she was aware of how like her father she was at this moment. Nothing had changed about her physically. She was as delicately featured as her mother, her wide green eyes as guileless, her expression almost serene, but she was setting up her trade with the shrewd business savvy of Jay Mac himself. "What is it you want?" he asked.

"A divorce."

She had the power to surprise him and this time it showed on his face. He set down his tumbler. "You marry me and then I divorce you."

"Yes." Now her tone was perfectly reasonable. "You get the land and I get what I really want."

"The divorce?" He didn't pretend to understand.

Maggie shook her head. "That's the means to an end. What I want is an escort to Colorado, specifically to a man named Dancer Tubbs. I want to know what he knows about healing. I have reason to believe he'll let me stay with him and learn from him."

Connor Holiday actually laughed. "Dancer Tubbs? You think you'd be welcome to stay with Dancer Tubbs?" Still smiling, he shook his head. He picked up his drink and took a short swallow. "I don't know how you've even heard his name, or know anything about him, but you don't know enough if you think you'll find a welcome there."

Maggie raised her chin a trifle haughtily. "A while back my father was thought to have died in a train wreck at Juggler's Jump in Colorado."

"I'm aware of that. Your father's an important man. News of what happened reached my ranch the same as it did everywhere else. As the crow flies, Juggler's Jump's about twenty miles from the Double H. I was part of one of the first search parties to go over the area."

Maggie hadn't known that. "Then thank you," she said sincerely.

"For what? I didn't find him."

"You looked. There were others on the train besides my father. You must have helped them."

Connor didn't want her misplaced gratitude. He brushed it aside with a wave of his hand. "I never heard how your father was found, only that he reappeared one day."

"Rennie and her husband found him. No, that's not quite true. Dancer Tubbs found him first, took care of him, and kept him safe. Rennie never believed Jay Mac was dead. She made Jarret take her to the site of the wreck and from there, on a hunch, he took her to Dancer's place. They found Jay Mac working in one of Dancer's mines."

"It's rather hard to imagine."

She smiled faintly. The image of her father on his hands and knees, picking ore out of a vein of gold, was not an easy one to maintain. "I know. But it's true nonetheless. In the months before he was found he and Dancer Tubbs forged a binding friendship."

"That's even harder to imagine." He leaned forward in his chair.

"Look, Maggie, Dancer is something of a legend in that part of Colorado. People know *of* him, but not many people *know* him. That's the way he prefers it."

"I'm aware of that. But he made an exception for my father. Rennie says he does that for all hurting animals. That's why he healed Jarret's shoulder. If you're hale and hearty he won't have anything to do with you, but if you need him, *really* need him, he won't turn you away."

"Are you ill?"

"No."

"Then what makes you think—"

"I need him. I think he'll understand." She saw by Connor's expression that she wasn't explaining herself well enough. "I've always wanted to be a doctor," she said softly. The ache from her shattered dream was still there. She realized belatedly that she couldn't expose herself to Connor Holiday. No matter what she had done with him, this was exposure of a different nature. One had only left her naked, this would leave her defenseless. "Never mind," she said. "It's not important."

Connor had no problem translating that. She didn't want him to know. Sensing it would be futile, he didn't press. "Rumor has it that Dancer Tubbs is rather . . ." He searched for a way to say it. ". . . Rather difficult to look on."

"So I understand. But it wouldn't bother me. It didn't bother Jay Mac. And it didn't bother Rennie."

"You've never seen him then."

"I've never been west of Pittsburgh. Have you seen him?"

"Never. He's a hermit and he shows most trespassers the dangerous end of a shotgun. For all practical purposes he's a neighbor of mine, but I've always respected his privacy."

Maggie was surprised when she felt the tug of humor. "It probably has nothing to do with the dangerous end of his shotgun," she said dryly.

"Not a thing," he deadpanned.

Comfortable silence descended briefly before she remembered she didn't like him, was a little afraid of him, and the first feeling at least was mutual.

Connor watched her withdraw again. "Have you mentioned this idea of yours to anyone?"

"Who would I talk to?"

"Your sister."

"Skye?" Maggie thought of Skye's reaction at the breakfast table. "No, she wouldn't understand. I don't share everything with her." *I've never shared everything with anyone,* she thought.

"I was thinking of the other one, the one who's a nun."

"Mary Francis. No, she wouldn't approve of me setting about so deliberately to get a divorce.

Connor's voice was terse. "I would think divorce would pale in the face of abortion."

In her lap Maggie's fingers knotted together. She managed to keep her voice steady. "It does," she said. Her dark green eyes were haunted. "And I have to live with my decisions."

He stood. At six-foot-two Connor Holiday towered over Maggie Dennehy. In every other way she had managed to make him feel small. "So you and I are the only ones who know about your plan."

"That's right. We're the only ones who should ever know."

He nodded shortly.

"You agree?" she asked anxiously. "To everything? The escort to Dancer's? The divorce?"

"Yes."

"And I'll never have to see you again? I mean, I didn't know that you lived so close to Mr. Tubbs."

"As the crow flies."

"It's closer than I'd hoped," she said bluntly.

"You're assuming that I might want to see you," he said just as bluntly. "Don't flatter yourself."

She flushed. "I'm sorry. You're right, of course. It would be as if we were still separated by two thousand miles instead of only twenty."

"Exactly." He kept his remote gaze on her face. "Well then, Miss Dennehy, let me put the question to you again. Will you marry me?"

"Yes, Mr. Holiday, I believe I will."

Chapter Six

She didn't quite believe she'd said it. Maggie stared at Connor Holiday and waited for him to take back his proposal. He didn't. He merely returned her gaze until she grew uncomfortable and looked away. Now that she had what she wanted she hardly knew how to proceed. Connor took matters out of her hands.

"I'm leaving for home in four days," he said. "I've already had to delay my departure once. I'm not doing it a second time."

"What about the wedding?"

"What about it?" One eyebrow lifted. "You're not suggesting that we have a big affair with all our parents' society friends?"

"N-no. I . . . I was just wondering when we would do it?" The uncertainty in her own voice added to her distress.

"What's wrong with the day after tomorrow? That leaves us with only one night in New York and then we're on our way west the next day."

"The day after tomorrow," she repeated without inflection. "Yes, that would be all right, I suppose."

"Good, that's settled."

"I won't marry you in church," she said.

"You couldn't anyway. I'm not Catholic." He watched her bite her lower lip. "I'd think you'd be relieved."

She was thinking of confession. Father Flynn was going to recognize her voice and she was going to get a lecture on excommunication. Her cheeks burned. Maggie didn't think she could summon enough courage to go to the confessional in the first place. "There's no relief with any of this."

Connor picked up his tumbler and went to the sideboard. He poured half as much as Maggie had given him the first time. He didn't keep it for himself. He handed it to her. "You don't need to knock it back," he said. "Just sip it."

Maggie took a tentative sip to appease him. It worked because he sat down again. "Who will marry us?" she asked.

"Most anyone, I suspect."

"Judge Halsey married my sister Michael. He's her godfather. Perhaps he'll do the same for us."

"Do you want me to arrange it?"

"Please."

Connor indicated with a short gesture that she should take another sip of her drink. This time she did little more than wet her lips with the whiskey. "I'm not trying to get you drunk," he said, "only a little more relaxed than you are now."

Maggie nodded her understanding, though it didn't change her actions. She held onto her drink but didn't taste any more of it.

Connor leaned back in his chair. "What about our wedding night?" he asked.

Whiskey sloshed over the side of Maggie's tumbler as she jerked stiffly. "Oh!" Without thinking, she sucked droplets of whiskey from her knuckles.

He watched her. The dark centers of his eyes absorbed her artless action but he was remembering the suck of her mouth on his flesh. He felt his body stir almost immediately in response. She didn't have to touch him to make him hard. Beryl would hate that. Connor got up and took the tumbler from Maggie's hand. "It's a shame to waste good whiskey."

Maggie noticed he didn't drink it, though, merely put it aside. She cleared her throat and managed to get out rather raspily, "You were saying?"

Connor sat on the sofa beside her this time. He felt her draw her curled legs closer to her body. "I was asking about our wedding night. Since we'll be going away the following morning, I think we should spend it at my father's house."

"I thought we'd spend it here," she said.

"Why?"

Because I'll feel safer, that's why. She said, "My dressing room has a day bed. You can sleep there."

"Like hell. It's probably comfortable for your friends but I'd hang over at both ends." He saw by her slight smile that he had guessed correctly. "On the other hand, the chaise in my dressing room will accommodate you."

She didn't relish the idea of sleeping on a chaise but she was grateful he didn't expect her to share his bed. She avoided looking at him. "That . . . that will be fine."

"Good."

"I want to talk about the divorce," she said.

"In a moment. I want to talk about the journey west. I wasn't planning on first class accommodations. It will be days and nights of sitting up in—"

Maggie shook her head, interrupting him. "Jay Mac will let us take the private Northeast Rail cars. He'll insist on it, actually, so there's no sense in thinking we'll be doing anything different."

"And he always gets his way."

Maggie stared at her hands, thinking about what she was going to do. "Usually," she said hollowly. "He usually gets his way."

"This time I don't mind."

She turned to look at him, her smile a little lopsided, a little sad. "It's hard to mind when Jay Mac throws money at you." Connor looked as if he might interrupt and Maggie stopped him. "No, don't explain. I understand. Believe me, I understand. Jay Mac's money is very seductive."

So is Jay Mac's daughter. Connor didn't much like the direction of his thoughts. His eyes strayed to Maggie's slender waist. Thinking about the child that might have been, he found the common sense that had momentarily deserted him. "You wanted to talk about the divorce," he said tightly.

She supposed she had angered him with her talk of money. He probably didn't like being reminded that twelve thousand dollars had bought him. "I think we should begin proceedings as soon as we arrive in Denver. It could take a while and I'd rather not draw it out longer than necessary."

"You don't think it would be better to wait, say a year or so, before beginning?"

"No!"

"It's hardly flattering that you're so horrified."

"Good," she said stiffly. "I don't mean to be flattering."

Connor considered that. "You'll have to get over this aversion to me at least for one day."

"My family won't expect that I've suddenly fallen in love with you," she said. "That would make Jay Mac suspicious. He imagines love will come in time. We need only be civil."

"All right," he said. "That'll make things easier for me, too."

Maggie blinked. For a moment she had forgotten she wasn't the only one with an aversion. "Then it seems we're agreed."

He stood. "I'll talk to my father tonight and yours tomorrow."

Maggie also stood. She looked at him uncertainly when he held out his hand.

"A shake," he said. "To seal our bargain."

Maggie's slender fingers were swallowed by his as she extended her hand. Long after he was gone she could still feel the warmth of his skin against hers. She'd struck terms with a man, she thought. Why then did it seem as though she'd made her bargain with the devil?

For three days Maggie lived in fear that someone would see through to her heart. Everyone, even Jay Mac, asked her why she was changing her mind about marrying Connor Holiday, but they all accepted her explanation that Connor himself had helped her see the sense in it. Perhaps because it was a little of the truth or perhaps because they all found it remarkably easy to believe she could be led about so simply, there was no unpleasant interrogation.

True to form, Jay Mac was congratulating himself for being so foresighted in his estimation of both his daughter and Connor Holiday. Knowing that she was going to thwart his plans, Maggie almost felt sorry for him. Almost. For three days she permitted herself the small satisfaction that accompanies revenge. She understood herself well enough to know that she would live with guilt after that.

She saw little of Connor. He spoke to her once, as a formality, after speaking to her father. Their conversation was stilted on that occasion. She was invited to dine at his home by his father and Beryl but during that ordeal Maggie felt oddly protected by Connor's presence. He called for her to go riding in Central Park. They sat side by side in an open carriage, more to be seen than see, laying rumors concerning their hasty marriage to rest. She smiled. He smiled. Their hands never touched.

Maggie remembered that leisurely ride through Central Park as she stood beside Connor in Judge Halsey's private chambers. The last time they met they hadn't exchanged a single word and now they were exchanging vows.

She had thought it would be the hardest part. She had forgotten about the kiss.

Maggie raised her face. Connor was studying her, his dark eyes sliding over her forehead, over the tiny crease between her brows, over her pale cheeks and anxious eyes, until they settled on her mouth. She had drawn in one corner of her lower lip, worrying it gently. He shook his head slightly and she released it. Somewhat self-consciously the tip of her pink tongue peeped out and dampened the line of her lower lip. She saw her reflection in Connor's darkening eyes as he lowered his head.

His mouth was firm on hers. He didn't press but the pressure was there. Her lips parted yet he didn't invade. As a kiss it was chaste and Maggie knew that because the one she was comparing it to had been filled with carnal promise.

She shivered slightly as memory prodded her senses. She could feel his mouth on hers, insistent, hot in its seeking. She could taste him as his tongue wedged itself between her teeth and she opened her mouth wider. He teased her, his lips mobile on hers, sucking, plundering. Then playful. He released her. And his mouth went lower. He touched her . . .

"Maggie?"

She came out of her reverie with a start, blinking widely. Connor's face was very close to hers. His breath was warm against her skin as he said her name. "Oh," she said softly, dazed.

"Oh, indeed," Judge Halsey broke in, his tone knowing. He beamed hugely at Jay Mac and Moira, who returned his fulsome smile. Skye giggled. Mary Francis grinned. Rushton nodded, pleased. Only Beryl looked thunderous.

Feeling foolish, Maggie stepped back, slipping out of Connor's light hold on her elbows. She was grateful he let her go. She turned away from his cool and distant gaze and faced her family.

She was enveloped in their loving arms, in their fierce congratulations. Jay Mac and Moira hugged her warmly while Skye danced around her happily. Mary Francis was more subdued but just as affectionate. Judge Halsey made certain he got to kiss the bride. Rushton also stepped forward to welcome Maggie into the family.

Beryl moved to stand beside Connor. She looped her arm in his, securing him in case he wanted to make a scene of fighting for his release. "It seems the bride is getting all the attention," she said softly, provokingly. "Perhaps the groom would like a kiss?"

"It's not necessary."

"I *know* that. Still, I wouldn't mind congratulating you."

"I'd mind." He didn't even look at Beryl. His gaze swept Maggie and her family and for the first time he appreciated the difficulty of the task she had set for herself. It wasn't easy going against a force like Jay Mac and now that she had drawn others in with the deceit of her marriage, it was going to be even harder. Connor didn't think Maggie was by nature a deceitful person. She had told him plainly about the abortion when it would have served her just as well to lie. She caught him looking at her and when he refused to look away it was she who flushed and turned her attention to his father.

"She's a pitiful thing," Beryl said, following the direction of Connor's gaze. She witnessed Maggie ducking her head in embarrassed confusion.

"Do you think so?" he asked.

"She doesn't even like you looking at her. What are you going to do in the bedroom?"

"Turn back the lamps, I suppose."

Finding it impossible to goad him, Beryl almost stamped her foot in frustration. Across the room she saw that Mary Francis was watching her. "I don't think I like the nun," she said under her breath.

"It isn't hard to imagine why."

"Oh God, here she comes." Beryl managed a credible smile as Mary Francis approached.

Mary Francis was struck first by the proprietal grasp that Beryl Holiday had on Connor's arm. She was struck secondly by Connor's complete indifference to it. "I don't know that anyone's officially welcomed you into our family," she said softly to Connor.

"Thank you." He eased out of Beryl's arm by pinching her surreptitiously on the soft underside of her wrist. When he was free he leaned forward and kissed Mary Francis on the cheek. It was impossible not to feel warmth from her smile. "I regret we won't have a chance to get to know each other better."

"Connor," Beryl said, drawing out his name disapprovingly. "Shame on you lying to Sister Mary Francis that way." Her pale blue eyes darted over Mary's placid and thoughtful expression. "He was just telling me how happy he'd be to get back to his ranch."

Mary Francis didn't rise to the bait and addressed her remarks to Connor. "That's understandable. Even on brief visits you must find New York terribly confining."

Beryl wasn't used to being ignored. "I think he meant that going home was preferable to spending another minute in the company of your family."

Mary Francis laughed. It was no light, musical trilling sound that came from her either. Mary Francis had a deep and hearty laugh that usually shocked people with its robustness because it was so unexpected. She saw Beryl's beautiful features contort with surprise and she laughed harder. Tears formed at the corners of her eyes and she didn't bother trying to brush them away. Across the room Skye began laughing without even knowing what was funny. It had always been that way. Mary Francis's laugh was completely contagious.

Connor saw his wife was smiling. He grinned back at her and this time her smile broadened. It was the first spontaneous moment they had shared all day.

Mary Francis caught her breath. She found a handkerchief tucked beneath the sleeve of her habit. Treating Connor to a watery smile, she dabbed at her eyes. "I'm sorry," she said to Beryl. "Did you think I was laughing at you?"

"I—I . . ." Completely bewildered by Mary's frankness, Beryl stuttered to a halt.

"Of course you did. How could you help it?"

Beryl's eyes sought out Rushton's. She was frantic to escape. "If you'll excuse me," she said. "My husband wants a word with me."

Mary Francis nodded serenely. "By all means." She watched her go, then turned to Connor. Her smile was gone and her forest green eyes were hard. "That woman's a witch," she said with quiet fierceness. "What is she to you?"

Connor found himself admiring his sister-in-law's directness. "My father's wife," he said. He watched Mary Francis consider that, wondering if she should take it at face value. He helped her out. "That's all she is to me."

Mary Francis continued to stare at him, her eyes narrowed and thoughtful. "She could hurt Maggie."

"I won't let her."

Maggie joined them then. Her glance darted between her husband and her sister as she tried to divine the nature of the conversation she had interrupted. She asked Connor, "Has Mary Francis threatened to break your kneecaps?"

Connor's brows rose slightly and his glance at Mary conferred greater respect.

"We were just coming to that," Mary Francis admitted shamelessly.

Maggie's nod was wise. "I thought that might be what was going on." She looked at Connor. "I suppose it's because she's the oldest that she's taken on the role as everyone's protector, but she takes it very seriously."

"I'm beginning to understand that," Connor said. He was careful not to smile. Not only would it have been condescending but he believed he risked the chance of never walking again.

"Mary Michael and Ethan were married in this very room and she threatened his kneecaps."

"So it's something of a tradition," Connor said. "Then I *do* feel welcomed."

Mary Francis couldn't help smiling. "As long as you don't hurt my sister you have nothing to fear." She paused a beat. "Otherwise . . ." On that note she walked away.

Maggie turned so that her back was to her family. Her face, which had been animated moments earlier, was drained of color. She couldn't appreciate the irony that it was only with Connor that she could be herself. "Please," she said quietly, "can we leave soon? I can't bear much more of this."

"We'll leave now," he said. He took her hand in his and tucked it against his side. Her fingers were cold, her skin like ice. He wondered that she wasn't shaking. "I reserved a suite for us at the St. Mark."

Panic paralyzed her for a moment. "But you said—"

"My father's idea," he told her. "A gift to us, actually."

It was not so much Connor's words that calmed her, but the way he said them. He managed to communicate that he was no more pleased about the arrangement than she was. That made her feel better. She thought she might be able to go on a little longer. "We're expected to join everyone for a wedding dinner at my parents' home," she said. "The judge is going to join us."

He sensed the change in her, the way she had tapped into some reserve of strength she hadn't been able to find moments earlier. "Are you certain?" he asked. "I can make our excuses."

"I'll be all right," she said. "That is, if you don't mind."

A decade ago, as a young man, Connor had had to choose between a ravenous wolf pack and a forty-foot drop down the sheer face of a cliff. He knew precisely why he was remembering that incident now. His choices seemed equally unpleasant, though perhaps not as potentially fatal. His glance wandered to Mary Francis in deep conversation with his father and he reconsidered his last thought.

"I'll do whatever you want," he said, then added significantly, "but not always. This time I don't mind."

The wedding dinner was not the painfully stressful event Maggie had feared. The tension that always seemed to exist between Rushton and Connor had eased to a tolerable level and Beryl was properly attentive to her husband. Mary Francis and the judge were responsible for the liveliest conversation and Skye for the ribald humor. Moira made certain no one's plate was ever quite empty while Jay Mac filled their glasses with samplings of the best wines from his cellars.

Maggie and Connor extricated themselves from the gathering after only two hours, their parting made easy since the real farewells would happen at the train station in the morning. A light rain had started and pattered gently against the carriage roof. By the time they reached the St. Mark Hotel it was a downpour.

"Do you want to make a run for it?" Connor asked. "Or wait it out? It doesn't look as if the doorman intends to come out with an umbrella."

"I don't think an umbrella would help much," she said doubtfully. "Let's run for it."

Connor shook his head. "I wasn't thinking. You'll ruin your gown."

Maggie looked down at herself. The bodice of her gown was embroidered with beads the color of sapphires. Everywhere else, including the square train that swept the floor around her when she stood, was pale blue satin. Even her delicate shoes had been specially dyed to match the gown. She sighed. "You don't mind waiting? I rather liked this gown."

Connor was thinking that he rather liked it himself. Or at least he liked the way Maggie looked in it. He knew she didn't suspect that he felt that way. He had been successful hiding his appreciation behind his remote gaze, but it had been as much a strain as any other part of the day's charade. "We'll wait." He craned his neck so he could get a better view of the sky. It was unrelentingly gray and night was closing in early. "It's got to let up sometime."

Maggie rearranged her train and settled back. The combs that kept her carefully coifed hair in place were uncomfortable when pressed tightly to her head. She removed them and combed out her hair with her fingers. "That's better." She leaned back against the leather cushions again and closed her eyes.

Connor's eyes fell on the vulnerable line of her white throat and his fingers itched to close around it. He thrust his hands into the pockets of his jacket and tried to think of something besides the uncomfortable swelling in his groin. Nothing occurred to him. In his mind's eye he could only see the repetitive sultry motion of Maggie's fingers threading through her hair.

He took off his jacket. "Here," he said roughly, pushing it in her direction. "Put this on."

The sound of Connor's insistent voice jerked Maggie out of her peaceful musings. She frowned, her head tilting to one side. "But—"

"I've changed my mind," he said. "I told you we wouldn't always do things your way." Maggie fumbled with the combs, trying to jab them back into her hair. He took them from her nerveless fingers and made her take his jacket. As soon as she had it on he jumped out of the carriage, then turned to lift her out.

Maggie expected to be put on her feet again and prepared for the rain to seep into her shoes and stockings. It never happened. Connor Holiday swept her and her train in his arms and carried her straight into the St. Mark. He was the one who had done the work but somehow she was the one who was breathless.

Once inside he set her down. Maggie was aware of guests in the lobby watching them, smiling knowingly, nudging one another. She supposed the spectacle had looked romantic after a fashion but the reality felt nothing like it. She removed Connor's jacket carefully and handed it to him. Her reflection in the full-length mirrors that graced the St. Mark's entrance bore out the fact that she had been protected from the deluge while Connor had borne the brunt of it.

Curling ends of his dark hair dripped water onto his collar and his white shirt clung wetly to his shoulders. Even his lashes were spiky. He shrugged into his damp jacket.

"Wait," she said when he started to go toward the registration desk. She stood on tiptoe and brushed away a droplet of water from his cheek with her index finger. "There. That's better."

It wasn't, but he didn't tell her that. He took her wrist in his hand. He saw by the look on her face that the pressure of his fingers was more than he had intended. He eased his hold slightly, forced a smile, and for the benefit of their onlookers, kissed the back of her hand.

Maggie had no choice but to go where he led though she didn't feel as much escorted as she did dragged along. She removed herself from his hold while he confirmed their arrangements with the hotel manager and looked around the lobby.

The St. Mark had a certain grandeur that made one feel awed and comfortable at the same time. The intricately plastered ceilings drew the eye upward while the muted reflections in the polished wood-work kept one grounded. Maggie had been in the hotel many times, especially when her sister Michael had made her home there. The St. Mark catered to families and long term boarders with its open and inviting dining and sitting rooms.

Maggie turned back to the manager who was assuring Connor that everything would be to his liking. She only listened with half an ear. Her attention fell on the open registration book in front of her.

Mr. and Mrs. Connor Holiday.

It was as though she had ceased to exist.

Caught in his own dark thoughts, Connor didn't notice Maggie's pensive, withdrawn mood as they rode the steam lift to the fifth floor. He ushered her inside the suite and they were followed in short order by the bellboy carrying their bags.

The spacious suite was appointed tastefully with dark walnut furniture. The sitting area had two wing chairs and a long, stiffly stuffed sofa. The area rug carried out the room's color theme of cream, maroon, and hunter green. The dining space was marked by a small walnut table and two side chairs, all of them polished so they reflected the occupants of the room. An enormous cut glass vase had been set in the middle of the table and the sweet fragrance of a dozen long stemmed red roses lay heavily in the air. Above the mantelpiece was an elaborate gilt-framed mirror which magnified the gas jet lighting in the room.

The bellboy placed their bags in the bedroom which was to the left of the dining area. He showed them the armoire, the dressing and bathing rooms, and the balcony that overlooked Broadway when one opened the French doors.

As she stood on the threshold of the bedroom, Maggie took note of these things with only one small part of her mind. Her attention was riveted on the bed and when the bellboy left and she was alone with Connor again she said the first thing that came to her, the only thing she'd been thinking about for ten minutes.

"There's only one."

Connor paused in removing his jacket. He looked at her oddly. "What?"

"There's only one," she repeated.

He finished slipping out of the jacket and hung it on the brass coat rack just inside the door. "I understood that part," he said, running one hand through his dark hair. He plucked at his damp shirt. "I don't understand what it means."

"One bed," she said. "One bedroom! There should be two. My sister had a suite here. *She* had two bedrooms."

"I'm sure she did," Connor said evenly. "But she lived here, didn't she? She wasn't married then."

Maggie found his calm infuriating. "So? What has that to do with anything? The St. Mark has suites with two bedrooms and I want one." Even to her own ears she sounded like a spoiled child on the verge of a temper tantrum.

Connor was thoughtful for a moment, watching her, then he shrugged. "Fine," he said. "But you'll have to arrange it."

In spite of his indifferent tone, Maggie sensed he was challenging her. "Fine," she said. "I will." She smoothed her hair in the mirror above the fireplace and when she was satisfied with the hasty repairs to her appearance she turned to go. Connor was standing in front of the door, blocking her way.

"You know they realize we were just married," he said pleasantly.

Maggie would have realized it if she'd thought of it. "So?" she asked carelessly, pretending it didn't matter.

Connor stepped aside to let her pass. "If you're not embarrassed to request a second bedroom on your wedding night, then I'm not going to stop you."

Determined to brazen it out, she said, "It's the lesser of two evils, isn't it?"

He opened the door for her. "Be my guest. I look forward to hearing your explanation."

She sniffed haughtily and swept past him, gracing him with a sour glance when he chuckled under his breath. Maggie took the lift but she asked the operator to let her out on the second floor. She stepped off confidently, pretending she had a direction in mind. When she heard the gate close behind her and the lift move upward again, she stopped and leaned against the wall in the dimly lighted hallway.

What *was* she going to tell them at the front desk? Bridal nerves? The groom was a wife beater? One of them was ill? The marriage was a farce? They were only comfortable sharing a bed in brothels?

Maggie's laughter was a trifle hysterical. Down the hall a door opened and a man stepped out. She ducked her head, covered her mouth with her hand, and pretended to cough. She began walking, her head bent, and felt the stranger's inquisitive eyes on her. Maggie went to the end of the hallway and opened the door to the stairwell. Once she was safely away from curious glances she paused on the steps, leaning lightly against the iron rail banister. She looked down. There were twenty-four steps circling down to the first floor. She remembered the smiling hotel manager, the good wishes of the desk clerk and porter. *Mr. and Mrs. Connor Holiday.* Maggie looked up. Three flights of stairs loomed above her. Seventy-two steps.

Well, she thought, if she walked slowly she might just have her story in place by the time she reached the top.

Connor wasn't in the sitting room when she returned. She dreaded walking into the bedroom, afraid to find him there in some state of undress. Calling herself all manner of fool and a coward, Maggie went into the bedroom. He wasn't there. She said his name, quietly at first, then more loudly. He didn't answer. She peeked in the dressing room and knocked on the bathing room door. There was no response.

Had he gone looking for her when she took so long? Maggie frowned, wondering how that might complicate the story she had planned. She lighted the bedside lamps and turned off the gas jets. Sitting on the edge of the large four-poster, Maggie removed her shoes and carefully rolled off her stockings. She opened her valise and found it empty. The armoire was filled with her clothes—and his. It made her stomach flutter oddly to see his shirts on a peg beside her chemises, her stockings beside his socks. Her colorful hair ribbons shared space with his black bow ties. His vest nudged her corset.

Maggie pulled out her nightshift and laid it at the foot of the bed. This morning her mother and sister had helped her with her gown. Now Maggie struggled with the tiny row of buttons at the back.

Watching Maggie from the balcony, Connor felt like a beggar urchin with his nose pressed to the bakeshop window. Only his wife wasn't a hot cross bun and it wasn't his mouth that was watering. The cool night air wasn't as effective as a cold shower on his aching groin, but then Connor wasn't willing to turn his back on Maggie in favor of the view of Broadway. He sat tensely on the edge of the stone balustrade, his arms crossed in front of him. His usually remote gaze had taken a sleepy, heavy-lidded turn as his eyes wandered over Maggie.

She was twisting and turning, trying to get at the buttons at the back of her gown. Still, there was something inherently graceful in her movements. She had managed to free one shoulder and the bare curve of her skin caught the lamplight. Muted shades of orange defined her collarbone. The combs that had held her hair back were dislodged by her struggles. She tossed them aside and plaited her hair quickly so a single thick coil of copper fell down her back. For a moment she looked too young to be the wife of any man.

Then she slipped out of the beaded blue gown.

The cambric chemise molded her figure. It was a plain garment with no flounces to emphasize the curve of her breasts or hips. She pulled at a ribbon and the garment fell silkily past her arms, her waist, her thighs, and circled her bare feet. She stepped out of it.

Connor shifted his weight on the stone railing as Maggie reached behind her to tug at the laces of her corset. The movement thrust her breasts forward. He watched her sigh as the corset fell away. She reached under her camisole and rubbed her flesh with the flat of her palms. Connor wondered why she bothered with the contraption when it served no purpose except to make her uncomfortable. He could nearly span her waist with his hands. The corset merely kept him from feeling the softness of her the way he wanted to. Then again, perhaps that's why she wore it.

Connor stood up and pushed away from the railing as Maggie touched the hem of her camisole and began to lift it upward over her midriff. He tapped lightly on a pane of glass in the French doors. He saw her freeze.

Like a doe sensing danger, Maggie became still and alert. The sound was not repeated but it didn't matter to her. She knew she had heard it and she knew where it had come from.

Maggie raised her head slowly, her fingers dropping away from her camisole at the same time. It modestly fell over her bare skin but it hardly mattered. She felt naked and exposed. She saw his shadowy outline on the balcony, the dark profile that was still dangerous and threatening despite the fact that she knew his identity. She didn't have to see his eyes to know their cold, fathomless depths, or see his face to be aware of his mocking half-smile.

Maggie was pleased with her composure; pleased that she didn't scream as instinct prompted her to. Turning her back on him, she picked up her nightdress and slipped it over her head.

Connor tapped again. He jiggled the door handle for good measure.

When she turned back around she was smiling. He was locked out. It was a delicious irony and made her feel infinitely more in control. She took her time getting to the door and grinned cheekily at him.

"There won't always be a door between us," he reminded her. He knew she wouldn't have given him such a smug look if she wasn't feeling safe *and* superior.

"You're right," she said. "If you take the street exit I'll be a widow and rid of you permanently."

"Don't count on it."

Even through the distortion of the glass his voice maintained its peculiar menacing quality. He'd probably take the leap and live just to spite her, or worse, die and haunt her. Maggie turned the jammed lock and opened the door.

"Thank you," he said coldly, stepping inside.

Maggie ignored him. She went to the armoire, removed her dressing gown, and disappeared into the bathing room.

Connor's eyes narrowed at the militant set of her shoulders. His fingers curled into a tight fist, enabling him to keep from grabbing her swinging braid and yanking her solidly against him. He didn't know what he would have done with her then. He wanted to believe he would have shaken her but he suspected he might have been persuaded, with no provocation on her part, to kiss her.

Cursing softly, Connor went to the armoire and removed his own nightshirt and dressing gown. It seemed likely that Maggie was going to spend the better part of the evening in the bathing room.

An hour later and for the second time that night, Maggie stopped cold on the threshold of the bedroom. Connor was sitting up in bed, occupying the entire middle section as he read the New York *Chronicle,* effectively claiming the four-poster as his territory.

Maggie cleared her throat. "I don't recognize squatter's rights," she said.

"What?"

"You heard me."

"I always hear you," he said patiently, not looking up from his paper. "But I never seem to understand what you're saying."

Infuriated by his inattention, Maggie leaned across the bed and yanked the newspaper out of his hands. She stared at the crumpled paper in her clenched fists and was appalled by her behavior. When she raised her eyes to Connor she saw he was watching her with that fascinated, studied look that completely unnerved her.

"I'm sorry," she said, unable to quite convey how sorry she really was. She unfolded the paper, laid it on the bed's goose down duvet, and attempted to smooth it out. She was only marginally successful.

"Let me," he said, removing the paper from beneath her fingers, "before you destroy it." He folded it neatly and placed it on the bedside table farthest away from Maggie. Then he gave her his full attention. "You were saying?"

Maggie took a step back from the four-poster. "I don't recognize squatter's rights," she said again, pointing at him then gesturing to the entire bed. "Just because you got there first doesn't give you ownership."

One of his dark eyebrows kicked up. "It doesn't? Do you mean there's somewhere I have to go to stake my claim?"

"That's not amusing."

"I hadn't meant it to be. I'm serious. Do I have to apply in the lobby for rights to the bed?"

"You're doing this on purpose," she said, frustration edging her tone. "Where am I supposed to sleep?"

He looked around him as if taking note of his complete possession of the bed for the first time. "Did you think I wanted the whole thing for myself?" he asked, baiting her. "I'm willing to share." He patted the bed. "Either side."

Not quite believing that she'd heard him correctly, Maggie stared at him for a moment. "Go to hell," she said finally.

He watched her go, his derisive smile flattening as she slammed the door on her way out.

Maggie winced as the door thudded shut. When Connor didn't respond to her second childish tantrum of the evening, she eyed the sofa in the sitting room as if it were her enemy. Pillows and blankets were in the other room and she refused to return for them. Turning off the gas lighting, Maggie curled in one corner of the sofa, discovering unhappily that it was as stiff and as uncomfortable as it looked. She took off her robe and tried using it first as a pillow, then as a blanket. It was not particularly satisfactory as either.

She stretched out but her relatively short height was no benefit— her feet still dangled or curved her body unnaturally if she tried to rest them on the far arm. Noise and light from the street below filtered into the room. She couldn't do anything about the revelers, but she could shut out the light. She got up, padded over to the window, and drew the drapes. She tried both wing chairs as possible sleeping nests. Neither worked.

She stubbed her toe on the footstool as she went back to the sofa, then turned her ankle as she danced around. Frustrated, she kicked the stool which only served to magnify the pain in her foot. "Dammit," she swore, collapsing onto the sofa. She held her injured foot between her hands and massaged it. Connor Holiday would never be accused of being a gentleman, certainly never by her.

The door to the bedroom opened. Connor leaned against the jamb, backlit by the lamps. "Are you quite finished?" he asked.

"Finished doing what?" she asked impatiently.

"Making noise."

Even though she hadn't been doing it deliberately she asked, "Why should you sleep when I can't?"

"Why indeed?" he asked dryly. He pushed away from the jamb and came into the sitting room. His eyes adjusted to the lack of light and he noticed for the first time that Maggie had hurt herself. "What happened?"

"Nothing."

Connor sat on one arm of a wing chair and cinched the belt of his dressing gown more securely about his waist. "Are you going to be this miserable the entire way to Colorado?" he asked. "Because if you are I'm going to reconsider my promise to escort you."

Maggie didn't consider his threat a real one. "We have a deal."

"People break deals all the time."

"Not you." She didn't think he was a gentleman, but then neither did she believe he was without some shred of honor.

Connor simply stared at her for a long moment. "All right," he said at last. "Not me. But that doesn't mean I can't be miserable right back."

"You've already proved it," she said under her breath.

He heard her and ignored the comment. "Do you really want to travel two thousand miles like that?"

As a matter of pride she pretended to think about it. Finally she shook her head.

"Very well then," he said. "How did you hurt yourself?"

"I stubbed my toe on the footstool."

"And?" he asked, not satisfied.

She wondered how he knew there was more. "And I think I've sprained my ankle," she admitted reluctantly.

Connor lighted an oil lamp on one of the walnut endtables. He found the overturned footstool, set it in front of Maggie, and sat down. Without asking permission, he took her foot and rested it on his knees. He examined the toe first, flicking it lightly with his finger, then gingerly probed her foot and ankle.

Maggie winced and jerked reflexively, trying to withdraw her foot when he managed to find the tender part.

His hold was firm but gentle and he didn't let her go. He felt her relax, wary still, yet trusting him more than she just had a moment earlier. "It's a sprain, all right." His fingers absently stroked her warm skin as he spoke, lightly going over the bones of her foot. "What do you want to do about it?"

"Why ask *me?*" Her voice was slightly breathless, something she didn't like and hoped he hadn't heard.

"You want to be a doctor, don't you?" He felt her stiffen again, less trusting, though for different reasons and it made him angry. "You told me that much yourself. I asked Skye about it this afternoon. She says you didn't get accepted by the medical school. Is that why you came to me?"

"Perhaps you can get some ice for my foot," she said.

"Did you go to Madame Restell before or after your rejection?"

"Never mind," she said, sitting up straighter. "I'll get the ice myself."

Unconsciously Connor's fingers pressed more tightly on Maggie's injured foot. "Did you think of anyone but yourself when you made your decision?"

Maggie's breath caught at the back of her throat as pain shot through her foot. It seemed to travel all the way through her spine and exploded in her head. "Please," she gasped. "You're hurting me."

It all registered belatedly: his grip, her tears, his painful questions, her fear. Connor released her foot. "I'm sorry."

She got up from the sofa and backed away from him, limping. "Don't touch me," she said hoarsely. "Don't ever touch me. I hate it when you do. You always hurt me. You don't know any other way." She was trembling now and her eyes were accusing. "I don't care if you *do* hate me and I don't care what you think of me. You got what you wanted out of this marriage. I'm not the only whore in this room!"

She shrank back as Connor came to his feet.

"Maggie," he said quietly. He watched her press herself more solidly against the wall. Connor had no clear idea what he wanted to say. He despised what she had done. Didn't that mean he despised her as well? But perhaps not well enough. If he didn't want her, if he wasn't attracted to her, he wouldn't have to remind himself so often how much he disliked her. Self-loathing eclipsed any hint of color in his eyes. They were flat, black, and cold as a winter night. "I'll get the ice," he said. "Excuse me. I have to change." When he came out of the bedroom a few minutes later, Maggie was no longer pressed to the wall although she was still leaning against it. Out of the corner of his eye he saw her flinch as he passed. "This is never going to work," he said quietly.

Once she was alone Maggie felt as if she were melting down the length of wall. She was dry-eyed though she had never felt more like crying. It was difficult to swallow and there was a pressure in her chest that made it hard to breathe. What had he meant? What wasn't going to work? He wasn't talking about their marriage, certainly. It wasn't supposed to be a success. They had wed for failure. Anything else was unacceptable to either of them.

Maggie drew her legs up to her chest and locked her arms around them. Was he going to back out of their arrangement? Earlier in the day she had seen Jay Mac take Connor alone into the library. Neither her father nor her husband had mentioned it later but Maggie knew what had taken place. Jay Mac had handed over the deed to the Double H. The land was Connor's again, safe from the tyranny of Northeast Rail and the robber barons. And all he had had to do was take a wife he didn't need, didn't want, and didn't like.

Connor wasn't long in getting the ice. The restaurant staff wrapped shavings of it in a linen napkin and gave him a bucket of it besides. There was no one at the St. Mark who wasn't willing to accommodate the newlyweds.

Connor placed the shavings on the sofa and the pail of ice on the marble apron of the fireplace. "Come here," he said, holding out his hand.

She hesitated but he didn't withdraw. Maggie placed her hand in his and let herself be pulled to her feet. He motioned to her to sit on the sofa. Instead of taking the stool for himself this time, Connor knelt on the floor and lifted Maggie's injured foot on the stool. He raised the hem of her nightdress a few inches than lightly pressed the napkin full of ice on her ankle.

"Too cold?" he asked when he saw her grimace.

"I can stand it."

"That isn't what I asked. I can get another towel to wrap the ice in if it's too cold."

She strove to be civil. "It's fine."

Connor sat back on his haunches. "I apologize for what I did earlier," he said. "I didn't mean to cause you pain."

Maggie knew he was talking about the physical pain. The other had been purely intentional. "I know. It's all right."

"Do you always let people who hurt you off so easily?"

Surprised, Maggie's eyes widened. "I don't understand."

"I don't either," he said, studying her face. The cat-like shape of her eyes was more pronounced as she tilted her head. Her lower lip was drawn in, caught between her teeth in a habit that could indicate thoughtfulness or anxiety. There was the tiniest vertical crease between her brows as she drew them together. He had a sudden vision of her sitting up in a wide bed, her slender body somehow both edgy and eager as he walked into the brothel's bedroom. "If I had realized . . ." His voice trailed off. Would he have done anything differently? he wondered. Would he really have crawled into her bed that night? He had asked for someone quiet, someone who wouldn't ask too many questions, or worse, bore him with the story of her miserable life. He hadn't wanted to know anything about the woman under him, the woman who took him into herself and let him pound his frustrations against her slight and supple body. He hadn't meant it to be that personal.

"Never mind," he said. The mask that imprisoned his features was back in place. He stood. "What did they say at the front desk when you asked about another room?"

Maggie was caught off guard. It was a question she had expected much earlier. She nearly forgot what she had planned to say. "The hotel's full," she said. "The manager said there aren't any rooms to be had."

"None at all?" A half-smile played at the edge of Connor's mouth. "I wish I had known that," he said.

Maggie frowned. "Why?"

"I wouldn't have bothered asking for one." He disappeared into the adjoining bedroom and when he returned he was carrying his valise. The sleeve of one shirt peeked out through the closure, pinched in his hasty packing. "Room 313," he said. "The manager had no trouble accommodating me when I told him I didn't want to disturb you. He offered me my choice of rooms, actually. Several were two bedroom suites, but I explained I didn't see the point of aggravating your injury by moving you."

Maggie groaned softly, her face flushed with embarrassment at having been caught in her lie. "I hope you looked suitably frustrated when you spoke to him," she said, struggling to maintain her dignity. The thought that Connor might have revealed he was content, even delighted, to be rid of his bride for the night was humiliating.

Connor didn't respond until he was in the hallway, well out of Maggie's hearing. "Looking frustrated was the easy part," he muttered.

Chapter Seven

In the morning Connor joined Maggie for breakfast in her room. "Did you sleep well?" he asked, thinking of his own restless night.

"Yes," she said quickly, not quite able to look him in the eye.

"Your foot didn't hurt you, then?"

"What? Oh." Maggie hadn't been thinking about her foot. It wasn't her ankle that had kept her up most of the night. "No . . . no, it didn't bother me . . . not at all. I'm not limping this morning."

Connor lifted the silver dome that covered their bacon and eggs and began serving himself. "You're able to travel?"

"Yes, of course."

He nodded, not entirely satisfied but willing to be convinced. "Bacon?"

"One, please."

He gave her two and a generous serving of scrambled eggs. When he broke and buttered his biscuit he gave her the larger half. Connor made certain Maggie's coffee was always warm by adding a little more to her cup every time she took a few sips.

His attentiveness made Maggie nervous. While the aroma of the food teased her senses she discovered that under Connor's watchful eye everything had become essentially tasteless.

He observed her pushing her eggs around her plate rather than eating them. "You're going to have to do better than that," he said. "I realize we're not going west by covered wagon, but you'll be surprised how this trip's going to sap your strength. You'd better eat up."

She ducked her head and stared at her plate. "I can't eat when you're hovering," she said. "You're acting like a mother hen with your chick." The silence that followed her statement went on so long Maggie was certain she'd made him angry. She dared a glance upward.

Connor burst out laughing. Her shock was so palpable that he laughed harder. It finally became necessary to raise his napkin to his eyes to wipe away the tears.

"It wasn't that funny."

He sobered gradually. "No one's ever accused me of it," he explained. "That's all. I've been called a—well, you can use your imagination. You've called me a few unsavory things yourself."

Maggie felt heat rising in her neck and face.

"But a mother hen? No, no one's ever accused me of that." He took a quick bite of his eggs and stole another strip of bacon from the serving dish, then rose from the table. "I left my things in the other room," he said. "I'll get them now so you can finish eating in peace. We're expected at the train station at eleven so we have some time."

When he was gone Maggie realized what a perverse creature she was. She actually missed his companionship. Meals in her home were never taken alone unless one was ill. There was always conversation, some exchange of ideas or general story telling. She was going to miss it even though she was rarely the one to initiate a debate and even less likely to take a major role. The chatter had always gone on around her and it had been agreeable to be the quiet one. Her sisters thought she was as inscrutable as it was possible for a New Yorker to be. A faint smile touched Maggie's lips and her eyes held the faraway look of someone capturing childhood memories.

She shook her head slowly, laughing at herself, and began eating.

Connor was surprised when he heard the door to his suite open. He didn't think he had been very long getting his things together. "You decided you missed the mother hen already?" he called from the bedroom.

Beryl followed the sound of his voice. *"Mother hen?"* she asked. "Is your poor little wife already homesick for her mama?"

Connor dropped his valise back on the bed and turned to the doorway. He made no attempt to hide what he was feeling or thinking. His black eyes speared Beryl. "What the hell are you doing here?"

Beryl untied the scarlet ribbon that secured her bonnet. A fringe of her dark chestnut hair fluttered against her forehead as she fanned herself casually with the brim. "You shouldn't talk to me that way," she said, unperturbed. "I could be here because something's happened to your father."

"Are you?"

She smiled and moved into the bedroom. "No." Beryl caught her reflection in the full-length swivel mirror. She was confident enough of her appearance not to dwell on it or try to rearrange it. No matter what Connor said she knew he found her attractive. Beryl's walking dress was the same shade of scarlet as her bonnet ribbon. The bodice was a modest cut emphasizing the length of her neck and the narrowness of her shoulders. It was also tightly tailored, molded to her breasts and cinched in at the waist. She dropped her bonnet on a rocker and came to stand at the foot of the bed, inches from Connor. "Rushton's in good health." Her smile became sly and touched her eyes in the same way. "Vigorous health, actually."

Connor had no difficulty taking her meaning. He wished his father would take Beryl to bed all day long. It was the surest way of keeping her out of his. "Does he know you're here?"

"I told him I might stop by. He's gone to his office at the mill. He plans to meet you at the train station to say his farewells along with everyone else."

"And you?"

"I plan to say my farewells now." Her delicate hands came up to her throat and she began to unfasten the silk-covered buttons. "Don't worry," she said. "I know your wife's in a separate room. They told me at the front desk. It's a shame about her foot. Do you think she did it on purpose? To stay out of your bed?"

"Beryl, I told you before that when you married my father it was over between us. You can't have his money and me in your bed. There's been no love lost between Rushton and me but I won't do this to him. Credit me with something you don't have yourself—morals." He turned away and continued packing.

"It *is* over between us," she said. She undid another button. The lace that edged her camisole was visible now. "You're going back to Colorado and we'll probably never see each other again. This is about good-bye, Connor."

"I don't want you, Beryl."

"Do you expect me to believe you want *her?*" she demanded. Beryl's short laugh was hollow and spiteful. "Don't talk to me about morals, you sanctimonious hypocrite. If I married Rushton for money then what the hell was it *you* did yesterday? I suppose when Jay Mac pulled you into his library he didn't give you a deed worth twelve thousand dollars and thank you for marrying his insipid, green-as-grass, too-smart-for-her-own-good daughter?" Beryl's fingers worked over the buttons until her scarlet bodice was completely open. Her corset pushed her breasts up and forward and she flaunted the invitation. "Dammit, Connor, do you think I'm going to make a stink if you take her to bed? That would be the pot calling the kettle black, don't you think, since I have Rushton and enjoy making love to him? I've never sought to deny you your pleasures. I only asked you to share them with me. What's the harm? We're both married. We'll share the sin."

Connor deliberately finished folding his shirt before he answered. "Share the sin?" he asked. "I don't think that's the way it works, Beryl. I believe they compound that sort of thing in heaven, not divide it equally among the black sheep."

She gave her head a furious little toss. "Don't make fun of me."

He turned on her angrily. "It's either that or hurt you."

Beryl Holiday stood on tiptoe and slipped her arms around Connor's neck. She pressed herself against him and buried her face in the curve of his neck. "Then hurt me," she whispered against his flesh. "I don't mind."

One of Connor's hands was placed on her waist, the other curled roughly in her hair. When he tried to pry her away her head was tilted back and her lips, slightly parted now, damp, hinting of secret pleasures, invited his mouth. She looked up at him, daring him and drawing him in with the darkening centers of her pale blue eyes.

"Damn you," he said through clenched teeth.

Beryl closed the distance between them. Her mouth worked over his lips, her tongue probed. Her fingers threaded in his hair, securing him for her eager and hungry touch. Her breasts swelled against his chest and she stretched trying to expose them above the line of her corset and camisole. His fingers bit into her waist and the coil of hair at her nape. She felt captured by his bruising embrace, vulnerable even as she was the aggressor. His skin was warm, his mouth hot. She welcomed the pressure, the hardness, and against her thighs she felt his need.

Maggie didn't realize she had done anything to draw their attention. Connor could have told her that she only had to be in the same room to command his. She didn't ask what made him look toward the doorway and he wasn't given the opportunity to explain. By the time he extricated himself from Beryl's grasp Maggie was gone.

Connor found Beryl's bonnet and thrust it at her. "Take this and get out," he said roughly.

Dazed, Beryl dropped down on the bed. She glimpsed herself in the mirror. Her hair was disheveled and her lips swollen. There was heightened color in her fashionably pale face and her eyes were dark and languid. "What's wrong with you?"

Connor grabbed his valise and left.

Beryl heard the door slam. She lay back on the bed, stretched slowly, arching her spine in a movement that was peculiarly feline. She turned her head toward the mirror again. The bedroom doorway was entirely visible to her. Beryl's smile shifted from shrewd to satisfied.

Maggie wasn't in their suite when Connor got there. Her bags were also gone. Cursing, he chose to take the stairs rather than wait interminably for the vertical steam lift. Slightly out of breath by the time he reached the lobby, Connor was relieved to find her calmly waiting for him in one of the areas partially secluded by its arrangement of chairs and greenery.

He dropped his bag beside hers and sat in the chair opposite her, then pulled it closer for privacy. Maggie was studying the hands folded neatly in her lap as if they were not her own.

"Look at me, Maggie," he said. His tone, while not quite a demand, fell far short of coaxing. "Do you think I don't know why you chose to come down here?"

She raised her eyes. There was a dullness in them that was at odds with her fixed, bright smile. "I'm glad you're so perceptive, Connor. It saves explaining."

"Then I wish you were as perceptive," he said. "Because you require an explanation. What you saw back there was—"

Maggie shook her head. "I don't want anything from you," she said quietly. "Especially not an explanation."

Connor glanced around. Maggie had chosen her setting wisely. He couldn't very well make a scene in the lobby of the St. Mark. "Sooner or later you're going to have to listen to me," he said.

"Then I choose later."

He didn't like it but he was coming to recognize the stubborn, unyielding thrust of her jaw. "Very well," he said, coming to his feet. "I'll see about getting a hansom to the station."

Everything was quickly arranged by the manager. Their bags were taken out to the street and the hansom appeared within minutes. Connor offered his arm but Maggie pretended she didn't see and preceded him out of the hotel. She let the cab driver assist her into the hansom and seated herself in the far corner. She didn't believe Connor would impose himself by sitting beside her. He knew she wanted nothing to do with him.

The ride to the station was accomplished in silence. Maggie concentrated on how she would behave in front of her family and Connor's. By the time they reached the train Maggie had convinced herself she could touch her new husband without losing her breakfast or her dignity.

Events of the morning had caused them to arrive earlier than planned. Two of Northeast Rail's private passenger cars had just been coupled to No. 454 and they were adding the freight cars from a side track. An amiable porter began loading their baggage along with the trunks that had arrived the night before.

Connor pointed to the pyramid of satchels, valises, and trunks. "All of that's yours?" he asked Maggie. He knew the answer, of course, but he couldn't credit her with that much foolishness.

"Mama and Skye packed for me. I told them it was too much but no one listened."

Connor got the impression it was a state of affairs she was used to. "Dancer Tubbs won't have room for everything you own."

Maggie sat on one of her trunks, making herself comfortable. Her gown was tailor-made, cut with a masculine bias from the dark gray color to the bodice that resembled a man's waistcoat and jacket. "I'll leave some of the things with Mary Michael in Denver. If we see

Rennie I'll give some things to her. You don't have to worry about carting my belongings all over Colorado. I'm not going to be a burden to you."

"Where do you get these ideas?" he asked. "I only said that Dancer couldn't accommodate your things. The train's going to take us as far as Queen's Point and we'll use wagons and horses from there. Traveling isn't the problem. Dancer's cabin is."

"I'm sorry," she replied. "I misunderstood." Maggie turned her face away from him and watched the station traffic instead. The platforms and ticket counters were beginning to crowd with passengers and well-wishers. The available benches were already taken by people who enjoyed nothing so much as watching the trains come and go, sometimes placing a friendly wager on which arrival would be late and which engine would come thundering in under the clock. Seasoned travelers dressed for it, ignoring spring and summer fashion and wearing darker colors that could hide the offending smoke, soot, and cinders. Women herded their children together, counting brown, black, and towheads as they hurried along the platform. Husbands distanced themselves from the flock to keep an eye on the baggage handlers and the occasional unescorted and attractive female. Salesmen held onto their cases of product with white-knuckled intensity, protecting the life's blood of their work. A sketch artist went by, carrying his pad and easel, looking for customers who might pay a few pennies for a farewell portrait.

Connor didn't like the station. It was everything he disliked about New York: too crowded, too noisy, too hurried. It reminded him again how much he was his mother's son, not his father's. Had things been different, the Colorado ranch wouldn't have interested him as anything but a source of capital, just as it was to Rushton.

He glanced at Maggie, watched her take in the sights, welcoming the very same things he detested, absorbing the nervous pulse of the station, breathing in the crowd and the confusion as if it were vital to her very existence. She wouldn't last two weeks on the Double H and probably less than that at Dancer's—if he let her stay there at all. Connor was relieved Maggie had proposed divorce, otherwise the onerous task of bringing it up would have been left to him. She had given him back his ranch but she'd never survive there.

She felt his eyes on her and she turned. It unnerved her when he watched her so intently and gave nothing away of what he was thinking. "What are you looking at?"

At that moment he was looking at her throat. Beneath the jacket-bodice of her gown she was wearing a starched white shirt with a pleated front, pearl buttons, and a black silk bow tie at the collar. Somehow she managed to look entirely feminine wearing an outfit that should have given her a mannish appearance. He pointed to the bow tie. "That's mine," he said, his voice indicating something close to astonishment. "I wondered what happened to it."

She smoothed the tie neatly. "You packed in a hurry last night," she said. "And this morning?" She shrugged, her smile indifferent. "This morning, I'm not surprised you didn't think of it. Do you want it back?"

He shook his head. There was something oddly intimate about her wearing what belonged to him. It surprised him more that she had chosen to do it, and after what she witnessed with Beryl, that she kept it on.

For once she was able to divine his thoughts as his glance became less impenetrable. "It looked better with my dress than any of the ribbons I owned," she said.

"Then keep it."

She suspected it wasn't simple generosity that prompted his gift. It occurred to her that once they were west of the Hudson River Connor never planned to wear a tie again. "Thank you," she said politely. Connor looked as if he were going to say something, but the arrival of the porter for the trunk she was sitting on interrupted him. Maggie stood and let her seat be taken away.

Connor looked around for a bench where she could sit. There was none available.

Because he looked as if he might enjoy clearing a few of the sightseers off their benches, Maggie laid a light restraining hand on his forearm. "It's not necessary," she said. She pointed to the far end of the platform where a small, noisy group of people were mounting the stairs. "Anyway, I think the family's arrived. That's Mary Francis laughing."

Connor had recognized the unmistakable hearty laugh as well. He held out his arm for Maggie.

"Don't worry," she said, her smile fixed in the direction of her approaching family. "Unless you or Beryl say something to Mary Francis your secret and your kneecaps are safe."

His reply was filled with soft menace. "You're very brave when your family's around."

Maggie ignored him although she knew it was true. She reached out for her mother, hugging Moira with only a fraction of the desperation she felt. Over her mother's shoulder she saw Rushton and Beryl arrive. Her touch went cold.

Moira drew back, holding Maggie a few inches from her. "You look wonderful, dear."

"Mother," Skye said, rolling her eyes. "You just saw her yesterday. And if you ask me, she looks a little peaked, though I like the bow tie." She kissed her sister on the cheek. "Where did you get it?"

Happy for the diversion from her appearance, Maggie pointed to Connor. "Pilfered it, I'm afraid."

Frankly astonished, Skye looked at her new brother-in-law. "You *stole* it?" she said.

Connor laughed. "No, brat. Your sister stole it from me."

Mary Francis poked her youngest sister in the ribs. "You don't have to act so stupid around him now, Skye. He's Maggie's husband, not a potential suitor."

"Girls," Moira said in a maternal tone. She sighed. Neither of her daughters was particularly abashed by the reprimand. "Was the St. Mark as lovely as I remember?" she asked Maggie.

"Quite lovely, Mama."

Jay Mac clapped Connor heartily on the back. "You look as if you can't wait to be rid of the lot of us," he said.

Connor wondered how much honesty Jay Mac would accept before he was insulted. He chose a tactfully truthful response. "I'm looking forward to seeing my ranch again," he said. "I miss the space and silence."

Rushton joined them as Connor was speaking. His son's reply made him think of Edie, his wife who wouldn't be moved from her valley. His attention went to Maggie. She was lithe and delicate, with fine-boned features and a smooth complexion. He tried to imagine her on the Double H, riding the range beside Connor, cooking meals for the hired help, birthing children in the same bed where Edie had birthed Connor. None of it seemed possible to him. She was very different from Edie, Rushton thought, but in one important way she was exactly the same: she was a native flower, no more able to flourish in the harsh Colorado setting than Edie could have in the hostile New York air.

Rushton took his son's hand and shook it, wondering all the while what Connor really thought of his new wife. He drew Connor aside, letting Beryl fend for herself, and held his son's gaze with his own. "Don't let her die out there," he said quietly.

Connor's remote expression didn't change, though he felt a coldness seep through his skin to his bones. "What's that supposed to mean?"

"Your wife," Rushton said. "She'll never survive the Double H. Let her go before it kills her."

"You mean let her run out in the middle of the night the way you did?"

Some of the color left Rushton's chiseled features. A frown creased his brow. "Is that the way you think it was?" he asked. "Did Edie let you believe that all these years?"

"My mother never talked about you deserting her," Connor said coldly. "But Old Sam made sure I knew."

For a long moment Rushton didn't say anything, then he nodded slowly, resignation in the faint, tired movement of his head. "He would," he said, more to himself than to Connor.

"Are you going to suggest it was somehow different? That you didn't leave in the middle of the night? That you didn't hate living on the ranch?"

Rushton looked at his son, then across the way at his daughter-in-law. "No," Rushton said finally, staring at Maggie. "I'm not going to tell you different. You couldn't hear it from me." His attention came back to Connor. "I pray to God you don't have to learn it from your wife."

Connor accepted his father's enigmatic reply because Beryl chose that moment to join them. "Rushton," she said, "you can't keep Connor all to yourself over here. Other people want to wish him well."

Rushton Holiday smiled, patting Beryl's arm as she wound it around his. He thought he'd chosen his second wife well. She was a beautiful flower but not fragile, common without being coarse, a survivor because it was her nature. He never told her why he sometimes called her Daisy. "Come along, then," he said. "We'll join the others. Connor's heard all the paternal wisdom he's willing to tolerate." They moved away, leaving Connor standing by himself.

"Are the cars to your liking?" Jay Mac was asking his daughter when Connor came up behind her. He rested his hands lightly on her shoulders and her tensing was so slight that he was certain he was the only one who noticed it. There was a fragrance to Maggie's hair that teased his senses. Lavender, he thought. It was subtle, delicate. It suited her.

"We haven't been inside yet," Maggie told Jay Mac. "I'm certain everything's fine." She tapped her father lightly on the chest, smiling. "I know you like comfort when you travel."

Jay Mac's face took on a ruddy hue as Moira and his other daughters laughed. He took off his spectacles and made a show of cleaning them. John MacKenzie Worth was a wealthy man but he didn't surround himself with ostentatious reminders of it. His private railway cars were his only exception and he was still self-conscious enough about it to be embarrassed. "Not a word, Rush," he warned his business friend. "I've seen your carriages and your matched pair of cinnamon mares."

"We all have our vices," Rushton said. Beside him Beryl's pale eyes rested on Connor.

The boarding of No. 454 was announced up and down the platform. Moira drew closer to Jay Mac. "I can't believe it's happening," she said. "First Michael, then Rennie, now you." She twisted a handkerchief in her hands. "And so far away, all of you. I wish . . ." She bit her lower lip, a gesture so like Maggie's that Connor was taken back by it for a moment.

"I'll write, Mama," Maggie said, stepping free of Connor. She took her mother's fidgeting hands in her own. "You know I will."

"I'll hold her to it," Connor said.

For the sake of everyone, Moira pretended to be relieved by the promise. She kissed Maggie on the cheek. "You can always come home," she whispered in her daughter's ear.

Maggie's eyes closed briefly. Her heart ached. "I know, Mama. I know."

The next few minutes passed in a blur as Maggie was handed from one person to the other. The farewells were personal, wrenching, but somehow she got through them. She knew she had because she was finally standing on the balcony platform at the rear of the second private car, Connor beside her, her family and his on the station platform below. She grabbed him instinctively to steady herself when the train began to move. He put an arm about her shoulders.

They held that pose until they were out of the station and there was no one left to see them.

Maggie opened the door to the private car and preceded Connor inside. She had rarely traveled in the car but her father used it extensively. Although Jay Mac had had a second car commissioned he seldom used both when he was traveling alone. The car that Maggie and Connor were in had been fitted for Jay Mac's comfort, but also for the practicalities of his business.

Everything in the car was built in or secured in some fashion. A mahogany desk, polished to bring out the hint of red in the wood, took up a large area at the head of the car. A heavily padded burgundy leather chair accented the desk. A map of the United States, indicating all the rail lines, existing and proposed, extended between two windows. Bookshelves lined a portion of the wall behind the desk from floor to ceiling and two wing chairs were situated near the small wood stove. The work area of the car gradually gave way to other furnishings. A dining table, no larger than the width of the window under which it was secured, meant that Jay Mac could take his meals in privacy. An Oriental carpet kept the cold from seeping through the hardwood floor and added warmth with its patterned splash of colors. Drawers were built in under the berth-like bed and a trunk with extra blankets was against one wall.

Maggie noted immediately that her father had added some touches just for the newlyweds. Several glass vases had been attached to the sides of the car with brass fittings. They alternated with the milk-glass globes that covered the oil lamps and each one was filled with carnations, greenery, and baby's breath. The wine rack was stocked and a bottle of champagne sat in an ice bucket on the table. A cloth banner had been draped from one side of the car to the other, announcing their just-married status, and the towels and bed linens, neatly folded on the unmade bed, had already been mono-grammed with an elaborately curled H. Maggie could only imagine that her father had hired seamstresses to work day and night to embroider the linens in time for their departure. She hated to think

Jay Mac was so certain of the outcome that he had had the work done months ago. Sighing, she turned away and nearly collided with her husband. She ducked to one side and followed the direction of his gaze.

Connor wasn't looking at the linens. He was critically examining the size of the bed.

"It's three-quarters size," she said.

"Cozy."

"I was thinking it was a little big."

Connor's attention shifted from the bed to Maggie. They obviously weren't thinking about the bed in the same light. "I suspect we have a problem," he said calmly.

"I don't think so," she said carelessly. "I'll take the bed and you'll use the sofa in the forward car."

"As I said, I suspect we have a problem."

Maggie refused to argue about it at the moment. She removed the towels from the bed and stacked them in the cupboard near the curtained-off toilet; then she took off her mantle and hung it on a brass and porcelain knob just inside the rear door. The private car swayed slightly as the train gathered speed and Maggie held onto the secured mahogany side table as a sudden wave of nausea caught her off guard.

"Are you all right?" asked Connor. Under the circumstances he thought he deserved the brief sour look she shot him. It had been a stupid question since she was obviously *not* all right. Her face was wretchedly pale, her eyes were pained, and her mouth had flattened. "What's wrong?"

Maggie didn't answer immediately. She waited for the sensation to pass as she knew it would. She straightened slowly and eased her grip on the anchoring table. "Nothing," she said. She didn't ask herself whether she deserved Connor's disgusted look; she simply ignored it. "Would you like to see the other car?" she asked. Without waiting for a reply, she headed forward.

Passage to the next private car required stepping outside and across the coupled balconies. Overhangs on both cars made the brief journey protected from the elements. While the private car they had first entered was furnished so that Jay Mac could use it alone, the second car was meant for taking influential investors and business colleagues on day-trips from New York. The round mahogany dining table in this car seated eight comfortably. There was a large open basket of fruit at the center and another covered basket sitting on one of the chairs. The wood stove was embellished with brass fittings and the iron wine rack held a full dozen bottles. Four burgundy wing chairs and two sofas were arranged for easy conversation and small side tables were especially fitted with ashtrays and oil lamps. Two Oriental rugs were used this time, one under the dining table and the other in the parlor area.

Connor looked around and whistled softly. He pointed to the dining table. "Hell of a place to play poker."

Maggie smiled. "You're exactly right," she said, looking at him sideways. "Jay Mac told us it was so he could serve his friends dinner on their day-trips but no one's ever believed it. Every few months he gathers five or so friends together and they leave New York, supposedly on business. The only deals they make, I think, are from a deck of cards. Your father's gone with Jay Mac a number of times."

"He's never mentioned it," Connor said.

She wasn't surprised. "You're not very close, are you?"

Connor shrugged. "We hardly know each other."

It was not what he said, but the way he said it, that warned Maggie that conversation on that topic was ended. She glanced around the entire room. "Well? What do you think? Can we manage satisfactorily? Between the two cars there's plenty of space. And there *is* the rest of the train. You'll be allowed access to all the other cars. I don't see why we have to be in each other's pockets."

Connor's soft grunt was noncommittal. He was mentally measuring the length of the sofa against his own. The accommodations were far superior to anything he would have arranged for himself but it was difficult to remember that when he kept thinking he was giving up a comfortable bed for an uncomfortable sofa.

"If you don't mind," Maggie said, "I'm going back to the other car to unpack my things."

"And if I do?" asked Connor. "Mind, that is?"

"I'll do it anyway," she said stiffly. "I was merely trying to be polite."

"I thought so." When she started to go he put his hand on her arm lightly, stopping her. He felt her recoil and his dark eyes became colder and more remote as she stepped back. "I was going to tell you not to exhaust yourself trying to be polite. It seems you're not going to do that after all."

Embarrassed that she had made her distaste of his touch so blatantly apparent, feeling somehow that it showed a weakness on her part, Maggie lowered her head and hurried out of the car.

Connor stretched out on the sofa. As he suspected it was about eighteen inches shy of restful. Every muscle in his body would be curved taut as a bow if he had to sleep on it until Denver. The floor was preferable and he thought it was probably where he would end up. His wife clearly was not willing to share a bed.

His wife. Connor ran his fingers through his hair and rubbed the back of his neck. He remembered how she had shied away from him, but on the heels of that he remembered another time when she had only been shy with him. What the hell did he really expect from her? he wondered. What the hell did he really expect from himself?

He glanced over his shoulder at the door where Maggie had exited. For a moment he considered following her but he had no clear idea what he wanted to say. Did she really need him to damn her for aborting their child when she looked haunted all the time? Was he supposed to apologize for what she assumed about Beryl's visit at the St. Mark? What in God's name was it she wanted from him?

Nothing.

He hated that it bothered him.

Connor ignored the full wine rack and went in search of hard liquor and companionship in the forward passenger cars.

By the time Maggie finished unpacking her own belongings she was more tired than could be easily attributed to the task she had accomplished. She hadn't slept well the night before and the farewell to her family had been especially wearing but it was more than that as well. As soon as the thoughts surfaced she resolutely buried them and immersed herself in another mindless task, this time taking care of Connor's bags and trunks. It was an intimate, wifely sort of duty, just the kind of thing she thought she would abhor, and it surprised and pained her to discover there was nothing inherently distasteful about it. She supposed that had she been doing it for someone she loved, the ritual of folding and smoothing and stacking and packing might even have been a comforting one. She imagined the faint scent of him clung to his clothes and had she felt differently she might have held them closer, taking an odd reassurance from them.

Maggie shook her head, clearing away the vague yet unsettling fantasies. She stuffed the last of Connor's things in the narrow armoire and eyed the unmade bed. Instead of snapping out the monogrammed sheets to make it up crisply, Maggie stretched out on it the way it was. She struggled with one sheet, covering herself haphazardly, and was asleep within minutes of her head touching the pillow.

Connor found her just that way an hour later. Her hair, freed from its ivory combs, fell over the curve of her neck and shoulder and curled around the pearl buttons on the pleated front of her shirt. She had loosened the bow tie but not taken it off. The hem of her gown had climbed up her calves and where the sheet didn't reach Connor had a glimpse of the smooth line of her legs. She had one hand tucked under her face, pressing her cheek, and the other lay flatly against the sheet just where the monogram H had been elaborately stitched. Her plain gold wedding band caught streamers of sunlight as the train rolled past fields of Pennsylvania corn. He had chosen the band without consulting her or asking his father. The ring had been Edie's, his mother's, and he wasn't certain why he had wanted Maggie to have it. He hadn't told her its significance and he hadn't warned his father, but when he pulled it out of his pocket at the ceremony he had looked past Maggie's gentle, cautious smile and seen Rushton's brief anguish. For a moment he had felt powerful, being able to force that emotion on his father. Then Maggie's hand had stirred in his, the delicate bones shifting in his palm and beneath the thumb that was passing over her knuckles, and he knew that if she was using him, he was also using her, using her in ways she didn't clearly understand. The feeling of power passed. He felt petty.

Connor rearranged the sheet over Maggie. There were faint shadows under her eyes that were not caused by the dark fan of her lashes. He touched her forehead with the back of his hand. She stirred slightly, wrinkling her nose.

"I didn't mean to wake you," he said softly. He had found hard liquor and companionship in the forward cars and had indulged in neither. Each of the three second-class cars had friendly poker games in progress. Connor had been invited to join but he chose to watch instead. He wondered what the players would have thought if he'd told them about twelve thousand dollars he had won and lost in the space of a single evening. His black eyes drifted over Maggie. They might have believed he'd won the money. They'd never believe how he lost it. "You have the face of an angel," he said.

She was sure she was dreaming and her smile was unguarded. Maggie turned slightly, rubbing her cheek against the back of her hand, the movement lazy and vaguely feline.

Connor drew up a chair and sat down, resting his feet on the frame of drawers supporting the bed. He rocked back in the chair so it was balanced on the two rear legs and crossed his arms in front of him.

Maggie came awake by slow degrees and found her dream disconcertingly real. Her smile vanished. "What are you doing?" she asked. It was disappointing to her that her voice was husky and breathless. Connor did not look at all threatened or inclined to respond. "Well?" she demanded, more firmly this time.

"Are you always so prickly when you first wake up?"

"You'll never know," she said sweetly. Maggie sat up and rubbed her temples. The nap hadn't been refreshing; it had left her with a headache. "Because I'm not waking up with you this close to me again." She sighed. "Would you please move away from the bed so I can get up? I need a headache powder."

"I'll get it for you."

Maggie didn't argue because she didn't want to move. She lay back down and told him where he could find the packet. There was a keg of fresh water beneath the washstand. She heard him rummage through cabinets until he found a glass and a spoon. Almost immediately after that he was handing her the medicine. She raised herself on one elbow long enough to drink it down.

"Is it the motion of the train that's making you ill?" he asked.

"Something like that." She closed her eyes.

"You should have told me."

"I didn't think of it," she said tiredly. "I don't travel that often."

"Yet you're going halfway across the country with a man you hardly know to study with a man you've never met. It must be important to you."

She didn't answer immediately. There were things about herself she didn't want to give up, not to Connor Holiday who despised her as a thief and a whore and now, because of what she'd told him about Madame Restell, as a murderer. Yet she heard herself say, "It is."

Connor took the glass from her hand and sat on the edge of the bed. Maggie's panic was immediate and he made no move to touch her or try to prevent her from rolling closer to the wall. "I'm not going to hurt you," he said quietly. "I want to feel your forehead. You're still flushed."

She automatically touched her face with her hand, but her fingers were still cool from holding the glass of water and her skin felt much hotter than it probably was. Still, she was cautious of moving toward Connor. The situation had a curious familiarity, as if she had played out a similar scene with her husband before. She remembered she had been ill in the brothel when they had first met. Was the peculiar sensation prompted by a memory from that time?

Connor was patient. Had she been a filly he might have enticed her with a bit of apple or sugar sprinkled in the palm of his hand. But she was a woman, all woman, reluctant and wary of extending her trust, and the only proper substitute for the apple and sugar was patience. Connor simply sat there, doing and saying nothing, waiting her out.

She slid toward the middle of the bed. The sheet and her gown tangled in her legs and she pushed at them, getting rid of the sheet but sliding the gown modestly over her legs. She lay on her back and stared up at him.

"Has this been anything like the marriage you imagined?" he asked. His question raised a ghost of a smile. "I didn't think so."

"I never imagined I'd marry."

That surprised him. His black eyes became less remote as they flickered with interest. "I supposed every young woman thought about it."

"I didn't." At her sides Maggie's fingers slowly unclenched and her breathing came a little easier. Connor watched her hands and wondered what he could say to draw her out. It surprised him when she added, "I don't think my sisters thought about it either."

"Really?"

"Perhaps that's why Jay Mac pushes us into it."

Connor raised his hand and touched Maggie's cheek lightly, then her forehead. Now that the flush had faded from her cheeks she was less warm. "You can breathe again," he told her as he removed his hand. "I don't think you're sickening for anything."

"I could have told you that. It's just a headache and motion sickness."

"Do you want me to pull the blinds?" he asked.

She shook her head. The movement gave rise to the sick sensation in her stomach. "I just need to lie here. It will pass."

"I can massage your scalp." Connor expected her to shudder. It was a measure of how poorly she felt that she agreed after only a moment's hesitation. She started to sit up. "No, stay where you are," he said. "I'll move." He shifted his position so she could place her head on his lap. His fingers threaded in her hair and moved gently against her scalp. Some of the tension lines at the corner of her eyes eased almost immediately. He watched her lids flutter closed.

"Tell me about Beryl," she said quietly. She felt his fingers still and knew she had caught him off guard. "I wasn't jealous, you know."

"I know," he said. "This would have to be a different kind of marriage for you to feel that." His fingers resumed their gentle circling. "I imagine you thought I was trying to make a fool of you."

"It occurred to me, though I rather thought it was Beryl, not you. Mama told me you were engaged to her once."

"How did she know that?"

"Beryl told her, I think."

Connor's mouth pulled to one side in disgust. "That doesn't surprise me."

"Do you still love her?" she asked.

He paused, thinking. It was the way she had asked the question. It made him wonder if he had ever loved Beryl Walker. "No," he said at last.

But Connor's hesitation had cost him the chance to be believed and reaffirmed all of Maggie's convictions that she had been right to choose the course she had. It would have been intolerable to be married to someone who was in love with another woman. What sort of husband could he have been to her? What sort of father to a child? No, as painful as they were, she had made all the right decisions. She might have actually fallen in love with him herself, with his gentle fingers and his coaxing drawl, and then where would she have been?

"Don't you have anything else you want to ask me about Beryl?" he asked.

She thought about it. "No," she said. "Nothing else."

That bothered him. "Don't you want to know why she was at the St. Mark? If she was there all night?"

"I think I saw why. And it doesn't matter if you arranged that room for yourself to be with her. I told you I'm not jealous."

Because she didn't want to know Connor found himself wanting to explain. Perverseness made him want to speak out, pride kept him silent. He continued kneading her scalp.

Moments before she fell asleep again she whispered, "I'm glad we can be nice to each other."

Connor sighed and leaned back against the inlaid mahogany headboard. Maggie's head turned. Her cheek rested against his thigh. He wondered how long *nice* could possibly last.

Until dinner.

The train stopped in Philadelphia and Connor made arrangements with one of the restaurants to deliver dinner to their private car. Maggie was touched by his thoughtfulness and because he had gone to so much trouble, and because she had been so miserable most of the day, she took the time to dress her hair and find something suitable in her wardrobe.

She didn't notice that the waiters turned to watch her as she entered the dining car, and she certainly didn't notice that they didn't turn away. Maggie knew the claret velvet gown was elegant; what she didn't know was how she looked in it.

Connor knew. He tipped the waiters, told them to come back for the serving dishes, and dismissed them curtly. The looks they exchanged, and the single, knowing wink one of them shot in his direction set his teeth on edge.

"What the hell do you think you're doing wearing that?" he demanded roughly.

Maggie was startled by the harsh question. The waiters were not even out of earshot. Frowning, she looked down at herself, then at her faint reflection in the windows of the car. She liked the cut of the rounded neckline, the fullness of the short velvet sleeves. The peplum bodice made her waist look fashionably small without wearing a corset and by contrast, her hips looked more curved. The trained skirt was stiffened with a lining of muslin so the gown held its elegant line and there were velvet bands and satin pleatings at the front. The claret highlighted the same rich hues in her hair and gave her cheeks color without any artifice.

Whatever small confidence she had gained by putting on the gown was effectively shattered. She blinked several times, holding tears at bay, then she raised her chin, her mouth set stubbornly, and sat down at the table. "I didn't dress to please you," she said quietly, not meeting his eyes. "I dressed to please me."

Jesus, Connor thought, running his hand through his dark hair. She didn't understand. What the hell did she see when she looked in a mirror? he wondered. Not half of what he saw, obviously. He dropped his hand to the back of the chair and yanked it away from the table. It scraped against the Oriental rug, causing a ripple. He kicked at the rug and sat down on Maggie's left.

Connor lifted one of the silver serving domes and passed the platter of sliced roast lamb to Maggie. She took a small piece and added mint jelly to her plate. Out of the corner of his eye Connor watched her reach for the covered bread basket. He waited to see if she would fall out of her bodice. When she didn't he didn't know whether to be relieved or disappointed.

"Saloon girls cover more of their breasts than you," he said tightly.

Maggie did not think anyone had ever said the word *breast* in front of her before, not if they weren't referring to game hen or turkey. Mortified, her fingers tightened around her fork to keep from dropping it. She swallowed hard and replied with credible calm, "I don't know about saloon girls. *This* is the latest fashion in New York." She hadn't wanted to take the gown at all, she almost said. She'd known she wasn't going to have many opportunities to wear it, perhaps none at all. Skye had insisted and Maggie had given in. "And don't tell me we're not in New York any longer," she added, "because I already know that. I won't have occasion to wear it again and my . . . my—"

"Breasts."

"My *bosom* will be adequately covered in the future." As far as she was concerned the subject was closed.

Not so with Connor. He grasped her chin and forced her to look at him. The hardness of his features was tautly defined. "Make certain that it is, Maggie, or accept the fact that we'll be sharing a bed before our divorce." His eyes burned her with their coldness. "And if you get pregnant again I'll make damn certain there's a baby this time."

Chapter Eight

Maggie jerked away from Connor's grip and stood. Her hand swung back in a wide arc and came rushing forward.

A hair's-breadth away from making contact with his face, Connor seized her by the wrist. His grip pressed bruisingly against her pulse until her fingers uncurled. The fork clattered on her plate.

The sound of it caught Maggie's attention. She stared at it lying on the fragile bone china, a fork again, not a weapon that could have scarred Connor permanently or blinded him. She was trembling with fear.

He was shaking with anger.

"I'm sorry," she said, her voice small and choked. She didn't meet his eyes. "I've never——" She stopped because he wasn't standing beside her any longer. The rear door to the private car was slammed so hard that Maggie felt the shudder roll through her.

She sat down slowly. The aroma of their dinner seeped out from under the silver covers. What had been appetizing was now only nauseating and Maggie, careless of convention or the elegant line of her gown, huddled in her chair, her knees drawn up to her chest, trying to smother all feelings of sickness. She sat that way for a long time, her mind very nearly a blank as she stared straight ahead, her withdrawal from everything around her complete.

When she finally moved Maggie was stiff from her contorted posture. She limped and stretched on her way back to the sleeping car. She let out a breath she hadn't known she'd been holding when she found the car vacant. She didn't give another thought to where Connor might have gone to vent his terrible anger; she was simply grateful to be alone.

Maggie lit one of the oil lamps and pulled down the blinds in all the windows. Her eye caught the "Just Married" banner and she tore it down, balled it up, and pitched it under the desk. She was in the middle of undressing when she heard the waiters returning. From their laughter and sniggering in the other car she knew the scenario they had assumed from the untouched meal. Maggie's troubled eyes fell on her empty bed. They couldn't have been more wrong.

After she finished undressing and put on her nightgown and wrapper, she made up the bed and found extra linens for Connor. She took them to the dining car and laid them on one of the sofas. After a brief hesitation, Maggie arranged the sheets and blankets on it and found some throw pillows for her husband to use. She tested the comfort of the sofa, stretching out and turning on both sides to measure its length and width. It only took her a few minutes to realize that Connor would be hopelessly uncomfortable with the arrangement.

She thought of the bed and of the things Connor had said to her earlier. There was no question of sharing it. It was a matter of giving it up. The decision was taken out of her hands as she fell asleep thinking about it.

When Connor returned to the station it was minutes before midnight and only seconds before No. 454 was scheduled to leave. He had no sooner boarded than the train started to pull away. He stood on the balcony a moment, wondering if he should retire to the sofa or enter the sleeping car and risk another argument with Maggie. The muted light slipping out from under the drawn blinds warned him that Maggie was waiting up for him. He wondered if she had been worried that he was going to miss the train—or praying for it.

Connor stared at the door to the sleeping car for several long moments. He thought about having to sleep in his clothes, about not being able to wash, about not being able to stretch all night long if he chose the sofa, or not being able to relax all night long if he chose the floor. Then he thought of Maggie's eyes, the hurt and haunted look, the pain of betrayal. He turned to his left on the balcony platform and entered the dining car.

The car was dark and he didn't bother lighting a lamp. The aroma of their uneaten meal still clung to the air but a quick sweep of the dining table told him that everything had been taken away. His stomach rumbled and his mouth watered but there was no satisfying either. He sat down on one of the sofas and began taking off his shoes. His grin was self-mocking. He was getting used to his needs going unsatisfied.

His shoes hit the floor with a mild thump. He removed his socks, then stood up to shrug out of his jacket and waistcoat. Both those items were tossed in the direction of a wing chair. One hit, the other missed. Connor tugged at the tails of his shirt and pulled them free of his trousers. He unfastened a few buttons and rolled up the cuffs. A haphazard search for some pillows turned up nothing. He didn't find any blankets or sheets but then he hadn't really expected Maggie to think about his comfort.

He stretched out on the sofa, wondered if the other one was in any way more suitable, and fell asleep thinking he should have given it a try.

Sunlight filtered in under the drawn blinds. Maggie could feel it pressing at her eyelids, trying to slip under her lashes. She shifted her position and placed a forearm over her eyes. The rolling motion of the train was comforting, the steady clacking of the wheels over the track, reassuring. Maggie yawned, stretched. She raised her forearm and started to get up.

Connor turned on his side. His shoulder was braced uncomfortably against the curved arm of the sofa, his neck supported at an unnatural angle. One of his calves dangled over the side of the cushions, the other foot over the far end. He stretched, rolled again, and this time landed facedown on the Oriental rug.

Maggie bolted upright while Connor groaned. She slid off her sofa and knelt on the floor beside him, placing a hand on his back. "Are you all right?" she asked, alarmed when he didn't move. "Is there something I can do?"

He didn't raise himself to look at her, but merely shook his head slowly.

Maggie touched the back of his neck with her fingertips. His hair looked nearly black against her pale skin. Afraid of a rebuff, her touch was tentative as she sifted through his hair searching for abrasions on his scalp.

Connor held himself very still as her fingers threaded through his hair. Her touch was a whisper against his skin yet he felt it all the way to his toes. He stood it as long as he could, then he turned on his back and stared up at her. Her hand hovered just above his cheek, suspended momentarily before she began to withdraw it. Connor took her by the wrist and drew it back.

Maggie winced when his fingers closed over the delicate underside of her wrist. He released her immediately and let her cradle her hand protectively in front of her.

"Did I hurt you?" he asked. His touch hadn't been rough, merely firm. He sat up. "Let me see."

She shook her head. "No, it's all right."

Connor's eyes narrowed. Where they had been sleepy a moment before they were alert and biting now. "You really can't stand for me to touch you, can you?"

Surprised by the terse accusation, Maggie's mouth parted slightly. Defenses rushed to her mind but all were left unspoken. She put out her wrist instead and let him look. He didn't deserve protection from the consequences of his actions.

Connor's eyes dropped from Maggie's pale face to her extended arm. Her skin was mottled with a bracelet of ugly blue bruises. He could make out the placement of his fingers by the dark shadows that colored her skin. He knew he hadn't done the damage a moment ago, but hours ago, when she had raised her hand against him.

Maggie removed her arm from his line of vision and stood. There were not going to be any apologies because they would have been meaningless. They would hurt each other again, not physically perhaps, but in more deeply profound ways they would draw blood.

"Did you sleep here all night?" he asked, running a hand through his hair.

She nodded. "I left the bed for you." She didn't add that it had been unintentional.

Connor leaned against the sofa. He rubbed the back of his stiff neck, shutting his eyes briefly. "That won't be necessary from now on."

She didn't argue. "Very well." Her voice was stiff, almost priggish. She couldn't seem to help herself.

"I was thinking that I might wait for another train at Pittsburgh."

"That isn't necessary."

"We'd probably arrive in Denver only a few days apart. You could wait with your sister until I get there."

Maggie tightened the belt on her robe. "I would have to wait in a hotel," she said without inflection. "I can't go to Michael's without you."

He was silent a moment. "So no one in your family's going to know about the divorce until after the fact."

"That's right."

"Are you certain you want it that way?"

Coldness seeped back into her voice. "Very certain."

"Then I'll stay," he said after a moment.

Maggie didn't acknowledge his decision. She simply turned to go. She was on the point of leaving when she heard him say, "But there have to be rules."

Connor got up off the floor and released some of the blinds. They flew upward, rattling in their shuttle. Sunlight was burning off the fog as No. 454 made the last slow descent from the Allegheny Mountains in central Pennsylvania. He looked over his shoulder and saw Maggie was still at the door, her hand curled around the knob. She was waiting for him to expound on his idea about rules. He offered her fruit from their bon voyage basket instead.

"I wish I had been able to find this last night," he said, extending an orange toward her. When she remained where she was he shrugged and began peeling it himself. He nudged a chair away from the dining table with one bare foot and sat down. "I was starved."

Maggie's hand dropped away from the doorknob but she didn't move into the room. She fiddled with the end of her braided hair. "There's a covered picnic basket on the wing chair over here." It was partially hidden under his discarded jacket. She was surprised he hadn't found it last night. "I think it was meant for our lunch yesterday."

"I'll look later. This is fine for now." He split open the orange. Droplets of sweet juice splashed his knuckles and he sucked it off.

Watching him, something twisted inside Maggie. Her mouth,

which should have watered at the sight of the orange, went dry instead. "What sort of rules?" she asked hoarsely.

"That we spend as little time together as possible," he said. "That you don't wear fancy ball dresses. That you don't stand there playing with your hair, looking sleepy-eyed and desirable and beautiful. That you don't touch me or let me—" He stopped because Maggie had fled the room. She hadn't heard everything he had to say but he thought she had gotten the message. He stared at his hands. They were shaking.

For the remainder of the journey Maggie rarely left her car. It had become hers by virtue of the fact that she had taken one of Connor's absences to move all his belongings to the forward car. With the exception of the monogrammed sheets, she had managed to erase all other traces of him. They ate meals together when the train stopped along the route but Connor never made another attempt to have their dinner served to them privately. They shared meals in hotels in Columbus, Indianapolis, St. Louis, and Kansas City. Breakfast and luncheon baskets were brought to them by the porters, but as soon as they were gone Maggie retired to her car with her portion and Connor remained alone in the dining car.

As No. 454 rode the rails inexorably toward Denver, Maggie struggled with loneliness. In her family she had often been the one off by herself, often alone, but never lonely. She had always had somewhere to turn, someone waiting who was eager, even happy, to include her in their adventure or hers. Connor had made it clear that he wanted nothing to do with her, that as far as he was concerned she was a pariah. For the first time in her life, cut off from her family, Maggie found herself physically sick with the pain of separation.

She never let on that it made her ache to be so isolated. The only person she could have told was the same person who wasn't interested in hearing it. Maggie knew that Connor often went to the forward cars. He played poker with a changing succession of travelers in second class, found conversational companions in first class, and even played with some of the poor children confined with their immigrant parents in the crowded third-class cars. She knew this because he mentioned it in passing sometimes and though she wanted to hear more, she never asked.

She found herself crying at odd times, for no readily apparent reason. She blamed Connor at first, but it seemed unfair, so in the end she took the burden on herself, accepting it as more of the ripple effect from her painfully-made decision.

Maggie paid attention to what she was wearing when Connor was around. She chose simple, modestly-cut day dresses even if she was meeting him in the evening. The colors were gray and brown, sometimes with a small print and cuffs and collars in contrasting fabrics. She didn't mind his edict about her wardrobe because she was wearing precisely the clothes she was most comfortable in, the ones she had thought were suitable for her work with Dancer Tubbs. She arranged her thick hair in a single braid, sometimes coiling it at the back of her head, most often letting it swing loosely at her back. There were days when she knew she wasn't going to see Connor that she didn't bother dressing at all, days, in fact, in which she did not rise from her bed.

Self-pity was something new to Mary Margaret. Sometimes it frightened her that she might live her life that way. Sometimes she didn't care.

They were less than twenty-four hours outside of Denver when Connor made an unannounced visit to Maggie's car. She was curled in the large leather chair behind her father's desk, reading a book. It was late in the afternoon, too early for dinner, but her eyes automatically strayed to Connor's hands to see see if he was bringing her something. She couldn't imagine any other reason for his visit.

He watched her eyes dart to his hands and knew what she had expected. "Does it matter?" he asked. "You wouldn't eat it anyway."

He sounded almost angry, Maggie thought. "If you've come to pick a fight then you may as well leave," she said. She was pleased with her tone, pleased that she could manage the right amount of indifference. She opened her book again and began to read. Maggie didn't comprehend a single word but she took comfort in the fact that *he* didn't know that.

Connor sat on the arm of one of the wing chairs. "We're going to be in Denver tomorrow," he said. "I've asked the conductor to wire your sister at our next stop so she'll know when to expect us. The question is, what are we going to do about you?"

In spite of her desire to ignore him, that drew Maggie's attention. She closed the book and dropped it on the desk. There was enough force behind her action to make it slide halfway across the polished surface. "What about me?"

Connor began to wonder which of them was really spoiling for a fight. He kept his voice carefully neutral but said bluntly, "Frankly, Maggie, you look like hell."

Knowing it was true didn't make it any more palatable. She wished she could have said the same of him but the reality was that the further they traveled from New York, the more Connor Holiday seemed to thrive. He no longer wore black waistcoats and tailored jackets. His shirts weren't starched and his studs weren't gold. He had abandoned brushed flannel trousers in favor of the ubiquitous pants of the west: jeans. Silk shirts were replaced by cotton and chambray and his short vest was scarred brown leather. The most jarring difference in his appearance was that somewhere between St. Louis and Kansas City, Connor had begun to carry a gun.

Maggie knew without a doubt that if this was the man she had seen in New York she would never have made her proposal. The confinement of a city like New York had not set well on Connor's shoulders, but she had not realized how much until she had seen him shrug it off. She'd heard him say at the train station, in response to a question from her father, that he missed the space and silence. Looking at him now she understood it better, understood how contained he had been by convention, how crowded he had been with the choices forced on him by her father and his own.

She thought about the space and the silence he wanted and was more certain than ever that divorce was the best way to give both those things back to him.

Maggie had been silent so long that Connor wondered if she had heard him. "Maggie?" he asked. "Do I have to repeat myself?"

"No," she sighed. "I heard you. I look like hell." She swiveled in the chair and gave him a dead-on look. "Are you going to shoot me?"

One corner of his mouth lifted and he said dryly, "They shoot ugly women in Kansas. We're in Colorado now. We string 'em up."

Maggie stared at him for a moment. She blinked as his words registered, then she burst out laughing.

Connor had not expected her laughter. It washed over him like a refreshing spray of mountain water. It seemed to have substance, touching his face, his neck, the back of his hands, sending a skittering sensation down the length of his spine. For the brief span that her laughter lasted Connor had to revise his opinion. With her bright green eyes, with her wide smile flashing her teeth, with the flush of color that suffused her cheeks, Maggie was simply beautiful.

Maggie's laughter faded as she felt Connor's critical gaze. Uncomfortable beneath it, her hands fell to her lap. "I gather you're concerned because my sister might suspect there's a rift between us."

"I'd have thought that would be your concern," he said. "I'm more worried she might think I beat you." He got up from the arm of the chair and approached Maggie. She tried to brush his hand away when he reached for her chin but he was insistent. She let him cup her jaw and raise her face for the cold and distant scrutiny of his dark eyes. "How much weight have you lost?" he asked.

Maggie wasn't certain that she'd lost any. She'd been so inactive lately that she thought it was more likely that it had merely been redistributed. "I have no idea."

"At least ten pounds," he said. "When you couldn't afford to lose one. You're not going to be strong enough to make the journey from Queen's Point to Dancer's." He drew her to her feet and made her go with him to the mirror above the washbasin. "Look at yourself," he said, standing behind her. "There are hollows under your cheeks and your eyes look bruised." He plucked at the shoulder seams of her charcoal-gray day dress and demonstrated how loose the material was. "What are you going to tell your sister?"

She shrugged. Because Connor was still holding parts of her dress her action gave her the appearance of a marionette. She didn't like the effect at all. Knocking his hands aside, Maggie pushed away and put some distance between them. "I'll think of something to say to Michael," she said.

"If you don't *do* something about the way you look, you're going to have to tell her you have the plague."

"Bastard," she snapped at him under her breath. "You're the one that told me to—"

He held up his hand. "I never told you to hole up here like some damned prairie dog or hermit. Unless you've been trying to anticipate what life will be like with Dancer Tubbs, then you've got no excuse for what you've become. I told you to stay out of my way, not

crawl underground. You've never once come forward to meet anyone on the train. Passengers think you're a regular blue-blooded
Eastern bitch, too good even for the first-class folks. Did you expect
me to come back here to try to coax you out of bed or out of your
self-pitying mood?"

Her green eyes flashed with anguish. *"What is it you want from me?"*
she cried.

Something snapped in Connor. He closed the distance between
them. His hands snaked around her waist and he pulled her up
against him. Caught off balance, her body laid flush to his. His
fingers bit into her waist as he secured her against his chest and
thighs. Her head snapped back and he cradled it with his palm.

"I want you to remember," he said tersely. Then his mouth covered
hers.

Connor's lips moved over Maggie's, his tongue probing the line of
her lips, pressing for an opening against her teeth. Her small gasp
gave him the entry he sought.

Maggie's arms hung loosely at her sides. They rose slowly and her
hands touched Connor's shoulders first, lightly, not pushing him
away and not pulling him closer. Gradually they looped around his
back. Her fingers closed over the soft leather of his vest and held on.
His mouth was warm and firm and the movement of his tongue was
causing her heart to slam. Her breasts swelled against his chest. She
rubbed herself against him and a ribbon of heat curled between her
thighs.

Connor's mouth was insistent, hungry. It moved over her greedily.
He felt her body stir, respond, then blatantly match his own need. He
backed up to the desk, leaned on it, and pulled Maggie intimately
between his open thighs. She fit against him the way he remembered,
her arms around his neck, her breasts curved against his chest, her
thighs supporting his.

Connor's hands cupped her buttocks, pressing her closer so that
she was ground against the fly of his jeans. The sound of his groan
was absorbed by her mouth. He tugged on one of her arms and
found her hand, folding it in his. He brought it along the side of his
chest, rested it against his hip, then moved it between their bodies,
over his swollen groin. He held it there, letting her feel his need as
he turned them both and began backing Maggie over the desk.

Maggie tore her mouth away and pushed hard at Connor's chest.

He backed away immediately, his breath coming hard, his feral glance harder as he fought for control of his body. Maggie slumped forward, her head in her hands. She stared at the floor. The intricate pattern of the Oriental rug shifted and blurred in front of her eyes.

It wasn't fear of pregnancy that had brought her to her senses. It was the realization that she was letting Connor Holiday take her on her father's massive desk. It seemed somehow shameful that she had been willing to let him and shame is what gave her the strength to push him away.

She looked down at herself and saw that Connor had unfastened most of the buttons on her bodice. Her breasts rose and fell with each of her ragged breaths. Maggie closed the buttons with fingers that trembled.

Connor watched her. Her cheeks were flushed, her mouth swollen. She refused to look at him. He didn't think she remembered what had happened on the occasion of their first meeting but she couldn't have any doubts what he wanted from her. "It won't happen again," he muttered, his voice harsh with the frustration of denial. "It shouldn't have happened this time."

He slipped out of the car and went looking for the whiskey drummer.

Maggie leaned on the edge of the desk and cried.

Connor sat with Maggie on a bench outside the Denver depot, a few valises stacked on either side of them. From time to time he glanced at her but couldn't see any particular effect from his impulsive and ill-conceived attempt to make love to her. She had taken his advice about her manner and mood and had managed to look brighter and happier. There was nothing she could do about the weight loss, though when Connor considered it later he thought perhaps he had misjudged the situation. She had felt surprisingly full in his arms, her breasts actually larger than he remembered and her bottom more rounded. Her cheeks were still gaunt, however, and where her gown was open at the neck he glimpsed the pronounced line of her collarbone. The shadows beneath her eyes hadn't disappeared either, but her hair was shining, and her faint smile seemed less nervous.

"Michael's not usually late," Maggie said, glancing up and down the platform. No. 454 had left the depot an hour earlier. Their private cars had been uncoupled and were standing idly on side tracks in the rail yard.

"Maybe she didn't get my wire," Connor said.

Maggie leaned back against the bench and tried to relax. "Have you been to Denver often?" she asked.

"Not often."

"What do you like about it?"

"Not much."

She glanced sideways at him. "Are you provoking me deliberately?"

He realized how tersely he had answered her questions. He grinned. "Not intentionally."

Maggie laughed.

The grin had transformed his face, the laughter hers. When Mary Michael came upon them, her young daughter in tow, she wasn't surprised they hadn't noticed her. It eased her mind. There was little about Maggie's marriage that didn't trouble her. "Madison," she said to her daughter, "you and I are intruders on a private moment."

Maggie and Connor looked away from each other simultaneously. Maggie's expression was almost guilty as she turned her face in Michael's direction; Connor's was merely remote.

Recovering quickly, Maggie jumped up from the bench and threw her arms around her sister. They hugged fiercely, young Madison squeezed between their skirts. "Oh, Michael, it's *wonderful* to see you!" The sentiment could not have been more heartfelt. Tears gathered in Maggie's eyes and she didn't have to look at Michael to know it was much the same with her. It was only the tugging on their skirts that separated them.

"Someone wants to be noticed," Michael said, laughing. She made a swipe at her eyes to brush away tears and picked up her daughter. "Do you want to go to your Aunt Maggie?"

The flame-haired youngster displayed no shyness. She struggled to get out of her mother's arms and into her aunt's.

"Traitor," Michael whispered. She dropped Madison into Maggie's eagerly extended arms and turned to Connor. "Would you like to be noticed, too?" she asked. Her smile was playful and engaging. Her dark green eyes radiated warmth.

Some of Connor's natural guardedness faded. "I think I'd like that," he said.

Over the top of Madison's bright head, Maggie watched her husband's easy response to Michael. She felt a tug of sadness that she couldn't coax a smile from him so simply, then another tug that she had never tried. She turned away and gave all her attention to Madison.

Mary Michael was several inches taller than Maggie. She didn't have to raise herself quite as far to place a kiss on Connor's cheek. "Welcome," she said feelingly, then confided with characteristic honesty, "Frankly, I don't know what to think about this marriage, but I'll have time to sort it out over the next few days."

"I take it I'm only being accepted for inspection," Connor said dryly.

Michael's laughter was bright. "Something like that." She glanced at Maggie. "Now don't glower at him." Her attention darted back to Connor. "You're doing a credible job of hiding your surprise, but I know you've met Rennie and I can see that no one's thought to tell you about me."

Looking at her, Connor had no difficulty understanding what she meant. "You're right," he said. "No one thought to tell me you were Mrs. Sullivan's twin."

"Actually, she's mine," Michael said, dimpling, "but you can't get her to admit it."

Maggie watched Connor study Michael for a moment. She knew that he was making a comparison to Rennie, searching for differences in the twins. But she also knew where his comparison would finally rest and that he would find her, as was always the case when she drew scrutiny next to Rennie and Michael, a pale and unexciting replica of her older sisters. Their hair was dark copper and wildly curling, while hers was merely red. Their green eyes were several shades darker than her own, more deeply emerald while hers were green glass. The shape of their mouths was similar and they all shared a serious nature that flattened the full outline when they were deep in thought, but Rennie and Michael had dimples when they broke into smiles, while Maggie knew hers was unadorned.

Maggie felt her face flush as Connor finished studying Michael and turned his eyes briefly on her. Angry at herself for caring what he thought, she stared back at him defiantly. His glance narrowed in response and she found herself using Madison as a distraction and a shield.

Connor's attention rested on Michael again. "The resemblance is striking, but I didn't mistake you for your sister."

Michael was used to hearing how much she and Rennie were alike. "Rennie and I take pleasure in our similarities," she said, "but we're always complimented when people notice how different we are. We can't fool our husbands for a moment."

Maggie put her wriggling niece on the platform. "I can't believe you tried."

"Once," Michael said. "It was an ill-conceived plan from the beginning."

"Rennie's idea, then," Maggie said with complete confidence.

"Of course." She shrugged. "You'd think I'd learn, but I went along with it."

Madison wasn't particularly interested in the adult conversation floating above her head. She'd been there when her mother and Aunt Rennie had decided to switch places and she'd seen how her father and Uncle Jarret had pretended to be fooled. But she hadn't really liked it when Uncle Jarret kissed her mother in a way that only her father did. Aunt Rennie hadn't liked it much either. There had been some arguing after that and then some laughing and then some scolding. It had been very confusing and really not very much fun.

Connor was also only listening to Michael's account with half an ear. He hunkered down on the platform and patiently waited out young Madison's shy approach. The two-year-old smiled coyly in response to his encouraging grin. Her glance was shaded by long lashes that were much darker than her bright red hair. Her head was tilted to one side as she inspected him and made her judgments.

Connor crooked his index finger and she leaped into his arms, nearly bowling him over. Laughing, Connor stood and gave Madison a little toss above him. She giggled joyfully as her dress fluttered and her curls bounced.

Watching them, Michael shook her head in amusement and confided to Maggie. "She's an incurable flirt," she said. "I'd like to blame it on Skye but Madison's only seen her a few times. Though, come to think of it, it might have been long enough for her to teach—" She stopped as she noticed Maggie's stricken look. "What's wrong?"

Maggie barely heard her sister. Her complete attention was caught by Connor and Madison. *This is what it would be like with our child.* She watched him toss Madison into the air again, his enjoyment so genuine that Maggie was momentarily wrenched with grief. *He never let me think he might want our child.* And, on the heels of that thought, as he tumbled and tickled Madison, *I never really asked.*

Michael took her sister by the wrist and gave her a little shake. "Maggie? What is it?"

Michael's concern drew Connor's attention. He held Madison in the crook of his arm and took a few steps toward Michael and Maggie. His wife was pale, the shadows beneath her eyes suddenly more pronounced. She was looking at him as if she'd never seen him before and Connor was not flattered by the almost accusing, horrified cast of her eyes. For a moment he wondered if she had suddenly remembered everything about their first meeting. "Maggie?" His voice was gentle but his eyes were sharp and they held a warning.

Maggie managed to make the sob she was choking back sound like laughter caught in her throat. Under the hard probing of Connor's dark eyes, she came out of her reverie. She shook her head, clearing it, and smiled with self-mockery. "I'm sorry," she said, her mind working quickly as she tried to find an excuse for her odd behavior. "I thought you were going to drop her. I just froze." She saw immediately that Connor didn't believe her but accepted the excuse for what it was. Maggie was relieved when Michael latched onto it.

"Then you won't want to watch Ethan play with her," Michael said, kissing Madison's downy cheek. "I can tell you that my heart sticks in my throat when he pitches her skyward. And she just laughs and laughs." She hugged her daughter. "Don't you, Maddie? You laugh and laugh . . ."

Madison giggled obligingly.

"Where is your husband?" Connor asked, chucking Madison lightly on the chin. She batted at his hand while her eyes begged him to do it again. "Maggie thought he might be with you."

"Ethan's gone to Stillwater to testify in a murder trial. I'm hoping he'll get back before you have to leave for your ranch." She pointed to their bags. "That doesn't look like very much to me. You're planning on staying more than a couple of nights, aren't you?"

Maggie spoke up quickly. "We're anxious to get to the Double H,

Michael. Connor's been away for a long time and I'm excited to see my new home."

Connor saw that Michael's eyes had narrowed faintly and that she was studying her sister more closely now. He'd heard more desperation in Maggie's tone than enthusiasm and he thought Michael was perceptive enough to have heard the same. "We're grateful for the invitation," he said, slipping one arm around Maggie's waist, "but Maggie's right. I'm anxious to get to the Double H. I'll try to get her back here at least once before winter sets in."

"That's October," Michael warned Maggie, wagging a friendly finger at her. "Winter comes early to the Rockies."

"Winter comes early," Madison mimicked in a sing-song treble. She wagged her finger at Connor.

"Flirt," he said, grinning at the child.

Michael sighed. "It must be Skye's fault," she said again to Maggie. "I know *I've* never been accused of being one." She hefted Madison in her arms again and glanced backward at the bags. "It's not a long walk from here to home, but you don't want to carry those. We'll hire one of the porters to bring them."

"I have some trunks in the car that I want you to take," Maggie said. "I'm not dragging all my belongings to the Double H."

Michael was immediately sympathetic. "You don't have to explain," she said. "Mama and Skye did all your packing. I still have some of Rennie's things in my attic because she and Jarret move around so much with the railroad. I can put your trunks there until you decide you want them." She put Madison down and took the little girl's hand. She started to lead the way, then stopped, giving Connor a flirty sidelong glance that was remarkably like her daughter's. "Did Mary Francis threaten to break your kneecaps?" she asked.

"That's all been taken care of," Connor said gravely.

"Oh, good. Then you really *are* one of the family." She tugged on Madison's hand and began walking.

Behind her, Maggie and Connor exchanged glances. Neither one of them was smiling.

Denver fascinated Maggie. While Connor and Michael barely glanced around as they walked, Maggie looked in every direction, craning her head to see up and down the length of the side streets and into every shop and mercantile along the main thoroughfare. She had imagined the town would be rougher then New York but she only found it more rough-hewn. The buildings weren't as tall, the storefronts weren't as large, but there was a variety of services and entertainment available including a theatre and an opera house. She had known from Michael's letters that shootouts didn't occur in the heart of Main Street on a daily, or even a monthly, basis, but she realized that secretly she had been expecting something like that. No outlaws came running from the bank they passed; no drunks wandered out of the Lucky Seven saloon. Men tipped their hats as they strode along or nodded and smiled in brisk, friendly greeting. Many of them didn't wear guns and those who did didn't seem particularly anxious to use them. Women and children weren't haunted with fear as if they were expecting an Indian raid or a cattle stampede. It was a warm, sunny day and everyone seemed to be enjoying it.

Maggie was a little disappointed.

Michael's house was two blocks from her husband's office. When she let go of Madison's hand the little girl ran alongside the white picket fence bordering the yard until she came to the gate. There, she stood on the gate rail and swung back and forth, doing the very thing she was forbidden to do. She thought having guests would save her the embarrassment of a scolding. It didn't. Michael gave her a severe, knowing look and Madison climbed down, hanging her head with more sheepishness than she actually felt. The adults were hard-pressed not to laugh.

"Quite the actress," Connor remarked, pulling back his smile. He added innocently, "And whose influence could that be?"

"Not *my* side of the family," Michael said with playful haughtiness. She opened the gate and scooted Madison inside the yard. "She gets it from her father. He once pretended to be an outlaw." Michael saw Connor's genuine surprise and interest and looked at Maggie, her feathery brows drawn downward. "Didn't you tell him?" she asked.

"No, it didn't come up."

Michael laughed at her assumption. "Of course it didn't come up. I'm sure you had better things to do on your trip here than talk about how I met Ethan."

Maggie blushed, not quite able to meet her sister's eyes. Connor saved her by giving her a faint squeeze and saying with just the right inflection, "Much better things."

Michael laughed again. "Let's go inside, shall we?" She nudged Madison up the two wooden steps and across the wide porch front. To the left of the door the porch swing swayed gently as a breeze cornered the white frame house. Michael opened the door and ushered everyone inside.

There was nothing about the house that reminded Maggie of their palatial home on Broadway and 50th but they hadn't always lived there. Before Jay Mac had moved his mistress and children uptown they had lived in a pleasant, unassuming house near Union Square. Michael had managed to capture the charm of their childhood in her new home.

Madison had grabbed Connor's hand and was taking him on a solo tour. Maggie hung back with Michael. "It's lovely," she said, wandering into the parlor from the hallway. "It reminds me of—"

"I know," Michael said, finishing her sister's thought without having to say it aloud. "Rennie thinks the same thing. So did Mama when she came to visit. I didn't do anything intentionally, it just happened. Some of the furniture is like what we had growing up and I suppose it's the colors I've used in the rooms that give that effect."

"No," Maggie said. Her eyes drifted over the mantelpiece, cluttered with photographs in gilt and pewter frames. The furniture was comfortably plump with pillows scattered across the back of the sofa and chairs and more piled haphazardly on the floor. Copies of the *Rocky Mountain News* were lying in disarray on one end table and in a stack beside the pillows. "No," Maggie repeated, smiling warmly, "it's more than that. It's a *feeling*. It's not what's in the room. It's *how* it's in the room."

Michael's mouth screwed comically to one side and she gave her sister a frank, dry look. Her gesture encompassed the room. "You're referring to my housekeeping."

Maggie looked around again. "I suppose I am," she said, surprised. "How did Mama ever manage with five of us and no Mrs. Cavanaugh?"

"Mama asked herself the same thing, but she was very happy to see that I've carried on the tradition. She calls it 'homey chaos.' Jay Mac called it a mess. He wanted Ethan to hire a housekeeper for me."

Maggie's eyes widened.

"Oh, it didn't end there," Michael said, picking up newspapers from the end table and dropping them on the floor stack. "Not with Jay Mac. He practically ordered Ethan to order me to quit my position with the *Rocky Mountain News*. Then he ordered me himself. He also thought it would be more suitable if we built a new home for ourselves in another section of town farther away from Ethan's office and the courthouse. He decided it was too dangerous for a Federal Marshal to be so accessible. Mama couldn't get him to stop. I think there was a twenty-four-hour period when no one was speaking to him."

"Poor Papa."

Michael laughed. "That's just it, we all forgive him even if we don't give in." She saw the shadow that briefly clouded Maggie's expression. Michael impulsively grabbed her sister's hand and pulled her toward the kitchen at the back of the house. "Come on, I'll make you some tea and you can tell me everything. Madison has your husband securely in her thrall for the time being."

Maggie's face crumpled. She was more surprised than Michael when she began to sob.

Michael pushed out a chair at the kitchen table and sat Maggie down. She didn't rush to comfort. Instead she found a handkerchief for her sister, thrust it in her hand, and set about making tea. By the time she was finished Maggie had regained her composure. Michael put a cup of tea in front of her and joined her at the table. Above-stairs she could hear Connor and Madison playing in her daughter's room. "He's doing me a favor by wearing her out," she told Maggie. "I was afraid she'd be too excited to take a nap today."

Maggie's small smile was still a trifle watery. "He's good with her, isn't he?"

"Some people have a special knack with children," she said. "Ethan does. I'm catching up."

Maggie's brows lifted. *"You're catching up?"*

"Hmm-mm. Don't misunderstand me. I love Maddie. I always have. But Ethan's more relaxed with her. I suppose I'm afraid I'll do something wrong. Ethan's fearless or confident, I'm never really sure, but she responds like a flower to sunshine around him." She sighed. "Sometimes I wish I had Mama here to help me, or at least reassure me. I don't have her way. You're the one who got that."

"Me?"

Michael nodded. "You," she said firmly, but didn't explain. She urged Maggie to drink some of her tea. "So tell me how this marriage came to pass. When I saw Rennie last she was kicking herself for ever mentioning Connor Holiday and his land to Jay Mac. She had no idea that a few extraneous comments about the man would start Jay Mac's interfering wheels in motion. She's afraid you won't forgive her."

Maggie raised her teacup. Its warmth felt good around her cold hands and the security kept her hands from trembling. She carefully took a deep breath and met her sister's watchful eyes over the rim. "There's nothing to forgive," she said evenly. "Everything's worked out for the best. Connor and I are deeply in love."

Michael stared at her sister. She was silent for a moment. "I thought that when I first saw you at the depot. I've been wondering ever since."

Maggie sipped her tea. "It's true," she said quietly. "We began horribly. Neither of us wanted to have anything to do with Jay Mac's suggestions."

"Suggestions?" Michael scoffed. "You're kinder than I would be in your place."

"That's because I'm happy to be in my place—now."

"Then what were those tears about a few minutes ago?" Michael reminded her bluntly. "My God, Maggie, your eyes are still red from crying."

Maggie put down her cup and self-consciously made another swipe at her eyes with the handkerchief. "Better?" she asked.

"A little. Though you won't hide it from Connor. You'll have to think of something to tell him, but I'm coming to believe that you're getting used to covering your real feelings. Not getting much better at it, but at least getting practice."

"That's not fair, Michael," she said quietly, tucking the handkerchief away. "I'm telling you the truth."

Michael was not convinced. "Why were you crying then?"

"I don't know." And because it was very nearly the truth, it had the proper resonance of that quality. "It's all so new to me, I suppose. I'm a little afraid."

"Does he beat you?"

"No!"

"Because if he does—"

"No!" Maggie's teacup rattled in the saucer as she jerked away from the table. "Never! He wouldn't—"

"All right," Michael said calmly. She tapped the table lightly, encouraging Maggie to sit again. "That, at least, I believe." She paused. "What about your dreams, Maggie? Have you given up medicine to be Connor Holiday's wife?"

"You've got it backward," Maggie said. "I became Connor's wife because medicine gave up on me. I wasn't accepted by the medical school."

Michael's expressive eyes communicated her sympathy. "Oh, I'm sorry, Mag. I didn't know."

"It's all right. Everything's happened so quickly, there wasn't time to write it all to you."

"So tell me now," she prodded gently.

Upstairs Connor sat with Madison until she fell asleep. The youngster had surrendered reluctantly, yawning so hard at times that Connor had difficulty not following suit. Smiling, his expression not at all remote, he touched her small bright head, tousling the curls with the tips of his fingers. Would his child with Maggie have had those same flame curls?

He deliberately pushed the thought away and rose from the bed. He straightened a few of the things their play had disrupted then left the child's room quietly. He poked his head into the adjoining room and saw it belonged to Ethan and Michael. Their personal items were strewn across the top of the dresser and the open door to the wardrobe revealed their clothes. Connor moved along the hallway. The next door opened to a narrow, treacherously steep and winding staircase that led to the attic. Looking at it, he shook his head. He'd need Ethan's help or a pulley system to get Maggie's trunks up there. The final door along the hallway opened to the guest room and Connor walked inside.

His first thought was to wonder why he hadn't thought of it before. His second thought was the realization that Maggie probably hadn't considered it either.

Hell, he thought, they'd managed to avoid each other for nearly two thousand miles but the next two nights didn't look so promising.

"Maggie," he called from the top of the steps. "I need to see you for a minute." And because he remembered where he was, he added significantly, "Alone, please."

Chapter Nine

Maggie put off going to bed as long as she could. It was the middle of the night when she and Michael had finished trading every piece of information they could think of. Madison had climbed into bed shortly after dusk and Connor had retired at midnight. Maggie had promised she would join him soon but it hadn't been difficult to keep Michael engaged in conversation. Their discussion may have been prompted by Maggie's desire to avoid the bedroom, but it was perpetuated by her desire to share.

Michael yawned hugely, not even bothering to cover her mouth. "Is there anyone we haven't talked about?" she asked, collapsing dramatically against the pillows scattered around her. "What time is it?"

Maggie glanced at the clock on the mantel behind her sister. There was no chance she could avoid the inevitable any longer. "Twenty minutes after three." There was every reason to expect that Connor was sleeping soundly. She remembered he'd been resigned by the prospect; she had been frustrated. "I didn't mean to keep you up so long."

"I don't know which one of us is at fault," Michael said. She yawned abruptly, laughed at herself, and jumped to her feet with more energy than she'd shown two minutes earlier. She held out her hand to Maggie. "Up with you, Mag." Maggie came to her feet in a fluid, graceful motion. "I wish I could move like you," Michael said enviously.

Maggie's dark brows lifted. "You're the one who can dance, not me. I have two left feet."

"When you're self-conscious, you have two left feet," Michael told her. "When you're not, you're like a deer."

Maggie was too tired to think about that. She helped Michael turn back the lamps, then climbed the stairs ahead of her sister. They hugged briefly at the top. "Good night," Maggie said softly.

Michael ducked into her room. "Good night." She shut the door.

There was no more avoiding. Maggie went inside.

Except for moonlight filtering through the lacy curtains the bedroom was dark. After a moment Maggie's eyes adjusted enough to move without bumping into things. Connor was lying on the bed, turned on his side away from her. She knew that's where he would be because there really was no other choice. Between the washbasin, the highboy, the armoire, and the rocker, there was virtually no floor. A cat would have had trouble finding space to curl on the braided rug. There was no possibility that Connor or Maggie could.

Although he had been sleeping soundly, Connor was aware of Maggie the moment she entered the room. He lay very still, conscious of his breathing and his heartbeat as she prepared to join him in bed. She was trying hard not to disturb him, moving almost stealthily as she gathered her nightclothes and performed her evening ablutions. He couldn't watch her in the course of undressing or washing but his imagination filled in the movements that were hidden from his eyes. After a few minutes of that he began wishing he *could* see her, reasoning there was no possibility the reality could be as interesting as what he was imagining.

As Maggie washed herself at the basin she found herself glancing over her shoulder to make certain Connor still had his back to her. She breathed shallowly, quietly, conscious of making any noise that might inadvertently wake him. She tiptoed across the braided rug to her side of the bed. Each time the floor creaked she paused and waited, nearly faint with anxiety that he would turn over and grin at her and announce he'd been awake all the time. When that never happened, Maggie cautiously turned down the covers on her side.

Even under her slight weight the bed dipped as Maggie pressed one knee on the mattress. She slipped under the covers rather awkwardly and made no attempt to get comfortable. Instead she lay stiffly on the very edge of the mattress, the sheet and comforter drawn protectively to her chin. She realized, somewhat unhappily, that unless sheer exhaustion took its toll there wasn't the slightest chance that she was going to be able to close her eyes.

After several minutes Connor understood that Maggie wasn't going to fall asleep. In that same breadth of time Maggie became aware that Connor was awake.

Without a word passing between them they turned simultaneously to face each other and stared.

"I'm not going to attack you," Connor said quietly.

"I know."

"Do you?"

She didn't. Not really. She was surprised when her thoughts were given a voice. "I'm afraid of you," she said. Maggie wished she could take it back, more afraid now that she had given him something so powerful to use against her.

"Are you?" he asked. "Or are you afraid of what you want from me?"

"I don't want anything from you."

For several long moments he simply looked at her. A pale wash of moonshine caressed her features, the curve of her cheek, the pared line of her nose, the fullness of her mouth. "Be honest about that at least," he said finally. "Do you think I like it any better than you?"

Maggie bit her lower lip as Connor turned on his side away from her. He punched his pillow, slipped an arm under it, and yanked the comforter up to his shoulders. "I don't understand," she whispered when he had quieted. "What is it you don't like? That you think I want something from you? All I want from you is a divorce."

"Go to sleep, Maggie," he said tiredly. "I'm not going to touch you."

As Maggie had suspected, it was sheer exhaustion that finally made her close her eyes.

Under the covers her legs tangled with his. The hem of her nightgown had slid to her hips and the length of her bare leg lay flush to his, a sensual contrast of texture and warmth. One of her arms rested across his chest, the other had slipped under his pillow and helped to prop both their heads. His palm curved over her hip. His fingers pressed against the soft skin of her bottom. Her breath mingled with his. Her movement stirred the sweet fragrance of lavender in her hair. His heartbeat accelerated. Sensation seem to gather in his groin. Fullness followed, an aching heaviness that was neither pleasure nor pain but made him long for release.

She rubbed against him when he moved. Her back arched, then her throat. His lips were light on her neck, his tongue damp on the outline of her jaw. Her mouth opened when his came across it. Their lips pressed, tasted, explored with sucking hunger.

His kisses seemed to steal her breath. Her head twisted as she gasped for air. His hand closed over her breast and it swelled in the gentle hollow of his palm. Her mouth was greedy, her tongue pushing, surging against his, playing out a sweetly urgent battle. Her fingers moved to his hair and held him captive while her lips touched the corner of his mouth, his jaw, and teased the lobe of his ear.

She lay more fully against him and her movements became more insistent, more frantic, as if she were trying to get *under* his skin and feel what it was he was feeling, as if she needed to know everything, feel everything.

His mouth was hot on her neck, moist where he touched the hollow of her throat. His tongue trailed across her collarbone then dipped, spiraling around her breast to the dusky rose tip. His teeth gently worried the nipple, each tug shooting crackling sparks of sensation across the surface of her skin, then more deeply beneath her skin, where they moved in waves that pulled at the center of her as they receded.

There was an aching between her thighs, not heavy, but hollow, and then his hand was there, pressing and searching, intense without relief, and she moved against the heel of his palm, wanting it also. His fingers dipped inside her and she moaned softly, wanting this but wanting more. Her cotton nightgown was too heavy on her skin, too much of a barrier against the need to feel his hand on her naked flesh.

She pushed at her clothing, struggled. He was helping her, sliding the material past her hips and waist, pushing it past her breasts. Free, she coiled around him and was frustrated by the drawers that kept her from touching him. Her fingers pulled at the drawstring; her hands slipped beneath the material. He arched as she pushed the drawers over his hips, past his thighs, his knees. They were lost in the tangle of sheets.

His hand found hers, guided her to his thighs. She cupped him first, exploring, then his hand closed over hers again and moved it slowly along the length of his hardness. She stroked him in her fist, drawing a gasp from deep inside him. Her mouth moved over his chest and his flesh retracted in anticipation of her touch.

They moved in unison, arching, seeking. Their touch was blindly needy, consciousness barely tapped, conscience not at all. They felt pure pleasure, shared it, but didn't understand it.

And at the moment when they might have surrendered to it an insistent rapping separated them.

Connor groaned as the terrible pleasure of frustration became pain. Bleary-eyed, he tried to sit up and found himself covered by Maggie's lithe body. She raised her head, her eyes horrified as awareness speared her like a poison-tipped arrow, replacing excitement with waves of painful humiliation.

The rapping came again and they identified it at the same time.

Maggie was paralyzed, taut and unyielding across Connor's body where she had been supple and searching moments earlier. It was left to him to remove her, taking her by the hand again and guiding her away. The sound at the back of her throat was anguished as she realized where her hand had been and what she had been about. With his help she rolled away.

There was no time to bury her face in a pillow. The door to the bedroom was being opened cautiously. Connor yanked the comforter over Maggie and pulled the tangled sheet around his middle. His drawers slipped over the side of the bed along with Maggie's nightgown. He made a swipe at them, pushing them under the bed as the door opened wider, but there was no possibility of pretending they had been sleeping. Maggie was sitting up, clutching the comforter against her chest.

Michael poked her head through the crack in the door. She did not need anyone to tell her what she had interrupted. Connor's expression was rigid with the frustration of denial and Maggie's looked as if she wanted to crawl under the comforter instead of using it as a shield.

"I'm sorry," Michael said, genuinely embarrassed. She hoped this was something they would all laugh about some time in the future.

Looking at Connor and Maggie now, though, it appeared that that future would be a long time coming. "Maggie? Could you stay with Madison while I go for the doctor?"

Those words twisted Maggie out of her stupor. "Doctor? What's wrong?"

Michael stepped in the room. She cinched her robe about her waist and ran a hand through her tangled hair. There was a crease between her brows, a worried, harried look in her eyes that belied her next words. "I don't think it's anything serious," she said. "She's flushed and her skin's warm to the touch. I'm probably making too much of it."

Uncaring of his modesty, Connor stood and hitched the sheet more securely around his waist. "You stay with Madison," he said, beginning to gather his clothes. "I'll get dressed and go for the doctor."

"But you don't know—"

"You'll give me directions," he said calmly.

Michael hesitated.

"Go," he said. "Unless you want me to drop my—" He didn't have to finish. Michael was gone. Connor looked over his shoulder at Maggie. She was getting out of bed, struggling with the comforter and her modesty. "Your nightgown's under the bed on my side," he said. He turned back, dropped the sheet, and began dressing.

Maggie's frosty glance was wasted on Connor's back. She found her nightgown and slipped it over her head, then put on her robe. She brushed past Connor on her way to the door.

"Nothing happened," he told her softly as her hand closed over the knob. "And nothing's settled."

Maggie didn't pretend not to know what he was talking about. The hollow ache and moist heat was still between her thighs. Her breasts felt swollen and heavy. She could sense the outline of her lips without touching her tongue to them, and when she did, she could taste him there. "Something happened," she said, her eyes tormented. "But you're right, nothing's settled."

Maggie sat with her sister and Madison while Connor went for the doctor. She used a sponge dipped in a mixture of alcohol and water to cool Madison's skin and prepared some camomile tea to soothe Michael's nerves.

Michael's fingers lightly raked Madison's hair, smoothing it over her scalp as Maggie sponged her. "I'm sorry about the interruption," she said. "I didn't know what else—"

"Don't give it another thought." Maggie avoided her sister's eyes. She was afraid Michael might see there was no reason to be sorry, that she was grateful for what had happened.

"Connor looked as if he might like to strangle me."

Better you than me, Maggie thought. Keeping her head bent, she shrugged and said, "He got over it as soon as he realized what you wanted."

"I'm not completely sorry," Michael said. That brought Maggie's head up. "I was worried there might be some . . . some problem in the bedroom. It's good to know there isn't."

Maggie's cheeks flamed. "What made you think there was a problem?" she snapped. Her hands twisted hard as she wrung out the sponge but when she returned to bathing her niece, her touch was gentle. "And even if there was I can't see that it's any of your concern. You may be my sister, but you can't dictate the relationship I have with my husband!"

Michael's fingers had stilled. "Maggie!" she said softly. "I'm sorry if I offended you, but I know things can't be easy between you and Connor. The circumstances of your marriage must put a strain on both of you."

"I told you," Maggie said tightly, "that we've managed to put that behind us. We both have what we want out of our marriage. Can't you accept that?"

Michael fell silent. In spite of her tender touch and Maggie's delicate ministrations, some of their tension was transmitted to Madison. The child stirred restlessly between the two adults and brought an uncertain peace.

When Connor arrived with the doctor it was Maggie who went downstairs to let them in. "I think it's chicken pox," she told the physician. "She only has a few spots on her bottom, so faint that I would have missed them if I hadn't been looking."

Dr. Hamilton nodded, thanked Maggie, and went to Madison's bedroom. Maggie would have followed but Connor stopped her.

"This may be the only opportunity we have to talk in private," he said. "Let's go in the kitchen."

Maggie's fingers twisted in her hair, plaiting it as she followed him to the rear of the house. "The water's still warm from the tea I made Michael," she said. "Do you want something to drink?"

He shook his head. "And you don't either," he said, pointing to one of the chairs at the table. "Have a seat." He expected her to bristle at the command but she obliged him, if not meekly, then with no fussing. Connor pulled out one of the ladder back chairs and straddled it, his forearms resting on the top rail. His dark eyes were steady on Maggie's. He noticed that she didn't turn away from his scrutiny. "I'm not going to apologize for what happened in our bedroom," he said finally.

Maggie's voice was quiet and calm. "I didn't ask you to."

"When I said that nothing happened, I meant that we didn't—"

"Consummate the marriage," she said politely. "I know what you meant. Still, it was something to me. I've never . . ." She stopped, her voice trailing off because she knew it wasn't true. She *had* done things like that before and with this man. She couldn't keep hiding behind her memory loss. "I didn't mean for this to happen again."

"Neither did I." He took in a breath and let it out slowly. "I don't want to stay here one more night that we have to."

Maggie nodded, her smile faint. "Sometimes we *do* agree." She sighed. "If you'll speak to a lawyer tomorrow, I'll go to the depot and arrange for our cars to be attached to the next train out of Denver headed for Queen's Point."

"I'll do it all," he said. "Where's our marriage certificate? I might need it to help us secure a divorce."

"There's a strongbox beneath Jay Mac's desk. The key's in the middle drawer."

"Maggie, you understand that even though we both want it, this divorce isn't going to happen overnight?"

Her eyes dropped to her hands folded neatly on the tabletop. "I know." There was a certain amount of pain in her tone. "Just please get it started." She got up. "I'm going to check on Madison. I want to hear what the doctor has to say, then I'm going to bed."

"I'll be up in a little while."

It was the first of three nights that Connor Holiday spent sleeping in a rocker because he couldn't keep his hands off his wife.

*   *   *

They delayed their departure until Ethan returned from Stillwater. As much as Maggie wanted to leave, she couldn't go while Madison was ill. Connor's understanding and willingness confounded her and complicated matters in her heart. Maggie watched him develop an easy friendship with Michael, a loving one with Madison, and a comfortable one with Ethan. She didn't know what to make of the man who would not always be her husband. He was stiff and unyielding with his own father, cold to Beryl, and angry with her, but Maggie saw that he was rarely any of those things with other people. She thought that even a lifetime of living with him wouldn't provide the explanations she sought.

There were moments when that thought relieved her, others when it tore at her heart.

Maggie stood on the small platform balcony leaning against the iron rail. They were miles outside of Denver and she still couldn't quite bring herself to go inside. She and Connor had had to say goodbye to Ethan and Madison at the house, but Michael escorted them back to the depot.

The farewell had been wrenching for both sisters. Maggie had come so close to begging Michael to allow her to stay that she could taste blood on her lip where she had bitten back the words. And Michael, without knowing the cause of Maggie's torment, felt the pain almost as keenly as if it were her own.

Connor stepped out on the balcony and stood directly behind Maggie. The air was cool as their train climbed the tree-lined side of a mountain. On their left, blue spruce pines erupted from the earth at impossible angles and on their right the mountain fell away so steeply that stepping off the train in that direction would have been like stepping into the sky.

"Are you sorry you didn't ask her if you could stay?" he asked quietly. He was close enough to be aware of the fragrance of her hair.

She didn't turn around and when she felt his hands settle lightly on her shoulders, she didn't resist. "You knew?"

"It was pretty obvious for everyone to see."

Maggie closed her eyes. She hadn't wanted *anyone* to see. Tears pressed against the back of her lids.

"Maggie?" His fingertips nudged her gently, urging her to turn without demanding that she do so.

As the train continued to climb, drawing them inexorably closer to the moment they would part, Maggie turned and leaned against Connor, not afraid of his strength, but wanting it. Tears fell from the corners of her eyes as he held her in a loose embrace and let her sob against his chest.

Moira Worth turned the corner in the upstairs hallway and nearly collided with the housekeeper. Mrs. Cavanaugh had a polishing cloth tucked in the pocket of her apron, a broom and dustpan in one hand, and a black leather satchel in the other.

"Was that Maggie's room you just came from?" Moira asked.

"Sure and it was," Mrs. Cavanaugh explained. "I've been meanin' to get around to takin' care of it since our little girl left. I only had time to give it a spit and promise before today." A smile split her round face. "And look what I found when I did the thing right." She dropped the dustpan and leaned the broom against the wall. "Don't you know, it was under her bed." She held up the leather bag. "Sure, and so far under that I had to use my broom handle to push it out."

"You're nothing if not thorough, Mrs. Cavanaugh," Moira said. She glanced at the satchel. "I don't remember seeing Maggie with that before. It looks a little like a physician's bag."

"That's what I was thinkin'. Do you suppose the poor darlin' bought it before she heard from the medical school?"

"Entirely possible," said Moira. "Did you open it?"

Mrs. Cavanaugh pursed her lips. "That's not for me to do," she said stiffly. "I was bringin' it to you."

Moira accepted the bag. She fingered the clasp but it didn't release. "It's stuck."

"I know." The housekeeper realized her error too late, but she had the grace to look sheepish. "I was certain Maggie wouldn't mind if I tried to take a peek."

Moira laughed. "You're incorrigible." She gave the bag back to Mrs. Cavanaugh. "It doesn't really matter what's inside. It's Maggie's. Why don't you pack it up and send it to her? She'd like that. She may even have cause to use it where's she going."

"Where should I send it? To the Double H?"

Moira shook her head. "Send it to Michael in Denver. She'll know the best way to get it to Maggie."

Mrs. Cavanaugh hefted the bag and picked up her broom and dustpan. "It's as good as done," she said, as she hurried down the hallway.

The livery in Queen's Point had boarded Connor's horse during his trip east. Maggie stood in the entrance to the stable and watched the reunion with a great deal of amusement. It was difficult to know who was happier, Connor Holiday or his horse. She made certain she let him know it, too.

"Tempest's been with me three years now," Connor told her, not apologizing in the least. "He's the best range horse I've ever had and . . ." His voice dropped to a whisper so that only she could hear. "And my mares like him, too." He laughed when Maggie blushed predictably. "Now go wait outside while I wrangle with the owner over the fee." He gave Maggie a push toward the door.

Fearful that it wouldn't hold up under scrutiny, Maggie didn't examine the camaraderie that had developed between them. She accepted it at face value, assuming that it was impossible for tension to sustain itself indefinitely. The breaking point had been when he simply held her and let her cry until she was exhausted. He never questioned. He let it be.

That freed Maggie as nothing else could have. She didn't know if Connor had changed his opinion of her; it didn't matter. What mattered was that she was no longer afraid of him.

Connor purchased a wagon at the livery and two mares to pull it. Their belongings, reduced considerably since Maggie had been to Michael's, were loaded in no time. Connor purchased supplies for their journey and additional staples for Maggie to take to Dancer Tubbs as well as supplies for the Double H. He tethered Tempest to the rear of wagon since Maggie couldn't manage the reins of the team and he was afraid Tempest would throw her.

"Take a good look at that mining town," he told her as they were preparing to leave. "There's nothing like it between here and Dancer's. We'll be on our own."

Maggie kept her eyes on Connor, not on the town. "I'm ready to go," she said. "Everything I want is ahead of me."

Connor Holiday couldn't help wondering if she meant him as well. "All right," he said. "But there's no shame in changing your mind."

Maggie had no intention of changing her mind. Connor snapped the reins and the team began a slow walk on the dirt track road leading from Queen's Point.

Dancer Tubb's claim was a three day's journey from the mining town. Connor had warned Maggie that the trip would be difficult. Once they were underway he never mentioned it again. It would have been disrespectful to try to protect Maggie from the consequences of her decision and Connor didn't try. With the exception of not expecting her to drive the wagon, Connor demanded that she share every chore.

Maggie could not have anticipated what the travel would really be like. If Connor had taken the time to describe each aspect of the trip, she wouldn't have believed him. It only took an hour on the hard seat of a buckboard wagon to convince Maggie that she was ill-prepared. Her back ached from the wagon's steady jouncing and her bottom, in spite of the skirt, underclothes, and cotton duster she wore, felt bruised. Her wide-brimmed bonnet shielded most of her face from the sun but she still felt the tip of her nose reddening. Her corset bound her uncomfortably but it also supported her breasts. Without it she imagined she would have popped a button on her blouse each time they hit a bump.

When they stopped to rest the horses Maggie helped draw water and feed them. She climbed over rocks and waded through streams to reach water that was inaccessible to the horses while they were hitched to the wagon. She knelt on the bank and drank from an icy spring with her cupped hands, washing a half-day's dust from her face and neck.

Through his hooded and remote glance, Connor watched her. He made no move to help her or indicate in any way that he might want to. He only had to take inventory of his own stiff bones and cramped muscles to understand how Maggie was aching, yet she never mentioned it then or at any other time during their journey.

When Connor announced they were stopping for the day he

noticed she was not particularly relieved, merely agreeable. After a rather awkward climb down from the wagon Maggie began gathering kindling for a fire, and at Connor's direction, pine branches for a softer place to sit and sleep. She hauled water to make coffee while Connor cooked their meal of smoked ham and beans. He showed her how to make pan cornbread over an open fire and Maggie watched over his shoulder, standing while he hunkered in front of the flames.

"You can sit down, Maggie," he told her. "There's not another thing for you to do right now."

"If I sit down now I won't be able to do another thing later."

His attention was back on his cooking, but he was smiling. "You're going to eat standing up?"

"If that's what it takes," she said philosophically. As it turned out, she compromised, leaning against the trunk of a sheltering pine to take her meal. Even that small amount of inactivity made her so stiff that cleaning their dishes and pans was a painful chore. When Connor roughly ordered her to lie down on the bedroll he had laid out, Maggie obeyed without taking exception to his tone. She slept almost instantly.

The following morning the steamy aroma of coffee a few inches from his nose teased Connor to wakefulness. Maggie was kneeling beside him, fresh-faced and smiling, holding out a mug. It occurred to him that he could enjoy being awakened in just such a manner for the rest of his life—even without the coffee.

He sat up slowly, rubbing his eyes and the bridge of his nose with his thumb and forefinger. He took the coffee in one hand and ran the other through his tousled hair. "Is it your intention to spoil me?"

"No," she said, genuinely surprised by the question and his gruff, almost angry manner. "It's my intention to be kind to you. Like you were to me yesterday." Maggie sat back on her heels and smoothed her skirt over her bent knees. "Thank you for finishing up the chores and letting me sleep. I meant to be more help."

He sipped his coffee and shrugged carelessly. "You did enough."

"I'll do better today."

His only response was a soft and skeptical grunt.

Because of Maggie's early rising and preparation they were underway within a few hours of sunup. At each stop Maggie helped Connor, often without direction. She prepared lunch and he cleaned up and at dinner they shared both tasks. Her movements were a little slower than his as she worked out the stiffness. She stretched and arched her back as she climbed in and out of the wagon and occasionally she rubbed her neck, but Connor was forced to admit to himself, if not to Maggie, that she had managed the second day's travel and chores with more grace and energy that he could have possibly expected.

The small fire they laid that night was less for warmth than to keep curious creatures away. In the brush beyond the circle of light Maggie could hear the scurry and flutter of small animals searching out food. She turned on her side, her back to the fire, and gazed at Connor's profile. He was lying on his back a few feet from her, his head cradled in the palms of his hands, staring at the great expanse of black-velvet sky. She followed the line of his vision and was struck by the vastness she had never seen before, with brilliant star patterns that she had only seen in books.

"We don't have these stars in New York," she said in awe.

Understanding exactly what she meant, Connor smiled faintly. "I know," he said. "I missed them. All the glitter's on the ground in the city. Any city."

Maggie said nothing. She let herself feel the space and the silence and began to comprehend in a more profound way how Connor was linked to the majesty of these surroundings. Streams ran clear and cold in this country. Water talked back as it rushed over smooth rock. Aspens whispered in the wind. Leaves shimmered, lustrous green on one side, silver gray on the other, alive to the slightest breeze. Blue spruce covered the mountainsides, painting the Rockies with rich and radiant color.

Connor turned on his side and slipped one arm under his head. With the fire at Maggie's back her figure was a slender silhouette. Only her hair captured the fire's light, giving her a burnished halo of copper and gold. She was too still to be sleeping, too quiet to be doing anything but thinking. Not for the first time he realized what a private person she was in some ways, and how at odds she must have been with her nosy and noisy family.

"A penny for them," he said.

Maggie smiled and extended her hand toward him, palm up.

Connor stared at her hand a moment. When it dawned on him what she wanted, he dug into his pocket, found a penny, and dropped it into her palm. Her fingers closed over it immediately and she withdrew her hand. "I suppose you learned that it pays to be quiet in your family," he said.

"That's right," she said serenely. "Jay Mac says that collecting a penny for my thoughts is the only business sense I inherited from him." She held up the penny so she could see it better in the firelight. "This makes eight dollars and twenty-seven cents."

Connor whistled softly. "That's a lot of thoughts."

She nodded. "And this penny's special," she said, "because you're the first person outside of my family who's thought my thoughts might be worth something."

"I haven't heard one yet," he pointed out. "I'm beginning to think I was robbed. I don't suppose you give refunds."

Maggie slipped the penny in her skirt pocket. "No refunds, not ever."

He didn't have to see her cheeky grin to know it was there. "I'm still waiting," he said.

She was quiet a moment. "Very well," she said softly. "I was thinking what a hard thing it must have been for you to leave this place, even in order to secure it."

"Why do you say that?"

"It seems to me that you belong here and you shouldn't have to live anywhere else. It's too cruel."

"That's a rather fanciful, romantic notion, don't you think?"

"Perhaps it is," she admitted. "But it's not exclusively mine. You've thought the same thing about me, haven't you?"

Connor was struck again by her perceptiveness and the knowledge that his thoughts were not always so safe from her. "I suppose I might have," he hedged. It was as much of an admission as he was prepared to make. "Our situations aren't all that similar. I've been east a number of times, for years at a time, and I managed to live to tell the tale. You can't make the same claim. You told me once that you've never been farther west than Pittsburgh."

Maggie was intrigued by what she didn't know. "For years at a time?" she asked. "I thought you'd only ever really lived at the Double H."

"When I was fourteen my mother sent me to live with my father," he said, unaware of the faint edge of bitterness in his tone. "The war was over and it was safe to travel again. Edie got it in her head that

I should get to know my father better. I was supposed to stay a year but after three months I managed to get myself packed off to boarding school. I finished the year there, then went back to the ranch." He hadn't thought about that experience for a long time. Recounting it made him realize how much responsibility he bore for having to go to boarding school. He'd been an angry young man, trying to antagonize his father and prove that Rushton wasn't needed or wanted. "I might have stayed at the school longer but my grandfather died and I was allowed to go back."

Maggie heard it in Connor's voice—the thing that said he would have gone back whether or not he had been allowed. Rushton would have been a fool to try to keep him and though her acquaintance with Connor's father was brief, she didn't think that "fool" was a word that could be applied to him. "You were close to your grandfather?"

"Old Sam was my best friend."

Maggie knew there would be no elaboration. There was a certain finality in Connor's tone again, a warning that this subject was closed, as if he had expressed all that he could about his relationship with his grandfather in that single, simple sentence. She quelled her curiosity about Old Sam. "You said you were east on other occasions," she prompted.

"Four years later my mother and father arranged for me to attend Princeton. Edie wanted me to be able to choose between her world and my father's. She said a good education required both east and west and I'd had more than my share of one and not nearly enough of the other."

"You did four years at Princeton?" she asked.

"Your shock is hardly flattering."

"That's not an answer."

"All right," he conceded. "I did two. I raised so much hell they asked me to leave."

"*Asked* you?"

"Showed me the door."

"As in *escorted?*"

"As in *kicked out.*"

Maggie laughed. "Now *that* I believe. What did you do then?"

"I went to New York and finished my eastern education—not quite in the manner my mother had intended and—"

"And not in a way that your father approved," she finished.

He paused. "Something like that. I started working for William Barnaby."

Because Maggie grew up with Northeast Rail she knew William Barnaby's business. He was a steel manufacturer, and, along with Andrew Carnegie, Rushton Holiday's fiercest competitor. There was no censure in her voice when she responded. "So you learned your father's business from another man."

"That's what I did."

Maggie rolled on her back and stared at the sky. "It's ironic," she said softly. "It seems as though Jay Mac's had an impact on every moment of my life, just as Rushton's had on yours. Who would have thought an absent father could exert the same influence as one who was nearly always around?"

"I don't know what you're talking about."

She didn't let him get away with that. "Yes, you do."

Connor pushed himself to a sitting position. "Then you damn well don't know what you're talking about. Until I agreed to marry you I've never done anything Rushton wanted."

Maggie's smile was a trifle sad, her eyes knowing. "And you don't think that's influence?" she asked quietly.

Connor stared at her. Pale yellow flames from the fire caressed one side of her face. "What I think is that the next time I'll keep my penny."

She nodded.

Unaccountably angry, Connor got to his feet and stalked away. When he returned Maggie was sleeping.

He was still angry the next morning. He didn't say more than ten words to Maggie as they prepared to depart. It made him even angrier that she didn't seem to notice, or if she noticed, didn't seem to mind. They rode in silence for most of the morning. It wasn't until they stopped for the horses to rest and attend to their own needs that Maggie broached the silence. And when she did it was to speak of the divorce.

"Why do you want to know now?" he asked tersely, patting down his horse. "I met with the lawyer almost a week ago."

"But you never told me what he said."

"He said it would take some time."

"How much time?"

Connor shrugged.

Maggie's brows rose. "Didn't you ask?"

"It'll take as much time as it takes," he said roughly. "Does it matter? You'll be at Dancer's. I'll be at the Double H." But he could see that Maggie wasn't satisfied. She was adjusting the bit on one of the horses, but her eyes were anxious and the corners of her mouth were pulled down. He sighed. "Look, Maggie, documents have to be drawn up that will need our signatures."

"Documents? But how will we get them?"

Connor frowned. Maggie's agitation was quite real. She was twisting her wedding band as if she wanted to yank it off. "They'll be sent to Queen's Point. Someone from the ranch will pick them up when we get supplies."

"When will that be?"

"Since I'm taking supplies with me now we probably won't need another trip until the end of summer."

"The end of summer?"

"That's right." He climbed onto the wagon. "And once they're signed they have to go back to Denver to be presented to the judge. That will take a few months. Then there's a waiting period of another six months."

Maggie pulled herself up and sat down hard beside Connor. "But that means we're still going to be married this time next year."

"Probably."

"But—"

Connor's head swiveled sharply. "Unless you're planning on marrying Dancer Tubbs I don't see the problem."

"I'm not planning on marrying anyone," she snapped. "That's just it. I don't want to be married!"

"That makes two of us!" His air of finality brought down a curtain of silence. After a long, uncomfortable minute Connor jerked the reins and the team started forward. "I'm sorry," he said quietly.

Maggie shook her head. "No," she said. "I'm sorry."

"You're scared."

She bit her lower lip. "Petrified." She was only hours away from meeting Dancer Tubbs and though she didn't believe he'd turn her back, she didn't know for certain. The thought that she might have to go with Connor to the Double H, along with the realization that she might have to endure months of his hard-tempered silences, increased her anxiety tenfold. She laughed uncertainly. "You'll be glad to get rid of me."

"You're trying very hard to make sure I'm glad."

She looked at him and said rather primly, "I don't know what you're talking about."

He grinned. "Yes, you do."

She smiled reluctantly, supposing it was true. It had started to get a little comfortable between them as they shared the same routines and the same space, but for Maggie the comfort itself was unsettling. "Why where you at the brothel that night?" she asked. She caught his surprised glance. "It's another thing I've never asked you. I mean, you know why I was there. It only seems fair that I know what took you to Mrs. Hall's."

Connor's laughter made him snap the reins and the team stepped up their pace. "What explanation do you want beside the obvious? I wanted a woman."

Her cheeks pinkened. "Had you been there before?" she asked. "Is that why you chose Mrs. Hall's?"

"I'd been there before," he told her.

"Was there someone special?"

"No." He paused, then said impatiently, "If you really must know, I went there because that morning Beryl had crawled into my bed while I was still half-asleep. I pushed her out, but that night, after I'd won my stake, I still had whores on my mind. I decided to do something about it."

"Oh," she said softly.

He shrugged. "You asked."

"I know."

Connor looked straight ahead, his eyes on the winding road. "You were quiet," he said. "It's one of the things I liked about you. I told Mrs. Hall that I didn't want a chatterbox and she sent me to you. Of course, that was a mistake, but at the time it didn't seem like one. You were just what I wanted."

"I could have been anybody." She paused. "Any *body*."

Connor didn't answer. She was right. He hadn't cared at the time, hadn't wanted to care. It was one of the conditions. "I may have hurt you," he said quietly.

She frowned. "What do you mean? Because I was a virgin?"

He didn't know why he'd even brought it up. She didn't remember and perhaps there was no good reason why she should. "That's part of it," he said. He wished he hadn't said anything, hadn't raised the doubt in his own mind again. But he remembered how she had moved under him, pushing at his shoulders, shifting her legs, and as much as he wanted to believe that what she had done was done in passion, there were times when he wasn't so sure. "You may not have been as willing the first time as I wanted to believe."

Maggie's dark green eyes clouded and a vertical crease appeared between her brows. Her heart seemed to stop for a moment then slam against her chest so hard that she could barely catch her breath. "What are you trying to tell me?" she asked. "That you forced me?"

Connor continued to stare ahead. He felt Maggie's fingers on his wrist, just below his cuff, willing him to look at her. "I don't know what it was between us. The laudanum . . . the liquor . . . you didn't know what you were doing."

"The first time?" she asked.

"The first time," he said. "The second time . . . I don't know."

"Why are you telling me this?"

Connor lifted his chin in a gesture that indicated something in front of them. "See that ridge ahead?" he asked. "Once we're on the other side we'll be on Dancer's land. That divorce you want so badly is about to happen. It may not be legal, but it'll be real. We won't be seeing each other again and I wanted you to know in case you remember something. It wasn't fair to leave you thinking that somehow you were to blame for what happened."

Maggie didn't say anything to that. She raised her face and kept her eyes on the ridge.

Dancer Tubbs watched the couple on the wagon draw closer. Through his spy glass he recognized the man as Old Sam Hart's grandson and the owner of the neighboring Double H. "Hah," he muttered under his breath. His damaged vocal cords gave his voice a guttural, raspy quality. "Damn fool ain't got a right to trespass, Old Sam's kin or no." He turned his spy glass on the woman. She was a pretty thing, he thought, and familiar to him in a vague sort of way. Dancer spit on the end of his glass and buffed the lens with the sleeve of his gray jacket. He looked through it again, judging the woman with a critical eye this time, troubled by an odd sense of recognition.

Almost immediately she obliged him by removing her bonnet, giving her head a shake, and fanning herself with the wide straw brim. It was when sunlight glinted in her copper-colored hair that he finally placed her. She was one of Jay Mac's daughters, she had to be. It was the only explanation for the invasion of his land.

He glanced over his shoulder where his horse stood poking at the grass. "It's not Rennie," he said, "because that's not Jarret with her and Rennie ain't quite that dainty. And it ain't Michael 'cause I hear she's Rennie's look-alike. Can't be the nun 'lessen she's left the church. Now what's the name of the other two?" The horse continued to snuffle. "You ain't no help." Dancer collapsed the spy glass, slid down from his perch, and mounted. He jerked the reins and urged his horse over the line of the ridge so there was no chance of being sighted by anyone.

Dancer let them pass and then he followed, announcing his presence only when they were within sight of his cabin.

"You folks lost your way?" he asked. His pleasant voice was at odds with the shotgun he had pointed at them. He kicked his mount forward until he was beside the wagon.

Connor held the team steady and didn't try going for his gun. He looked at Maggie's hands. They were folded neatly in her lap, not a sign of trembling.

"We're not lost, Mr. Tubbs," she said to Dancer. "I'm Mary Margaret Dennehy." She felt Connor shift slightly beside her, a reaction to her use of her maiden name.

Holding the gun carefully in one hand, Dancer slapped his thigh with the other. "Damn me if I didn't know that," he cackled. "Knew you was one of Jay Mac's young'uns. Couldn't put a name to you."

"My family calls me Maggie."

He repeated her name. The scarred side of his face distorted his smile. His eyes shifted. "And you're Old Sam's grandson. Edie's kid."

Connor had no idea that Dancer might know him. "Connor," he said. "Connor Holiday."

"Ain't that somethin'," he said. "Knew Edie had a kid, never knew she was married. All these years I thought you was a Hart."

"Holiday," Connor repeated. "The same last name as Maggie, though she's apparently already forgotten."

Dancer saw Maggie frown. He lowered his Winchester. "Suppose we step inside the cabin and discuss it. Ain't gonna shoot either one of you . . . yet."

He relished their startled looks and laughed all the way to the cabin, his high-pitched cackle sounding as if it were breaking at the back of his throat.

Chapter Ten

The prospector's cabin was built with the timber that had been cleared to make room for it. It was situated on a small knoll, protected by towering pines and aspens on three sides and a wide, shallow stream on the fourth. They went inside as soon as the horses were tethered and cared for.

Dancer pointed to the two high-backed ladder chairs. "Sit," he said. "I'll manage just fine here by the door." He kept his shotgun lowered but he didn't put it away.

Maggie's eyes darted around the cabin. As far as she could see, it was mostly as Jay Mac had described upon his return to New York years earlier. A wood stove seemed to be the only addition the prospector had made. Judging by the size of the spider web connecting the andirons to the damper, the stone hearth looked as if it hadn't been used recently. There was still no pump, which meant hauling water from the stream. The furniture was pine and had been crafted with considerable care. Running her fingers over the table surface, Maggie found it smooth and cornered cleanly with hard right angles. Pots and kettles hung on the wall near the stove and there were empty pegs near the fireplace. A colorful rag quilt covered the narrow bed on the main floor of the cabin, but there was also a ladder leading to the loft where Maggie knew Dancer slept.

What interested Maggie most, however, were the tiered shelves filled with herb pots at the cabin's rear window and the dozens of small glass bottles that were stored haphazardly in the open pantry along with staples like flour, sugar and salt, jams and bacon grease. She squinted, reading the carefully printed labels. Slippery elm. Goldenseal. Peppermint. White willow bark. Ginger.

"What brings you here?" Dancer asked abruptly. "Can't be a sudden desire to see this old face."

Maggie and Connor contained their reactions when confronted by the prospector's ravaged face. Dancer was having none of it. He wanted them to look and look hard.

Dancer's scars were set in white relief against his skin, like a hundred twisted webs stacked thinly on one another. His half-ear was curled and flattened against his head. The left side of his mouth was pulled taut in a perpetually savage grin. His beard drew down from the right, but only covered three quarters of his face. It was thick and ill-kempt, black as boot polish and long enough to reach the second button of his blue-gray woolen overcoat. A gold braid epaulet dangled from his right shoulder. A saber swung from his waist.

His clear, frost-blue eyes would have been uncommon in any face, but in one so disfigured they were especially remarkable. Like twin points of searing light, they burned Maggie and Connor with their heat. "Well?" he demanded hoarsely. "You gonna puke?"

"Not if you don't talk about it," Maggie said primly. Beside her, Connor smiled.

Dancer leaned against the door. "All right," he said. "So you know about me and you was prepared. But that don't tell me what you're doin' here in the first place."

Under the table, where they were out of sight, Maggie's hands twisted nervously in her lap. "I've asked Connor to bring me here because I want to learn about healing," she said. "I know how you cared for my father when he was near to dying and Rennie's told me what you did for Jarret. She thinks you know as much as any three doctors."

"Hogwash," he said tersely. "I ain't no doc and I ain't likely to know what any of 'em knows." His eyes narrowed suspiciously. "Your father know you're here, girl?"

"Yes," she said.

"No," Connor said.

Dancer looked from one to the other. "Which is it?"

"Jay Mac doesn't know," Maggie said. "But then it's none of his business. Connor knows and since he's my husband that should be what matters."

Dancer gave a short bark of laughter and said to Connor, "Ain't it convenient how she remembers she's married when it suits her purpose?"

"I was thinking the same thing," Connor said dryly.

"You agree with her comin' here?"

Connor looked around the cabin and tried to imagine Maggie living in it. Her bedroom in New York was larger than Dancer's entire home. There were few amenities and the daily work of living would be more than she was used to. His eyes fell on the potted herbs and the jars of dried teas. "No," he said finally. "I don't agree. But this is what she wants and she was willing to do what it took to be here. Maggie's more resilient than she looks so don't be fooled by her appearance." *The way I was,* he almost added. "I want her to come to the Double H with me but she's not interested, perhaps not even if you turn her away."

"That true?" Dancer asked Maggie. "You're not goin' with him even if I turn you out?"

"That's true."

Dancer scratched the whiskered side of his face thoughtfully. His eyes drifted over Maggie. He looked hard at her wedding band. "It's a fact there's things I don't understand here." He laughed suddenly. "On the other hand, there's other things I understand better than one of you, maybe both of you." His hand dropped away from his face. He worked his puckered mouth back and forth as he considered Maggie's request. "Ain't got no special place for you, girl."

Maggie pointed to the bed. "I'll be fine there. It was good enough for my father."

Dancer was thoughtful again, then he spoke abruptly. "Don't like it. How'd I know you ain't lookin' to rob me?"

"Rob you?" Maggie asked. "Why would I want to do that?"

"Folks do," he said. "It's been tried more times than I got fingers 'n' toes. Rumor in the Rockies has it that I got gold and silver aplenty in my mines." He gestured to Connor. "Tell her," he demanded. "Tell her that's the way of it."

Connor turned to Maggie. "There's a widely held belief in these parts that Dancer's mined his claim and buried most of the treasure."

Dancer slapped his thigh and cackled. "What would be the sense in it?" he asked. "Bringin' gold up from the earth only to bury it again? But folks get it in their heads and I can't get it out. Damn me if I can be responsible for what folks is thinkin'."

"Do you understand what he's telling you, Maggie?" Connor asked. "There's a certain amount of danger here apart from the hardships of living. Tell her how many men you've chased off your land, Dancer."

"Can't say as how I've chased more than two off that were tryin' to rob me," he said. "But there's a score of 'em buried in the hills, though."

Maggie couldn't quite suppress her shiver. "I still want to stay," she said, resolute. "I can learn to protect myself."

"Now I ain't puttin' a gun in your hands," Dancer said. "Most likely I'd get my own head blowed clean off." He ignored Maggie's challenging look. "How long you expectin' to stay?"

"A year," she said. "Perhaps a little longer."

"I can teach you what I know in a month."

Maggie doubted that but she didn't argue the point. Her dark green eyes beseeched him.

"All right," he said. "You can stay. But when I say git, I mean git. That clear enough?"

She nodded.

Connor looked at Dancer. "You're letting her stay here?"

"Now that's just what I said, didn't I? You ain't gonna try to talk me out of it, are you? That makes no kinda sense either. What did you bring her here for if'n you weren't gonna let her stay?"

"I didn't say I wasn't going to leave her here," he said. "But I could hope that she'd come to her senses, couldn't I? Or that you'd see this for the folly it is."

Dancer's eyes narrowed on Connor's hard face. "You ain't one to be talkin' about senses," he said. "Leastways not until you got some of your own."

Connor's glance became more distant. "You're probably right," he said tersely. His chair scraped the rough floor as he stood. "I'll unload the supplies we purchased in town for you, then I'll be going. Maggie? Do you want to help me?"

Maggie felt his stiff, cold anger but she followed him outside. She noticed that Dancer didn't follow. "Did you really think I'd change my mind?" she asked.

"No." He began shifting sacks of dry goods from the wagon to the cabin's small front porch. "But I didn't think it'd matter." *To me,* he nearly said.

She put a different construction on Connor's words. "I told you Dancer would take me in."

"I remember," he said, letting her think what she would. "I didn't think you knew what you were talking about."

Maggie yanked at her valises and tossed them onto the porch. "That's plain enough."

"What I don't understand is why he's letting you stay." He pitched a sack of cornmeal hard enough that it split along one seam. Cursing under his breath, Connor reined in his frustration. "And it's not because you're Jay Mac's daughter or Rennie's sister. It's something else."

Maggie climbed into the back of the wagon and began pushing crates and sacks toward Connor for unloading. "I'm not one for looking a gift horse in the mouth," she said. "Is it so important for you to figure it out?"

"Strangely enough, yes."

They finished unloading Dancer's supplies and Maggie's belongings in silence. With the wagon load lighter now, Connor unhitched one of the mares and led it to Dancer's small lean-to stable. "You may need her," he said.

Maggie was speechless. Tears welled in her eyes.

Connor stood in front of her, his hands at his sides. He wanted to shake her; he wanted to hold her. "You can reach the Double H by following the stream due north. Veer left at every fork. You'll be on my land this side of three hours but don't try it when there's more than a few inches of snow. The ranch sits in a valley but the passes all drift. You won't make it."

She nodded, drawing in her bottom lip, knowing that she'd never try it at all. Her dark green eyes held his.

"That's it, then."

She nodded again.

"You don't have to stay," he said.

"No, you're wrong. It's the one thing I *have* to do."

Connor searched her face and saw that the indecision had disappeared again. "I wish you luck." The words were inadequate, he thought, the sentiment too stiffly offered to seem sincere. He reached for her, realized what he was doing, and stopped. "Maggie?"

She responded to the heat in his eyes and the cautious uncertainty in his voice. She stood on tiptoe and placed her hands on his shoulders. She lifted her face and leaned into him, pressing her mouth full against his. Connor's hands cupped the inward curve of her waist, holding her tightly, supporting her against the length of his body.

Sunlight warmed them. A breeze lifted her hair so that it fluttered against his shoulders. Her skirt rippled between his legs. His mouth moved over her parted lips. Her fingers slipped around his neck and threaded in his thick hair. She returned the kiss measure for full measure.

It was Connor who drew away, Maggie who took the shaky breath and laughed a trifle uneasily. Sunlight still caressed them but the breeze had gentled. Maggie's hair fell back from Connor's shoulders and her skirt drifted along the slender line of her own legs.

"Goodbye, Connor," she said softly, inadequately. "Thank you." Other things she wanted to say were caught in her throat.

"Goodbye." He climbed onto the wagon and jerked the reins.

Maggie watched him until he was out of sight but he never looked back. She turned slowly, saw Dancer watching her from the window, and went inside.

"Seems like you weren't all that anxious to say farewell," he said, watching her closely. "He know about the baby?"

Maggie wasn't startled by the question. The baby was the reason Dancer was letting her stay and she had counted on him to recognize her condition and respond. "No, he doesn't know."

"He the father?"

"Yes."

Dancer reached in his pocket and pulled out a pouch of tobacco. He pinched some off and placed it between his lower lip and his teeth, pressing it down with his tongue. "Damn me if I know what's goin' on," he said. He tossed the pouch on the table. "Help me get these supplies inside. You can put your things under the bed and on those pegs by the hearth. No sense in you takin' the loft now. In a few months you won't be climbin' any ladders and that's a fact."

* * *

Maggie never climbed any ladders but she did everything else. As summer wore on she worked by Dancer's side except when he was working his claim. He rarely made demands on her. Instead he had expectations. He didn't ask her to do anything he hadn't done himself, nor did he ask her to do something she'd never done before without teaching her first.

That was how Maggie learned to wash clothes at the stream without having them float away on the current and split kindling without chopping off her toes. She hauled water and baked bread. She swept the floor, mucked the stalls, and cleaned the privy. She learned how to use acid to separate Dancer's gold from the ore without burning herself. She gathered blackberries and raspberries and learned how to make preserves. She weeded, hoed, and harvested vegetables from Dancer's garden and discovered that while some portion of the gathering went to the table and another to the root cellar, there was yet another portion that disappeared to a place not visible from the cabin. She followed Dancer one day as he was hauling potatoes away and came upon his still. That's when she learned about making moonshine.

In the beginning it seemed as though she was tired all the time. Dancer swore she could find a way to nap leaning against a hoe. She collapsed onto her narrow bed as soon as the dishes were cleared and cleaned and she was sleeping by the time Dancer climbed the ladder to the loft.

Maggie couldn't have said precisely when it changed, only that it did. Gradually she became aware that she wasn't cat-napping anymore, that she was strong enough to work more efficiently, and that some evenings she turned back the lamps after Dancer went to bed.

There were other changes that happened so slowly they were hard to notice. Maggie's breasts grew heavy and tender, her abdomen rounded. There was a nagging ache in the small of her back and her walk had become less graceful. Her moods were sometimes as unpredictable as the weather. She let out the fitted waistlines of her clothes and finally took to wearing a smocked overblouse. She had a habit of smoothing the material over her belly when she was deep in thought, smiling to herself when the baby kicked.

She'd had a lot of time to get used to having a child—ever since she'd dissolved Madame Restell's Infallible French Pills in the wash basin in her bathing room—but it was only since she'd come to

Dancer's that she began to think about being a mother. In Connor's company it hadn't been possible to dwell on that eventuality. Denial had been more important, a critical state of mind to keep him from knowing the truth. Now what she did best was worry.

She worried that she wouldn't know how to feed the baby or how to play with it. She worried that she'd drop it, or lose patience with it, or not know what its crying meant. She worried that she might spoil it, frustrate it, or not teach it what it needed to know. Was she clever enough to be a mother? Kind enough? Gentle enough? The only thing she didn't worry about was loving it.

Dancer didn't understand how Connor couldn't have known what Dancer himself had suspected almost immediately. Maggie had given up trying to explain because Dancer thought it was interesting that she came so quickly to Connor's defense. Dancer's high-pitched laughter was always more brittle and grating when he was being superior so Maggie didn't give him many opportunities to tease her. She let him think what he wanted because he would anyway, and satisfied herself that she had made the better choice by not telling Connor there had never been an abortion.

If Dancer needled her about some things, he was more than understanding about others. He was patient with her slowness and lack of agility as the weeks passed. He never berated her for not knowing something he attributed to plain old common sense. He asked questions but he rarely probed and he listened to the answers.

During the summer, intermingled among the tasks she *had* to learn, Dancer Tubbs taught Maggie about the things she *wanted* to learn. When he saw her press the heel of her hand to her back and grimace with pain, he showed her how to prepare white willow tea. When he realized she suffered occasional morning sickness he steeped goldenseal tea with a pinch of ginger to lessen the nausea.

Dancer was methodical in his approach, showing Maggie how to identify the plant in the wild first. White willow trees had olive-green branches and furrowed, dull-brown bark. A few teaspoons of the inner bark were placed in a cup of cool water to soak for two hours, then brought to a boil and divided into three doses. In midsummer they collected plants that grew in the wild or were specifically cultivated by Dancer. They always went out when the day was warmest, ignoring the heat in order to find plants free of dew and surface water. He showed her how to select a plant in its best condition, choosing the flower when it was about to open or when the shoot had reached its greatest growth point. The herbs were spread out and dried, some preserved in alcohol, others in sunflower seed oil. She learned how to make teas, tisanes, balms, washes, and poultices, and when and how to apply them.

The leaves and shoots of watercress were an excellent remedy for gout. A syrup made from the bark of the wild black cherry could be used for cough, colds, and diarrhea. Wintergreen leaves prepared in oil relieved a sore throat. As a tea, wormwood was useful for indigestion and heartburn but prepared as an oil it was a powerful poison.

Somewhat to Dancer's amusement, Maggie wrote everything she learned in a journal. She drew meticulous sketches of the plants, recorded their names, their preparation, and how they should be used. Some evenings she worked well into the night.

Maggie felt she earned Dancer's grudging respect. He never seemed to mind her curiosity or her questioning except when it inadvertently touched on the personal. She learned a great deal from Dancer Tubbs—except the origin of his knowledge. She suspected most of his sources were Indian but that his experience living among them had not been pleasant; possibly he had learned about healing to survive and had been driven out for stealing the shaman's powers. Dancer never confirmed her suppositions outright, but as they worked side by side, day after day, there were subtle indications that her conclusions were correct.

Keeping busy provided Maggie with a balm better than any herbal remedy, sustaining her during days when her thoughts would have otherwise been on Connor, exhausting her by bedtime so she didn't have to think about how things might be different if he were with her. Still, she remembered his parting kiss, the way his mouth had moved over hers, the texture of his hair beneath her fingers, the single breath they shared as they drew back.

"You missin' your man again?" Dancer asked as he stomped into the cabin. A clod of dirt dropped from the heel of his boot onto the floor. He put his Winchester on the rack by the door, picked up the broom, and swept the floor before Maggie could give him one of her prim, fussy looks. "Sure looks like you're missin' your man." He propped the broom against the wall and removed his saber.

"I don't have a man," she said.

"Had one, though." He laughed at his crude joke until Maggie stared him down. He ducked his head in a gesture of apology. "Sorry." He listened to himself and added, "Damn me if I ain't acquirin' manners."

It was Maggie's turn to laugh because Dancer Tubbs seemed quite unhappy about the notion. She stopped abruptly. "Oh!"

"The baby?"

Maggie nodded. "A powerful kick that time."

"Must be the heat that makes him so active." He wiped his brow with his forearm. "There ain't been an Indian Summer like this in years."

The kicking subsided and Maggie relaxed, tipping back and starting the rocker again. She picked up her sewing and began hemming the baby's nightshirt. In her haste to leave New York before her family knew she was pregnant, Maggie had not given much consideration to what her baby would wear at birth. Now she was set with the task of cutting down her slips and gowns to make a layette and needlework had always tried her patience.

Dancer watched her prick her finger and sighed. He washed his hands at the basin and took the sewing from Maggie's lap. "Can't understand how you can be so accomplished in most things and can't do a stitch to save your life." He plopped himself down in one of the chairs at the table and began the hemming himself.

For once Maggie let herself enjoy being idle. The last throes of summer were sapping her energy. She closed her eyes and rocked gently. "Did you see anyone coming this way from the Double H?" she asked. She'd been asking Dancer the same question most every day since the middle of August.

"Nary a soul," he said. "Maybe Connor Holiday decided he ain't gonna divorce you."

She raised her lashes a fraction and gave him a frank, skeptical look. "I don't think he'd decide that. He hates me."

"That what you call it when a man kisses you like he wants to gobble you up?"

"Connor agreed to the divorce."

Dancer shrugged, the scarred skin of his neck pulling with the movement. "A man can change his mind just like a woman."

"He won't," Maggie said with serene confidence. "He may be the most honorable man I know." Connor hadn't had to share the painful, intimate details of their first night together; he hadn't had to accept responsibility for what happened when it was easier to call her a whore. "He agreed and someone will arrive here with the divorce documents. You'll see."

"Hope it's soon," Dancer said casually. His eyes drifted to the loft. He pulled back his glance when he realized what he was doing. "I'm kinda tired keepin' watch for 'im just so you don't get sighted first." He bit off a short thread, examined his handiwork, and pronounced himself satisfied. Dancer placed the baby's gown on the table. "You figured on a name for the baby yet?"

"I'm still thinking."

"Dancer's a nice name," he suggested.

"I'm having a girl."

"Still a nice name."

Maggie smiled wistfully. Her expressive eyes were kind as they lighted on the prospector's disfigured face. "Yes," she said. "It's a very nice name."

Dancer ducked his head again, this time in genuine embarrassment. Usually he didn't mind when Maggie looked at him. There was never any pity in her glance. Feeling her gentle gratefulness, though, was almost as discomforting. He wanted to make her stop looking at him. His hoarse voice was challenging. "Know how I got it?"

"No," she said, still smiling. "How?"

"When the explosion in the mine set my face on fire they say I danced like the devil himself."

Maggie couldn't help herself. She blanched. When she recovered she saw his satisfied grin. "Sometimes you're a horrid man, Dancer Tubbs," she said, her eyes snapping at him.

"That's a fact."

Maggie rose from the rocker, put on her straw bonnet, and left the cabin. Dancer's laughter followed her onto the porch until she shut the door. The wide stream that bordered the cabin's yard beckoned her. She wandered down to its bank and began walking along the edge. On impulse she took off her shoes and stockings, dropped them in the grass, and continued her walk, dipping one foot or the other in the water every few steps.

She laid her hand on her rounded belly. "What do you think of Dancer for a name?" she asked. The kick seemed timely but she didn't know how to interpret it. She laughed. "Was that yes or no?"

There was another kick, this one right under her ribs. "No, I think."

Maggie lifted the hem of her gingham skirt and waded to the middle of the stream. She wiggled her toes over some smooth pebbles until they were buried. "Connor's mother was Edie," she told her baby. "I never asked, but I think it was short for Edith. Do you like that?" There was no response. "Well, I don't," she said. "At least not all by itself." She kicked at the pebbles, letting them fly, and finished crossing the stream. Keeping close to the bank she continued her walk north. "What about Mary Edith? Your aunts could argue for the rest of their lives over which of them you were named after." It seemed like a good joke on her sisters. "Mary Edith," she said more firmly. She tested the name a few more times. "I'll want to think—"

The sound of approaching horses and riders interrupted Maggie's musings. She scanned the area quickly, looking for cover, and darted toward some sheltering pines. The riders were upon her before she had covered half the distance from the stream to the trees. One of the riders blocked her escape with his horse while the other guarded her rear.

Maggie's forearm dropped protectively across her swollen abdomen as she was cornered. She turned so that the riders were on either side of her. They circled again, blocking another escape attempt.

The most frightening thing, Maggie thought rather giddily, was that the rider in front of her bore a passing resemblance to Connor. The similarities did not hold up under scrutiny, but his build, his battered leather vest, the dark hair and eyes, had fooled her momentarily. As insane as it was, she felt a fleeting sense of relief that the menacing stranger *wasn't* Connor Holiday.

She caught her breath and lowered her arm slowly. Darting a glance over her shoulder she saw the rider to the rear was older but bore enough similarity to the other that it wasn't difficult to recognize they were kin. "What do you want?" she demanded, standing her ground. Her hope that by being firm, even arrogant, she could shame them for frightening her, vanished as the rear rider laughed at her.

"Say, Tuck," he said pleasantly, "didya ever hear tell that Dancer had a woman?"

"Never did." Tuck's flat black eyes rested on Maggie's belly. He pushed back the brim of his hat a notch. "Look's like he's fixin' to be a father, too."

"What do you want?" Maggie persisted.

"Name's Freado, ma'am," the older rider said. "And we're looking for Dancer."

"Well, you can see that he isn't here."

"Sure, I can see that. What I'm thinkin' is that it would be a good idea for you to come with us to his cabin. Sit with us while we're waitin' for him."

"You can just as easily go on without me," she said. "You seem to know the way."

"Oh, Tuck and I been in these parts before," Freado said. "Only Jack was with us then. You don't see Jack with us now, do you?" Maggie shook her head. "That's 'cause Dance shot him."

"He can't ride with you now?" Maggie asked. "Is that what you mean?"

It was Tuck who answered. "What Freado means is that his brother's dead. That plain speakin' enough for you?"

Maggie understood enough to feel the knot of fear tighten in her stomach. Having no clear idea where she wanted to go, Maggie tried to move from between the horses. Her exit was immediately blocked. "Let me pass," she said stiffly.

Freado laughed. "She sure enough likes to give orders."

Without another word passing between the two men, Maggie found herself being herded toward the cabin. They didn't let her pick up her shoes and stockings as she passed the place where she dropped them, but kept her moving. The hem of her dress got wet as they hurried her across the stream and up the knoll to the cabin. Maggie hardly knew whether to be grateful or worried when she saw Dancer was waiting for them on the porch. She watched him lower his shotgun as they approached and for the first time she realized that Freado had his Colt leveled at her back.

"Toss that on the ground," Tuck yelled to Dancer. "Or Freado's gonna put a hole in your woman. Maybe put a hole in your baby."

Dancer didn't hesitate. He pitched the shotgun. "What d'you fellas want?"

Freado kept his gun aimed on Maggie. "That's real polite that you're askin' now. You didn't bother last time. Shot first, as I recalled."

Dancer rubbed the scarred side of his face. His bright blue eyes narrowed. "Guess that's 'cause you made no secret about bein' up to no good. The three of you was skulkin' around my claim like you was after somethin' particular."

"Know what?" Tuck asked. "We're still after somethin' particular. Only this time I think you're gonna show us just where to look."

Maggie didn't need to have it explained to her. Tuck and Freado were after Dancer's gold and they were going to get it this time because she was in the way. She tried to make eye contact with Dancer, to let him know that she didn't expect him to give up his gold because of her, but he refused to look at her. His brightly burning eyes were steady on Freado's revolver. She had to say the words aloud. "Don't do what they want on my account, Dancer. I knew the risks of coming out here. I accepted them. I still do."

"Good woman you got," Freado said. "All heart, no sense. Must be how you got her in the sack."

Dancer's grim, disfigured mouth thinned. The web of scars on his face whitened. "You gonna wait here while I get what you want?"

Tuck laughed. "Not likely. You're not gonna skip out on us. Your woman's nice, but she's not worth the kinda gold Freado and me figure you got. I'll go with you to make sure you give us every bit of what you got buried on your land."

Dancer Tubbs leaned against one of the porch supports. "You prepared to dig it out?" he asked. " 'Cause what I got buried is pretty deep."

"I think you'll dig it out," Tuck said, patting the rifle in the scabbard by his saddle. "Leastways this Remington says you will."

Maggie raised one arm, imploring Dancer. "You don't have to do this," she said.

He ignored her. "Who's comin' with me?"

Tuck urged his horse forward immediately. "I am. Freado'll stay with your woman, just so you know there's no point in tryin' to come back without me."

"I'll be bringin' you back," Dancer muttered. His eyes finally moved from Freado's gun to settle on Maggie's pale face. "Or someone just like you." His eyes moved past Maggie, not waiting to see if she understood his meaning, and onto Tuck. "You gonna make me walk?" he asked. "Or you gonna let me saddle up? We gotta piece to go to get what you want."

"You can saddle up," Tuck said. "You figure nightfall before we get back?"

"Sounds about right."

Tuck nodded, let Dancer walk off to the stable, and turned to Freado. His voice was loud enough to carry. "If you don't see me comin' 'cross that stream by nightfall, kill her."

Maggie saw the break in Dancer's stride and she knew he'd heard the threat.

Tuck rubbed his jaw with the back of a gloved hand. "I'll be comin' back alone," he said, mouthing words above Maggie's head. Only his partner understood the message this time.

Connor Holiday pulled off his gloves, leaned forward in his saddle, and patted Tempest on the neck. "Good climb," he said, praising his mount. He looked back over the rocky outcroppings and narrow ridges that Tempest had managed to negotiate and thought again his horse was half mountain goat. "Now we just have to find that cow. How the hell she got up here is a mystery." A wide section of the Double H was spread out below him— It was impossible not to be drawn to the sight.

The log ranch house was situated on the gentle curve of the valley's western slope. Its verdant setting of pine trees and thick grass giving the impression of emerald velvet. The corral, stable, and other outbuildings were closer to the water source; cattle and horses roamed the lower hillside freely. A curving ribbon of water ran across the property from north to south. Sunlight glanced off the water, giving it the reflective quality of a mirror, while a breeze made the aspens shiver and the hillside glow with color.

Even at his distance from the ranch Connor could make out the activity of his four hired hands. Ben was working just outside the forge, fitting shoes to the horses for the next drive. Buck and Patrick were taking turns getting thrown from Connor's newest addition to the stable and the smoke rising from the ranch house meant that Luke was starting their dinner.

"Or burning it," Connor said aloud. Tempest snorted. Connor patted him again. "You miss Woody as much as the rest of us do, don't you, boy?" Struck by a surge of wanderlust, the Double H cook had left for California three weeks earlier. No one was expecting him to return anytime soon, if ever. The four remaining hands and Connor took turns cooking. No one did a good job at it because no one wanted it as a full-time position. For three weeks they had just been getting by, tightening their belts as they began losing weight. More amused than frustrated by the situation, Connor decided he'd let it go on another week or so before sending Ben to Cannon Mills to hire a cook.

"Ben's looking just hungry enough that I don't think he'll spend three days whorin' when I need him back here." Tempest shifted restlessly. "Okay, let's go find that cow." He urged his mount away from the precipice.

It was a movement far below him that caught his eye. He halted Tempest, turned back, and surveyed the valley again. He didn't see the rider at first, protected as he was by the shelter of pines, but then horse and rider darted into the clearing, splashed wildly across the stream, and rode straight for the corral. Grazing cattle scattered and their lowing reverberated throughout the valley, rising to reach Connor and prick Tempest's ears.

Connor squinted, staring hard at the rider as he jumped down from his horse and met Buck and Patrick at the corral fence. It wasn't possible. He was just imagining that the rider was familiar. The sunlight was deceiving him. But the longer he stared the more he was convinced. He lowered his hat, shading his eyes against the sun's reflection on the water. He saw Buck and Patrick raise their right arms simultaneously and indicate his general location on the mountainside. When the stranger turned, Connor knew he hadn't imagined anything.

Dancer Tubbs had left his claim. It meant only one thing to Connor: something had happened to Maggie.

Under Connor's guidance Tempest made the descent recklessly. The horse was lathered, pushed to the edge of his endurance, by the time they reached the corral. Buck and Patrick were no longer alone with Dancer. Luke had come out of the ranch house and Ben had joined them from the forge. The four hired hands were sitting on the top rail of the corral watching Connor's brutally paced arrival with equal parts of interest and concern. They hadn't been able to learn a thing from Dancer Tubbs, but they knew the prospector's arrival had something to do with the reason that Connor was mostly a son of a bitch these days.

Connor leaped down and confronted the prospector, tension radiating through him. "What's happened to Maggie?"

Dancer had been drinking water from a ladle. He tipped out the undrunk portion, handed the ladle back to Luke, and wiped his mouth on the sleeve of his sweat-stained blue-gray jacket.

Connor's fingers curled into his palms, making white-knuckled fists when Dancer was slow to answer. "Dammit," he said, "tell me something before I lay you out, old man."

The prospector wasn't cowed. "This afternoon two men came lookin' to steal my gold. I've seen 'em before, killed one of their kin last time. They got to Maggie before they got to me. One of them, name of Freado, is holdin' her in my cabin until I get back with the gold. I don't figure she's safe ifn' I get back with gold or not and I don't like my chances of helpin' her alone."

"You said there were two men," Connor said.

Dancer's blue eyes grew slightly colder. "Other's dead." He spit. "He got too greedy for his own good. Forgot to watch his back." The prospector's mouth twisted to one side. "Thing of it is, you look a little like the one I killed. Tuck, he was called."

Ben spoke up. He was a thick-necked man, with hands like hammers, black from his work in the forge. He wiped them on his leather apron. "He's talking about Steve Tucker. I've seen him hangin' around Cannon Mills before. Dancer's right. He does look a little like you."

"Did," Connor said. "He *did* look a little like me." He turned back to Dancer. "How does that figure in your plans?" He had no doubt that Dancer Tubbs had a plan.

"Tuck meant to kill me," Dancer said. "Never thought for a moment he'd try anything else. He's the only one expected back at the cabin. If he isn't there by nightfall then Freado's goin' to kill Maggie." There was no need to add that it may have already happened. He could see that Connor was aware of that—and a lot more besides.

"We need to leave now, then," Connor said tightly. "Buck, get a fresh horse for me and one for Dancer."

Dancer stopped Buck when he started to lead his horse away. "Just a minute. That's Tuck's horse. Connor'll need to ride it back. Tuck's clothes are in the saddlebag." He looked at Connor. "You'll need to put 'em on. No sense takin' any chances."

Connor nodded. He pulled the clothes out and began stripping. "Buck, get two horses anyway. Dancer and I'll be able to travel faster if we're on fresh mounts and Tuck's animal will do better without a rider. I'll switch horses just before we reach the cabin."

Buck ran off, his long-legged, loping stride getting him to the stables quickly. Patrick pushed up the brim of his dusty black hat, revealing a fringe of bright red hair. With the shadow lifted from his face there was a sprinkling of freckles visible across the bridge of his nose. "You want us to come? Watch your back?"

Connor looked to Dancer. "Do we need that?"

The prospector shook his head. "My plan only calls for two. While Connor's distractin' I'll be reactin'."

Luke, who rarely smiled, thought that was worth a small grin. He dropped from his perch and scooped up Connor's discarded clothes and tossed them over the corral rail. "I don't mind being your flank."

Connor pulled on Tuck's shirt. "Thanks, but not this time, Luke."

Luke nodded, his gray eyes serious. He saw the tautness of Connor's jaw and recognized his friend's need to do this thing on his own. He leaned against the corral and deftly caught Connor's hat as it came sailing toward him.

Connor put on Tuck's hat, tugged on the brim, and turned to Dancer. "Is this going to fool him?"

"It don't really matter, does it? I reckon you'd come anyway."

"You're right."

Dancer studied Connor thoughtfully for a moment. "Then there's something else you should know," Dancer said. "Maggie's pregnant."

In the same breath that Connor was calling Dancer a bastard, he was drawing back his fist. Luke intervened, blocking Connor's punch with his forearm.

Dancer stood his ground, rubbing his jaw as if he'd been hit anyway. His lopsided grin pulled his face grotesquely and whitened his scars. "I'm flattered," he said. His high-pitched laughter crackled. "Damn me if I ain't flattered."

"What are you saying?"

"Isn't it obvious?" Luke asked, letting go of Connor's arm. He looked at Patrick and Ben, who were nodding. Dancer was waiting expectantly for Connor to comprehend what everyone else knew. Luke grew impatient. "It's *your* baby, Connor."

"That's not possible, she—" Connor didn't finish his sentence. Buck was coming toward them with the horses. "Let's go," he said tightly, strapping on his gun belt. He gave Dancer Tuck's Remington rifle. "Don't give me a reason to regret not using that on you." He tugged the reins of the bay sharply and didn't look back to see if Dancer was following.

Maggie rocked slowly. The floor made a steady creaking sound against the chair runners that she found soothing. Throughout the day she had looked up from her sewing to glance out the window. On this occasion a firefly glowed. Then another. She judged there was little more than an hour's daylight left.

She was actually surprised to be alive. Once Tuck and Dancer left she thought Freado would kill her, in spite of his instructions to the contrary. When he didn't she began to hope, and now that twilight was settling it seemed cruel that he had allowed her that. Maggie thought that if it hadn't been for her baby she might have simply begged him to kill her hours earlier and stop torturing her with the possibility.

Freado jerked his Colt in her direction. "You want to stop that?" he snapped.

Although Maggie's heart was slamming against her breastbone, her features were composed as she raised her face. "Stop what?" she asked.

"That goddamn rocking! Stop it or I'll—" He pulled back the hammer on his revolver.

Maggie set her feet flat on the floor and the creaking stopped. "Should I sit somewhere else?" she asked. "You told me to sit here."

"Sit there—only don't rock."

It was virtually impossible to do. She went back to her sewing but in a few minutes she was rocking again. The blast from Freado's gun propelled Maggie out of the chair. Wood splintered as a bullet sheared one of the rocker's curved runners, tipping it to one side.

Maggie's hand went over her heart as she tried to contain the beat. Her sewing dropped to the floor. She opened her mouth to call him every vile name she could think of.

"Save it," he said, putting the Colt away. "I got a wife, I heard it before. Now sit."

Color returned to Maggie's face slowly. She stooped to pick up the baby clothes and saw her hands were trembling. "I have to use the privy," she said quietly, mustering the threads of her dignity.

"Again?" His tone indicated complete disgust.

"I'm pregnant," she said. "I have different needs than you."

"All right," he said sourly. He pushed away from the table and opened the back door. He waved his arm, indicating she should precede him.

"You don't have to come with me," she said.

"I think I do."

And that was that, Maggie thought. She had made more trips to the privy than she needed to, hoping that just once he would let her go on her own. It hadn't happened yet and it wasn't going to happen this time. Freado escorted her to the privy, waited outside while she relieved herself, and followed her back to the cabin.

"Now sit," he said.

"I want to make some tea," she said, picking up the kettle.

"Then you'll be wantin' another trip outside. I know how it works."

"Let me make it for you," she said. Her wide green eyes implored her captor. "I need to be busy."

Freado impatiently raked his curly hair with thick fingers. "All right," he said. "Make the damn tea."

"Will you fire up the stove?"

"Oh, for God's sake," he said, frustrated. "This is why I didn't want no dinner. Too much fussin'. Do it yourself." Instead of returning to the chair he had occupied most of the day, Freado sat on the narrow bed where Maggie slept. He had a good view of the creek through the window and he could still see Maggie at the stove. In a little while he lost interest in Maggie's activities as the fireflies began to blink in ever-increasing numbers.

Maggie tried to ignore the relentless approach of night as she prepared Freado's tea. She listened for the sound of riders instead.

"Here it is," she said, coming toward him with the steaming mug.

Freado held out his hand, palm up, indicating she should stop. "Just put it on the table," he said. "I don't want you spillin' it on me and it's too damn hot to drink right now."

Maggie very nearly screamed her frustration. Some of the intense feeling showed on her face.

"D'you think I didn't know you had a plan?" he asked. "Now sit, dammit."

She sat. The rocker was tilted at an angle that made her back ache. Maggie swept her sewing from the table onto her lap and tried to clear her mind of all thought. When Freado's harsh voice pulled her to the present she had no idea how much time had elapsed since she sat down.

"Looks like no one's comin'," he said, getting up from the bed. He walked to the door, opened it, and leaned against the frame. "And that doesn't look good for anyone, does it? Tuck's either dead or he run off with the gold himself. Maybe he 'n Dancer cut a deal and decided to leave us both in the lurch. Don't see how it matters to you, though. I'm gonna have to kill you either way."

Maggie forgot what she was doing. She clutched the nightdress she was stitching and pricked the heel of her hand with the needle. At her slight cry, Freado turned away from the door.

"What the hell's wrong with you now?"

Maggie sucked on the injured area and said nothing.

Freado kicked the door shut and sat on the bed again. "Hell of a thing to have to do since you ain't done me a moment's harm." His abrupt yawn was incongruous with the murderous talk.

It took a great effort of will on Maggie's part not to allow her eyes to stray to the mug on the table. She lowered her injured hand slowly and watched Freado with greater interest. His eyes seemed vaguely out of focus and there was a thin line of beaded sweat above his upper lip.

They heard the approach of a single horse and rider at the same time. Their heads swiveled in the direction of the window simultaneously.

"I'll be damned. It's Tuck!" Freado jumped to his feet. And promptly dropped to the floor as if he had been felled by a woodsman's ax.

Maggie didn't hesitate. Scrambling from the rocker, she grabbed Freado's gun, drew back the hammer, and held the Colt in a tight two-handed grip.

Several long minutes passed, then the cabin's front door was pushed open slowly.

Chapter Eleven

Connor shouldered the door when it wouldn't open more than eight inches. Under his force it budged another two. Something was braced at the bottom of the door, holding it in place. Knowing the risk, he began to squeeze himself through the opening.

Maggie's extended arms trembled under the weight of the Colt. Freado's body blocked the door. She saw a jean-clad leg step inside.

"Stop right there."

For a moment Maggie thought it was her own terrified voice that had given the order. The hoarse, raspy quality was exactly as she imagined her own might be. Then she realized the voice had come from behind her, not through her.

"Maggie, put down the gun."

It was Dancer! She was afraid to turn around, afraid it was some horrible trick. She gestured with her gun toward the intruder at the front door.

"Put the gun down, girl, afore you shoot someone."

Maggie responded to the patience and firmness in Dancer's tone, dropping the gun beside her on the table just as Connor pushed his way into the cabin.

"Oh, my God." Maggie knew it was her voice this time. She sat slowly, her legs no longer able to support her, as Connor lowered his gun. Her hands moved to rest on her belly, not so much in an attitude of protection as with the intention of hiding her pregnancy.

Connor's features were rigid. When he spoke it was as if he were biting off the words and spitting them out. "So there *is* a baby."

His scorn lashed Maggie. She actually flinched under the cold, steady stare of his black eyes. The muscle that worked in his jaw underscored his tension and anger.

Off to the side Dancer watched the interplay with interest. He leaned the Remington against the wall. "You two ain't fit to be left by yourselves. No tellin' what you might say."

"Stay out of this, Dancer," Connor said.

Dancer rubbed his jaw. "Seems like I'm the one that invited you." He pointed to the unconscious miscreant on the floor. "First things first." He walked over to Freado and hunkered down. Placing his hand on the robber's neck, he searched for a pulse. "What did you give him, Maggie?"

Thankful for Dancer's question, she pulled her eyes away from Connor. It helped to think about what had already happened rather than what was going to happen. "Corn poppies," she said. "In some tea. He's not dead, is he?"

"No. Just out cold."

"I didn't even know he drank the tea. I let him think I meant to scald him with it and he made me put it on the table. I didn't see him take it. Is he going to be all right?"

Dancer and Connor exchanged glances. "Help me get him out of here, would you, Connor?"

Connor bent and took Freado by the shoulders. Dancer got the feet. They lifted him together and moved out the door onto the porch. "You want to take care of him?" Connor asked. "Or do you want me to?"

"I'll do it," Dancer said. "Let's get him on his horse. I don't want to do it where Maggie can hear the shot."

They slung Freado's body over his saddle and Dancer gave the horse a hard swat on the rear. Freado's gelding ambled off in the direction of the creek. Dancer mounted his own horse and followed.

Connor returned to the cabin. Maggie was standing by the window where she had been watching them. She turned when Connor came in. "What's Dancer going to do?" she asked.

"Escort Freado off his land."

"Shouldn't we report this to someone?"

"The law, you mean? Someone like your brother-in-law?"

"Yes."

"There isn't a lawman within fifty miles of here."

"So he goes free."

Connor merely shrugged. "Do you really want to talk about this?"

Maggie hardly knew what to say. She shook her head, not certain she wanted to talk at all. "Would you like some tea?" she asked nervously. When she saw Connor's mouth lift in an amused, cynical grin she realized how inane the question was, how it must have seemed to him. "Just tea," she said. "I wouldn't put anything in it."

"Just tea, then."

Maggie went to the wood stove, added some kindling to the glowing embers in the fire box, and stoked the fire. "You can have a seat," she said. When he didn't move immediately, she added, "It makes me uncomfortable with you standing there like that."

Connor removed his hat and tossed it on the bed. He ran a hand through his hair. Pulling out one of the chairs, he straddled it. "This better?" he asked. He noticed that Maggie was worrying her lower lip as she nodded. He couldn't guess the number of times he'd pictured that little fretful, thoughtful gesture in his mind's eye. "What happened to the rocker?"

Maggie set the kettle on the stove. "That man Freado shot it."

"Why?"

"He couldn't stand the sound it made when it was rocking."

Connor thought about that and his brows drew together. "You were sitting in it when he splintered the runner?"

"Well, yes," she said. "Otherwise it wouldn't have been making any noise."

Connor regretted allowing Dancer to mete out Freado's punishment. He swore feelingly under his breath. "I should never have let you come here," he said.

"You couldn't have stopped me." She stood on tiptoe, stretching to reach the mugs. Maggie set them aside while she prepared the tea for the strainer. "What happened to the other one?" she asked. "How did Dancer get away?"

"Tuck got careless," Connor said.

"He's dead, then."

"Yes."

Maggie was silent as she poured boiling water over the strainer and let the tea steep. She watched the liquid change slowly from clear to caramel color then added a dollop of honey to both mugs. She carried Connor's to him and set it on the table, then she went back to the stove to get hers, choosing to drink it standing up and keep her distance. "I'm not sorry Tuck's dead. He would have killed Dancer."

"But . . ." he said. He could almost hear her thoughts, they were so clearly expressed in her eyes, in the small vertical between her brows, in the way her lower lip was once again tucked between her teeth. "But you wish Dancer hadn't come for me."

Maggie ducked her head, not able to meet Connor's frank stare. The evening was still warm but Maggie's hands were cold. She wrapped her hands around her mug and lifted the steaming tea toward her face. "I didn't want you to know," she whispered, anguished.

"That's obvious," he said coldly. "You would have been willing to lose your life and the baby's rather than look to me for help. Thank God Dancer didn't see it the same way."

"I took care of Freado. We didn't need you."

"You were resourceful and you were lucky and if you hadn't been, you can be damn sure you *would* have needed me!" Connor wasn't aware of when he had come to his feet, only that he was standing now. His left hand was on the top rail of the chair, his fingertips pressed tightly to the wood. "How dare you not tell me about my baby! How dare you let me think you aborted my child!"

Her voice trembled. "My baby," she said. "My child."

"No, dammit! *Ours!*" Seeing Maggie flinch, he visibly reined in his anger. His voice was low and terse. "Of all the words I would have used to describe you, *selfish bitch* didn't figure into them until now."

Maggie gasped at the hard, hurting judgment. "No," she said softly, achingly. "That's not who I am. I was trying to do right by everyone."

"Convince me."

It was the arrogant challenge in his tone that set Maggie on edge. She lifted her face and glared at him. "I don't have to explain myself to you."

Connor came around the table. Maggie darted to the back door, flung it open, and ran outside. She veered away from the path that led to the privy and sprinted toward the hillside and the sheltering pines. The full moonlight revealed a fallen log blocking her way and she prepared to jump. Her feet rose—and didn't touch down again.

Connor caught her as she rose in the air and hauled her against him, dangling her several inches above the ground. Maggie had to brace herself by putting her arms around his neck; his hands were secure on the small of her back.

"Maggie," he whispered hoarsely.

She burrowed against him, pressing her face into the curve of his neck. His breath was warm on her ear as his mouth settled near her temple.

"Maggie," he said again. "Don't run from me. Don't ever run from me."

She tried to shake her head and sucked in a sob instead. She felt herself being lowered but her arms didn't move from Connor's neck. One of his hands left her back and touched her nape, then buried itself deep in the strands of her hair. He stroked her, supported her. He let her soak his shirt with her tears and he absorbed her fear, her pain, knowing that he had contributed to both.

"I couldn't . . . couldn't take those pills," she said, her voice breaking. "I couldn't get rid of the ba . . . baby. I couldn't have done that."

Connor simply held her.

"But . . . but you were right . . . I'm a selfish bi . . . bitch. I didn't—"

"No," he said gently. "I was wrong. I'm sorry I said it, Maggie. I was wrong."

She sniffed inelegantly and smiled against him. "We never agree on anything."

He set her away from him. Moonlight washed her fine-boned features. Connor rubbed at the tear tracks with the pad of his thumb. "Let's go inside," he said.

Maggie nodded, sniffed again, and gave Connor an embarrassed, watery smile. She let him slip his arm through hers and escort her back to the cabin. This time when he pulled out a chair, it was for her. He pressed her into it.

"When did you eat last?" he asked.

"I had something at noon. I wanted to fix some dinner but Freado wouldn't let me. He didn't want the fussing." She found a handkerchief tucked in the sleeve of her pale rose overblouse and wiped her nose. "It's been a trying day."

One of Connor's dark brows kicked up. "Only you," he said, his mouth curving in dry amusement. He turned away and started searching the pantry for something for Maggie to eat.

"What does that mean?"

"It means," he said patiently, cracking some eggs in a bowl, "that you've got a talent for understatement. You've stared down death most of the day and you describe it as 'trying'. That's not exactly what I would expect from one of New York's social princesses."

"That isn't who I was." She picked up his mug and took a sip from it. "Neither was any of my sisters. We were John MacKenzie Worth's daughters . . . his *bastard* daughters. I never wanted for anything, but outside my own home I was never wanted anywhere." Maggie saw Connor's hand momentarily slow as he beat the eggs. That small hesitation on his part made her feel listened to. "I don't think my life was exactly as you've imagined."

Connor stopped beating the eggs. He put a black iron skillet on the stove and added a bit of bacon grease. "And how do think I imagined your life?"

"Filled with social engagements. Private schools. Invitations to the theatre and skating parties and masked balls."

"Skye talked about all those things."

Maggie sighed. "At the dinner party," she said. "I know. Skye told me she rattled on about anything she could think of to be sure you knew she was an empty-headed twit."

"She was convincing."

"That's Skye." She smiled wistfully, recalling her sister's earnest description of her behavior that night. "The truth is, Skye charges ahead rather fearlessly. She forces people to take her in or tell her bluntly that she isn't wanted. She's had more invitations than the rest of us combined, but she does it just to make a point, not because she really cares for it, or believes that she's really accepted. We went to the parish's parochial school, not exclusive academies, and none of us is particularly welcome in certain homes along Fifth Avenue, even to fill out an odd-numbered dinner party."

"So what did you do?" Connor added the beaten eggs to the skillet and stirred them with a wooden spoon.

"I read."

"That's all?"

"Mostly." Maggie sipped from Connor's mug again. "Mary Francis left the house when I was twelve so she was never really a companion. Michael and Rennie had each other. Michael wrote a lot and Rennie talked about trains all the time. Skye dragged me around when she could, but mostly I just read."

"Where?"

Most people would have asked what she had read, not where she had read it. "In the library, in my room. Sometimes, when I was trying to get out of chores, I would slip up to the attic or out on the back porch roof. Mama would send my sisters out to hunt me down." She looked at him curiously. "Why do you ask?"

"I wondered if you had a tree house," he said. "With a rope ladder that you could pull up to keep everyone else away."

Her eyes widened faintly. "I used to ask Jay Mac for one. He said no one would ever hear from me again."

Connor lifted the skillet and spooned the eggs onto a plate. "He was probably right." He put the plate and a fork in front of Maggie. "Eat up. Do you want bread?"

She shook her head and picked up the fork. "Thank you."

Connor sat at the table. "Why a doctor?"

"It never occurred to me to want to do anything else. I told you once I never thought about marrying."

"Children?"

Maggie swallowed hard. "No," she said softly. "I never thought about children."

"So," he said heavily, "you gave in to a single impulse just once in your life, joined your sister in a game that you would rather have ignored, and found yourself accosted, prostituted, and—"

"Pregnant," she finished for him.

"With no memory of any of it."

"Little of it," she corrected.

Connor nudged the plate in front of her, encouraging Maggie to eat. "Little?" he asked.

"I remember some things," she said softly, avoiding his eyes. "The sailor . . . Harlan Porter . . ." The way Connor touched her. The hungry exchange of kisses as his mouth slid over her cheek, across her jaw, and made a damp line along her throat. His hands on her skin. His palm cupping the underside of her breast. The heat he infused in the center of her. " . . . there was a girl with a broom. She chased Harlan away."

"That's all?"

"That's all." She concentrated on her eggs. "I don't know anything about your money."

"I wasn't thinking about the money."

Maggie took a bite of food rather than respond to that. She hoped the heat in her cheeks hadn't given her away. "Dancer should be back here soon. Do you think something's happened to him?"

"Dancer can take care of himself." Connor gave a cursory glance out the window. "Who knows about the baby, Maggie?"

She should have known better than to think she could have sidetracked him. Maggie pushed away her plate and put down her fork, her appetite gone. "Dancer."

"Dancer?" Connor frowned. "You mean you haven't told anyone else? Not your mother? Not Michael?"

"No one. I didn't want anyone to know. Did you think I singled you out because you're the father?"

"It occurred to me."

"Well, I didn't," she answered testily.

"When do you plan to tell your family?"

"I don't know. Probably when I tell them about our divorce."

Connor looked at her pointedly but refused to be drawn in. "And when were you going to tell me?"

Maggie shrugged.

"Maggie?" he persisted.

"I had no plans to tell you," she admitted impatiently. She looked at him sharply. "Does that satisfy you? It's what you suspected, isn't it?"

"It's what I suspected," he said, his tone weary, "but not what I wanted to hear."

"Then why do you ask me these things?" she said, exasperated. "Why do you—" She stopped. The baby kicked her hard under the ribs and it brought her upright. Her face softened as she placed her palm over the spot where she felt the kick.

Connor watched Maggie anxiously. "Does he hurt you?"

She smiled, shaking her head. Her expression was shy, her green eyes veiled by thick lashes. "Would you like—" He was already leaning forward in his chair and extending his hand. She took it and laid it over her abdomen. "Wait," she whispered, matching her voice to the awe of the moment. "She'll do it again. There! Did you feel it?"

Connor nodded but he didn't remove his hand. "Are you sure it doesn't hurt?"

"It's mostly surprising."

The baby kicked two more times before Connor withdrew his palm. "You look well, Maggie." What she looked was beautiful. Her skin glowed, her hair was lustrous, her delicate features animated. Her hand, when she had taken it in his, was rough, the pads of her fingers calloused, but it was the only outward sign he recognized of any hardships she had endured. He wanted to cradle her cheek, touch its softness. He wanted to place his thumb against her lips, feel the dampness of her breath as her mouth parted. "It looks as if everything about your life agrees with you."

"You mean the pregnancy."

"I mean everything." He gestured to the cabin. "This. What you're doing here . . . the work with Dancer. And yes, I meant the pregnancy, too."

"I'm not unhappy," she said softly.

He thought it was an odd way of phrasing her satisfaction. "The baby must be due in December."

"Just before Christmas."

"Don't you want to be with your sister in Denver?"

"No. I'm where I want to be. Dancer will help me with the delivery."

"He knew about the baby from the very beginning, didn't he? That's why you were so certain he'd take you in."

She nodded. "He didn't understand why I wanted to be here. I'm not sure he agrees even now, but he wasn't about to turn me out." Maggie hoped that hadn't changed with Connor's arrival. She glanced at the window again, looking for Dancer. A curtain of moonlight still draped the surrounding trees. The prospector was nowhere in sight.

"Do you want me to look for him?"

Maggie was only partially successful in masking her anxiety. "Would you mind?"

Connor got to his feet. "This won't take long." He went to the door and opened it. "In the meantime, think about our sleeping arrangements for tonight, and understand that I'm not bedding down with Dancer Tubbs." He shut the door in time to miss the mug Maggie threw at him.

*   *   *

Dancer Tubbs heard Connor coming when he was still a distant mile off. He shot off his gun to guide him, then he rolled on his back again, groaning as his leg twisted under him. Freado's body lay a few feet from him, face down on the rocky ground. There was no movement nor any chance there would be now. The thief's neck was broken and Dancer had paid for it with a broken bone of his own.

Connor saw the two horses milling around on the hillside before he caught sight of Dancer. He urged his mount up the hill. Stones shifted beneath its hooves and the horse stumbled. Connor managed to stay in the saddle but he proceeded more cautiously.

"What the hell happened to you?" Connor asked as he rode up to the prospector. He dismounted and knelt beside Dancer.

"Got careless myself," he said tightly. "Shouldn't have expected that Freado would stay sleepin' forever. He woke up, realized what was goin' on, and led me a merry chase up this damn hill. I knocked him off his horse."

Connor sent Freado a cursory glance. The odd angle of the man's neck told its own story. "Is that how he broke his neck?"

"That's how."

"And what about you?"

"I just fell," he admitted hoarsely. He flinched when Connor began examining him. "Dammit, be careful how you move my leg!"

"I'm going to have to set it."

"Like hell. You don't know—" Dancer's intelligible speech vanished as he let loose a string of curses that nearly heated the air around them.

"All done," Connor said, ignoring the prospector's threats. "I'll find some wood for splints."

Dancer had recovered a measure of his dignity by the time they reached the cabin. Connor helped him down from the horse and supported him as they went inside.

"It seems like Dancer's solved our sleeping dilemma," he told Maggie as she rushed to assist. They put him on the narrow bed after Maggie turned down the quilts. "I have to take care of the horses now." His quick exit this time spared him from Maggie's sour look.

Dancer didn't miss it. He laughed shakily. "Half expected you two would have made up or killed each other by now."

"We're too stubborn to do either." She straightened from the bed. "White willow tea?" she asked. "It will help the pain."

"Hard liquor would help me more. Pour me some of that 'shine."

"White willow tea it is," she said.

Dancer made a disgusted sound. "I just had a feelin' that some day I'd regret teachin' you about healin'." He propped a pillow under his head, careful to move slowly, and watched Maggie go about making the tea. "He says you sent him out after me, girl."

"I was worried."

The prospector snorted this time. "You ain't my nursemaid, you know. Been a long time since someone worried about me."

Maggie kept working at the stove, placing the bark in a jar to steep once the water was hot.

"Can't say I like it," Dancer said. "I been takin' care of myself for more years than you got candles on a cake."

"Do you have a point?" she asked softly.

"If your husband wants you with him," he said gruffly, "then don't make me an excuse to stay here. I ain't no one's excuse for sheer wrong-headed foolishness."

Maggie's busy hands grew still and she turned away from the stove to face Dancer. "Are you telling me to git?" she asked. She saw his puzzled look. "When you took me in you told me that when you said 'git', I was supposed to git. Is that what you're telling me now?"

Dancer had to look away from the quiet anxiety in Maggie's eyes. She wasn't pleading with him, but there was a calm resignation in her expression that made him feel as if he was betraying her. "I'm sayin' what I'm sayin'," he said. "If Connor says go with him, then don't let my leg here stop you. That clear enough?"

It was clear enough. She returned to her work and slowly let go of the breath she had been holding. "How would you take care of yourself?"

"That's my affair."

Maggie wasn't satisfied with the answer but Connor walked into the cabin. "Have I interrupted something?" he asked.

"No," they said simultaneously, for entirely different reasons. Maggie didn't want to open the discussion to the subject of her leaving; Dancer didn't want to talk about the fact that he might need help.

Connor raised one eyebrow as he looked from one to the other.

"Liars," he said without malice. He kicked out a chair and sat down, stretching out. "How's your leg?" he asked Dancer.

"I've had worse."

"I'm making him something for the pain," Maggie said.

Connor nodded. His eyes drifted to the loft, then back to Maggie. He wondered if she had given their sleeping arrangements any more thought. As she turned in her work his attention was caught by her rounded profile, her full breasts, her swollen belly. He wanted to feel her against him again, feel the baby move under his hand, touch her breasts, and know the curve of her against his flesh. He wanted to hold her.

She caught his stare, the curious warmth in his usually remote eyes. She flushed and looked away. It was because of the baby, she thought, that he was looking at her with the kind of interest that made her shaky inside. It was only because of the baby.

Maggie poured the boiling water into the jar and let the bark steep. It would be an hour before the tea was ready for Dancer. She didn't know quite what to do with herself or her hands. She leaned back against the stove and crossed her arms in front of her. Her posture emphasized the distention of her belly and when Maggie realized it, her arms quickly dropped to her sides. "I'm sorry I drank the last of the tea," she said to Dancer. "I should have made more right away."

He brushed the comment aside. "You didn't know I was going to fall off my horse. You needed it for your back."

"Your back?" asked Connor. "What's wrong with your back?"

Dancer didn't give Maggie an opportunity to answer. "It aches her fierce most days."

"Not fierce," Maggie corrected. "It just aches."

Connor pointed to the chair opposite him. "Sit."

"I'm fine."

"Sit."

Shooting Dancer a disgruntled look when he chuckled, Maggie sat. "There's nothing wrong with my back," she said to Connor.

Connor ignored her and spoke to Dancer instead. "Has she been working like a ranch hand all summer?" he asked.

"More like a field hand," he said. "She ain't exactly been bustin' broncs or digging post holes. Not that I don't think she coulda done it. There just ain't no coddlin' her."

Maggie grinned, feeling rather good about Dancer's description. Her smile faded when she saw Connor's disapproving glance. "Did you think I came here to be waited on?" she asked him. "Of course I worked. I'm not incompetent, incapable, or an invalid."

"Now you got her dander up," Dancer said to Connor. "And you ain't even said anything."

"I noticed," Connor said dryly.

Giving them both an impatient look, Maggie left the table and went outside to the porch. She sat on the step, leaning one shoulder against the rough-hewn pine support. She didn't turn when the door opened and Connor stepped out. She felt him just behind her. He stood there for a long while before he reached down and touched her shoulder. The pressure of his fingers urged her to move down one step. She did so without protest and then he was sitting behind her, pulling her between his splayed legs so her head rested against his chest.

"Better?" he asked softly.

Surprisingly, it was. She had thought she wanted to be alone, but she hadn't, not really. She didn't think she wanted him so near, but she had accepted him easily. "Better," she said.

His fingertips touched the gentle curve of her temple. He brushed back a lock of her hair, but once it was out of the way his fingers strayed back to the spot, stroking her so lightly it was like a breeze against her skin. "Dancer says you've learned everything he has to teach you," he said.

"He tells me that, too. I'm not certain I believe him."

Connor heard what she wasn't saying, namely that she wasn't sure she was ready to leave. He wasn't going to be drawn into that argument. He changed the subject instead. "Have you written your mother?"

Maggie nodded. "Every day, not that she knows it. Dancer's only been to town once since I've been here. He posted some letters then, but I have another box full. Perhaps you could mail them when you go."

"Perhaps I could."

Maggie closed her eyes. His caress whispered across her cheek.

"I thought a lot about you," he said. "I didn't think I would, but it happened anyway. I wanted you to know that." The admission was made reluctantly, as if he was trying to hold back the words and they were being drawn out by a force more powerful than his will.

"I thought about you, too," she said.

It was the most either one of them was prepared to say. They fell silent. Connor's fingers threaded through her hair. The back of his hand brushed the nape of her neck. His touch raised a tingle across the surface of her skin. Maggie turned into him slightly so his fingers made the same movement again. He traced the exposed line of her throat and felt her racing pulse beneath his calloused fingertips. He bent his head and touched his lips to the crown of hers. Her hair smelled like lavender. He unwound her braid and released more of the fragrance. His hand dropped to her shoulder but the pressure was light, urging her upward, not holding her down.

When he stood, Maggie came to her feet with him. He was on the step above, towering over her, yet she felt no fear, only a sweet yearning that made her lift her moon-washed face and hold his gaze with her wide, expressive eyes.

"Come with me, Maggie," he said gently, a shade urgently.

She knew he wasn't talking about tomorrow or forever—he was talking about what he wanted now. He was talking about what they both wanted. She put his hand in his and let him lead her away from the cabin.

They paused briefly at the stream. Maggie had waded through it most every day since she had come to Dancer's. This time was different. This time Connor scooped her up and carried her across it and kept on carrying her, through the curtain of moonlight into the canopy of pines.

He set her on her feet on a soft bed of fallen needles. Her arms were still looped around his neck. He started to say her name again, this time in question, but she shook her head slightly and stood on tiptoe. Her mouth touched his, answering what he had only asked with his eyes.

The kiss was sweet and lingering. Maggie's lips moved over his. Her tongue traced the line of his upper lip, not seeking entry, merely tasting. She felt his hands at the small of her back, holding her to him, and the way he held her felt like security, not capture.

She kissed the underside of his jaw. His mouth slid over her temple and the fragrance of her hair teased him again. Maggie leaned against him more heavily when her knees couldn't seem to support her. He lowered her to the ground as the kiss between them deepened. They knelt at first, too greedy and demanding to break the contact. Connor's fingers twisted the buttons on Maggie's overblouse and slipped it over her shoulders. Her breasts pressed against the thin material of her camisole.

Maggie broke the kiss and pulled back slightly. She drew in a shaky breath as she looked down at herself. Her uncertain glance was finally raised in Connor's direction. He was staring at the shadowed curve of her breasts and Maggie raised her arms to cover herself. He stopped her, circling her wrists lightly with his fingers.

"No," he said. "You're beautiful. I wish it were the middle of the afternoon."

Maggie ducked her head, embarrassed. She watched his hands as they released her wrists and were raised to the level of her camisole. His fingers slid along the edge of the material, caressing the high arc of her breasts. He twisted a button and the material parted. He did it again. And again. Her breasts filled his hands. His thumbs drew slowly across her nipples. He heard her tiny gasp.

"Did I hurt you?" he asked.

Not looking at him, she shook her head.

"Maggie?"

"They're tender," she whispered.

His touch was even lighter this time. The tip of her breasts stiffened beneath his thumbs and Maggie's small shudder was one of aching, not pain. Connor leaned toward her. He bent his head and touched his mouth to her nipple. Maggie's fingers threaded in his hair, supporting him even as she held on as she was lowered the rest of the way to the ground. The pine needles at her back were an odd sensation, soft yet abrasive, the very same sensation that Connor's mouth was causing as it moved over her breast.

His lips slid in the valley between her breasts. Her racing heart pulsed against his mouth. He raised his head and stretched out beside her, curving one arm under Maggie's neck to cradle her. He looked at her for a long moment, his eyes searching her shadowed face, listening to the sounds of her tremulous breathing. He lowered his mouth over hers. Her lips parted.

Connor's tongue pushed against hers, deepening the kiss as a surge of carnal hunger swept them both. His lips pressed. Hers responded. They shared the same breath.

His lips touched the corner of her mouth, her cheek, the sensitive skin just behind her earlobe. He was drawn again and again back to her mouth, to lips that were sweet and yielding, to a response that was eager and searching. One kiss was not enough. Each kiss demanded another.

Connor's mouth touched her closed eyes. "Look at me, Maggie," he said hoarsely.

She opened her eyes slowly, shyly. His breath was warm on her face. One of his legs was lying over hers and his free hand twisted in her hair.

"You're not afraid?" he asked. He didn't give her time to answer. "I don't want you to be afraid."

"I'm not afraid," she said on a mere thread of sound. She reached up to touch his face. She liked the clean, solid lines of his jaw in the curve of her palm. "I want you to know about the first time," she said. "There was no force."

He started to open his mouth to speak but she stopped him by placing her index finger across his lips. "I was afraid then," she said quietly. "Waking up . . . realizing what I was doing with you . . . how much I wanted it . . . those feelings frightened me . . . but then . . ." It was difficult to look at him. "You didn't force me."

"You remember?"

She said the next words against his mouth. "I remember that much." Then she kissed him hungrily.

Their mouths fused with the intense pressure of their need. This time it was Maggie who was working the buttons. She fumbled with the ones on Connor's vest and shirt and pushed them both off his shoulders. He worked them down his arms and flung them to one side. Maggie caught the waistband of his jeans as he turned and fumbled with the buttons of his fly. She managed three before he placed his hands over hers, stopping her.

"I want to enjoy this," he said against her mouth. "If you touch me now I'll . . ." He didn't have to finish. In spite of her inexperience, Maggie understood. Her hands slid slowly up his chest to his shoulders, rubbing him with the heels of her hands. "How do you know so much?" he asked, nudging her nose with his.

"I read."

He didn't ask her what kind of books, but he bet they were ones she didn't read where just anyone could catch her. Connor groaned softly as her hands slid between them again and his skin retracted at her touch. Her mouth followed the path of her hands. The damp edge of her tongue made a line down his throat, across his collar bone. Her teeth raised his nipples to hard nubs.

They were on their sides again, Maggie's belly pressing against his hard abdomen. One of her legs was raised over his as their mouths worked. The baby kicked hard enough for Connor to feel it. He tore his mouth away from Maggie's. "My God," he whispered hoarsely, awed and a little frightened. She drew his face back to hers. "It's all right."

"What if I—"

"You won't."

He kissed her again, this time turning her so she straddled him. Her breasts spilled toward him. His hands slipped under her skirt, along her calves to her hips. He pulled at her drawers and she helped him so that while her skirt billowed around her modestly it was her naked thighs that touched him. He spread his hands over her hard belly. She sighed as he rubbed her stretched and sensitive skin, desiring in that moment nothing more than to curl against him contentedly. Then his hand slipped beneath her parted thighs and he touched her in another manner, manipulating the delicate bud at the source of her moist heat. She sucked in her breath as pleasure seemed to sear her senses. The heel of his hand pressed against her. Deliciously responsive to his touch, she rubbed and rode. She leaned forward as his finger probed and penetrated. First one, then another. Maggie closed her eyes, surrendering to sensation.

Her hair slipped forward over her shoulders. The auburn curtain surrounded his face. She was hot against him, moving, shuddering. Her breath came in short gasps as she sipped the night air. Then suddenly she rose up, dislodging his hand, and when he tried to hold her she avoided his grasp.

"I want more than this," she whispered, her voice husky. Her hands slipped to his jeans again, this time reaching under the material.

"No," he said.

She ignored him, releasing his tumescence.

"Maggie."

"Let me." She had touched him this way before, holding him in her hand, stroking. He had made a sound at the back of his throat, the way he was doing now. "Come into me," she said. "Just like before."

Connor was no match against her siren's call. She was innocence unraveled, and in her feminine heart she was all-desiring. His hands curved over her hips, lifting her. She guided him into her slowly, drawing out his entrance until he jerked his hips and made her take all of him.

She cried out, a breathy little sound that Connor didn't mistake for pain. His hands moved to her tender breasts, caressing them as she began to move against him. She didn't close her eyes this time, watching his hands instead as they slid across her skin, wishing, as he did, that more moonlight filtered between the overhanging boughs. The shadow of his movements and the calloused, slightly abrasive touch of his fingertips caused ripples of heat to spread through her.

Maggie felt the spiral of mounting pleasure. Connor's hands slid to her hips again as his own climax neared, his fingers pressing against her skin. She leaned forward, her breath coming in short gasps again. He guided her, watching, gauging the rise and intensity of her need, until he felt himself give way and could only react selfishly, jerking against her as pleasure spilled out of him, along with his seed.

A moment later, when he touched her intimately, Maggie slipped over the edge, climaxing hard as joy seemed to shatter her. She held onto him, said his name in a ragged, breathy sigh, then collapsed against him. He turned her so they could stretch out comfortably on the bed of pine needles, the curve of her buttocks cradled against his groin.

He kissed her neck, nuzzled her. Maggie pulled at the open throat of her camisole, trying to cover her breasts. "No," he said. "Leave it." One of his hands cupped the underside of her breast.

"But I have to get back to the cabin." Her protest wasn't said with much conviction. She added rather helplessly, "Dancer's tea."

"There's time," he said. "We've been gone this long. He'll understand."

"He'll know?" she asked.

Connor smiled. Their clothes were scattered to kingdom come; what they still wore was in disarray. Maggie's lips were swollen from his kisses, her hair sprinkled with pine needles, and he could still feel the heat from her flushed body. "I think he'll know," he said. "Are you sorry?"

"Not sorry," she said. "A little embarrassed." Now that the haze of desire was fading, Maggie could admit to herself that her embarrassment ran deep. "It was like this the first time we were together, wasn't it?" Her question wasn't really a question because she felt the answer in her bones, across the expanse of her skin, as if memory had seeped to a level below her consciousness. Connor's nearness, their posture, was familiar to her. His hand at her breast was not alarming, but comforting.

"Very much like this," he said, thinking of the intense desire that had existed between them.

"If I *had* been a whore," she said quietly, cautiously, "would you have come to see me again?"

He hesitated. The question was much more complicated than she thought and required something more than a simple yes or no. His hesitation cost him a chance to reply.

"I see," she said, starting to rise.

"You're assuming the answer's no," he said. He reached for her but she eluded his grasp. He sat up, righting the fly of his jeans as Maggie drew her camisole together and began to look around for her overblouse.

"Yes, I'm assuming that. Are you telling me I'm wrong?"

"No."

"Well then?" She stood and brushed off her skirt. The overblouse was caught in one of the boughs and she yanked it free.

"You're offended," he said.

That gave Maggie pause. She held the blouse in front of her. Reason asserted itself slowly. She sighed and smiled faintly, derisively, mocking herself. "I'm sorry. It was a stupid question. I shouldn't have asked."

Connor got to his feet and picked up his shirt and vest. "I wouldn't have returned because I would have been afraid," he told her. He wasn't looking at her but he felt her stillness. "I was angry that night . . . restless . . ." He remembered his winnings at the poker table. "And full of selfish pride. What I wanted wasn't meant to be personal. And I wouldn't have wanted it to be. I would have stayed away for the rest of my time in New York."

She opened her mouth to say something but he turned then and looked at her. A shaft of moonlight touched his face and his eyes were sharp, the blackness intense.

"And I would have spent the rest of my life thinking about you." Ignoring her sharp intake of breath, he shrugged into his shirt, tucking in the tails, then slipped into his vest. "That's what I would have done if you'd been a whore," he said. His voice was harsh as he began to shrug off his vulnerability. "I sure as hell wouldn't have married you."

Maggie flinched a little at his tone. "You sound as though you still regret it."

This time his hesitation was purposeful and he didn't bother explaining it, letting her think what she would. "Let's go," he said.

She didn't move. "You got what you wanted out of this marriage," she reminded him.

"Didn't you?" he asked. "You got your escort west. You've learned what Dancer could teach you. Or was there something else you wanted that I don't know about?"

"Yes," she said, her chin rising slightly. "But I got that, too." She began to walk past him, but he stepped in front of her, not touching her, just blocking her path. "I wanted a name for my baby." This time when she moved around him he didn't try to stop her.

Connor followed Maggie to the cabin, but at a slower pace. By the time he arrived she was serving Dancer the white willow tea. The prospector was pale, sweat beading the unscarred portion of his face. Maggie's own face was devoid of expression as she pointed to the wash basin. She made her wishes known with a brief gesture. Connor crossed the cabin and wet a cloth, returning to the bed to give it to her.

"He's fevered," she said.

"Ain't nothin'," Dancer said as she wiped his brow. "It's got to be expected with a break like mine."

"I shouldn't have left you," she said. "It won't happen again."

"Now, girl, don't go sayin' things like that."

"I mean it, Dancer. I'm not leaving you." She removed the empty mug from his hands and placed it on the table. When Dancer was lying comfortably again she began to bathe his face.

Connor brought the wash basin to her, then went to the loft and began arranging the bedclothes. He called down to Dancer. "Do you have extra blankets up here? Maggie steals the covers."

"In the trunk," Dancer said, grinning lopsidedly at Maggie.

"Just throw them down here," she said, glancing toward the loft. "I'll sleep on the floor."

Connor peered over the edge. "Like hell," he said pleasantly and returned to his work. Opening the trunk, he found a stack of blankets. He pulled out two and snapped them over the mattress. Dancer's bed was nothing more than a straw-filled tick spread out over the floor, but Connor smoothed it out, tucked in the blankets, and plumped the goose feather pillows. It was when he started to shut the trunk lid that an envelope caught his eye.

He recognized it immediately. It was addressed to Maggie and her name was scrawled in his handwriting. He didn't have to open it to know what it contained. Nearly two months ago he'd sent Buck to Dancer's to deliver the divorce documents for Maggie's signature. He thought the papers had gone on to Denver by now.

He opened the envelope and pulled out the papers. There was only one signature on any of them: his. He slipped the documents back inside and put the folded envelope in his rear pocket. It was something they'd have to discuss but he doubted she was any more prepared to talk about it now than he.

Connor leaned over the loft again. He saw that Dancer was sleeping and Maggie had moved to the broken rocker. "Turn back the lamps, Maggie. It's time to come to bed. I want to get to the Double H before noon tomorrow."

"I'm not going to stop you," she said.

"No, but Dancer's going to hold us up a little."

"Us?"

He nodded. "You and me. We're leaving in the morning." He made a circling motion with his finger. "All three of us. And if you want to discuss it, you'll do it up here. I'm going to bed."

Chapter Twelve

Connor held the ladder steady as Maggie climbed to the loft. He helped her over the edge. "You managed that rather gracefully," he said.

"Don't lie. I'm as big as a cow and twice as clumsy." She crawled onto the mattress, dragging her nightshift with her. "I can't get up and down that ladder all night long," she told him. "You'll have to see to Dancer when he needs more of the tea."

"Precisely what I had in mind. You need your rest." He fiddled with the loft's single oil lamp, adjusting the wick until there was only a suggestion of a flame. Darkness gave Maggie the privacy she craved. "Do you want help with your buttons?" he asked.

"No," she said shortly. "You undressed me once tonight. That was enough."

"You'll understand if I think otherwise."

She didn't understand. "I thought you didn't want anything else to do with me," she said stiffly.

"I never said that."

Maggie started to argue but an abrupt, wide yawn took the wind out of her sails.

"Bedtime," Connor said, pulling off his shirt. He turned back the lamp the rest of the way and crawled onto the mattress. The straw crackled. Maggie finished putting on her nightshift and followed him. She turned on her side, drawing her legs upward in a position that was comfortable for her in her pregnant state. When Connor curled against her, fitting his contours to hers, she didn't push him away. His chest and legs were actually a welcome support against her back and thighs.

"The tea has already been separated into doses," she told him, stifling another yawn. "You can give it to Dancer cold every four hours. It's on the table beside him."

"I'll take care of it."

"Don't break your leg going up and down the ladder."

He chuckled, his breath ruffling her hair. "You sure are bossy." He made the point with a certain amount of affection.

"I'm not going anywhere with you in the morning."

This time he didn't respond. He slipped his arm around her and closed his eyes. He felt her stiffen, then relax. In minutes they were both racing toward pleasant dreams.

By noon the following day Maggie found herself on a horse headed in the direction of the Double H. She hardly knew how it had come to pass. The best explanation she could have offered was that Connor Holiday simply didn't take no for an answer. Throughout the morning he had chosen to ignore her rather than discuss it. He simply began packing supplies and clothing on Dancer's mule and their mounts. Since they had no wagon for Dancer, he built a travois and hitched it to the prospector's horse. Dancer, confined to the bed, kept asking Maggie to fetch his shotgun so he could kill the bastard. She noticed Connor had the good sense to watch her out of the corner of his eye as if she could be tempted to do it. There were moments when she thought it would have served him right.

She supposed she could have dug in her heels and absolutely refused to leave but Connor's high-handed tactics made it unwise. After he had everything packed, he picked Dancer up and carried him to the travois. Maggie, if she was really going to take care of the prospector until his leg mended, had little choice but to follow. Her herbs and medicines might have been another sticking point, but Connor had carefully packed all of the jars and bottles she had collected and prepared with Dancer's help. He had even gone to the garden to take fresh plants. Connor promised to send one of his hands the following day for the items they couldn't take with them.

Maggie noticed that he had everything very well planned, a fact she mentioned several times. Connor was right to note that her observation was more suspicious than complimentary. He merely responded with an enigmatic smile that suited his dark and distant expression.

They followed the stream north, veering left each time it forked. Connor stopped frequently, as much for Maggie's comfort as Dancer's, and he kept the pace slow. Though he had said he wanted to reach the Double H by noon, Maggie realized he had only used that to move them along. Except for the acknowledgement that she and Dancer needed to rest, Maggie thought her husband approached their journey with the same single-mindedness he might have had for a cattle drive.

It was the middle of the afternoon by the time they arrived at the threshold of the valley. Connor held his horse and let Maggie draw up to his side. He said nothing. His ranch would rise or fall in her estimation on its own merit.

Maggie had no expectations concerning the Double H. She had never thought she would see it and, in truth, had avoided thinking about it. Now, standing at the gateway to the valley, she understood that anything she could have imagined would not have been grand enough for what confronted her. It quite simply took her breath away.

The colors of the earth were rich, the colors of the sky, bright. Hues of green defined as emerald, jade, and pine shifted and blended when the wind chased a shadow across the hillside. Blue and white were the only colors in the sky. There was no hint of gray at the edge of the puffed clouds or on the horizon. In the distance, peaks rose sharply, their white caps glinting in the sunshine. Where the stream widened and water rushed over stones and fallen logs, diamond droplets sprayed in all directions.

The ranch house spread out over the land as if it *were* part of the land. It didn't rise up with the majesty of the surrounding mountains, but held to the earth with its stone foundation and pine walls. Cattle and horses ignored the boundaries of the corral and were scattered throughout the valley. A rider moving along the western rim saw them and waved. Connor raised his hand in acknowledgement. "That's Luke," he told Maggie.

She barely heard him. "It's nothing like Dancer's place," she said, her voice awed.

Connor smiled, but it was Dancer himself who answered. "Hell, girl, Connor's privy is bigger than my cabin."

It was an exaggeration, but from what Maggie could see, not much of one. "Is all this yours?" she asked Connor.

"It is now," he said, pride and satisfaction mingling in his tone. "My grandfather came out here when Pike was exploring the Louisiana Purchase in '06. He was the youngest man on the expedition. He broke away to marry one of the Indian guides and against everyone's advice, decided to make this his home. Most of what he learned about ranching my grandmother taught him. They captured wild horses in the canyons to begin their stud. They farmed for their daily existence and traded with the Indians for supplies. There was no market for what they were doing. He did it because there was pleasure in it, he said, and he suspected that some day the rest of civilization would find him again, and then he'd be ready."

Connor's hand swept the valley. "He was still out here forty years later when Fremont came through to map the territory. My grandmother was dead by then but he had three sons and a daughter to help him run the ranch."

Maggie was doing some mental calculations. "Your father was part of Fremont's group, wasn't he?"

Connor nodded. "My uncles took off when the Fremont expedition moved on, but Rushton stayed behind. He married my mother the same year and I was born a few years after that."

"Just about the time gold was discovered in California."

"That's right." His smile changed to a grin. "Civilization didn't exactly catch up with Old Sam Hart then, but it sure did move through here. This land has one of the best passes through the Park Range."

"Which is why Rennie was interested in it for Northeast Rail."

Dancer snorted, drawing attention to himself on the travois. "Y'all got the rest of your life to jaw about family history. As for me, damned if I ain't tired bein' dragged behind a bad-mannered horse what swats me with his tail every twenty feet. Can't even see what you're talkin' about, only see where we been. Ain't the same thing," he grumbled. "Ain't the same thing at all."

"I guess we should be moving along," Connor said, winking at Maggie. He saw that she was trying to hide a smile behind her hand.

He thought it was a good sign that they were starting their trek across Holiday land sharing something like laughter.

By the time they reached the ranch house Luke had left the ridge to join the other hands in greeting them. Connor helped Maggie down from her horse and made the introductions. He noticed all the men studiously avoided looking at his wife's swollen abdomen as if they thought he still hadn't accepted the idea of fatherhood.

Maggie leaned on Connor for support as he led her up the porch steps and into the house. In spite of the frequent stops, her legs weren't too steady on solid ground. Just inside the door, Connor actually picked her up. "But I want to look around," she protested. Behind her she could hear Dancer grumbling more loudly as Ben and Buck tried to help him off the travois.

"You can look around," Connor said, "but you'll do it like this."

"If you're going to order me around, we're not going to get along."

"I'll risk it," he said dryly.

Maggie noticed he was smirking. The half-grin transformed his face, making him seem more mischievous than dangerous, and on top of that, more handsome than he had any right to be. She simply stared at him.

"Something wrong?" he asked.

She blinked. "No," she said rather breathily. "Lead on."

His grin deepened. "All right. Through here is the parlor." He stepped through a wide archway leading from the hall. Fringed area rugs were scattered on the hardwood floor. The furniture was pine, plain and serviceable, but crafted by skilled hands. Overstuffed cushions, covered in fabrics woven in the same colors as the valley, were placed on the furniture frames to make comfortable seats. The fireplace had a thick wooden mantel set into the stone and there were photographs in handmade frames crowding the surface.

Connor stepped out of the room and crossed the hallway. "This is my study," he said. He turned slowly so she could see the built-in shelves lined with leather bound books. "In my grandfather's day this was a bedroom and the parlor was a kitchen. Even when my mother was a little girl there weren't enough books west of the Mississippi to fill shelves like these. Most of them began arriving after the gold rush. Travelers would leave one or two as payment for a night's lodging on our land. Later, after my father took off for New York, he'd send a crate of books for Christmas or my birthday. When Old Sam was alive we kept them in the attic because he didn't like much of anything Rushton did. I converted this bedroom into a study after my grandfather died."

He drew back out of the room and continued down the hall, showing her the bedroom that Dancer would use, the dining room, kitchen, and at the rear of the house, the large bedroom where Connor slept. "This used to be several small bedrooms but I didn't need them all so Ben helped me take out the walls."

Maggie wished he had left them up. "I didn't expect your house would be so large."

"This ranch house has been changing since my grandfather settled here and laid the first stones. Every few years something gets added or altered." Connor carried Maggie over to the large bed and set her on the colorful quilt. "Old Sam used to say his wanderlust vanished the moment he saw this valley. He planted himself here and never thought about living anywhere else." He sat on the edge of the bed and took Maggie's straw hat from her hands, placing it on a chair. "Is there anything I can get you?"

She shook her head. "I'm fine."

"Then I'm going to help unload our bags while you nap."

"I'm not tired," she said.

"Liar. You were practically asleep in the saddle." He reached for the light cotton blanket folded at the foot of the bed. "Lie down and I'll put this over you."

She did as he suggested, thinking she was entirely too compliant. She supposed it was because she *was* tired. "We still have a lot to talk about, Connor."

"But we don't have to do it right now." After he covered her, he leaned over and kissed her on the forehead.

"And you're entirely too familiar."

This time he placed his palm over her abdomen and patted lightly. "I'm your husband."

"That's one of the things we have to talk about."

It seemed to Connor that it was as good a time to leave as any. "I'll wake you for dinner," he said and got out of the room before Maggie could object.

As it happened Maggie was up in time to prepare dinner. No one suggested that she do it; in fact, the kitchen was empty when she started, but no one asked her to stop. Connor, when he first came upon her, looked as if he might tell her to go back to resting, then he lifted the lid to the stew pot, sniffed, and seemed to think better of it. Maggie noticed that soon after Connor left the kitchen there was a veritable parade of ranch hands through the back door.

They came on different pretexts. Ben showed her a burn on his finger from a shower of sparks in the forge. Patrick limped in to sit at the kitchen table while he shook a few stones loose from his boot. Buck said he was looking for the hat he'd left behind when he helped bring in Dancer's belongings. Luke asked for a drink of water from the pump.

Maggie saw to each of their needs, enjoying the brief chance for conversation. She also noticed, however, that to a man they sidled up to the stove and lingered next to the stew pot, taking in the aroma of carrots, onions, potatoes, and meat simmering in its own juices. Luke stayed long enough to help her cut out the biscuits and get the oven ready.

When the kitchen got too warm for comfort, Maggie joined Dancer on the front porch. Connor had taken a cot outside and let the prospector stretch out on it. It was, in Dancer's words, better than bein' cooped up like some damn chicken.

"Is there anything I can get you?" she asked before she sat down. Dancer merely pointed to the porch step and gave her a firm look. She sat. Her eyes were drawn to the corral where Connor was leaning against the top rail talking to Buck and Patrick. A stallion the color of smoke was pacing off the length of the corral, shooting nervous glances in the direction of the men. "What are they doing?" she asked.

"Decidin' whose turn it is to take a fall," said Dancer, chuckling. "Buck's gone down twice and Patrick just kissed the dirt for the third time. Can't say when I've had a better time doin' nothin' but watchin' a couple of fools try to outsmart an ornery animal."

"If they're smart they'll get Connor to take a turn," she said dryly.

Dancer's gleeful, high-pitched laughter gave the horse a start and the three men glanced in the direction of the porch. "You'd like that, wouldn't you," he asked, slapping his good leg.

Smiling, Maggie waved at the men and said through her teeth, "I'd very much like to see Connor Holiday take a good swift kick in the—"

"Looks like you'll get the chance," Dancer said gleefully. "There he goes now."

Maggie's smile vanished. She sat up straighter, perching on the edge of the step as Connor approached the stallion. She could see that he was talking to the horse but couldn't hear what he was saying. Not that it mattered, she thought, because she knew Connor's tone was more important than his actual words. It was easy to imagine the gentle, calming cadence of his voice. She knew first hand how soothing it could be. It was a little galling to realize he probably practiced that whiskey-soft cadence breaking mares. It was something to remember the next time she heard those same tones being whispered near her ear.

"I hope that horse pitches him over the fence," she told Dancer.

He chuckled at her lie—even in profile he could see the anxiety in Maggie's face.

Maggie watched as Buck helped steady the skittish animal while Connor mounted. The ranch hand managed to clear a safe distance before the stallion tried to unseat its rider. Connor used only one hand to hold on, balancing himself with the other. His body met the rise and fall of the horse's frantic attempts to throw him. Buck and Patrick yelled encouragement. Dancer whooped his enjoyment. Maggie simply held her breath.

The stallion snorted and bucked, kicking up dust and clumps of dirt. Connor's hat fell on the ground and was trampled. Buck and Patrick vaulted the corral as the horse charged the fence then ran the perimeter of the rails. Connor swayed in the saddle, bounced and jolted by the stallion's arching, but managed to stay in his seat.

"Damn me if his teeth ain't rattled," Dancer said.

Maggie came to her feet as Connor was dipped dangerously to one side. He righted himself momentarily, took the next attempt to throw him nearly standing in the stirrups, then was pitched head over heels as the stallion abruptly ground to a halt. Maggie was already running in the direction of the corral as Connor made his ignominious somersault from the saddle. Patrick opened the gate for her.

Maggie dropped to her knees beside Connor as he was trying to pick himself up. "Don't you dare move," she said, placing her hand at the center of his back.

Groaning, Connor obligingly collapsed again. He felt her hands moving along his shoulders and arms, at the back of his neck, then along his legs. He knew nothing was broken but he let Maggie discover that for herself. Connor tucked one gloved hand under his cheek and stole a glance in Maggie's direction. She was worrying her lower lip, her face pale. Connor realized she wasn't merely concerned, she was scared.

"I'm probably going to live," he told her, trying to inject a note of humor.

Maggie sat back on her haunches and glared at him. "No, you're not," she said stiffly. "I'm going to kill you." Behind her, one of the hands snickered. She ignored him, getting to her feet. She brushed herself off, turned her back on Connor, and marched off in the direction of the house.

Watching her go, Connor sat up slowly. He took the trampled hat that Buck handed him and beat it against his thigh, shaking off the dust and making a half-hearted attempt at reshaping it.

"Whooo-eee," Buck said under his breath. "Look at her go. She sure is mad at you."

Connor didn't look at all bothered. He was actually grinning. "I know."

"You had your face in the sod that time," Patrick said.

The stallion had ambled to the far corner of the corral. Connor's glance was a mixture of gratefulness and respect. He got up, shook himself out, and dared a quick look toward the house. The screen door was swinging closed behind Maggie. "This time I think it was worth it," he said. In a sweeping motion he placed his hat back on his head and jerked his thumb toward the stallion. "Your turn."

Patrick rubbed his chin with the back of his hand, frowning. "Bet she doesn't come runnin' to check my bones," he grumbled.

Buck laughed but Connor said seriously, "You better hope she doesn't."

Patrick shook his head and walked off in the direction of the stallion, muttering, "Hard to tell which one of them has it worst."

Maggie was subdued at dinner. The conversation went on around her and she only listened with half an ear as Buck and Patrick regaled everyone with a recounting of Connor's fall and Patrick's subsequent success with the stallion. She was complimented several times on her stew and biscuits and she accepted the accolades rather absent-mindedly, her thoughts clearly elsewhere.

When the men pushed their chairs away from the table and stretched, Maggie began to clear.

"Luke and Buck will do it," Connor said, stopping her by placing a hand lightly on her wrist.

"I don't mind," she said.

He shook his head. "It's their turn."

Luke was already on his feet, pulling Buck up with him. "Connor's right. It's our turn."

Maggie looked at the two men skeptically. Buck didn't seem to know anything about it being his turn. His sudden enthusiasm appeared to have something to do with Luke's elbow in his ribs. Maggie surprised herself by not calling attention to that fact. "Excuse me, then," she said quietly. Connor's hand slipped from her wrist and Maggie left the kitchen.

She settled in Connor's study. The clatter and laughter from the kitchen was subdued as she closed the door, ceasing to exist once she was alone with her thoughts.

It occurred to her that she could love him. The thought both thrilled and frightened her and turned her stomach inside out. She felt weak and trembly and mocked herself for both. She told herself to be sensible, that she had no real understanding of her own feelings and could not hope to know Connor's. There was no indication that he returned any finer feeling at all and, Maggie realized with sudden insight, it probably didn't matter. Whatever she felt, Maggie knew it wasn't conditional, dependent upon what he thought about her or what feelings he might have for her.

Out of the corner of her eye Maggie saw a movement on the porch. She looked up from the unopened book in her lap and watched Connor cut across the front yard and head toward the stable. She set aside her book and went to the window. After a few minutes she saw him leave on his horse and suddenly, unexpectedly, she felt a wave of incredible loneliness.

Maggie laid her hand on her abdomen, smoothing her smock over the curve of her belly. She stroked absently, watching Connor ride across the valley until he disappeared into the forest of pines, turning away long after she lost sight of him.

Night had fallen by the time Connor returned. The hands had

gone to the bunk house and Dancer had retired to his room. Maggie was in the kitchen heating water at the stove. A copper-lined hip bath had been pulled close to the pump but in spite of its nearness to the source, and in spite of Maggie's caution, puddles of water dotted the floor.

Connor was too surprised to say anything immediately. Then he was too intrigued. He stood in the doorway and watched, waiting for Maggie to notice him. Steam from the boiling water had flushed her face and created a rosy sheen across her cheeks and brow. Tendrils of hair curled damply at the nape of her neck and her temples. Her skin was glowing. She was humming softly to herself, a lullaby, he thought, and her mouth was curved in a tender smile. He wondered if she was thinking about the baby, then decided she couldn't be. She wouldn't have been prepared to lift another kettle filled with hot water if that were the case.

Maggie wrapped a towel around the handle of the kettle and got ready to swing it toward the hip bath.

"Don't you dare," Connor said.

Maggie nearly scalded herself as she dropped the towel and bumped the stove with her hip. She placed the back of one hand against her forehead and offered Connor a faint smile. "You scared me," she said. "I saw you headed this way but I didn't hear you come in."

"What do you think you're doing?" he asked.

Maggie's smile faltered, reflecting her embarrassment. "I thought it was obvious. I'm preparing a bath."

"That much *is* obvious," he said dryly. "What I want to know is why you're doing it alone."

"Then that's what you should have asked," she said primly. She picked up the towel and wrapped it around the handle again. Before she could lift the kettle Connor was beside her and taking it from her hands.

"For God's sake, let me do that. You'll hurt yourself." He poured the water in the bath. "You should be more careful with the baby."

Maggie was tempted to drown him. Instead she took the empty kettle and placed it in the sink. "I'm fine," she said, rounding on him, hands on her hips. "And the baby's fine. A little hard work hasn't hurt either one of us." She brushed past him. "I'm going to bed."

"What about your bath?" he asked.

"*My* bath?" she asked, pausing in the doorway. "I drew that for you."

Connor recognized a parting shot when he heard one. He didn't attempt to call her back or follow her. He was managing, with disturbing frequency, to rile Maggie. It was not entirely intended.

Shaking his head ruefully, Connor stripped off his clothes and tossed them on the floor. He sank into the tub slowly, drawing his knees toward his chest. Water lapped against the sides. He scooped a few handfuls of hot water and sluiced his shoulders, then he dipped his head in the water, thoroughly wetting his dark hair and shook off the excess with the natural abandon of a soaked puppy.

From the doorway, Maggie laughed.

"I thought you were going to bed," Connor said, looking up in surprise. He raked his wet hair with his fingers and gave her a sheepish grin.

"I was, then I remembered you didn't have any towels." She placed two on the table where Connor could reach them and started to go. She stopped when she felt Connor grab a handful of her dress and tug. Maggie looked over her shoulder. "Yes?"

"Are you still mad at me?" he asked.

"Irritated," she said. "Annoyed. Frustrated."

"But mad?" His tone was hopeful.

"No," she said after a moment, sighing slightly. "Not mad." As far as Maggie was concerned it wasn't a good sign. In the space of a single evening, indeed, in the span of a few hours, she had gone from concluding that she *could* love him, to the realization that she probably *did* love him.

Connor's fist opened. He dropped the skirt of Maggie's gown. "I don't suppose you might consider scrubbing my back?"

"I might," she said, "if you don't think it will hurt the baby."

Connor winced, understanding at last what he'd done to arch her back. "I'm sorry," he offered belatedly.

Maggie shrugged. She knelt beside the tub and took the brush and soap he handed her.

"I really *am* sorry," he repeated.

She began to lather his back as he leaned forward. "I wouldn't do anything to harm my baby," she said softly. "I didn't think I would have to say that to you. I thought you would know that now."

"I'm not used to it yet," he said. "The idea of you having this baby

. . . it's still new to me. You've had a lot of time to become accustomed to it. I've only known since yesterday."

Perhaps it was asking a lot, she thought, for Connor to accept that she meant to be a mother, that she had always meant to be one. She had done quite a bit to make him think differently and she quietly admitted as much to him.

"Why?" he asked.

Maggie's scrubbing slowed. "I didn't know you," she said. "And I didn't know what you would do. You may have wanted to marry me for all the wrong reasons."

Turning his head a little, Connor gave Maggie a dry, skeptical look. "Do you think we married for all the right ones?"

She tapped him lightly on the back with the scrub brush, just hard enough to let him know what she thought of his comment. "You know what I mean," she said. "The marriage would have been because of the baby and there would have been no agreement to end it." She didn't mention that he hadn't sent the divorce papers to her.

He didn't mention that she hadn't signed the papers he'd sent.

Maggie began scrubbing again. "You were right when you called me selfish," she said. "I didn't want anyone to stand in the way of me becoming a doctor. That included my family and my baby and, most especially, you."

"And now?"

It was a moment before she answered. "Now I'm here. I still don't know what it means."

Connor reached behind him and took the brush from her hands. He twisted in the tub so he could see her better. "What do you want it to mean?"

Show some courage, she told herself. Tell him that you're thinking you might want to be his wife, that your insides are all fluttery with the possibility of loving him. Maggie's eyes dropped away from his and she shrugged. She called herself a coward.

Connor let the silence stretch between them. Finally he said, "It's all right, Maggie. I don't know what it should mean either."

Not sparing him a glance, she nodded.

He touched the back of her hand which was resting on the tub rim. "Go on to bed," he said. "I'll only be a few minutes."

Maggie felt awkward as she got to her feet. She dropped the soap back in the water.

"Thank you for the bath," he said as she turned to go.

"I thought you might be sore from your fall."

"I was."

She hesitated. "I made a liniment." She pointed to a brown bottle on the table. "I gave some to Buck and Patrick but I saved enough for you. It would be better if you put it on while you're still warm from your bath."

"Thank you. I will." He watched her go, then leaned back in the tub, stretching as much as he was able. For a moment, he thought, Maggie looked as if she might offer to put the liniment on him herself. Connor closed his eyes, smiling. It was a notion worth pursuing.

Once she was in the bedroom, Maggie quickly changed into her nightshift. She turned back the bedside oil lamp until only a flicker remained, then climbed in bed and pulled the quilt and comforter up to her neck.

"I know you're not asleep," Connor said as he came into the room. He was carrying the liniment and had one towel hitched around his waist. The other was rolled and hanging from his neck to catch water dripping from his hair. When Maggie didn't open her eyes he approached the bed more quietly. She didn't stir. "Maggie?" he inquired softly. There was no response. "I'll be damned." She really had fallen asleep.

His smile rueful, Connor sat on the edge of the bed and uncorked the bottle of liniment. Expecting an odor strong enough to make him flinch, he was pleasantly surprised by Maggie's concoction. He rubbed it on his arms and shoulders, then his legs. It burned pleasantly into his skin. He rubbed a little into the back of his neck, taking his time in the hopes that Maggie would wake and offer to help. Thinking about her hands on his naked flesh made it a difficult idea to abandon. He kept glancing over his shoulder to see if he could catch her playing possum.

Sighing, Connor stoppered the bottle and set it aside. He dried his hair more thoroughly, then lifted the covers and slid into bed beside Maggie. Yanking at the towel around his waist, he pitched it in the direction of a chair, then extinguished the oil lamp. Connor gave Maggie a small nudge and she obligingly turned in her sleep, presenting him with her back. He curved his body against hers, spoon fashion, and groaned softly as she snuggled into him.

He fell asleep even while he was thinking it was going to be a long, torturous night.

In the course of any given day over the next four weeks, Maggie found herself watching Connor. Her eyes welcomed him as he approached the house at meal times and followed him when he left to do chores. She was discovering that she liked the way he walked, liked the confidence in his long-legged stride and the manner in which he sprinted up the porch steps to be the first one in the door for dinner.

He was a leaner, too, she noticed. He leaned against the corral rails, as if he were indifferent to what was going on. He leaned in doorways, the whip-cord, muscular strength of him postured casually in a frame of light. He leaned against the kitchen table, one hip resting on the edge, his legs stretched out before him, while he nursed the last mug of coffee after breakfast. At night, when everyone had gathered on the front porch to trade stories or listen to Ben play his harmonica, Connor leaned against the rough-hewn supporting columns and tapped his foot lightly against the floor.

Maggie liked to watch him ride. Sometimes she would walk outside for no other reason than to catch a glimpse of Connor and Tempest weaving in and out of the trees on the mountainside. Sometimes horse and rider would tear across the valley with the wild unpredictability of the wind itself, Connor bending forward in the saddle, urging Tempest on, man and animal becoming a singular blur in the sunlight or as dusk fell.

He was a hard worker. Most mornings he was the first one up and often the last one in bed. He inspected the fences, counted the herd, rescued trapped cows, pitched hay, tended the late fall garden, and mucked out the stalls. There was nothing his hired hands did that he wasn't willing to do beside them. He had responsibility for everyone and everything and he took it all seriously, going over the accounts, seeing to the safety of his men, planning improvements for the ranch.

She learned he liked the smell of bacon frying but rarely ate more than a single strip, but he could put away half a dozen pancakes before the coffee was brewed. He liked his potatoes mashed, strawberry jam on his bread, and roast beef well done. He could eat two apple dumplings but passed on rhubarb pie. He seldom added salt at the table but Maggie could barely keep enough pepper ground to suit him.

At night he slept beside her, their bodies touching but never joined. Sometimes she'd wake in the middle of the night and discover he was gone. She would find him in the study, reading. He always invited her to join him but she never did, respecting the peace he had been searching for.

His dark eyes, when they rested on her, were no longer entirely remote or completely unreadable. She began to know the flicker that signaled amusement, the warmth that meant humor. She knew when he was suspicious, when he was worried, and when he had his temper on a short leash. She loved to hear him laugh.

And she wished he would kiss her.

Maggie was sitting at the table, arms raised and elbows on the edge, supporting her chin on the back of her hands. Flour dotted her fingers and cheeks and dusted her hair where she had pushed it back at the temples. The pie crust in the pan in front of her was fluted on only one side, forgotten as she stared off into space.

She didn't so much as blink as the back door opened and closed and Connor stepped into the kitchen.

"Maggie?"

At the sound of her name, her elbows slipped off the table's edge, her head jerked, and her chin fell. Her cheeks filled with color at having been caught daydreaming. The deeper hue was the result of *what* she had been dreaming. "I wish you wouldn't sneak up on me, Connor."

His eyes widened a bit and one side of his mouth rose in a quirky grin. "I said your name three times."

"Oh," she said, deflated. "Well, what did you want?"

"Luke says there's a storm heading this way. He's not usually wrong about these things."

Maggie nodded. She appreciated the warning though she wished she'd been able to keep her fear of thunderstorms a secret. "I'll be fine," she said. "You can go back to whatever you were doing." When he didn't move, she asked, "Is there something else? Are you afraid the stream's going to flood?"

Connor rested one hip on the edge of the table and brushed a dusting of flour from Maggie's hair with his fingertips. "It's not that kind of storm," he said. "Snow's coming. Lots of it, according to Luke."

"Lots of it?" she asked hopefully. "You mean three or four inches?"

He found her eagerness amusing and naive. "I mean three or four feet."

Maggie's brows came together as her eyes darted to the window. The sky was solidly gray and the wind was picking up. She had been so wrapped in her own thoughts that she hadn't even noticed the change. "Feet?"

He laughed. "Yes," he said, tapping the end of her nose. "The miracle is that it's waited this long. Or did you think we were pulling your leg about winter starting in October?"

Since she'd been at the ranch for nearly a month and since the only snow she'd seen had been on the mountain peaks, Maggie had thought exactly that. "Tomorrow's November first," she said.

Connor pretended to wipe his brow. "Thank God we beat the deadline then." He had expected Maggie to smile. When she didn't, and continued to stare gravely out the window, he asked, "What's wrong? I can almost guarantee there won't be any thunder or lightning."

She tore her eyes away from the gathering clouds. "It isn't that," she said, shaking her head. "I supposed I've just finally realized that I'm going to have my baby here. Dancer's hobbling around so well these days that I thought we might leave soon."

"Leave?" Connor had straightened a little at Maggie's reference to the baby as hers, but her next sentence made him stiffen. "What are you talking about? Where did you get the idea that I'd let you leave?"

She started at that, her eyes glittering. "Where did you get the idea that you could stop me?"

The combatants were squared off as Dancer limped into the kitchen on his single crutch. "Never mind me," he said, "I can see there's a storm brewin' here, too." He turned to go back to the parlor.

"Don't go," Connor said. "I have to head back outside and help round up the cattle." He gave Maggie a significant look. "Our discussion isn't over."

*   *   *

Snow started falling just before noon. It came down in small, stinging flakes that swirled across the valley in powerful eddies and obscured the view of the corral from the house. After only two hours there were four inches on the ground and drifts that rose sharply toward the porch. Dancer watched the storm's raging from the parlor window. Maggie paced the length of the house from the kitchen to the front door, peeking out the windows in the bedrooms and study.

Luke and Ben were the first to return from securing strays in the northern end of the property. They were cold and wet with snow, their eyebrows and lashes white enough to make them look like old men, but they only stayed inside long enough to warm their hands around a mug of coffee. They ran rope lines from the ranch house to the bunk house and from there to the privy to keep anyone from straying too far. They equipped the stable and smoke house with a similar lifeline.

Buck and Patrick stumbled in later, clumps of snow dropping from their boots and pantlegs as they stomped around the kitchen trying to get warm. A snow drift had already reached the kitchen windowsill and they took turns sweeping off the porches and steps for Maggie's benefit.

Connor was the last to arrive at the house, only a short time before dinner and only minutes before Luke and Buck were preparing to leave in search of him. He brushed snow from the shoulders of his coat before he shrugged out of it. "Everyone in?" he asked Luke.

"You're the last," Luke said, taking off his own coat and hanging it on a peg beside Connor's. "We were getting worried."

Connor's eyes immediately searched out Maggie. She was taking a pie out of the oven. If Luke was including her among the worried, he had clearly mistaken the situation. "Tempest and I ran into a wolf pack," he said, taking off his hat. "They followed us for a while, trying to get at the stragglers I was bringing in."

Maggie set the apple pie on the window sill to cool. "Ben, would you stir the bean soup?" she asked. "I'm going to lie down." She left the kitchen before anyone could ask about her health.

In her bedroom Maggie took off her shoes and curled in the middle of the bed. When Connor tiptoed in almost an hour later she was still lying in the same position, dry-eyed and wakeful, hugging a pillow to her middle.

Connor put his boots down inside the door and padded over to the bed. "Ben wants you to know that dinner's ready," he said. "He's pretty proud he didn't burn your soup."

"Tell everyone to go ahead without me," she said dully. "I'm not very hungry."

His eyes drifted over her, searching for the cause of her listlessness. "All right," he said finally. He left the room, ate his dinner in silence, and managed to make everyone feel unwelcome at the table. The hired hands retreated to the bunkhouse and Dancer cleared the dishes. Connor pushed away from the table sharply, his favorite dessert largely uneaten. "I'm going to have it out with Maggie," he said.

Dancer shrugged. "Ain't none of my business."

"In case it gets loud, see that it stays that way." He couldn't prove it but he thought the prospector was grinning.

Maggie was sitting up when Connor returned to the bedroom. The pillow she'd been hugging was now supporting the small of her back. She looked quite regal sitting in the center of the bed, her chin thrust forward, her dark red hair coiled smoothly at the back of her head. "You'd better shut the door," she said coolly. "I don't want the others to hear us."

At first Connor thought she had overheard his comment to Dancer about having it out, then he realized that she had come to the same decision independently. "Dancer's cleaning up in the kitchen," he said. "He can't hear us. The others all went back to the bunk house." He pushed the room's sole chair closer to the bed and sat down, propping his feet on the iron rail frame. "Do you want to start?" he asked. "Or shall I?"

She lost her confidence momentarily. "You have something to say?"

He nodded. The change in Maggie's expression let him know that she had been preparing her speech while he was eating dinner. "Quite a few things, actually, but you go ahead. I think you've given it more thought and there's no telling what I'm liable to blurt out."

"Very well, then," she said, feigning composure if not precisely recovering it. "I think we should make some different arrangements in our living situation. I'm not prepared to share this bed or this bedroom another night, and since I can't live in the bunk house with the others, and neither of us wants to put Dancer out of his bed, then you'll have to go."

"I see," he said slowly. "And this new arrangement would be because . . ." He let his voice trail off as he lifted one dark eyebrow in question. When she didn't answer, but only looked away, he asked, "Because of the baby?"

Her head jerked around and she looked at him sharply. "The baby? Why do you think everything has to do with the baby?"

He opened his mouth to answer but she cut him off.

"You don't see me at all anymore, do you? Just me." She pointed to herself. "Separate from this baby. You're afraid if I work too hard or walk too far or sleep too much or sleep too little, I'll hurt the baby. It's never just about me." Tears sparkled in her eyes and she brushed them away impatiently, angry with herself for not being able to keep them back. "I *am* selfish," she said, swallowing a sob. "Sometimes I want it to be just about me."

"It's always about you," he said quietly.

Not certain she had heard him right, she stilled in the middle of wiping away her tears. "What?"

"It's always about you," he repeated. "I just didn't know any other way to say it." He dropped his feet off the iron bed rails and leaned forward in his chair. "Do you really think I don't see you except for the child you're carrying?" He shook his head, not really believing it. "I watch you all the time. I know how many brush strokes you give your hair at night. I know that when you're thinking or anxious or uncertain, you pull in your lower lip and worry it between your teeth. I see the smile you have for Luke in the morning when you serve up his eggs and the patience you have for Dancer when he's being clumsy on his crutch. You're gentle with Buck when he's not quick to get the joke.

"Sometimes I just like to watch your hands when you're talking," he said, smiling faintly. In his mind's eye he could see the graceful turn of her palm as she gestured. "Sometimes I just like to listen to your voice." He shrugged. "I know the arch of your brow, the way your chin comes up when you're angry, and the set of your jaw when you're determined. I know every curve of your body—and I remember the ones that were there before this baby. Whatever you think, it's not true that I don't notice you."

The words spilled out of her before she knew she was going to say them. "But you don't want me anymore."

Connor's eyes narrowed a fraction. "Where do you get that idea?" His voice was husky. "Every night since I brought you to this ranch I've slept with you against me. I have to leave our bed in the middle of the night because sometimes I wake up wanting you so bad I'm shaking with it."

Outside the wind was whistling through the valley, bending the aspen and bowing the pines. The windows rattled in their frames as shards of snow pelted the house. In contrast to nature's sounds, Maggie's tone was hushed. "Then why don't you reach for me?" she asked, struggling to hold his glance. "I would let you. I did at Dancer's."

"I know," he said quietly, partly on a sigh. "But I don't want it to be about need any longer."

"What are you saying? I don't understand."

"Don't you know?" he asked. "The next time I reach for you I want it to be about love."

Chapter Thirteen

"Love?" Maggie asked.

"You don't need me to explain that, do you?"

She shook her head. "You need to know whether or not you can love me," she said softly.

Connor's head tilted to one side, his eyes narrowing slightly as he considered her. "You have the oddest way of looking at things sometimes," he said. His observation was casual, not critical. "I wasn't talking about my feelings at all," he went on. "I was referring to yours. I don't know what to make of you, Maggie. When you didn't sign the divorce papers I—"

"Didn't sign?" she asked, bewildered. "How could I? You didn't send them to Dancer's."

It was like a fist closing over his heart, an icy fist. "I sent them," he said tersely.

"Oh." There was a hollowness in the center of her that kept expanding, as if she were filling up with emptiness. "I thought perhaps you had changed your mind."

"We had an agreement," he said, getting to his feet. "I thought perhaps you had changed yours." Connor crossed the room to the chest of drawers and rooted through two of the middle ones. He pulled out the divorce documents and brought them over to the bed. He handed them to Maggie. "I suppose Dancer has something to answer for," he said. "I found them in a trunk in Dancer's loft when

I was looking for blankets. I thought you'd put them there. Seems I was wrong. Looks like he decided to keep them from you."

Maggie glanced over the papers, her emotions numb. The handwriting blurred in front of her as she blinked back tears. The only other time she had seen Connor's signature was on their marriage certificate. That seemed painfully ironic now. "It's all in order, isn't it?"

"Appears that way."

"You never mentioned that you had these," she said.

"You never mentioned that you missed them."

Maggie smoothed the papers in her lap. The movement helped to hide her trembling hands. "I told Dancer once that you'd honor our agreement. He was probably hiding these from me even then."

"I suppose he has his own ideas about how things should be."

She forced a smile, though the edges of it were sad. "I suppose he does," she said. "It's a good thing we can think for ourselves."

Connor nodded. He watched Maggie finger the edges of the papers, her head bowed. "Maggie?"

"Hmmm?" She didn't look at him.

"What are you going to do?"

She stared at his signature. He had intended to divorce her, just as she'd asked. He hadn't had any second thoughts, never reconsidered it as she'd begun to believe he had. "I guess I need a pen," she whispered.

Connor hesitated a moment, then he turned on his heel and left the room, returning a minute later. He handed her the pen and placed the inkwell on the bedside table.

"I should have something to write on."

There was a book on the dresser. Connor got it for her and slid it on her lap and under the papers.

Maggie twisted the pen in her fingers. She reached for the inkwell, pulled the glass stopper, and dipped her pen. "Signing this right now doesn't mean we're divorced," she said. It was difficult to push the words past the lump in her throat.

"No, it doesn't."

She looked out. Night had turned the window into a black mirror. Her own reflection was all she saw but beyond her shimmering shape she knew nature was drawing a white curtain over the valley. "It's not as if we can take them to Queen's Point tomorrow."

"Probably not until spring."

"And you said it would take another six months after these were returned to the lawyer."

"That's right." Connor sat down on the edge of the bed. He reached for Maggie's chin, cupping it gently in his thumb and forefinger, and lifted. "So what are you saying?"

What *was* she saying, she wondered. She stared at him mutely, trying to read the expression in his reflective eyes.

"If I took back those papers now," he said, "you would always wonder if it was because of the baby."

"Wouldn't it be?"

He shook his head. "It would be because my signature on those documents represents the only promise I ever made that I regret." His hand dropped away from her chin, but he held her eyes. "And I regretted it before I knew you were still carrying my . . . our child. I regretted it when it was just about you."

"But you're giving me these papers now."

"I thought you'd already made your choice about what to do with them. You hadn't. This has to be your decision, Maggie. The terms were yours."

A droplet of ink splattered on the signature page, a dark blue exploding star. Maggie stared at it for a long time before she lowered the pen to the paper.

Connor watched her hand, a certain tightness in his chest. He was not aware he was holding his breath.

Maggie's focus moved from the line where she was supposed to sign to the place where Connor had put his name. "I don't think I knew your middle name was Hart," she said. Then she very deliberately used her pen to obliterate all evidence of his signature. She looked up at him. "I've made my decision."

He took the papers from her, crumpled them in his hands, and pitched them into the far corner of the room. "And I've made mine."

Maggie put the pen and inkwell aside. Her tentative, shyly offered smile brightened her face.

Connor leaned forward and kissed her lightly on the lips. Her breath was soft, sweet. His face was very close to her when he said, "I figure this means I can keep my bed."

The dark centers of her eyes widened. Her lips parted. "I figure it does," she said softly.

"Anything else you want to say to me?" he asked. He kissed the corner of her mouth, then the sensitive spot just below her ear. "Before I kiss you within an inch of your life?"

She liked the sound of that. One of his hands was already at her throat, fingering the buttons of her white overblouse. His fingers slipped inside and touched her skin, skimming the neckline of her chemise. Her flesh tingled with the light passing of his hands. "I love you?" she asked. "Is that what you want to hear?"

"Is that what you want to say?"

Her breath caught as the damp edge of Connor's tongue touched her ear. "It's what I want to say," she said. His mouth pressed gently against her neck. "I love you."

He felt her words vibrate against his lips. She said it again, more loudly this time and he pressed his mouth tightly to her skin as if he could absorb the words and the feeling. After a moment he raised his head. He touched her cheek with the back of his hand. "I didn't want to leave you at Dancer's," he said.

"I know."

He shook his head. "Not because I didn't think you'd survive it," he told her. "Because I loved you then."

Maggie's hands slid up his chest and slipped around his neck. She drew him closer and this time it was her mouth that closed over his.

Their lips pressed, clung. Maggie's fingers threaded in the hair at Connor's nape. She tugged gently, lightly scraping the back of his head with her nails, and absorbed the shudder of his body as he leaned into her. The pillow was removed from the small of her back and flung aside as Maggie was pressed to the mattress. Connor stretched out beside her and pulled at the buttons on her blouse. It parted over her breasts and belly.

He raised his head, breaking the kiss. His mouth touched her again, this time on her jaw, then below it, then along the vulnerable line of her throat. She arched her neck. He placed a kiss in the hollow and felt the vibration of her satisfaction. His mouth went lower, tracing a damp line down her breastbone. The faint stirring of her heart increased. His teeth captured the lace edging of her chemise. He tugged. His fingers pushed at the straps and eased them over her shoulders. He stopped short of revealing her breasts.

His lips wandered over the thin cotton fabric. The material was taut over her hardened nipples. His tongue dampened one. He worried it between his lips. Maggie moaned softly.

Then he heard the breath catch at the back of her throat. It wasn't the sound of pleasure; it was the sound of pain. He lifted his head and swore softly. "I hurt you."

She shook her head, but she was biting her lower lip.

Connor raised himself on one elbow. "Don't lie to me," he said. "Not about this."

Maggie touched his face. "No," she said, willing him to believe her. "You really didn't." Her slight smile was self-mocking. "The baby moved. She's sitting on my spine." The smile vanished as she winced. "And taking my breath away."

Connor helped her sit up. He rolled off the bed, found the pillow and stuffed it behind Maggie's back again. "Better?" he asked.

She hardly knew how to answer. It was true she could breathe again. And the discomfort was gone. But she was miserably frustrated. She looked down at herself, her open blouse, the damp circle on her chemise where her nipple was outlined, then at the swell of her belly.

Connor sat beside her again. "Maggie?"

"There must be something wrong with me," she said.

He had to strain to hear her, she spoke so quietly. His own fear rose and showed in the set of his jaw and the tiny muscle working in his taut cheek. Was she ill? Was it the baby? "What do you mean something's wrong with you?"

"Look at me," she said mournfully.

He was. He couldn't help himself. She drew his attention even when she didn't mean to. He was tantalized by her fragrance as she passed and intrigued when sunlight glinted in her hair. He knew she was approaching when she was still a room away and recognized by her sigh if she was frustrated or wistful. "I like looking at you," he said. "Is there something particular . . . ?"

Her tone was distressed. "I'm pregnant."

Connor's instinct was to laugh but some good sense told him that it wouldn't have been appreciated. His response maintained the gravity he believed the situation required. "Yes, you are."

Maggie continued to stare down at her abdomen. "I'm so ripe I'm ready to burst and I've still got two months and it doesn't seem like I should want you so very much, but I do, so then I wonder if there's something wrong with me that I like it when you touch me, even now that I'm so . . . so . . . , well, you can see how I am, and then I wonder if there was something wrong with me then, at Mrs. Hall's, I mean, when I was sleeping next to you and dreaming that I was touching you and then finding out that I was and not stopping because I liked it." She took a deep breath and risked a glance at Connor.

He stared at her, fascinated.

She sighed. "So I'm very much afraid I might like it too much, that maybe I *am* a whore because no decent woman would have stayed in bed with you at that brothel and I did." Her voice dropped to a husky whisper. "And I did it twice."

Connor touched Maggie under the chin. He leaned his forehead against hers. "We're going to sort this all out," he said softly. "But not right now."

"Not now?" she asked a little breathily.

He shook his head. "Right now we're going to make love."

"We are?"

"It's what we both want."

She nodded, the movement a trifle uncertain. "But—"

"There's nothing wrong with either of us for wanting it."

"There's not?"

He smiled. His lips brushed hers as he spoke. "I'll show you."

Maggie gave herself up to him. His mouth closed over hers and Maggie returned the kiss fully. She felt his fingers nudge the neckline of her chemise lower, then lower still, until her breasts were bared. His palms covered her, stroking gently, raising the flush of heat just beneath her skin. His thumbs spiraled toward her nipples and passed lightly across the hardened tips. This time her indrawn breath was pleasure's gasp.

Connor eased Maggie down on the bed, this time on her side. He reached for the bedside lamp and blew out the flame.

"Thank you," Maggie said quietly as Connor stretched out at her back, curving his body to her contours.

"I would have a hundred lamps in here," he said. "All of them lit." He brushed aside a lock of hair at Maggie's nape and kissed her warm skin. "You're beautiful." His mouth moved along her bare shoulder. "We have too many clothes on," he said softly.

"Mmmm," she hummed her pleasure, pushing back against him

so he cradled her bottom with his groin. She could feel the taut ridge of his fly against her. "Too many clothes."

Neither of them was moved to do anything about it right then. Connor continued to nuzzle Maggie's neck. His arm slipped under hers and curved beneath her breasts. He teased the nipples with his fingertips. The barrier of their clothes was deliciously frustrating.

Up to a point.

Without a word passing between them they knew when that point had been reached. Maggie pushed at her own clothing while Connor released the buttons on his fly. Her skirt was swept to the foot of the bed. His jeans caught the arm of the chair when they were tossed. His shirt and her chemise tangled as they were pitched in unison. Her drawers slipped over one side of the bed. His went to the other.

They came together, curved again on their sides, exertion and excitement making them breathe a little harder, racing their hearts.

Connor's hand slipped between her legs. The heat of her surrounded him. She was damp. His fingers stroked her intimately. She moved against him, her breath catching as his touch radiated fire that flushed her skin. Reaching behind her, she caressed his hip and thigh. She felt him shudder. His breath was warm against her skin.

He came into her from behind, torturing her with the slowness of his entry, stopping her even when she would have pushed against him and taken all of him quickly. She felt filled with him, his body flush to her, his chest against her back, the backs of her thighs soft in contrast to the hardness of his.

His first movements were cautious, a slow rocking rhythm that tested the limits of pleasure. The tiny sounds she made at the back of her throat hinted that it was too much and not yet enough. He whispered in her ear, low and husky, and asked her what she wanted. She didn't answer; she couldn't answer. Words failed her, but she showed him with her body, with movements that were bolder than his.

Excitement built in both of them. They moved in unison, opposing forces with a single goal. He encouraged her in raspy tones that vibrated his chest against her back. Blood rushed in her ears and made a roaring sound that accompanied the slamming of her own heart. She said his name in low, throaty tones that made him want to bury himself in her.

The insistent caress of his hand brought her to the edge. Tension was coiled in every part of her. "Connor," she whispered, beginning to arch. "Please."

He touched her again, driving into her. She gasped, then shuddered, reaching down to hold his hand against her. She felt him withdraw slightly, then fill her again. His rhythm quickened and his stroking became more shallow. She tightened around him as she climaxed, the moist center of her holding him a heartbeat longer before he moved again. His free arm slipped under her. She was secured to him, joined by his arms, by the tangle of their legs, and in the moment by their desire.

Connor buried his face against her neck as his climax brought him up against her hard. It seemed to go on forever, the release and ripple of tension, the suspension of time as pure sensation flooded through him.

His hold on her relaxed slightly, but he didn't let her go. "If you loved me any better," he whispered, "it would kill me." Then on a wishful, youthful note, he added, "But if I could pick the way I want to die . . ."

Her elbow came back and caught him gently in the ribs. His exaggerated groan mingled with her husky laughter. She snuggled against him, liking the weight and strength of him at her back.

His breath parted strands of her auburn hair. "There's nothing wrong you," he said softly. "Not a thing."

"I'm not—"

"Not a thing," he repeated. "Except maybe that you argue with me."

She smiled at that.

He eased out of her and brought the quilt over their bodies as he took up the spooning position again. His arm curved around her. "We'll talk about it later."

"All right," she said. She closed her eyes, stifling a yawn with the back of her hand.

They fell asleep together.

Denver

Ethan Stone was shrugging out of his coat as he walked in the door of his home. Snowflakes dusted the foyer rug briefly, then melted. He hung up his hat and coat, listening for a sound that would indicate the whereabouts of his wife. He heard the oven door close in the kitchen and started in that direction. Two steps forward and he was tripping over a package that had been placed as an obstacle in his path.

"Michael," he yelled, catching himself on the banister spindles before he pitched to the floor. "Are you trying to kill me with this thing?"

She appeared at the end of the hallway. She had a potholder in each hand and her mouth was set seriously. "I just put Madison to bed," she said. "Please don't shout." She disappeared again.

The package was large enough to have held a pair of boots and just about as heavy. Ethan nudged it to one side and continued on his way to the kitchen. "Something smells good," he said, sidling up to his wife as she worked at the stove. He tried to lift the lid on one of the pots but Michael tapped his fingers with a wooden spoon. A dab of brown gravy fell on his knuckles. He sucked it off and pondered for a moment. "Tastes good, too."

Michael's mouth pursed to one side as she gave him a skeptical look.

He leaned over and stole a kiss. Michael's lips parted briefly in surprise. The kiss lingered a moment longer than it might have otherwise. "That tastes better," he said, grinning.

"You're incorrigible."

"And I'm late."

"That, too." Michael pointed to the plates and silverware on the table. "If you'll set, I'll serve."

Ethan laid out the plates and utensils. "Jeb Morgan was drunk again tonight. His wife asked me to lock him up."

Michael looked her husband over, making certain he was still all of a piece. "No bruises this time. Jeb must be getting docile."

Ethan grinned. "Maybe I'm getting more agile."

Serving up the meat and potatoes, Michael's glance was gently disbelieving. "You just tripped over a package the size of a small stump for the third time this week," she reminded him.

He sat down and helped himself to the basket of bread. "If you wouldn't keep putting it in my way . . ."

Michael set the gravy boat and a bowl of succotash on the table. She sat down and bowed her head. Ethan joined her in prayer. When the brief grace was over, she lifted her head and without missing a beat said, "One would think that a federally appointed marshal, especially one who's college educated, would have sense enough to know that when the same package appears in his way on three different occasions, his wife is trying to tell him to do something with it."

Ethan served himself some of the vegetables and passed the bowl to Michael. "What am I supposed to do with it?"

At first Michael looked at him as if she couldn't believe her ears. Then she merely shook her head, sighing. "I told you what to do with it before I started putting it in your way."

He looked at her blankly.

Michael pointed upward. "To the attic," she said. "I want you take it to the attic."

"I'll do it right after dinner." He took a bite of roast beef. "What's in it?"

"You really ought to act a little abashed when you ask that question," she said. "You're making it quite clear that you didn't hear anything I was saying to you last Monday night."

"What was I doing?" he asked.

"Reading the paper."

"Perhaps I was reading one of your articles," he said hopefully, trying to extricate himself from the doghouse.

"I didn't have an article in the *News* that day." She patted the back of his hand. "But that was a good try."

"Thank you." He speared a small, buttered chunk of potato. "So the package contains . . ."

"A black leather bag," she said. "Mother is sending it to Maggie but she wasn't sure of the best way to get it to the Double H."

"We can send it on to Queen's Point."

"I thought of that, but then I got to thinking that the weather was too uncertain this time of year. You *did* notice, I suppose, that it's snowing this evening."

"Jeb Morgan slammed me with a few snowballs when I tried to take him in," he told her dryly. *"I* noticed."

"Then you realize that Maggie's probably snowed in at the ranch. That package is likely to sit in some storage closet at the station until spring. I'll feel better if it's here."

"What's in the bag?"

Michael shrugged. "Mama didn't say and I didn't peek. It looks a little like a doctor's medical bag."

Ethan's dark brows furrowed. "Medical bag? I thought Maggie had put doctoring behind her."

For a moment Michael stared out the kitchen window as if she could see past the curtain of night and falling snow, as if she could see her sister, and more importantly, as if she could see into her sister's mind. "Maggie was always the guarded one," she said softly, looking back at her husband. Her emerald eyes only hinted at the depth of her concern. "But I keep thinking that she hasn't given up the idea completely."

Maggie slipped out of bed and put on her nightgown and robe. It was still relatively early in the evening and her growling stomach reminded her she hadn't had any dinner. She stepped on Connor's thick socks lying on the floor and put them on. They felt comfortable and warm. Slipping quietly out of the bedroom, Maggie padded to the kitchen.

The house was silent. Sometime while she and Connor were napping, Dancer had retired to his own room. The wind had stopped whistling overhead but snow was still falling. A quick look out the back door revealed that the steps were once again obliterated and a small drift seemed to be crawling inexorably toward the door itself.

Maggie was familiar enough with the kitchen that she didn't bother lighting a lamp. She thought wistfully of home, of how surprised Mrs. Cavanaugh would be that she had learned her way around a kitchen. Home, she thought. *This is my home.*

She was not aware she had spoken aloud until Connor said from the doorway, "That sounds a little bit like a revelation."

Maggie gave a small start. She paused in picking up a loaf of bread and glanced over her shoulder. "I suppose it is. A happy one, though." She placed the bread on the table. "Would you like something to eat?" she asked, searching for a knife.

Connor pulled out a chair and sat down. "Nothing for me."

She sliced through the bread. When she skirted the table to get the butter, Connor captured her and brought her down on his lap. "I'm too heavy for you," she said, trying to scoot off his thighs.

Laughing, he held her still. "My saddle weighs more than you."

"But *you* sit on that."

"I also toss it around. Anyway, I'd sit on your lap if you had one." Both of his large hands flattened over her belly. His fingers spread out. Maggie's stomach rumbled. "I was hoping the *baby* would move," he said. "Not you."

"The baby," she said tartly, "is weak with hunger. Just like her mother."

Connor set Maggie on her feet again and let her get the butter. "Then feed that boy."

She managed to elude him on her return to the table, taking the chair across from him. "Our baby is a girl," she said.

"How do you know that?" he asked suspiciously.

"I don't know it," she said. "Not with I'll-bet-my-last-two-bits certainty. I just have a feeling."

"Then feed our daughter," he said. "I'll bank on your feeling."

Maggie put a dollop of sweet butter on her bread and spread it out. "You won't mind if it's a girl?"

"No. Did you think I would?"

She hesitated. "I don't know," she said softly. "I don't really know what you think about things like that . . . about girls growing up to be women and wanting to do things men usually do. Some men think girls are mostly useless." Even though she couldn't see his eyes in the darkness, she could feel him watching her closely.

"Useless except for taking to bed and bearing children," he said. "Is that what you meant?"

"Something like that."

"You're right," he said after a moment's thought. "You really don't know what I'd think." She had every right to question him, every right to be contemptuous. "I haven't done anything to make you realize I'm not one of those men."

Maggie said nothing.

"My mother ran this ranch. She worked beside my grandfather and my uncles and for a while she worked beside my father. When they were all gone she did it alone. She worked harder than any two hands she ever hired. She could rope and brand and shoot and she wasn't much bigger than you are. This ranch was in her blood and keeping it going was her dream. I suppose I never gave much thought to what women could or couldn't do, not at least until I spent some time in the east." He paused. The deep rasp of emotion was in his voice when he spoke again. "So no," he said, "I don't mind at all if we have a daughter, and if she wants to run this ranch someday, I'll have kept it going for her. And if she decides she wants to be a doctor, like her mother, then we'll figure out a way to make that happen, too."

Maggie's eyes glistened with tears. She left her chair, came around the table, and simply let Connor sweep her up in his embrace. She rested her head against his shoulder. "I'm not a doctor," she said.

"Yet."

And the way he said it, Maggie almost believed it could still happen. She kissed him on the jaw, then the mouth. The kiss deepened, lingered.

He pulled away reluctantly. "I thought you were hungry."

"I am. But I don't want the bread anymore."

Connor came to his feet, bringing Maggie with him. He carried her into the bedroom and they made love this time with their hands and mouths, touching and tasting with fingers and tongues. It was the contrast of textures that they enjoyed in their loving, the gentle abrasiveness of his hands in the silky lengths of her hair, the rough pad of his thumb sweeping across her tender skin. There was a soft spot at the nape of her neck, that when he lifted her hair and kissed her there, she shivered. She felt his skin leap just beneath her fingertips in anticipation of her touch.

His flesh was warm, her hands were cool. She thought he tasted both salty and sweet. He thought of the wild scent of musk when he pressed his mouth between her breasts.

It was an exploration, a discovery. This time there *was* time. She found him curiously exotic: the planes and angles of him so different from her, the width of his bones, the inherent strength, the dark hair that arrowed down from his flat belly, the dimples at the base of his spine that seemed incongruent with his maleness. Riding had given him thighs like steel but he was ticklish at the back of his knees. He liked her fingers combing through his hair, liked her teeth tugging on his earlobe, liked her mouth at the curve of his shoulder, sipping his skin. He liked her mouth elsewhere as well.

It was satisfying, this exchange, this sharing. Pleasure was mutual but they took it in turns. She brought him to a climax first, then his attention was all for her.

She wasn't ticklish anywhere, but there was a sound that she made at the back of her throat when he kissed the soft inner skin of her elbow. She liked the hot suck of his mouth on her breast, the touch of his hand on her inner thigh, the whisper of his breath near her ear. Engulfed in his, her hands were small. His tongue teased her fingertips as he kissed them one by one. His mouth pressed in the palm of her hand. His mouth pressed her elsewhere as well.

They lay together then, facing each other this time, their knees drawn upward and touching. Beneath the quilt their hands were clasped, fingers intertwined.

"The first time we met," Connor said, "you sat up in a whore's bed and looked as if you were expecting me. Do you remember that?"

"No," she whispered.

He squeezed her hand gently. "I've thought about it now and then. It stays there, in my mind, a niggling thought that won't go away. You were shy, but trusting, and knowing later what you went through that night with the sailor and Harlan Porter, it's struck me as odd that you would offer me—another stranger—trust so easily."

Maggie wished she could remember. "I don't know why I did," she said. What she did remember was the way she had turned to him in that bed, the way she had touched him with no invitation on his part, only a deeply buried need on hers. "You had every right to think I was a whore."

"And you had every right to think I was a doctor," he said.

The knot in her middle unwound a little. The notion that she might have mistaken Connor Holiday for a physician tickled her fancy. She grinned, laughing huskily at the back of her throat. "Your bedside manner is not precisely ethical," she said. Her laughter faded. "You're serious, aren't you?"

"You were sick and had been badly used by Porter. Mrs. Hall said she was going to send for a physician. I walked in carrying a leather satchel—"

"Filled with money."

"That *could* have been confused for a medical bag," he said. "I don't know what was in your mind, Maggie, but I know there's nothing wrong with you. There never was. Your curiosity was as natural as your desire. But the next time I saw you I set out to make you feel coarse and ashamed because it was easier than admitting I felt either of those things myself. It was easier to hide behind the fury about losing my fortune than to admit I may have hurt you that night, easier to call you a whore than to believe I may have taken you against your will. Your virgin's blood was on the sheets, on me, and I still found it more convenient to think you'd played a cheap whore's trick on me than accept the evidence in front of my eyes."

Connor pulled her hand closer to his chest. His voice was soft, earnest. "I was wrong about you," he said. "I was *always* wrong. I know why you didn't tell me the truth about the baby. You have a mother's instinct for protecting her young and you had no good reason to suppose that I'd make anything but the worst kind of husband and father."

"Connor," Maggie said gently. "You don't have—"

"No," he said. "I want to tell you these things. This summer, when you were at Dancer's, I came to realize that if I had treated you differently you might not have aborted our baby. When Dancer came here looking for help and told me you were pregnant I accused him of being the father."

Maggie gaped at him. "You didn't."

"I did," he said, sighing. "Then I saw you again and my best intentions fled. There was a bandit at your feet, you were pointing a gun at me, your eyes were consigning me to the lowest circle of hell, and you were still wearing your wedding band. I couldn't think straight."

"I wasn't thinking very clearly myself," she admitted.

Connor stroked the back of her hand with his thumb. "I wasn't sorry when Dancer broke his leg. It gave me the excuse I'd been wanting. I couldn't get you back to the Double H fast enough." He stretched his legs and insinuated one of them under Maggie's calves. "I'd also found the unsigned divorce papers. They gave me reason to hope." He chuckled. "False hope, as it turned out."

"It turned out just fine," she said. "Although it's not precisely comforting to discover Dancer Tubbs is as meddlesome as my father." She thought a moment. "Rushton had a hand in this as well, you know."

"I know," he said. "That's why I'm here and he's there. Everybody's happier that way."

* * *

New York

Beryl cinched her satin wrapper more securely about her waist. She stepped in from the balcony outside her room and shut the French doors quickly. A dervish of dried leaves followed her inside. She kicked at them.

"I don't see why we can't go to the Double H," she said. Her lower lip was thrust forward in a way that she knew was still attractive. She'd practiced the expression in front of the mirror. "Or at least to Denver."

"Homesick?" Rushton asked. He didn't look up from the newspaper he was reading in bed so Beryl's expression was lost on him.

"Yes," she said. "Homesick. Exactly that. I miss the mountains and the sky. I haven't seen my mother in nearly two years."

"You couldn't wait to get away from there. As I recall, your mother was included in the things you despised about Denver."

Beryl sat on the edge of the bed. Her pale blue eyes flashed. She yanked the *Chronicle* away from Rushton and threw it on the floor. "At least have the courtesy to look at me when we're talking," she snapped.

Rushton looked up politely, his dark eyes unfathomable. His voice was cool and patient. "Anger doesn't really suit you, Beryl. Your cheeks flush quite unattractively."

"Damn you, Rush." Beryl pushed at a lock of dark hair that had fallen over her shoulder. "I don't want to talk about the way I look."

There was a flash of something in his eyes that hinted at his amusement. "That would be a first," he said dryly. Rushton wasn't disappointed as Beryl rose to the bait instantly. He reached for her hand, holding on when she would have jerked it away. He pulled her closer so she was sitting beside him and tucked her arm under his. "All right," he said soothingly. "All right. Tell me again what you have in mind."

Beryl laid her head on her husband's shoulder. The wide lapels of her dressing gown gaped, revealing the perfect roundness of one breast. She didn't cover herself. "We haven't been back to Colorado. We never even talk about going. I love New York, Rushton, but I have family in Denver that I haven't seen since I married you."

"I thought that's the way you wanted it," he said.

"I did . . . I *do* . . . I don't know."

"You rarely write to your mother."

"I don't like to write. It doesn't mean that I don't want to see her."
She rubbed his arm with the palm of her hand. "You don't write to
Connor and I know you'd like to see him again."

"You know that, do you?"

"Credit me with some sense," she said. "You may not get along
with him for more than two minutes, but I don't think for one of
those minutes that you wouldn't like it to be different. Don't you
wonder how he and Mary Margaret are faring? Aren't you the least
bit curious?"

"I know how Maggie's doing," he said. "She writes to *her* parents.
Jay Mac told me he and Moira received a stack of letters just a few
weeks ago. Some of them date back to the middle of the summer."

"No one at the Double H must be going to town much to post
them."

That's what Rushton had thought, too. At first. Jay Mac had let
his friend read Maggie's letters and Rushton found them curiously
lacking in detail in regard to the Double H. In some cases, when
description was supplied, it was just plain wrong. His daughter-in-
law's letters were also lacking information about his son. Maggie
never wrote about the things that Connor did on the ranch that
might have interested her parents. She never mentioned any odd bit
of laughter that may have passed between them. She never sought
her mother's advice about an argument. If Maggie were to be believed it was the most idyllic marriage on the face of the earth.

Which made Rushton Holiday wonder if it existed at all.

He had said nothing to Jay Mac. He didn't want interference from
that quarter. But he had been curious and now he listened to Beryl
with more interest than she might have believed. "Tomorrow's the
first of November," he said idly.

"Hmmm. The Double H is probably buried in drifts."

"Probably." He let silence settle between them for a moment. "I
could leave the mills later in the winter."

"Christmas?" she asked hopefully.

"No. Later than that. February, maybe."

Beryl raised her head and looked at her husband. She made a
small moue. "But that's so long from now. And we still couldn't get
to the Double H."

"I wasn't thinking so much of the ranch," he said, "as I was of
your desire to see your mother. The train should make it quite easily

to Denver. We'll stay with Grace until the spring thaw clears the passes."

Beryl almost wailed, "But that could be March, even April."

"I know, dear," Rushton said solicitously, his eyes grave. "But I can't get away any earlier. And this way you'll have all the time you need to spend with your mother." He saw Beryl blanch slightly but he managed to temper his smile. "Why don't you do something with the lamps, Beryl?" he asked, brushing his lips against her forehead. "You've gotten what you want." His hand slipped inside the gap in her dressing gown and cupped her breast. "Now it's my turn."

She moaned softly when his mouth covered hers.

Maggie sat up in bed as Connor brought the feast to her. He showed her the tray, teasing her with the contents before he set it on the side table. Her mouth watered from the smell of silver dollar pancakes and bacon, hot honeyed tea and warm muffins.

"I can't eat all of that," she protested. However, her eyes followed the tray hungrily.

Watching her, he laughed. "I'll finish off what you can't, though I don't think I'll get much." He gave her a fork and the plate of pancakes and bacon. She tucked into it while he pressed a napkin into the neckline of her chemise. It was a pleasure to watch her eat with such relish. He said as much to her.

Maggie spoke around a mouthful of food, surprised by his observation. "I eat all the time," she said. "I'm as big as—"

"As a woman carrying a child ought to be."

She swallowed, smiling. "You're very gallant. But I like it."

"Then I'll do it more often."

Biting off the end of a crisp strip of bacon, Maggie was moved to add, "You're also a very good cook."

He grinned. "You're not going to get me to say I'll cook more often. Before you came to the ranch we hadn't had a decent meal here in weeks. No one wanted the job permanently."

"It's a job?" she asked innocently. "I hadn't realized. There's no wages."

Connor's smile faded. "You're right," he said. "We haven't been fair."

"It's not as if I could help out here in any other way," she told him. "Really, I haven't minded."

"No matter what it looks like, I didn't bring you to the Double H to cook."

"I'm not a good rider. And I don't know anything about roping and branding. The truth is, I don't think I want to learn. What I know about cooking, I learned from Dancer. He's been keeping a low profile around here, playing up his injury, but when no one else is around he's the one giving me direction in the kitchen. So you see, Connor, I'm something of a fraud."

He took one of the pancakes, rolled it up so it looked like a cigar and dipped it in some syrup. "Imagine that," he said. "I wonder if Dancer would want to stick around after his leg's healed?"

"Why don't you ask him? He's settled in here more comfortably than I would have thought. Ben and the others have been very kind and no one stares at him. He can't get back to his cabin now anyway, especially not with the snow, and he wouldn't leave before the baby's born. He might like hiring on as the Double H cook, at least until he can return to his mines."

"I'll talk to him."

Maggie reached for her mug of tea. "I suspect I'll be a lady of leisure again," she said, sighing.

"Somehow I don't think that will happen. You'll be plenty busy until the baby's born, then you'll be busier."

Three days before Christmas Maggie's thoughts drifted back to Connor's words. He'd been right, of course. Work on the ranch didn't stop just because the valley was blanketed with snow. The men still worked long hours feeding the cattle, clearing the stables, smoking meat, and forging tools for the spring. When wolves threatened the herd they went out to run them off. They hunted and fished and practiced rope tricks in the corral.

Maggie's days had been equally full. She washed and ironed and mended clothes, chores that were not entirely unsatisfying once they were actually completed. She made things for the baby. She no longer did the daily cooking but no one tried to stop her from baking. When Buck was laid low with coughing and chest pains it was Maggie, not Dancer, who tended him. Pressing garlic cloves in a tablespoon of honey, she made him take the mixture four times a day to loosen the congestion in his chest. She prepared chamomile tea for him at bedtime and added an extract she'd made from wild cherry bark.

Maggie sanded and repainted a cradle she'd found in the attic. She worked sporadically on a new quilt for their bedroom and let Ben teach her how to play the harmonica. She read a little in the evenings, sometimes sharing the space in front of the fireplace with Connor. She usually fell asleep with the open book on the floor beside her. She liked it when Connor carried her to bed.

Now, remembering his words about staying busy, she wished he was around to carry her to bed. She straightened slowly, tightly gripping the jar she was holding as another pain struck her lower back. When the pain faded Maggie returned the jar to its place on the pantry shelf. The task of rearranging the contents suddenly faded in importance.

Maggie backed out of the pantry and looked around the kitchen. Dancer wasn't there. She opened the back door, wincing as another pain, a cramp this time, took her by surprise. "Dancer?" There was no answer. She wondered where he had hobbled. Shrugging, she returned inside.

She went to the bedroom and stripped the bed of its good sheets and quilts and replaced them with three old sheets she found in the linen closet. She chose two books from Connor's study that she had been meaning to read and set them on the bedside table. She stood in front of the wardrobe for several minutes, debating about the nightshift she wanted to wear. She finally chose one with a narrow band of lace on the neckline and laid it out at the foot of the bed. She started to unbutton her gown. Her water broke when she sat down in the chair to remove her shoes. The cramp that followed took her breath away. It was all very interesting, she thought, as long as she could think about what was happening to her and not have to feel it. She padded back to the linen closet, found some towels, and began to clean up.

Connor discovered Maggie on her hands and knees in their bedroom. She had a towel in each hand and her chemise was stained dark with water. Most interesting to him, however, was the silly smile on her face when she glanced over her shoulder to look at him. "I'm sure there's an explanation," he said casually, leaning against the door jamb. "Did you overturn a bucket in here?"

Her smile widened. "Do you see a bucket?"

It took him a moment to take her meaning. "Oh, my God." He didn't hesitate after that. Scooping Maggie up, he put her beside the bed, stripped off her chemise and drawers and helped her wriggle into her nightgown. He waited until she crawled into bed and was comfortable before he left to find Dancer.

"She's got hours yet," Dancer told him after he'd examined Maggie. "She's reading now." He stepped into the hallway outside the bedroom and shut the door. He saw the worry creasing Connor's brow and shook his head, scratching the whiskerless side of his scarred face. "Ain't no cause to look like that," he said. "You delivered foals before. It don't happen all at once."

The waiting was interminable. Connor stayed with Maggie until Dancer threw him out, then he waited in the parlor, taking turns pacing the floor with Luke, Ben, Buck, and Patrick, looking toward the hallway expectantly each time the door to Maggie's room opened.

Her cries were the hardest for them to bear. When Connor wasn't pacing he was slumped in one of the armchairs trying not to hear her sporadic cries of pain. Buck was pale. Ben and Patrick knocked back shots of whiskey. Luke, usually stoic, actually winced.

Then there was the cry that was unfamiliar, yet known to all of them. Connor came to his feet, shot from his chair like a cannonball. Buck's face was flushed again with color. Ben and Patrick began pouring drinks for everyone and Luke's handsome features were creased by a grin.

When Dancer appeared on the threshold Connor didn't wait to hear what he had to say. He rushed past the prospector to get to Maggie.

She was sitting up in the middle of the bed. Her hair was damp and dark around her forehead and temples. There were shadows just beneath her lowered lashes and her complexion was pale, but when she raised her face her eyes were bright and her smile was simply radiant.

She raised her cradled arms as Connor approached the bed. "I want to name her Meredith," she said. "Mary after my sisters and Edith after your mother."

"Meredith," he repeated softly, reverently. He looked down at his daughter. There was a sheen of tears in his eyes. "I like it."

Chapter Fourteen

Meredith Dancer Holiday was six weeks old when the weather broke long enough to forge a pass out of the valley. The hired hands, all a little stir crazy, drew cards for the privilege of making the trip to Queen's Point. Luke and Buck won. Dancer decided to take the opportunity to make sure his cabin was still standing and he followed the others. Except for Meredith's lusty mealtime cries, the ranch house seemed oddly quiet after the trio's departure.

That was why Maggie was surprised when she heard footsteps pound across the front porch and then the door open and slam shut. She stopped rocking and Meredith was dislodged from her breast. The baby gave a mewling cry and began rooting again. Maggie held her protectively as the door to their bedroom was flung open.

Patrick stood in the doorway, clutching his hat in his hand. He sucked in air in great gulps and stuttered as he tried to speak and catch his breath at the same time. His freckles stood out even on his flushed face. "There's been an accident, Mag. You've got to do something. Connor's bringin' Ben now. He said to get Dancer's bed ready and then you'd know what to do."

Maggie didn't know what had happened, let alone what to do. She stood up, turning modestly to remove Meredith from her breast, and covered herself. She ignored her baby's wail though she felt her breast leak immediately. Cradling Meredith, she shooed Patrick out of her way and made him follow her to Dancer's vacated room.

"Help me make up this bed," she said. "I can't do it with only one free arm. And tell me what happened."

Patrick grabbed the sheets and snapped them over the bed, tucking in the corners while he spoke. "Something popped in the forge and shot a ball of fire at Ben. Connor tackled him when he came runnin' out, put him right down in the snow, but he's burned bad."

Maggie closed her eyes a moment and thought of Dancer's face. Her stomach turned over. "Help Connor get Ben in here," she told Patrick with more calm than she felt. "He didn't mean for you to dawdle with me." She realized she could have saved her breath. Patrick was off like a shot at her first command.

Maggie put Meredith in her cradle and carried it to the kitchen. The baby was still squalling but Maggie pretended she didn't hear. She set a kettle of water on the stove, fired the kindling, then began searching her pantry for dried elder flowers, leaves, and berries. She was putting out what she needed when she heard the front door open again. She met the men in the hallway. Ben was supported between Connor and Patrick. His large, barrel-chested body sagged and his head lolled forward. The odor of burned clothing, hair, and skin could be smelled in the air. Patrick kicked the door shut with his heel.

Maggie pointed to the bedroom. "Take him in there. Try to get some of his clothes off but don't pull them where they're burned to his skin." They disappeared into the room. She went to the parlor, retrieved a pair of scissors from her sewing basket, and gave them to Connor. His hands, she noticed, were steadier than Patrick's and fear had settled over him with a rigid calmness that was helpful in a crisis. "Cut his clothes where you have to," she said. "Patrick, get the hip bath and bring it here. Fill it a quarter full. Cool water. Don't bother to heat it. And you might find some bandages, too!" She had to call after him. He was quick to respond to the first order and barely heard the second.

Maggie gave Ben a cursory glance. His condition wouldn't be clear to her until Connor removed most of his clothes. She could see that his left leg was badly burned, mostly from the knee to his ankle. The leather apron he'd worn protected his chest, groin, and thighs from injury, but both his arms were scorched. "I'm going to make a wash for his skin from elder leaves," she told Connor. "It will take a little time. When Patrick gets back here with the water, use it to soak the threads of clothes sticking to Ben's skin." She thought Connor blanched. "Or I can do it," she offered.

"No," he said tersely. "I'll manage."

She hesitated, saw that he was determined, and nodded. "All right." Meredith was sleeping fitfully when Maggie returned to the kitchen. Maggie rocked the cradle with her toe while she prepared the wash. By the time she was finished Meredith was deeply asleep.

The wash had to cool before she could apply it to Ben's burned flesh. She used the time to prepare a variety of teas that would ease Ben's pain as well as help him sleep.

"You've done well," she told Connor when she returned to the bedroom. He moved off the bed to make space for her. A sheet covered Ben's unburned middle and left his arms and most of his legs free for her inspection. She picked up the sponge that Connor had been using and dipped it in a pan of cool water. She cleaned the burns carefully, looking for bits of thread that might cause infection later. In spite of her cautious ministrations, Ben jerked and groaned under her touch.

"Give him some of the white willow tea, Connor. It's in the blue spongeware mug." She returned to cleaning the burns. "You're lucky, Ben," she said gently. "These aren't nearly as bad as Patrick described to me."

"Probably told you I looked like a damn fireball," he growled. The effort to talk made him cough and the coughing shook him on the bed. He groaned again in pain.

"Don't say another word. Use your energy to drink what Connor's giving you."

Connor listened to the quiet authority in his wife's voice and saw Ben obey. Over the course of the next week Connor heard it again and again and saw the effect of her unassuming confidence in Ben's gradual recovery. He watched her sit at Ben's bedside, comforting her patient with her presence, holding the unburned palm of his hand when Ben could do nothing but cry in agony. She changed his bandages, cleaned his wounds, and applied the cool and soothing elder wash to his raw flesh. She prepared garlic balms for infection and brewed cups of poppy and white willow tea. Sometimes she sat with him alone. Other times she breast-fed Meredith at his bedside.

She was available to Ben at any time. She spooned broth to him when he couldn't manage himself, read to him while she cradled

Meredith in her arms. She bathed him, combed his hair, and shaved his broad and craggy face.

At night she fell into bed, into Connor's arms, exhausted. He liked those times. He liked having her close, all to himself. Knowing how rare they were and rare they were likely to be, Connor counted those moments as precious and savored them.

After watching Maggie at Ben's side, healing with her skill and her will, the one thing borne home to Connor was that his wife didn't belong at the Double H.

"Dancer would be proud of you," he told her as she was readying for bed. Connor was already lying on the edge of the mattress, his head propped up by an elbow. His eyes drifted from his wife to the nearby cradle where his daughter was sleeping soundly, her tiny bottom pushed in the air. At eight weeks Meredith was getting too big for the cradle. He and Patrick were working on a crib for her. It was still in the barn where they were hiding it as a surprise for Maggie, too. Ben's accident had given them more chores and less time for finishing the crib.

Maggie knelt beside the cradle as she closed the last button on her cotton nightshift. She touched the cap of Meredith's downy head. Her daughter's hair was even darker than Connor's. She stroked it lovingly, curling the ends between two fingers. "In a way I'm glad Dancer wasn't here," she said. "I think it would have been hard for him to see Ben's burns." She stood slowly, stretching as she yawned. The front of her nightshift was pulled tautly across her breasts. "But I missed him, too. I was afraid I wasn't doing it right."

Connor found himself staring at Maggie's chest. The full shape of her breasts was perfectly revealed through the thin cotton. The lamp at her back made a silhouette of her narrow waist and hips. Ben's injuries had put a damper on more than just getting the crib completed. Maggie had only just healed from childbirth when the accident happened. In the weeks since then it seemed either she was too tired or he was.

Connor Holiday hadn't made love to his wife since before their baby was born. His body was reminding him of that in a most natural and elemental way.

He rolled on his stomach as Maggie climbed into bed. The pressure on his groin kept him from seizing her on the spot. "I think you do most everything right," he said huskily.

She smiled. "Do you? I like it that you told me." She reached for the oil lamp but Connor's hand on her wrist stopped her.

"Not tonight," he said.

Maggie turned to look at him. His eyes simply burned into her.

"I've never made love to you in the light," he said. "This time I want to see."

It occurred to Maggie to tell him it wasn't decent, but in fact, she thought it was a very decent thing to do. She leaned toward him. "What if you don't like what you see?" she whispered.

"Not possible," he whispered back.

Maggie sat up and picked up the hem of her nightshift. In one sweeping motion she pulled it off and let it flutter to the floor behind her.

He liked what he saw very, very much. She was giving him a bold, almost defiant look that he suspected was more bravado than brave. He smiled, reached for her hand, and held it. His thumb passed lightly back and forth over the soft underside of her wrist. He felt her pulse race.

The tilt of her chin drew his eye to the length of her throat, the hollow, then the defining line of her collarbones. Her shoulders were drawn back, emphasizing the shape of her breasts. Under his gaze a rosy flush spread across her skin. Her nipples seemed to become a darker shade of coral.

His eyes drifted lower, along the inward curve of her waist, the flatness of her abdomen, then the flair of her hips. He released her wrist and let his hand drift along her naked thigh from hip to knee. His palm curved to her contours. She didn't move, yet he could feel her trembling.

"Shouldn't you . . ." she whispered.

His voice was even huskier than hers. "Shouldn't I what?"

"Shouldn't you take off your . . ."

Since she didn't seem capable of completing a sentence, Connor helped her. He lifted the sheet covering him to the waist.

Maggie's eyes widened slightly. He was already naked. He was also aroused. "You were pretty sure of me," she said.

"Let's just say I was hopeful."

Laughing, Maggie yanked back the covers and subjected him to the same scrutiny that had just fired her senses. She took in the breadth of his shoulders, the smooth expanse of his chest, the flat plane of his belly. And then she studied his erection. "Oh my," she said softly.

He pulled her toward him then rolled so that Maggie was trapped beneath his body. He rested his weight on his forearms. "I'll take that as a compliment."

"You should."

Then his mouth was closing over hers. He kissed her deeply, hungrily. She accepted the sweep of his tongue and pushed against him with her own. Her thighs were parted by his knee. She lifted her hips.

"Help me," he said.

She did. Her hand closed over him intimately. He eased into her. She was already wet for him. Their eyes locked, held. Joined, they didn't move.

The centers of her green eyes widened, darkened. His were like liquid onyx. Their breath mingled, hot and sweet.

They kissed again, slowly. Mouths fused. Tongues working the same rhythm their bodies would. Her thighs cradled him. She pressed against his hips, wrapped her legs around him, securing his body. Then the kiss broke. His lips grazed her chin. She arched her neck. His mouth touched her throat, sipped her skin. She caught her breath and trapped a sound of pleasure.

He moved. Hips rising and falling, pressing deeply into her. Her arms were raised. Hands alighted on his shoulders. Fingertips moved across his skin like a whisper. She rubbed against him, her breasts flush to his chest, nipples abraded pleasurably by the heat and hardness of flesh. Her thumbnail traced the length of his spine. He shuddered, groaned, buried his face in the curve of her neck. She smiled.

He bit her skin lightly. Her smile vanished. She touched the dimples at the base of his spine. He moved against her, hard this time. Her hand swept across his back. Her fingers twisted in the hair at his nape. His face lifted. He nudged her nose with his. He kissed her cheek, kissed the spot just below her ear, kissed her feathered brows.

She arched, pressing into him. Tension held her still for a moment. Pleasure was a drawn-out sensation, pulling her tautly, lifting her.

They moved together, slowly at first, catching a rhythm that satisfied and prolonged their mutual pleasure. There was a tightness in his chest as excitement rose with such intensity that it threatened to take the breath from his body. He held her closely, surrounding her, protecting her. She cried out, saying his name as she shuddered against him. His body seemed to absorb her pleasure until it was his own. He groaned softly, whispered her name against her skin.

Their bodies were flushed and warm. Neither of them wanted to move so they didn't.

"We started this way," she said, her voice husky, amused.

"So we did."

His weight was comfortable on her for a moment. She closed her eyes and simply felt him all around her. "I like this."

He kissed the corner of her mouth then moved off her, sliding onto his side beside her. He propped himself on one elbow and looked down at her. Her eyes were still closed, a faint smile on her lips. Her cheeks were flushed, her mouth slightly swollen from the pressure of his kisses. Her skin was smooth—the crease that was sometimes between her brows had vanished. The shadows beneath her eyes were caused by the fan of her dark lashes.

The tightness in his chest was back again; this time it was the sense of loving her that overwhelmed him. Tears touched his eyes. He blinked them back.

She seemed to know. She opened her eyes and asked, "What is it?"

"Nothing."

She was quiet, watching him, searching his face. She reached for him, cupping the side of his face with her palm. His dark eyes were neither remote nor cold. She felt drawn into them. They seared her and sheltered her, and it did not seem strange to Maggie that they could do both. For an instant she was touched by his soul.

"I love you," she whispered. Her hand dropped away, drifted across his chest, fell back to the mattress between them.

His throat closed on him. He touched her hand, drew her fingers between his. He said nothing; she didn't seem to expect that he would. They shared the silence.

Maggie snuggled closer. Connor drew up the sheet and comforter.

The baby stirred for a moment, mewling softly, then sighed and slept. Connor reached for the lamp and blew out the flame. Maggie rested her head in the crook of his shoulder.

As they slept, snow started to fall.

The passes were blocked again by morning. Maggie served pancakes at breakfast. Patrick had stumbled through drifts up to his hips to get eggs from the hen house. Batter bubbled on a greased iron skillet as she laid the first stack of flapjacks on the table. Connor speared three with his fork before passing the plate to Patrick.

"Save some for Ben," Connor cautioned as Patrick began to sweep most of the cakes onto his plate.

"I've already served Ben," Maggie said. She turned back to the griddle and flipped two more pancakes. She glanced toward the window. The ice flowers on the panes were slowly melting. "Buck and Luke aren't going to make it back, are they?"

"Not today," Patrick said. "Probably not this week."

"Dancer?"

Connor shook his head. "He'll be fine at his cabin until the weather breaks." He was cradling Meredith in the crook of his arm. He gave her a little bounce and she made a happy sound, not quite a laugh, but something that made every adult in the room smile.

"Don't you dare feed her a pancake," Maggie warned as Connor teased their daughter with a forkful of food.

"I wouldn't." Instead he put down his fork and stuck his forefinger in the honey jar. He let Meredith suck on the tip, which she did greedily. Connor looked at Maggie as if to say, *Is this what it feels like?* She merely blushed. Connor laughed.

Meredith and Patrick, each interested in their breakfast, were oblivious.

As the winter weeks passed it was the small moments that she held close to her heart: the laughter they exchanged, the smiles that were intimate and the ones that were open. She saw Connor with Meredith on his knee, watching her intently as she made tiny bubbles between her dewy lips. His hand engulfed their daughter's head when he cradled her. Sometimes he buried his face against her little belly, blowing gently or making smacking noises, and Meredith would smile and giggle.

Maggie remembered when she and Connor went sledding, and he bundled her up in layers of blankets until she was just a shapeless mound. Tempest pulled them on the long sled into the trees and they made a splendid run down the hillside until they tumbled into a snow bank. Sun glinted sharply off the snow—and off Maggie's hair, as threads of copper captured the light. Connor stole a kiss as she made an angel in the snow. "Your hair's like a flame," he said and pulled her to her feet.

In the evenings they sat in front of the fire, sharing a blanket with Meredith. They talked to her as if she could understand. Maggie consulted her about the garden she was planning. Connor spoke of her first horse. There was a moment, as they were discussing her future, that she wrinkled her nose and grimaced, and they both laughed until they cried. "She suspects we're like Jay Mac," Maggie said, wiping her eyes. But Maggie admitted in her heart that John MacKenzie Worth had done all right by her.

She remembered other things: Connor's and Patrick's presentation of Meredith's crib; Ben's move back to the bunk house; the snowball battle that left Connor defending his fort alone when Maggie surrendered to a fit of laughter that left her quite useless as a helpmate.

Maggie remembered the nights when she lay beside him, comforted by his closeness, by the shelter of his arms, and he talked to her in that low, whiskey-soft voice.

Living in the moment, she wove a tapestry of memories that winter.

Denver

Mary Michael Stone and Mary Renee Sullivan sat on either end of the sofa like a matched pair of bookends. Beryl Holiday was seated across from them. When Beryl's eyes lowered to lift her teacup the twin sisters exchanged identical, frustrated glances. When Beryl looked up again they were flashing perfectly beautiful smiles.

"It was kind of you and Rushton to make a point to visit us during your stay," Michael said. Michael, like her twin, wished she were still in the dining room with her husband. Conversation there was not likely to be so tedious or difficult. Several times she had heard laughter coming from that room as Ethan, Jarret, and Rushton traded stories.

"Rushton thought we should," Beryl said.

There was an uncomfortable silence. Rennie tried to help her twin. "I was happy to learn I was going to meet you," she said. "Jarret and I are only in Denver for the week, then we're heading for New York. We've been working on a project for Northeast Rail all autumn and most of the winter."

Beryl's pale blue eyes flickered. "I didn't realize you had been out here so long. I suppose I thought when you didn't get the Double H land, you would have gone home."

"We were in California," Rennie said. "But I'm still interested in the Double H tract, not that I think for a moment that Connor would sell it."

"Certainly not now," Beryl said. Her light laughter was brittle. "Not when he paid for it so dearly himself."

"You mean the wedding?" Rennie said, her hackles rising. "Connor Holiday should count himself fortunate that my sister was agreeable."

Michael's humor was not any better than Rennie's but seeing her sister's temper flare helped her keep her own in check. "Connor and Maggie were here soon after their marriage. They were quite happy." She didn't dare look at Rennie, who had already heard a different version of the visit. "It's hard to say who got the best of the bargain. More tea?"

Beryl held out her cup as Michael poured. "You'll understand if I think it was Maggie."

Rennie smiled sweetly. "I'm certain it's your position as his step-mother that prompts such allegiance." Out of the corner of her eye she saw Michael nearly choke on her tea. "After all, you chose his father over him." Rennie stood, put her cup down on the end table, and excused herself.

Michael could have cheerfully throttled her sister but she wouldn't apologize for her. She picked up the threads of conversation as if nothing untoward had happened. "I heard Rushton mention that you'll be going to Queen's Point in two more days."

The mottled color in Beryl's cheeks faded as she recovered her composure. "That's right." Now that Rennie was out of the room she found it easier to speak. All through dinner she couldn't forget that Rennie Sullivan was responsible for bringing Connor and Maggie together. It was Rennie's interest in the Double H, her offhand comments to Jay Mac about Connor, that had ultimately shaped events. "The passes should all be cleared by now. I swear I saw a daffodil yesterday."

Michael forced a smile. "I shouldn't wonder that Maggie's feeling in need of some company by now. Ethan and I have talked about going out. We'd love to see the ranch. And frankly, now that Maggie's this close, I miss her more than ever."

"The Double H is beautiful," Beryl said. "But I'm certain Rennie's told you that."

Michael could hear it in Beryl's voice again, the certain dislike of her sister. She kept her own tone carefully level. "Since Ethan and I can't leave anytime soon, I wonder if you and Rushton might do me a favor?"

Beryl set her cup in its saucer. She fingered the amethyst earring on her right ear, tilting her head to one side. "I'd be happy to, if I can."

"Maggie had to leave some of her belongings here. We have a few trunks, some valises, and—" she laughed, "—a package from my mother that's been gathering dust in the upstairs hallway all winter. Ethan's promised to take it to the attic once or twice a week since it arrived but it never happens. Now he's going to feel vindicated for his laziness." She smiled. "That's *if* you and Rushton are willing to take some of the things with you."

Beryl couldn't think of a good reason to object but she was working on it when Michael continued.

"I'll sort through everything, of course. I don't want to burden you unnecessarily. The physician's bag will have to go. Mama wouldn't have sent it if she didn't think Maggie would want it."

"Physician's bag?" asked Beryl. "Your sister isn't a doctor."

"No, she isn't." Michael shrugged. She didn't want to share Maggie's dream with this woman. "Actually I'm not certain that's what the satchel is at all. I never opened it."

"Black leather?" Beryl asked. She indicated a twenty-inch span with her hands. "About this big?"

"That's right. Just like a doctor would carry."

"I owned a bag like that once," Beryl said slowly, thoughtfully.

She remembered lending it to Connor and never seeing it again. She was careful to keep excitement out of her voice. "I kept odds and ends in it, for traveling purposes. Combs, brushes, perfumes. The sort of thing you don't want to be without."

"Maybe that's all it has in it," Michael said, although she was doubtful. Maggie would consider it frivolous to carry those things close by. "More likely it has books in it. Maggie's always reading. I know there are books in some of the trunks. I plan to make certain she gets those."

Beryl didn't care about the books. "Of course we'll take whatever you like," she said. "Rushton won't object, I'm sure."

Maggie rushed to the front door and flung it open. She raised Meredith from her hip to the crook of her arm. "Look there!" she said excitedly, pointing to the southern end of the valley. "It's Dancer!" Maggie called to Connor at the corral. She saw him look off in the direction she was pointing, then take off his hat and wave it, hailing the prospector as he approached.

Maggie jogged down the steps and across the yard. Patches of snow dotted her path like white lily pads and she skirted them. Connor came outside the corral to meet her, scooping Meredith out of Maggie's arms and holding her up even higher.

Dancer brought his horse right up to the welcoming trio as Patrick and Ben ran from the stable to greet him. "You all sure are a sight," he said, grinning widely. He leaned over in his saddle and tickled Meredith under the chin. "Ain't afraid of your old Uncle Dancer, are you? Look at her!" His laughter cackled. "She ain't afraid of this ugly face. Not a lick afraid."

"Of course she's not afraid," Maggie said. "Why would she be? She knows you love her."

Dancer dismounted. "Didn't say nothin' about lovin' her," he said gruffly. "Damn fool notion." He jumped around a little, shaking the dust off his clothes and the stiffness out of his bones. He tipped back his hat and gave Maggie a thorough looking over. "I can see you ain't come to any harm."

She supposed it was as affectionate a greeting as she was likely to get. On impulse she put her arms around Dancer and gave him a hug. "I've missed you," she whispered against his twisted and scarred ear. "We all have." Maggie stepped back quickly before he became too uncomfortable. "I see your leg's not giving you a moment's worry."

"That's a fact." He held out his hand to Patrick, shook it, then got a good look at Ben's scarred forearms. "What the hell happened to you?" he asked bluntly.

"Accident in the forge," Ben said. His thick neck reddened slightly and his face took on the same ruddy hue. Dancer was the last person he had expected to call attention to his scars.

"Ain't near as bad as mine," Dancer said. "Maggie take care of you?"

"Day and night."

"She ought to be a doctor, just like she wants." He took Meredith from Connor. "In case anyone cares what I think." He sauntered off in the direction of the house, cooing and chatting to the baby.

Smiling, Maggie looped her arm in Connor's and leaned against him. "It's good to have him back, isn't it? I really thought he might not come."

Connor motioned to Patrick to take care of Dancer's horse and Ben followed. "Hmmm?" he asked, realizing Maggie was waiting for an answer to a question he hadn't heard.

"What's wrong?" she asked, looking up at him. His features were drawn, the edge of his jaw cleanly defined. His eyes had a faraway look.

"Nothing." *She should be a doctor,* he thought. He looked down at her, smiled, and kissed her lightly on the lips. "Nothing," he repeated. "It's good to have Dancer back, isn't it?"

Maggie pretended she hadn't asked him the same question, pretended she believed there was nothing wrong. She squeezed his arm to her side more tightly, feeling desperate for a moment, as if he had slipped away from her. "Yes," she said. "And I'm going to bake something special to celebrate. A pound cake perhaps. Dancer's partial to pound cake."

Connor's hand slipped in hers, their fingers intertwining. She would make a cake, he thought. With her healing hands, his wife would make a cake. He wondered if he could get her to leave the valley, then he wondered if he could let her leave.

* * *

Queen's Point

Beryl stayed in the background while Rushton oversaw the loading of the wagon. Luke and Buck pushed the last trunk on and leaned against the buckboard to catch their breath.

"Damnable piece of luck running into them," Buck muttered under his breath.

"Rush isn't so bad," Luke said. *"She's* a piece of work though. Stay clear of her if you know what's good for you."

"Like I said. We should've left yesterday."

"You were busy yesterday, remember?" Luke asked. One of his dark brows kicked up and he gave Buck a rare half-smile. "Blonde. Brown eyes. About five foot two."

"Don't know how tall she was," Buck said, grinning. "I never seen her standin' up."

Luke gave a short bark of laughter and pushed away from the wagon. He saw a black bag on the wooden sidewalk and bent at the waist to scoop it up. "Missed one."

Beryl stepped forward. Her leather boots tapped lightly on the walk, her dark brown split riding skirt swung gently about her legs. "Don't bother with that," she said. "I'll take it with me."

Luke put the case in her hands. He moved out of her way or she would have brushed against him. He turned to Rushton. "We're ready to go, sir. Both wagons are loaded. Do you want Buck and me to each drive one or do you want to take a team yourself?"

Rushton's obsidian eyes narrowed slightly. There was a faint lift to one corner of his mouth. In that moment he looked very much like his son. "I'm not unfamiliar with driving a team," he said.

Luke knew about Rushton's stables in New York. Connor had told him about his father's matched driving teams. "Pardon me, sir," he said politely, "but this isn't Central Park."

"Have you ever been to Central Park?" asked Rushton.

Luke gave his hat a slight tip with his forefinger, conceding the point to Rushton. "I'll be responsible for the wagon with our supplies and Maggie's extras," he said, "if you'll take the one with your trunks and bags."

Rushton nodded. "Beryl? Do want to ride in the wagon?"

She shook her head. "I'll take the bay mare. At least for a little while." She looked to her husband for a leg up.

"Here, let me have that bag. You haven't let it out of your sight."

She smiled coyly and gave her head a little toss. Ringlets of dark hair swept easily past her shoulder. "A lady can't be without her combs, Rushton, even in this wilderness."

He laughed, shaking his head, and helped her step into the stirrup. "You look lovely as always. Fresh as a daisy."

Beryl wrinkled her nose at him. It was not an attractive expression. "I'm not a daisy," she said. "Daisies are common." She missed Rushton's low chuckle as he turned away and motioned to the others that he was prepared to start. Beryl gave the mare a kick and moved ahead of the group. She held the black bag in front of her and from time to time she twisted the catch. She'd oiled it so it would unlock easily and from time to time she'd do just that, easing the bag open so she could look inside.

From time to time, she'd smile.

Maggie carried Meredith in a sling on her back as she picked spring wildflowers. A clearing among the trees on the hillside was proving to be particularly abundant. The sunny patch of high grass and flowers was also invitingly warm. Maggie took off her straw bonnet, let it drop to the ground, and placed her collection of flowers inside the crown. She raised her face and let it be bathed in sunshine. "Oh, Meredith, this is a day to be enjoyed. Have you ever seen such a sky?"

She took off the sling and laid it out like a blanket, putting the baby down. She sat beside her and stroked her daughter's hair. At three and half months, Meredith was more recognizable as an individual in her own right. She squealed with excitement, chortled, and cooed. She made eyes at her father when he approached. She batted at things that were put in her way and when she got something in her tiny fist she held on stubbornly.

Lying on the blanket in the sunshine, Meredith turned her head in all directions, trying not to miss anything. Maggie unbuttoned her blouse, lifted Meredith to her breast, and let her daughter suckle.

"That's what you were really looking for," she said as Meredith sipped daintly. Maggie watched her lovingly, slightly awed by her ability to care for such a fragile life.

Connor came upon them sitting in the patch of sunlight. A light breeze ruffled Maggie's unbound hair while nothing stirred on Meredith's protected head. Maggie's features were serene. The merest smile touched her mouth as she looked fondly at her daughter. Her dark lashes were lowered, her brow untroubled. It was a profoundly private moment and Connor respected it, staying at a distance, content to have been part of it in his own way.

He never knew what alerted Maggie to his presence. He didn't think he'd made any sound or movement, but suddenly he was aware of her looking in his direction and the smile on her face was for him this time and it beckoned.

Connor stepped out of the sheltering pines into the clearing. His long-legged stride brought him quickly to Maggie's side. He was carrying a large wicker basket and a blanket over his arm. Hunkering down beside her, he kissed her, lingering on the mouth.

"What was that for?" she asked, aware her heart was beating rapidly in her breast.

He laughed softly. "Does it have to be for something in particular? I saw a beautiful woman sitting in the sunshine and I wanted to kiss her."

Maggie ducked her head at his compliment, embarrassed by it. She stroked her breast with her forefinger, helping Meredith take the milk.

"I mean it, Maggie," he said, lifting her chin toward him. "You are beautiful." Her smile certainly was. He could never get enough of it. He dropped the basket and blanket and kissed her again.

Meredith was jostled from her food source and made certain her parents knew about it.

Connor pulled back, grinning. "Brat," he said. He guided Meredith back to Maggie's nipple. "She doesn't want to share today."

"You're incorrigible," Maggie admonished.

He shrugged, unabashed. Picking up the blanket, he unfolded it and snapped it sharply over the grass. He helped Maggie move onto it, careful not to disrupt Meredith this time. "Dancer said you took off in this direction. He thought you might enjoy a picnic."

"That was thoughtful of him. And even more thoughtful to send you with the basket." She stroked her daughter's soft cheek. "Meredith and I wouldn't have liked it so much with just anyone." She gave Connor a sidelong glance.

"All right," he said. "It was *my* idea. Are you satisfied?"

"I don't know why you pretended it wasn't. It's a lovely idea."

He rolled his dark eyes and the hard, handsome lines of his face were suddenly boyish. "Maybe because you'd say it was lovely."

"Well, I won't tell anyone else, so your reputation won't suffer. Now show me what's in that basket."

Connor knelt on the blanket and opened the basket's lid. He pulled out cold fried chicken, thick slices of ham, baked beans, half a loaf of fresh-baked bread, and preserves.

Maggie's mouth watered as Connor made a plate for her, cutting the ham and chicken so it was finger food. She put Meredith at her shoulder and patted her soundly on the back. "Don't you think Luke and Buck will be back soon?" she asked. "I'm getting anxious to have material for some more clothes for Meredith and I know Dancer wants to restock the pantry."

Connor put some strawberry preserves on a slice of bread. "I wouldn't be surprised if they're back this week. There'll be mail for you from Queen's Point."

She nodded. "Letters that have been sitting there all winter. It's the one thing I can't get used to."

"I didn't realize it bothered you."

"It didn't when I was trying to avoid my family, but now I want them to know everything that's happening. You realize, of course, when Mama and Jay Mac learn about Meredith, they'll descend on us."

"Maybe I should reconsider Rennie's offer for that tract of land."

Maggie didn't try to hide her surprise. Her eyes widened and her mouth gaped slightly. "You're not serious."

"Not the land she wanted initially. I wouldn't sell that, but I might think about letting Northeast Rail lease a back tract that Rennie once considered for an alternate route."

"But—"

Connor shrugged. "The Double H has different needs than it did before. Maybe we can't remain isolated out here. If there was a track on the property we'd be connected to Queen's Point and Cannon Mills would be connected to us. Denver wouldn't seem like the other side of the earth to you."

"It doesn't," she protested.

He wasn't listening. "We wouldn't have to drive the herd so far and I wouldn't have to be gone for weeks from the property. It never mattered before, but now . . . with Meredith . . ." His voice trailed off thoughtfully.

"You grew up here without the rails. So did your mother."

"It was a different time," he said philosophically. "There are more choices now. And I'm thinking of you, too. You shouldn't have to wait half the winter for the things you want, not if there's another way." He looked at her and saw her face was ashen and that her eyes were wet with tears. "What's wrong, Maggie?"

"I don't want you to do these things for me," she said. "I don't want the valley to change because I came here. Meredith doesn't want it either."

He smiled faintly. "You can't speak for Meredith."

"Don't make fun of me, Connor. You know what I mean. You fought Rennie and Jay Mac because you were so opposed to having this valley cut by a rail line. You did whatever it took to keep your land just as it was meant to be. You sacrificed—"

He cut her off. "What did I sacrifice, Maggie?" he asked softly. "Loneliness? Dawn to dusk work with no one to make me smile at the end of the day? That's all *I* gave up." He put down his plate. "You gave me back this land. You gave me a daughter and you gave up your dreams. You're the one who made the sacrifice."

Though she didn't agree, she didn't know what she could say to make him see it differently. She wanted him to understand that she knew how he felt about the land, that she respected and admired his reverence for the space and the silence. She didn't want it altered on her account.

Connor picked up a small chunk of ham on Maggie's plate and fed it to her. "Eat," he said, brooking no argument. "You'll need your strength for what I have in mind."

Meredith belched loudly.

"That's what your daughter thinks of your suggestions," Maggie said. "It's the middle of the afternoon!"

"So?"

Under Connor's darkly searching glance, Maggie's objections were never voiced. "Incorrigible," she said affectionately.

His eyes dropped to her uncovered breast as she lowered Meredith onto her lap. "Encourageable," he said.

Maggie smiled and drew her blouse modestly over her breast. "In good time," she said. "Take your daughter and let me eat." She handed Meredith over.

Connor lay back on the blanket and allowed the baby to sprawl across his chest. Maggie dangled a sliver of tender chicken above his mouth. He took it with the enthusiasm of a fledgling chick. "I could get used to this," he said.

"Don't choke." She began to eat from her own plate. "And don't get used to it." Maggie let the silence fall over them. It made things seem close and comfortable. Gradually sounds from beyond the clearing made themselves heard. There was the sweet song of robins and the cry of the kingbird. A flutter in the trees high above them signaled a golden eagle taking flight. Squirrels moved in the underbrush. A pine cone was shaken loose and dropped to the ground. An intermittent breeze would shift the grasses, feathering them so a dozen different hues of green shimmered in the sunshine.

Maggie finished her meal and put her plate back in the basket. Meredith was sleeping soundly, comforted by the gentle rise and fall of Connor's chest and the steady beat of his heart. He was sleeping, too. Maggie's smile was indulgent as she stretched out beside him and snuggled.

It was the rifle shot that woke them. Connor caught Meredith as he bolted upright. Startled by the sudden movement, the baby let out a wail. He handed her to Maggie and got to his feet, looking toward the ranch house in the hope of seeing what had prompted the shot.

"I can't see anything from here," he said. "But it can't be an emergency or they would have fired again. I'm going further up the hill to the ridge. I'll be able to see over the trees there. Why don't you gather up everything? I'll be right back."

Maggie packed the basket, bouncing Meredith in one arm. The baby's wail calmed to a whimper. "I know, dear heart, you want changing and you want your papa," she said soothingly. "And you'll get everything you want in just a little while." Maggie returned her daughter to the sling and fitted it over her shoulders. Meredith's fingers tugged hard on Maggie's unbound hair until Maggie pulled it out of the way. She picked up the blanket, the flowers, and her bonnet and waited for Connor's return.

"I thought you said it wasn't an emergency," she said as soon as she saw his face. His expression was grave, his dark eyes distant. "What's happened?"

"Buck and Luke are back."

That was hardly cause for the hard cast to his features. "Surely that's good news," she said.

For Maggie's sake he forced a smile. It merely set his mouth in a grim line. "They didn't come alone. We have visitors."

"Guests! But that's won—"

"Beryl and my father."

Maggie's jaw clamped shut. She stared at him mutely for a moment. "Beryl," she said tonelessly.

"My father," he said.

But Maggie didn't mind seeing Rushton again. If not for his wife, she would have looked forward to his visit, in spite of Connor's apprehension. "It'll be all right," she said, as much for her sake as his own.

Connor said nothing. He picked up the picnic basket and led the way down the hill.

They met Luke and Buck first, unloading the wagons at the rear of the ranch house.

Connor looked over the trunks still on the wagon and imagined what had already been taken in. "I suppose this means they intend to stay awhile."

"Can't say as to that," Buck said. "They didn't offer and I didn't ask."

Connor held out his hand. "Good to have you back, Buck. You too, Luke. We didn't expect you'd be gone so long."

Luke swung a sack of flour off the bed of the wagon and tossed it toward Ben who was standing by the door. "We tried two different times to get back. There was a landslide in Jelly's Pass. The horses could have made it but not the wagons. We thought about getting mules, then figured what the hell, we'd wait for the miners to blast the route open. Besides that, Buck here was in love."

Maggie laughed. "Were you, Buck?"

He jammed his hat down over his forehead and applied himself to his work.

"I don't think he wants to talk about it," Connor said.

Luke hefted another trunk onto the porch where it was picked up by Ben and Patrick. "Some of these trunks are yours, Maggie. Your sister sent them along with Rush and Beryl."

Maggie gave Connor's sleeve a tug. "We should go inside. They're waiting."

Before Connor could object, there was a scream from inside the house. Seconds later, Dancer came stomping out the back door carrying his belongings in a blanket. "Hell," he said disgustedly, "I was plannin' to move to the bunk house anyway." He jerked his head toward the house, his look contemptuous, and marched off the porch.

Maggie was embarrassed for Beryl's poor manners, but Connor's expression was thunderous. "Connor, wait," she called after him as he started up the steps. "She was just frightened by Dancer. She wasn't expecting him."

"Then she should damn well wait for an invitation next time." He caught the sack of sugar Buck tossed him and headed into the house.

Maggie looked at Luke and Buck, sighed, and followed her husband. Inside, Ben and Patrick pointed down the hallway and toward the guest bedroom. She thought she heard them mention fainting as they passed in the kitchen. She could just imagine the scene Beryl might have made. "Poor Dancer," she whispered.

They came upon Rushton and Beryl in the guest bedroom. Beryl was lying down. Rushton was sitting on one of the trunks that made the room an obstacle course.

"Father," Connor said. His greeting consisted of that single word and a terse nod. "Beryl."

"Who *was* that man?" Beryl asked weakly from the bed.

Watching from the doorway, Maggie noticed Connor's step-mother looked quite beautiful with her chestnut hair splashed over the pillow and her pale eyes beseeching. Maggie felt like a voyeur; no one had noted her presence. Meredith, still slung on her back, was being blissfully quiet for once.

"Dancer Tubbs," Connor said. "And he was our guest."

Rushton cleared his throat as Beryl opened her mouth to take exception to Connor's answer as well as his tone. "I think what my son is saying is that Mr. Tubbs was invited to use this room and we were not."

Connor didn't respond, confirming his father's interpretation without saying a word.

Meredith chose that moment to make certain she wasn't ignored any longer.

Chapter Fifteen

Maggie was aware of every eye turned in her direction. She offered her smile tentatively as she brought the sling around and unfastened it. Cradling Meredith, Maggie turned and held her daughter so Beryl and Rushton could see. "Say hello to your grandfather, Meredith," she said.

Rushton was on his feet immediately, stepping over bags and around trunks to get to his granddaughter. "May I?" he asked.

Maggie didn't hesitate. His dark eyes had lost their distant look as he looked down on the baby. So much like Connor, she thought, and they don't even realize it. "Here," she said, lifting the baby. "Take her."

Rushton accepted the flailing bundle with the ease of someone used to holding babies. "She looks like Connor," he said. "Same hair, same eyes." Meredith wailed suddenly. "Same lungs."

Over Rushton's shoulder, Maggie saw Connor's reluctant smile. "I think so, too," she said. "She's beautiful."

"Babies all look alike," Beryl said. "I can't tell one from the other."

Rushton carried Meredith over to the bed. "That's because you haven't tried." He sat on the edge and showed the baby to Beryl. When Beryl sat up and leaned forward Meredith grabbed a handful of chestnut hair and tried to get it into her mouth.

"Oooh, the little—"

"Beryl," Rushton said firmly. "She doesn't know any better."

Connor came over and helped extricate Beryl. "I think she's wet," he said. "Maggie? Do you want to—"

"I'll take her," Rushton said, getting up. He walked back to Maggie. "Show me where you change her."

Maggie led him into the hallway. "We moved her crib back into our room when Dancer returned," she said. "It's just as well with you being here now."

"I know you had no warning," he said. "And I apologize for that."

"Really," said Maggie. "There's no need."

He shook his head, flashing the iron gray threads of hair at his temples momentarily. "There's every need. We could have stayed in Denver a few weeks longer, at least until we could get word to you about wanting to visit. I think I knew that Connor wouldn't want us here no matter what the circumstance. Frankly, I depended on you."

"Then I'm happy you did," she said. Maggie was careful not to compromise her sincerity by mentioning Beryl's name. She laid out the changing blanket on the bed. "You can put her down now. She can't roll from her back to her front yet; she'll be fine."

Rushton laid the baby down. "What did I hear you say her name was?"

"Meredith. Mary and Edith. Names from both sides of the family."

"Meredith," he repeated softly. "I like it."

She saw that Rushton was obviously touched. "That's exactly what Connor said when I told him." She stripped off the baby's wet diaper and dropped it in a pail of water. "Would you get me that basket over there on the dresser? I like to put a little cornstarch on her bottom." Maggie fussed over the baby while Rushton watched. She could hear voices coming from the other bedroom but she tried not to pay any attention. Rushton helped by keeping up a steady stream of nonsense chatter. Maggie was certain that if shareholders in his steel company heard him they would be moved to sell their stocks immediately.

"You're angry, aren't you?" Beryl asked.

He didn't answer her directly. "Whose idea was this, Beryl? Tell me that. Yours or my father's?"

"You *are* angry." Looking up at him, she coyly nibbled on the tip of one nail. "I suppose we thought of it together," she told him. "I wanted to see my mother in Denver. It would have been foolish to have come so far and not taken a little more time and effort to see the Double H again."

"You never liked the Double H."

"I liked it better than Denver."

"You hated Denver."

"That's what I mean." Beryl sat up further and put her legs over the side of the bed. She saw Connor's sour look when her gown didn't immediately fall over her knees and calves. "You used to like looking at my legs," she said, righting her petticoats modestly. "There's still nothing wrong with them."

Connor looked at the sea of baggage around him. "It looks like you brought everything."

"Don't be silly. We left a lot of things with my mother."

"Then you *do* plan on leaving sometime." Under his breath, he added, "I wondered."

Beryl stood. Looking in the mirror across the room, she fiddled with her hair. "It looks as if you recovered from your aversion to your wife," she said. "I seem to recall something about separate bedrooms at the St. Mark." She gave him a sidelong glance. "Or maybe the baby isn't yours?"

Connor didn't offer a response. "Anything in here belong to Maggie?" he asked. "Luke said you brought some of her things from Michael's."

Beryl looked around. She saw the black leather case sitting behind one of the trunks, out of Connor's line of vision. "It's all mine."

He shook his head. "Amazing," he said softly, taking a step toward the door. He was brought up short as Beryl slipped her arm through his.

She stood on tiptoe, falling against him as he turned. "No kiss, Connor?" she asked breathily. "You must really hate me for marrying your father."

He didn't hate her. He just didn't give a damn. Even while the words were forming in his head he realized he'd held onto them too long. Beryl was pressing her mouth firmly against his. He reached for her waist to push her away. Out in the hallway he heard Maggie's soft tread and his daughter's gurgling. He managed to wrench Beryl free before Maggie turned the corner into the room.

Maggie saw nothing but the step Connor took away from Beryl and the look of guilty pleasure on Beryl's face. "I came to see if Beryl needs anything," she said, keeping her voice carefully neutral. She couldn't look at Connor, though she could tell he was trying to meet her eye. "Rushton's going to take the baby while I start dinner." Rushton appeared in that moment and scooped Meredith out of her mother's arms.

"He's going to be absolutely silly about that child, isn't he?" Beryl said as Rushton disappeared again.

"I'll see to dinner," Maggie said.

"I'll come with you," Connor said, following her.

When she was alone Beryl sat on one of the trunks. She smiled to herself. Rushton might have been oblivious, but she was certain Maggie had seen enough.

"I don't need any help," Maggie told Connor once they were in the kitchen. "Go talk to your father in the parlor."

"There's time enough for that," he said. "Right now I want to talk to you."

Maggie opened the trap door to the root cellar and climbed down. "I'm listening," she said, her tone conveying quite the opposite. She filled a basket with potatoes and carrots and carried it up. Connor wasn't around when she reached the top. "Good," she said succinctly, satisfied and miserable at the same time.

With Dancer Tubbs in the bunk house, the hired hands were happy to eat there. Maggie served dinner for the family at the round oak table in the small dining room. There was a roast, carrots and potatoes, fresh rolls, and thanks to Luke and Buck's timely return with sugar and spices, there were sand tarts baking in the oven for dessert.

Meredith was sleeping when they sat down and Maggie realized belatedly how much the presence of the baby would have buffered the tension. It was just as well, she thought. It wasn't fair to Meredith.

"How is your mother, Beryl?" Connor asked rather stiffly as he passed the roast platter.

"She's doing well. She has a touch of bursitis in her shoulder that she likes to complain about."

"That can be very painful," Maggie said quietly. "Has she seen a doctor?"

"She doesn't like doctors," Beryl said, an edge to her tone. "She likes to complain."

Rushton spoke up. "Grace doesn't think anything she's gotten from the physician has been very helpful." He ignored the look Beryl shot at him. "Do you know something that may work? Luke and Buck were saying on the way here that you know quite a bit about healing."

"White willow tea may relieve some of the pain. Perhaps as little as a cup a day might be helpful. I could give you some of the bark to take to her. It's no trouble."

Beryl snorted. "I'm not giving my mother the bark from some tree. I don't hold to Indian remedies. When I get back to New York I'm going to send her some of that tonic they advertise in the *Herald*."

"It's likely to be alcohol with a few flavorings," Maggie said. "Most of those tonics aren't effective."

"She's *my* mother," Beryl said.

Maggie cut her carrots carefully, calling on her patience. "Of course," she said. "I'm sorry. You're right."

Rushton passed the rolls to his wife. "Here," he said. "Put one of these in your mouth." When she looked at him, startled by what she thought she heard, he merely smiled at her, his eyes giving away nothing. "They're delicious."

For the second time that day Maggie caught Connor smiling at something his father had said. She speared one of her carefully sliced carrots. "I haven't had time to read any of my letters. Tell me about my mother and father. Are they well?"

Rushton obliged Maggie's interest, filling her in on most every encounter he'd had with Jay Mac and Moira since the marriage. He watched the play of expression on Maggie's delicate features. Her eyes and mouth registered a myriad of emotion. She was amused, content, pleased, and wistful. And throughout his storytelling he was aware he was not the only one observing her. When his eyes darted in his son's direction he saw that the expression there was watchful, but carefully neutral, shielding his thoughts in a way Maggie could not.

"I had the opportunity to read some of your letters home," Rushton said with off-handed charm. "I hope you don't mind that Jay Mac shared them."

"Of course not." She busied her hands with buttering a slice of bread, desperate to remember what she had written that might prove embarrassing. Too late she realized that it was what she *hadn't* written that was going to cause her discomfort.

"You never mentioned a grandchild was on the way."

Maggie couldn't help looking uncomfortable. She was. She could feel Beryl's scrutiny.

Connor answered for her. "Maggie didn't want Moira to worry and I didn't want Jay Mac descending on us before the baby was born. Both of those things were bound to happen and neither was particularly desirable. The letters heralding Meredith's coming have all been sent. There'll be one waiting for you in New York."

"I see," said Rushton. He chewed thoughtfully. On his right he saw Beryl's fingertips tap on the table as she counted out the months from marriage to birth. He lightly placed his foot on hers, caught her eye, and cautioned her against speaking her thoughts aloud.

"Would anyone like more potatoes?" Maggie asked, thrusting the bowl in Connor's direction. Her cheeks flamed when she heard her own voice crack with nervousness. It didn't even help that no one looked in her direction or commented. She gave up the bowl and applied herself to her own meal, scarcely tasting what she ate.

Rushton steered the conversation to other topics and, to ease Maggie's discomfort, Connor contributed more than he would have under different circumstances.

Later that evening after Rushton and Beryl had gone to bed, Maggie joined Connor on the front porch. Wordlessly, he took her hand and led her away from the house and toward the stream. There was a perch of rocks on one embankment and they sat there, Maggie secured in the cradle of Connor's body, her knees drawn toward her chest, his arms folded around her. The night was unseasonably warm and the breeze that lifted strands of Maggie's hair also carried the fragrance of it to Connor's senses. He breathed deeply and rubbed his chin back and forth against the crown of her head.

"You were talking to him tonight," she said softly. Her hands covered his. Her thumbs passed across the back of his hands. "Really talking to him."

"What?"

"At dinner," she said.

Connor thought about it a moment. He had been trying to save the situation, make it less uncomfortable for Maggie, and somehow he and Rushton had actually exchanged ideas for the better part of thirty minutes without coming to verbal blows. "I suppose I was," he said, then added a little defensively, "What about it?"

"It was nice."

He grunted softly.

"It *was* nice," she whispered, smiling. "And I liked the way you came to my rescue. Rushton, too, for that matter."

"My father started it," he said. "If he hadn't brought up the letters you wouldn't have been embarrassed."

"I think that was just simple curiosity on his part. He wasn't purposely trying to make me uncomfortable."

Connor didn't say anything for a moment. "Why do you defend him?" he asked finally.

"Is that what I was doing? I hadn't realized."

He wished he could see her face. There was something a bit too innocent in her tone. "You like him, don't you?"

"Yes," she said. "I do." She paused a beat. "What is it that stands between the two of you? Beryl?"

"God, no," Connor said feelingly.

There was something comforting in knowing that. Maggie snuggled closer. "Then what?"

Moonlight was reflected on the surface of the water. Ribbons of blue and white light rippled and curled as the water rushed over rocks and a single fish leaped for the light. At Maggie's back there was a stillness about Connor. His chin had stopped moving in her hair. His arms held her but no more tightly than they had a moment before. His breathing was quiet.

"He killed her," he said at last.

The words simply hung there. There was no edge of bitterness, no accusation in the tone, only the flat conviction of truth.

"Connor?" She turned her head and looked up at him. There was a certain tautness along his shadowed jaw. She touched him there. "What do you mean?"

"I mean he killed her," he said. "He left the Double H in the middle of the night, skulked out of here like some damn cattle rustler, and never looked back. My mother wasn't the same after that. She was buried fifteen years later, but she died that night. It's hard to forgive him for that."

Maggie felt as if her heart were being squeezed. "How old were you?"

He shrugged.

"How old?" she repeated.

"Seven," he said, then added in a voice that seemed almost that young with its raw pain, "I watched him leave."

"Oh, Connor," she said softly.

"I don't want your pity."

"I'm not offering it."

Connor wasn't so certain. He started to move away but Maggie held onto his arms and kept him close.

"No," she said. "Don't go. I want you to know what I'm offering isn't pity." She hesitated, searching for the right words.

"I'm listening," he said.

"I suppose I do feel sorry for the little boy who lost his mother and father on the same night, but I keep thinking that he was *only* seven and he can't have possibly known what took place between his parents."

"You're wrong," Connor said. "You're forgetting I had my grandfather. He told me what my mother never would: that Rushton left with silver in his saddle bag."

"Silver? But what—"

"Old Sam struck a vein on the land years ago. He never did anything about it. Just kept the silver in a few jars in the root cellar. When he saw that my father wasn't satisfied with life here, when Rushton kept pushing my mother to leave, Old Sam offered him the money. My father took it and ran. It was enough for him to buy his way into the steel business. He parlayed it into a fortune while my mother worked herself into an early grave. That's what I know."

Maggie was silent for a moment, then she said, "I'll only say it this one time, Connor: you still don't know what was between your parents, and if you don't speak to your father about it now, you never will."

This time it was Maggie who moved. She released herself from Connor's arms and stood. She touched him lightly on the shoulder. "Good night." Maggie walked back to the ranch house and didn't look back until she reached the porch. Connor was still sitting on the throne of rocks, staring at the moon's reflection, surrounded by the space and silence.

The next morning after breakfast, Maggie found a few minutes for herself and her daughter. The hands were working on rebuilding some fences, Dancer was preparing the afternoon meal, and Connor had taken Rushton and Beryl on a tour of the property. Maggie and Meredith shared the braided oval rug in the parlor and played with a cloth ball and wooden rattle that Ben had fashioned for the baby. The wicker laundry basket beside them tumbled as Maggie rolled Meredith onto her stomach, then onto her back. The baby laughed and kicked her chubby legs when she was buried in a mound of clothes. Things scattered and a three-legged stool was overturned in their energetic play. Maggie blew kisses against her baby's smooth belly. Meredith giggled, puckered her lips, and made incoherent sputtering sounds. Maggie's thick hair was loosened from its pins and tickled Meredith with its curling ends.

"This is very touching," Beryl said from the parlor's entrance. Her voice suggested otherwise. She came into the parlor, kicking aside some of the clothes that lay strewn in her path, and sat in one of the chairs. "Please, go on. Don't let me stop you."

Maggie sat up and made an attempt to straighten her hair. She reanchored the pins and smoothed the crown. "I thought you were with Connor and Rushton," she said. Ignoring Meredith's whimper, Maggie began tossing clothes back into the wicker hamper.

"They were going farther than I wanted," she said, shrugging. "I've ridden most everywhere on the property anyway. There wasn't anything I wanted to see."

Maggie was sure Beryl might have thought differently if she'd been alone with Connor, but she decided not to say so. "I'm going to do some washing," she said. "Perhaps you would watch Meredith for a while?"

Beryl glanced at the baby, who was quietly sucking on the rattle. She didn't answer Maggie's question. Instead she asked one of her own. "How long were you Connor's whore before he married you?"

Maggie's breath was simply expelled from her lungs. Her brows arched toward her hairline. Her knuckles whitened around the clothes she clutched. "How long were you Connor's whore before you married his father?"

Beryl's slow smile was feral. Her pale blue eyes saluted Maggie's comeback. "Touché." She pushed at a lock of her dark hair, curling a tendril around her forefinger. "Let's just say that I never seriously worked the profession the way you did."

Maggie schooled her features. "I don't know what you mean," she said.

Beryl pointed to Meredith. "Is she Connor's child?"

"Your question's insulting."

"I'm sorry," she said coolly. "I don't how to pose it in any other manner. Is she?"

"You only have to look at her to know the truth."

"Which is not precisely an answer." She sighed. "Poor Connor. He wonders, you know."

Maggie's shoulders stiffened and her chin came up. She felt like a fish with Beryl dangling the bait. In spite of that knowledge she couldn't help herself. She bit. "How do you know that?"

Beryl's oval face was tilted to one side momentarily. The expression in her eyes was pitying, the set of her mouth soft. "How could I possibly know if he didn't tell me?" she asked quietly. "Oh, he *wants* to believe she's his. That's what makes it such an agony for him. He wishes he could be certain he was the only man you had, but . . ." Her voice trailed off. She studied Maggie's pale features. "When you work as a lady of the evening for Mrs. Hall, you're bound to have more than one partner."

Maggie's heart slammed in her chest. Beryl's revelation stunned her. "How do you—"

Beryl's dark brows rose again. "I've said it before. How could I know if Connor didn't tell me?"

Maggie wondered if she couldn't believe it, or if she didn't want to believe it. "When?" she snapped. "You haven't been here but a moment."

"You keep forgetting," Beryl replied calmly, "that my relationship with Connor goes back several years. I think I know when something's troubling him. I spoke to him last night."

"I was with him last night."

"I know you were," she said. "For a while. I saw you from my bedroom window. You left him sitting alone by the stream. I went out after you came in. We talked for a long time."

Maggie remembered waking when Connor came to bed. She had no idea what time it was when he joined her but she had been sleeping hard. He had warmed himself against her, sliding his cold hands along the curve of her hip and waist, teasing her until she poked him in the ribs. "You talked to him about Meredith?" she asked.

"I *asked* about him," she said. "He *told* me about Meredith."

"He actually told you about Mrs. Hall's?"

"He actually did." She smiled gently. "But you're beginning to realize the truth in that, aren't you? I really couldn't know otherwise."

Maggie couldn't think of an alternative explanation. She pitched the last of the clothes into the basket, added Meredith on top, and stood, scooping the basket under her arm. "I don't think I want to spend any more time alone with you, Beryl. If Connor told you these things then I'm certain he meant them to be held in confidence."

She laughed lightly. "Oh, I'm quite certain he didn't. Connor knows me as well as I know him. He told me because he *knew* I'd ask. Is the baby his, Maggie?"

She started to walk out of the room.

"Don't you want me to watch Meredith?" asked Beryl.

"Go to hell."

Beryl's smile rose slowly and smugly.

Rushton looked over the valley from the rocky ledge that he shared with his son. "You've done right by Edie's dreams," he said. His gaze turned from the breadth of the homestead laid out before him to Connor. "You love it the same way she did."

"What do you know about her dreams?" he asked. "Or about what I love? You weren't around long enough to know either one of us." It came out in the rapid fire of a machine gun burst and Connor regretted all of it immediately. "Never mind," he said tersely. "It's Maggie's fault. She got me thinking." He started to go but Rushton reached over and grabbed Tempest's reins. The horse pawed the ground nervously. Stones from the ledge slipped over the hillside, skittering and bouncing along the rocky incline. "Are you trying to kill me?" he demanded, taking his mount under control.

"No," Rushton said calmly, "I'm trying to make you listen. Just this once, hear me out."

Connor sat in the saddle stonily. He didn't move.

"That old man poisoned you against me," he said. "He couldn't stand the thought of his grandson leaving this valley the way his sons did. He pinned every hope he had on Edie, forced her to take up the commitment he had to this ranch and this land." When he saw Connor wasn't bolting, Rushton's tone became less earnest, less bent on convincing. "The thing of it was, your mother loved this place. For Edie, living here and loving it was as natural as breathing. Perhaps it was because she was a woman that your grandfather didn't trust her. Perhaps it was because he had already had three sons leave." He was quiet a moment. "Or perhaps it was because I represented a threat to him, someone from the outside who had elected to stay. Old Sam certainly didn't trust me. He thought I might give Edie notions about leaving, fill her head with what the city had to offer. Your grandfather never saw me as Edie's anchor here. He was sure I was going to take her away."

"You asked her to leave," Connor said. "I know. I heard you talking about it. So Old Sam was right."

"I asked Edie to leave more than a dozen times," Rushton admitted without shame. "But never once until she told me to go."

Connor's head jerked to the side. He stared at his father's chiseled profile. Rushton's mouth was grimly set, the edge of his jaw, hard. But the profile couldn't hide the glimmer of something wet at the corner of Rushton's eye. "My mother told you to go?" said Connor.

Rushton nodded once.

"You're lying." Connor spurred his horse around and left his father alone on the ledge.

Dinner that evening was a silent affair. Beryl offered a few conversation gambits but no one was interested. Meredith seemed to sense the tension and grew cranky as the meal progressed. Almost relieved for the excuse, Maggie left the table with her daughter and retired to the bedroom. Rushton went to the bunk house a few minutes later, ostensibly to play poker with the hands. Beryl began clearing the table. Connor walked out to the corral.

"Thought you might be out here," Dancer said as he approached the corral fence.

Connor continued grooming Tempest, stroking the stallion's flank with a hard brush. "Thought you'd be playing poker."

Dancer grunted. "No one around here has nuggets. It ain't worth playin' unless you got nuggets."

Laughing, Connor patted Tempest's hindquarters and sent him preening and prancing to the far corner of the corral. "Not everyone has a gold mine, Dancer."

"Don't I know it."

Connor leaned against the rail and stretched his legs. "Was there something you wanted?"

"Did you take your pa around the south end of the ranch today?"

"No. Some reason why I should?"

"Went down that way myself this afternoon. Frankly, I couldn't stomach the company 'round here, but that ain't my business."

Connor knew there was no love lost between the prospector and Beryl. "What is your business?"

"I think you got rustlers stealin' from your herd down that way." He saw he had Connor's complete attention. "Don't know it for a fact, but the signs look right."

"Why didn't you say something earlier?"

"I'm sayin' somethin' now."

Connor whistled sharply. Tempest's ear's pricked. The stallion trotted along the perimeter of the corral to Connor's side. Connor hefted his saddle off the top rail and slung it over Tempest's back. "You want to show me where?" he asked, fastening the straps.

"It's near dusk," Dancer pointed out. "It'll be hard to track."

"I don't plan on doing anything tonight," he said.

"All right."

They set out ten minutes later, taking the first part of the journey swiftly. Dancer was not a tracker by nature, but Connor had no trouble finding the signs. Grass was trampled. There were broken branches where horses and cattle had passed hurriedly.

"Not Indians," Connor said. "They'd never be this obvious. Looks like the work of two men. They picked out the grazing stragglers and didn't go for the heart of the herd."

"How many you reckon they got?"

"A dozen."

"They're long gone then."

Connor dismounted and went forward on foot for awhile. It took him less than ten minutes to find the remains of a fire. "They were pretty certain we wouldn't see the smoke from the house. This was a big fire and they weren't in any hurry to leave."

"Figure they plan to come back this way?"

"That's exactly what I figure." Connor glanced up at the sky. There was virtually no daylight left. "We'll start out tomorrow. They were headed for your property, Dancer. They could be holed up at your cabin."

"Like hell."

Connor grinned as Dancer spit to emphasize what he thought of rustlers using his place. "Come on," he said. "Maggie's going to be worried."

"Don't count on it," Dancer muttered.

"What?" Connor glanced over his shoulder. "Did you say something?"

"Never mind. Keepin' my nose out of people's business."

"Sounds more like your nose is out of joint." He waited to see if Dancer was going to reply. When the prospector didn't, Connor shrugged and led the way back to the ranch.

Beryl was waiting on the porch. When she saw them approaching she smoothed her lavender gown over her midriff and hips and tripped lightly down the steps and across the yard.

Dancer saw her coming first. "Here's trouble," he said under his breath. More loudly he added, "I'm goin' 'round to the bunk house and tell the others what we found. You take care of the animals." He dismounted and got out of Beryl's way before she reached them.

Connor slid out of the saddle and took both horses by the reins. Ignoring Beryl, he led them into the stable and into their stalls. "What is it now, Beryl?" he asked, lighting a lantern. He hung it on a hook just outside the stalls.

"You might make me feel a trifle more welcome," she said, sidling up to the first stall. Her face was bathed in the warm lantern light. She watched Connor work for a while before she said casually, "Your daughter's lovely. If she is your daughter, that is."

His head came up and he looked at her sharply. "What the hell is that supposed to mean?"

"Just that I know Maggie was the whore you met at Mrs. Hall's brothel. I imagine it's hard to know which dark-haired, dark-eyed patron fathered that baby."

"What the hell goes through your mind, Beryl?" he asked angrily, striking the offense before she cornered him.

She shrugged delicately. "Have I misspoken?" she asked. "I thought since Maggie shared it with me I could talk plainly to you."

Connor's eyes narrowed as he looked at Beryl for a long moment. "Maggie told you about Mrs. Hall's?" he asked, suspicious.

"How else could I possibly know?"

That was something worth finding out, Connor thought. "Meredith is my child and if you think Maggie told you something else then you misunderstood her."

"Perhaps I did," Beryl said softly, backing off slightly. "Tell me something, Connor, was she pregnant when you married her?"

"I didn't think so," he said. He rubbed down Dancer's horse. "It didn't have anything to do with why I married her, Beryl, so stop barking up that tree."

She laughed lightly. "What an unpleasant picture."

"It suits you," he said bluntly. "You're a bitch."

Beryl blinked. The line of her mouth hardened. "You'll regret saying that."

He stared her down. "A bitch in heat."

She slapped him.

Connor didn't respond except to become very still. He saw Beryl flinch. After a moment he pushed past her and went into the next stall to take care of Tempest.

Beryl recovered and followed him. "Your wife's not happy here," she said.

Most anything else Beryl could have said, Connor would have ignored. This barb struck an open wound. "Did Maggie say that?" he asked cautiously.

"What do you think?" she countered. Before he could reply Beryl went on. "When I was in Denver I spent some time with her sisters. There was talk of Maggie wanting to be a doctor. I confess I find the whole notion rather odd, but then she comes from a rather odd family, don't you think?"

Connor didn't reply.

"Do you think she resents you for getting her pregnant?" asked Beryl. She leaned against the side of the stall and crossed her arms in front of her narrow waist. "You might not have known she was carrying a child, but she knew, and with all the bastards in her family, what choice did she really have?" Beryl shrugged. "You have to admit, Connor, it seems Maggie gave up medicine to come out here. If I had a dream like that I wouldn't be happy with anything less."

Connor gave Tempest a slice of apple from the flat of his palm. He glanced sideways at Beryl, his dark brows drawn. "You did have a dream, Beryl. You wanted to marry money and get out of Colorado, and you'd almost given it up when you met my father. Strange, though, you got exactly what you wanted and you haven't been happy since. That doesn't leave you in a very good position to know Maggie's state of mind." He brushed his hands off on his jeans and started to move out of the stall.

Beryl blocked his path. "It was never just about money with your father," she said. "And never just about getting east." She put her arms around Connor's waist. "You wouldn't believe me if I told you what it was about." She raised herself on tiptoe and pressed her mouth against his.

Connor simply picked Beryl up and set her away from him. "Where did you get the idea I might love you? You're an astonishingly beautiful woman, Beryl—"

Maggie stepped into the stable holding Meredith in her arms. Her features were expressionless. In that moment she taught her husband about cold and distant eyes. "Rushton's looking for you, Beryl," she said flatly. "I told him I thought you were out here."

"And here I am." Beryl smiled coyly at Connor. "I guess that means I'll excuse myself." Her walk was deliberately provocative as she left the stable and slid one last, over-the-shoulder glance at Connor before she disappeared into the night.

Tempest snorted and moved restlessly. An owl in the rafters flapped its wings and hooted. A litter of kittens mewled for their meal in the loft. For more than a minute the animals provided the only sounds. Afraid that she'd sound like a harridan or a harpy, or start screaming and never stop, Maggie remained silent.

"Maggie," Connor said quietly, gently.

It was the voice he used on the horses, she thought. That low, lullaby tone that kept them calm while he reined them in. It was the soft, sweet cadence of capture. She wasn't having any part of it.

Connor raised his hand, reaching for her as she turned to go. His outstretched arm remained suspended, just inches from her. He could have extended himself and touched her. Instead he did nothing.

Lowering his arm, he watched her walk away. He'd wondered how he would convince her to leave the Double H. Now he knew.

Maggie was sitting in the rocker nursing Meredith when Connor came back to the house. She didn't look up as he entered the room or at any time while he was getting ready for bed. Meredith watched him, though, and to Connor's guilty conscience even his daughter's eyes looked faintly accusing.

"I heard we have rustlers," Maggie said, lifting Meredith to her shoulder.

"That's right." Connor slipped under the covers and rolled on his side, propping himself on an elbow. "Dancer found their trail. We're going after them tomorrow."

"Do you hunt them down or lie in wait for them to come back?"

"Either. This time, a little of both. Patrick, Ben, and Luke will wait for them. The rest of us are going hunting."

"The rest of us?"

"Dancer, Buck, and me."

Meredith burped. "There's a good girl," Maggie praised her. "Are you ready for sleep? Hmmm?" She kissed her daughter's cheek. "What about Rushton?" she asked Connor.

"What about him? My father's not going." He held out his arms as Maggie rose from the rocker. She handed him Meredith and he rolled on his back, letting the baby rest on his chest.

Maggie unbuttoned her dress. "He thinks he is," she said. "In fact, I'm certain he's counting on it."

"Then he should count on something else. It's too dangerous. He hasn't done any hard riding for years and I'm not sure he can handle a gun."

"He was examining your gun case earlier. He looked as if he knew which end to point."

Connor paused in stroking Meredith's silky cap of dark hair.

"What are you saying, Maggie? That I should take him along just because he can still get on a horse and hold a gun?"

"No, of course not." She unhooked her button shoes and rolled her stockings down and off. "You have to decide if he would be a help or a hindrance. I just don't think you should ignore him."

"Did he put you up to this?"

"No!" She let her dress drop to the floor, stepped out of the circle of material, and went to the wardrobe to get her nightgown. "I just think you should consider the consequences of not taking him with you. It would be a slap in the face."

Connor's reply was a soft, noncommittal grunt.

Maggie picked up Meredith, held her above Connor's face for a kiss, then laid her in the crib. She stood over the bed, patting Meredith's bottom gently while the baby squirmed and squealed. Connor blew out the lamps and the baby quieted almost immediately. Maggie gave it a few more minutes then crawled into bed.

She lay on her back and stared at the ceiling. She could feel Connor watching her. The very thing he expected her to talk about was the very last thing she wanted to talk about. Her emotions were too raw to bring Beryl into their bedroom. "What happened between you and your father today?" she asked quietly. Even though they weren't touching, she felt him stiffen and knew she had struck another nerve. "I know it was something," she said. "You and he went riding this morning in reasonably good spirits. You haven't exchanged five words since."

Connor didn't answer right away as his thoughts drifted back over the conversation with Rushton. "I asked him why he left," he said finally. "He made my grandfather the scapegoat, said Old Sam thought he'd take my mother away from the ranch. Convenient, since Old Sam isn't in a position to defend himself."

That hadn't settled well with Connor, Maggie knew that, but some sixth sense told her there was more. She waited, using silence to draw him out.

"He told me my mother asked him to leave the Double H."

Maggie expelled a breath she hadn't known she was holding. "You didn't believe him."

"I called him a liar."

"Oh, Connor," she said softly. "Can't you imagine any reason that Edie might have wanted Rushton to go?"

He didn't hesitate. "No," he said. "No reason. She loved him. He was everything to her—more important than Old Sam, or me, or this ranch. When you love someone like that you don't think about asking them to leave."

Her voice was gentle. "Don't you?" she asked. "Even if you thought they were miserably unhappy?"

This time Connor didn't answer.

Maggie and Beryl stood on the porch at daybreak, watching the men ride out. "There's no good reason for him to go," Beryl said angrily. "He could get himself killed."

Maggie gave her a sideways glance. Beryl's profile was stark, her skin pale. "There's every reason," she said. "It's not in him to ask others to do what he won't do himself."

"He didn't *ask* anyone."

"I suppose he didn't. But it's his land, Beryl. His responsibility."

"Not any longer."

Frowning, Maggie turned to face Beryl more directly. "What do you mean? Of course the ranch is his."

The line of Beryl's dark brows made her blue eyes seem even lighter. The corners of her mouth were pulled in a frown. "What are you talking about?" she asked, clearly bewildered. "He sold the ranch."

"Sold it?" Maggie's green eyes clouded, then cleared. "Sold it," she repeated softly. She realized then their entire conversation had been at cross purposes. Beryl wasn't worried about Connor. Her concern—and her anger—was directed at Rushton. "Of course," she said. "I don't know what I was thinking." Maggie hurried into the house before Beryl could see the smile she couldn't quite hide.

Dancer glanced over his shoulder in time to see Maggie return to the house. "Well," he told the others, "they ain't killed each other yet."

Buck laughed. Rushton and Connor made no comment.

"Course, if we're gone more than a day," he mused, "anything's likely to happen."

Connor shot the prospector a sour look. "You'd do better to think about what's ahead than what we left behind." It was his last word on the subject and Dancer took the hint.

The group split at the site where the rustlers had built their makeshift camp. Patrick, Ben, and Luke found places to hide among the trees and rocks while cows grazed on the grassland below them. Theirs was a waiting game. Connor led the others further south to Dancer's property. Theirs was a hunt.

From time to time during the trek, Connor's eyes shifted from the trail to his father. Rushton was holding his own, even, Connor thought, looking comfortable in the saddle. As the morning passed with no sighting of the rustlers, Buck and Dancer fell back on the trail and spread out, leaving Connor and Rushton to ride in tandem.

The sun beat down on them warmly while the breeze was cool. Connor brought the brim of his hat down to shade his eyes. "Maggie thinks I should listen to you," he said.

"Did she say that?"

"Not in so many words." His smile was brief and a trifle self-mocking. "Maggie never uses very many words."

"I've noticed that."

"She makes you think, then she makes you think it was your idea."

"Clever woman."

Connor shook his head. "Not clever. Wise. Maggie is wise."

Rushton glanced at his son. "You love her."

"You sound surprised."

"Shouldn't I be? This marriage wasn't to your liking and I'm not really sure it was to hers. I wasn't even certain that you and Maggie were still together. Her letters to Jay Mac didn't ring true of life here at the Double H, and she had next to nothing to say about you."

"Is that why you came out? To see for yourself?"

"Now you sound surprised."

Connor shrugged. His eyes scanned the narrow pass they were about to enter.

"Edie wanted me to leave the Double H," Rushton said, "but she never meant for you and me to be estranged. Why do you think she sent you east for your education? Why do you think she never willed the Double H to you? She meant for this land to be our connection."

"You were going to sell our connection," Connor said.

"It brought you home."

"This is my home," he said. "Your deal with Jay Mac took me to New York."

"You wouldn't have come any other way."

"And we both know why." There was no need to explain. Connor had invited Rushton to Denver to meet his fiancée and attend the wedding and Rushton was the one who got married.

Rushton's dark eyes studied his son's face. "Are you really sorry you didn't marry Beryl?"

There was no hesitation on Connor's part. "Hell, no."

"Then put it in the past." He looked ahead again. "When I left the Double H I didn't know I'd never live with your mother again. She gave me Old Sam's silver nuggets to start a business in the east."

"Old Sam said he bribed you to leave with those nuggets."

"You can call me a liar again, but that's not how it was." He waited a moment. Connor said nothing. "She was going to join me when I was settled and I was foolish enough to believe she meant it. I suppose she knew I'd never have gone otherwise." He was quiet and thoughtful. "Edie thought I was miserable here and Old Sam made certain she kept on thinking it. I never really understood then why she was so adamant that I get out. It took me a long time to realize she meant to be noble, sacrificing her happiness for mine." He glanced in Connor's direction again. "But the hell of it is, she never asked me if that's what I wanted."

Connor was quiet, thinking. He shook his head, his slight smile filled with self-mockery. "The apple doesn't fall far from the tree."

"So I've observed," Rushton said gravely.

Appreciative of his father's dry pronouncement, Connor's glance slid sideways. He missed the flash of sunlight in the ridge of pines above them.

Rushton didn't. He wasn't aware of any conscious thought on his part. He simply reacted, pushing Connor out of the way and shouting a warning at the same time. It was odd, he thought, how he could feel the impact of the bullet in the very moment he heard its report.

Chapter Sixteen

Connor grabbed his rifle from the scabbard and fired two shots into the tree line above him. He heard a shout, but in the pass it was difficult to know its origin. Using Tempest for cover, Connor helped his father down from the saddle. Rushton was holding his shoulder. Blood seeped through his fingers.

"Can you get to those rocks?" asked Connor, pointing to the boulders behind him.

Rushton nodded. His face was ashen and he was breathing hard, but he was game.

"All right. On my signal. I'll cover you." Connor fired into the trees again. "Now!"

Both men scrambled up the hillside. Stones slid under their feet as they searched for purchase. There was more gun fire. A rock shattered near Connor's left hand, showering him with shrapnel and dust. He pushed his father up the incline, rolled on his back, and shot again. This time something moved in the trees. Connor made it to cover just as one of the gunmen fell from the low hanging branches of a pine.

Rushton leaned back against the protecting rock. He pulled out his gun.

"You need that hand to hold your wound," Connor said. "You're damn well not going to bleed to death on me."

Rushton grinned. "Just as well. I haven't shot one of these in years." He passed his gun to Connor. "Where are Dancer and Buck?"

"Circling 'round. They were back far enough that they probably weren't seen." He took off his hat, put it on the end of his rifle, and raised the barrel slightly above the boulder that shielded them. A bullet struck the hat, spun it on the barrel. Connor lowered the rifle, took off the hat, and showed Rushton the hole by poking his finger through it. "Looks like we're stuck until the cavalry gets here," he said philosophically.

One corner of Rushton's mouth rose. "You sorry you let me come?"

Connor realized that his father had overheard some part of his conversation with Maggie the night before. He answered honestly, tearing off a piece of his shirt to bind Rushton's wound. "There's no one I'd rather have with me." He handed his father the strip of material. "Here, hold this while I look at the damage." He caught and held his father's eyes for a moment. "And thank you," he said huskily. "That's the second time you've taken something I thought was intended for me."

"The second?"

"Beryl was first," Connor reminded him. "And I don't think I've ever thanked you properly for that."

Rushton grunted softly as Connor examined the wound. "I didn't do that for you. I'm not that selfless." He tried to get a look at his shoulder while Connor probed. "And Beryl's not quite what you think she is," he said.

"We could get nose to nose," Connor said, "and never see eye to eye on Beryl." A bullet ricocheted off the boulder. Connor and Rushton ducked instinctively. "Hold this dressing in place," Connor said, reaching for his gun. "I want to have another look." He turned and knelt, facing the boulder. Instead of looking over the top he edged around the side.

The body that had fallen out of the trees was still lying on the hillside. The neck lolled sideways at an odd angle. Connor doubted it was a bullet that killed him. The man's hat had slipped off his head. His curly brown hair was powdered with rock dust. Even in grotesque death there was something familiar about the shape of the man's broad face and the color of his hair.

Whistling softly as he made the connection, Connor ducked back behind the rock.

"What is it?" asked Rushton. "More trouble?"

"Not exactly. I think I know who the rustlers are." He gave his father a brief account of his encounter with Tuck and Freado at Dancer's cabin, raising more questions than he wanted to answer. "Let's just say one of them looks like another of them. They're all kin and it would be hard to find a good apple in the barrel. My guess is they figured what happened to Tuck and Freado and came looking for Dancer. Somehow they tracked him to the Double H."

"Then they're not after your cattle."

"That was to get us out, but they'll take 'em." A shot was fired from their side of the hill. "I hope that's Dancer or Buck," Connor said, "otherwise we're not safe here." Several more shots were exchanged. None of them came near the boulder.

In spite of the pain throbbing in his shoulder, Rushton managed a dry grin. "It's the cavalry."

"Seems that way," said Connor. "I'm going to help." Without another word Connor left the safety of the boulder and scrambled higher up the hillside. Covering fire came from above as Connor dove behind another outcropping of rocks. From his new vantage point he could see Dancer. "Where's Buck?"

"Comin' at them from the other side," he called back. "Thought you might need some protection over here."

Connor ducked as a bullet came overhead. "It's appreciated."

"There sure as hell are more than two of them and I'm not countin' the one you got already. I reckon four, maybe five."

"They're kin to Tuck and Freado," Connor said.

"That a fact," Dancer drawled. "Then we got the whole clan."

Beryl sat at the kitchen table watching Maggie peel potatoes. "Aren't you worried?" she blurted out.

"Worried?" asked Maggie. She looked up at Beryl, her brows arched in disbelief. "That hardly describes it. I'm terrified."

"You have an odd way of showing it." As far as Beryl could see, Maggie had let nothing interfere with her routine. She'd done housework most of the morning, fed Meredith, prepared lunch, ironed, and was now preparing dinner. For her part, Beryl had found nothing could take her mind off things. "You haven't gone to the window once today."

"I'm letting you do that. I have to keep busy in other ways." Maggie reached behind her, opened a drawer, and pulled out a paring knife. She slid it across the table. "Try peeling some of these."

"You don't even know if they'll be home for dinner."

"I'm hopeful." She rolled a potato toward Beryl. "Peel."

Beryl peeled. "How could you let Connor go this morning?"

"How could I not?" She paused in her work, cocking her head to one side as she thought she heard Meredith. There was another whimper then blessed silence. "I can't stop him from running this ranch. It would be like asking him not to breathe."

Beryl tossed the peeled potato into a pot of cold water and picked up another. "That's what he asked you to do."

"What do you mean?"

"I always heard you wanted to be a doctor."

"That's true. But Connor never asked me not to do it. That was a decision I made on my own." Her smile was gentle. "Not quite on my own. Meredith was an influence."

Beryl shook her head slowly, studying Maggie with her pale blue eyes. "You're happy here, aren't you? You actually like the Double H."

Maggie stopped peeling. Without thinking about it, her gaze drifted to the kitchen window where she could see the tall trees and grassland, the distant peaks and azure sky. "It's different from anything I've ever known," she said almost reverently, "but I feel as if I belong here." She met Beryl's curious eyes frankly. "It's hard to know which part of it is because of Connor, which part is Meredith, and which part is just me. Perhaps there's no separating any of it. But, yes, Beryl, I'm happy here. Very happy."

Beryl Holiday merely shook her head.

"Wonder what Maggie's got cookin' tonight," Dancer said. The lull in the gunfire had already lasted more than twenty minutes. The prospector's thoughts had turned to dinner. "You think she's expectin' us?"

"I think she'd like to see us," said Connor.

"Reckon Buck's hungry about now." Dancer's head cocked to one side to catch the direction of the low rumble that caught his attention. "That your stomach, Rushton?" he hollered.

"It wasn't," he called back. His wound had stopped bleeding. It ached abominably but Rushton was happy to be alive. "But it could have been."

"Hear that, Connor?" Dancer said. "Your pa's hungry. Seems like we ought to settle this showdown by sundown." He cackled gleefully, scrambled to a kneeling position behind his rock, took aim, and ended the lull in the battle.

Maggie sat on the first step of the porch, teasing Meredith with a rattle. Beryl sat on the rocker behind them, pushing it back and forth with an intensity that wasn't meant to be relaxing, but to use up nervous energy. Listening to the incessant creaking, Maggie thought she understood why Freado had shot the chair from under her. Suddenly that whole encounter seemed wildly funny. Maggie's smile widened, a giggle erupted, then she was laughing deeply and heartily.

Meredith stopped her flailing to watch the play of expression on her mother's face. Her eyes widened and rolled comically. Her chin quivered. Then her mouth opened and the beautiful sound of baby laughter—clear, honest, and purely joyful—tumbled out.

Beryl's shoulders began to shake as she attempted to stifle her laughter. She didn't know what she thought was funny or what anyone else thought was funny—she only knew that suddenly it was impossible not to laugh. Tears gathered at the corners of her eyes and she didn't bother to brush them away. She tried to catch her breath between waves of hard laughter, gulping the air as though she were thirsty for it.

Maggie's lap shook, bouncing Meredith, as they laughed together. Beryl's own laughter made it difficult for them to stop. The three of them took turns instigating another round of helpless, healing laughter until they were simply unable to go on.

Maggie reached for the hem of her gown and drew it to her eyes. She dabbed at them, then at her wet cheeks. Then she sighed deeply, shaking her head, her smile rueful. "That felt good," she said.

It had, Beryl thought. And she still didn't know how or why it had started. The smile she offered Maggie was tentative, as if she expected rejection.

Maggie lifted Meredith so she could look at Beryl. "See that pretty lady there," she said softly to the child. "That's your stepgrandmama. Ooops, there went her smile." She paused, watching Beryl closely. "No, not quite. See, it's tugging at the corners of her mouth again. She's struggling, but . . ."

Beryl laughed and leaned forward in the rocker. She spoke to Meredith. "That's right. I'm your stepgrandmama and this is the only time I'm saying it. I'll never answer to it and if you call me anything but Beryl I won't send you presents from New York."

Meredith listened to Beryl, her small head tilted to one side. Her dark eyes were solemn and unblinking. One of her chubby hands unfolded and she made a reaching gesture in Beryl's direction.

"Imp," Maggie said fondly. "You heard the word 'presents' and you're ready to make friends." She held her baby out to Beryl.

"Little mercenary," said Beryl, scooping up Meredith. She tapped the infant on her button nose. "I think I like that." She glanced at Maggie through the fan of her dark lashes but continued to speak in singsong fashion to Meredith. "Your mama doesn't know whether to take me seriously. No, she doesn't. Wait. She's smiling just a little. Oooh, there it is. The whole smile. Just like yours."

Maggie leaned back against the porch support. Her smile gradually faded from fulsome to wistful. Twilight hung like a blue-gray shroud over the ranch. "It doesn't seem as though they'll make it back tonight," she said quietly.

Beryl's pale eyes looked toward where she expected the riders to appear. There was no sign of them. Anxiousness stirred in her again.

"Have you ever shot a gun?"

The question surprised Beryl. "A few times. I can hit the broad side of a barn. Why?"

"I just wondered." She hesitated, wondering what she could tell Beryl. "I wish I didn't have to stay here, waiting. I wish I could have gone with them this morning." She sighed. "At least I would know."

Beryl nodded. "Men don't understand about the waiting. They don't understand the toll it takes."

"Edie would have gone with them."

"Probably." Beryl's eyes drifted back to the baby she cradled in her arms. She touched Meredith's chin with her forefinger. "Rushton says that Edie could do most anything."

Watching Beryl's pensive expression, the knit of her dark and delicate brows, Maggie asked softly, "He talks about her?"

"All the time." Her half-smile was self-mocking. "I don't think he even realizes how often. Sometimes I think . . ." She shrugged.

Maggie waited, silent, but Beryl offered nothing else. "Are you tired of holding her?" she asked.

"No, I'm fine." She looked up, her features set softly in the dusky light. "That is, if you don't—"

This time Maggie realized that Beryl broke off purposely as something beyond Maggie's head caught her attention. Maggie's head swiveled as she strained to see what Beryl had seen.

At first it was only shadows, near-shapeless and shifting forms moving slowly through the fading light. The shadows were bunched, coming forward almost as a single mass; then they seemed to splinter, separating as they approached, becoming more recognizable. The lead horses and riders broke with the pack suddenly and thundered toward the ranch house. There were shouts that were not understandable but clearly communicating jubilation in volume and tone.

Maggie stood, listening for one voice in the midst of all the others. Behind her she sensed Beryl rising and moving to the lip of the porch. Turning, Maggie took Meredith into her arms. Both women stood silent and still, straining to see and hear.

Buck and Patrick reached the porch first, cheering and whooping as if it had been a race and they'd won the prize. Ben came in just behind them, stirring a dust cloud as he pulled his mare sideways to keep from colliding with the others.

Maggie was on tiptoe now, looking over them and past them, trying to see the rest of the party. Beryl had moved to the bottom step, her entire upper body leaning forward in anticipation.

Luke brought his mount up sharply, shaking his head at the antics of the others. Dancer loped in beside him. He tipped his hat to the women and grinned widely. "Sure hope you saved us some dinner," he said. "Hell of a thing, bein' late for dinner."

Beryl was running now, her sights set on the last two riders. Half the hands turned to watch her. The other half watched Maggie to gauge her reaction. What they saw caught them all off guard: Beryl's run never veered once toward Connor, and Maggie's features were serene and untroubled as though she had expected nothing less.

Maggie smiled at Dancer and handed Meredith to him. "Here, take her. She missed you." Then she followed in Beryl's wake.

Connor pulled up his horse, dismounting quickly as Maggie came upon him. She nearly leaped in his arms. He lifted her, laughing, and returned the kisses she scattered over his face. Her whispers of welcome and longing warmed his skin, touched his soul. He held her closely and then his mouth found hers. The kiss held, healing and deeply hungry in the same moment.

"Maggie," he said huskily. He kissed her again, this time on the corner of her mouth. He tasted the salty wetness of her tears and he said her name reverently this time, knowing the tears were for him.

Her smile was watery. "Next time, I'm going," she said.

Even in the deepening twilight, he could see that she was serious. He didn't say no.

"Are you two quite finished?" Beryl asked sharply, helping Rushton dismount. "Some people come home in one piece and some people don't. Put your arm around me, Rush. That's it."

Connor set Maggie away from him and went to help his father.

"It's just a scratch, Beryl," Rushton said gruffly as Connor took Beryl's place. "It hardly aches now."

"Scratch!" Her voice rose. "Maggie, look at it! He's got a hole in his shoulder and he can barely walk!"

"I've been riding and crouching the better part of the day," Rush told her, limping along. "I'm not stretched out yet."

Beryl grabbed Maggie by the arm and pulled her along as Connor helped Rushton to the house. "Stretched out!" she cried. "Any more of this damn foolishness and you'll be stretched out in a pine box."

"Pine box?" He grinned, turning his head to look at his wife. "I think we can afford better than that."

She raced around Rushton and Connor, forcing them to halt in their tracks as she turned and faced them. "No," she said firmly, fists on her hips. There was high color in her cheeks and her pale blue eyes glittered angrily. "There'll be no we then. So help me, Rushton, I'll have you buried in a pine box and I'll keep all your money." Through her haze of fury she saw his dark eyes widen slightly, his jaw loosen and drop a notch. "You can't be surprised," she went on. "It's what you expect from me, isn't it? It's all you've ever expected from me. I couldn't have married you because I loved you. That would have been inconceivable. It must have been for your money. It must have been because I wanted to live somewhere where the buildings towered over us and not the mountains. I couldn't have chosen you over your son for any reason but money and position." She looked from father to son and back again, tossing her head in agitation and disgust. "It's easy to live up to expectations when they're like either of yours." Beryl pointed to Maggie who was watching her calmly, letting her have her say. "*She* figured it out."

On that note Beryl spun on her heels and stormed into the house. Dancer laughed his high-pitched cackle as the door slammed behind her. Meredith burbled. Patrick pushed back his hat and scratched his head. "What the hell was that about?" he asked the other hands.

No one answered him. Maggie opened the door for Connor as he helped his father onto the porch and inside. "Take him to his room and get him out of that shirt. I assume the bullet went through."

"Clean through."

"And that Dancer's already taken care of it."

"As best he could."

"All right then," she said. "I'll get my herbs." She started to go, but a hand laid gently on her wrist stopped her. At first she thought it was Connor, then she realized it was Rushton.

"You figured it out?" he said quietly.

Maggie shrugged. "Beryl's giving me more credit than I deserve," she said. "It took me until you rode out this morning."

Rushton shook his head. Even through his pain he managed a rueful smile. "That's more than twelve hours ahead of me."

"She loves you," Maggie said simply. "When you think about it—both of you—you'll realize that it explains everything."

They watched her go. "Wise," Connor repeated softly. "Maggie's wise."

Maggie steeped washes to cleanse the wound and teas to relieve the pain. She showed Beryl how to apply the wash and the balm and let her give Rushton the tea. It was material from one of Beryl's petticoats that was fashioned for Rushton's sling. No one mentioned the lace edging around his elbow when Beryl slipped his arm into it.

Connor came up behind Maggie in the kitchen. She was standing over the stove, stirring clear chicken broth. His arms folded around her and he took her slight weight as she leaned into him. He kissed her lightly on the crown of her head. "Let Beryl do that," he said. "She's enjoying herself."

"So is your father."

"I've noticed." Connor slid his palms along Maggie's ribcage, past the curve of her waist, to her hips, then up again. "I'd like a beautiful woman to pay attention to me," he whispered.

"Beryl's busy."

He gave her a small squeeze, letting her know what he thought of that.

"Your daughter's sleeping."

Connor nuzzled her hair and removed the chicken broth from the stove. "You're the woman I want," he said gently. "And I know just where I want you."

Maggie's protest died away when she turned and saw the loving look in Connor's eyes. "For all time," she returned quietly. "You've got to want me for all time. I won't let you send me away."

The merest flicker of his darkly mirrored eyes gave him away. "How did you know?"

She searched his face, the stoic features that no longer kept secrets from her. She touched the side of his jaw, her thumb brushing just beneath his lower lip. "How could I *not* know?" she asked plaintively.

He reached for her hand, stilling it. His fingers closed around her wrist. He drew it away from her face and toward his side, then he led her out of the house and toward the stable.

Night cloaked the valley. Lantern light flickered from the bunk house. There was a shout of laughter from that direction, followed by Dancer's distinctive cackle. Maggie looked sideways at Connor. "Someone's embellishing your standoff with the rustlers," she said. "I've heard the story from Dancer and Rushton and they're both twists on the truth. No one *really* finishes a shootout because they're hungry."

"If they get hungry enough they do. We were and we did." He saw she didn't quite believe him and Connor was fine with that. He didn't want to talk about killing rustlers or debate western justice. Dancer's random firing into the trees brought down another cattle thief. Buck, in the rear position, wounded still another. Connor wounded two as they scrambled for higher ground and better cover. Surrender of the last uninjured man came quickly after that. Two of the wounded were mere boys, thirteen and fourteen, and even knowing that he'd likely have to face them again as men, Connor let them go. The others hanged.

"It had to be," Maggie said, responding to things left unsaid.

He put his arm around her shoulder and pulled her closer as they walked. "Do you always know the right thing to say?"

"Hardly ever."

"Then maybe it's the way you say it. Your voice is as soothing as one of your special teas."

Maggie thought she liked the sound of that. She kissed him on the cheek as they entered the stable. Connor gave Maggie the lantern to hold as he lit it, then he hung it on a hook by the doors. "Where are we going?" she asked as he began to lead her away from the entrance.

He pointed to the loft and nudged her toward the ladder.

She dug in her heels and gave him a saucy glance. "You're going to tumble me in a hayloft?"

"I certainly hope so," he said feelingly.

Grinning, Maggie hiked up her skirts and climbed the ladder. Connor gave her a boost over the top by palming her bottom and pushing. She obligingly went down in a thick mound of hay. Laughing, she held out her arms to Connor.

He knelt beside her. A rush of emotion left him without a voice for a moment. Her face was simply radiant. She stared at him with eyes that were like twin jewels. Her smile beckoned him. And her laughter cleansed his soul.

His fingers touched her temple. She turned her cheek in to him, rubbing against him in a sensual feline gesture. His hand delved more deeply in the dark coppery fire of her hair. He stretched out beside her, hay cushioning their bodies.

"Love me," he whispered. "Heal me."

She took him into her arms. Into her heart. Then into her. She bathed his face in soft, sweet kisses. Her fingers fluttered along his shoulders. She cradled him with her body. And he gave her pleasure. Her flesh vibrated with sensation as they moved together.

Fierce need drove him into her again and again. She accepted the force of him because her need mirrored his. She wanted to feel him everywhere. His hands in her hair. His mouth on her breasts. She needed to feel him between her thighs, in her and against her.

Her legs wrapped around his flanks. She ground against him. He knelt back, lifted her bottom, looked at their joined bodies, withdrew and plunged into her again. The stab of pleasure was intense enough to make her cry out. Her neck arched, then her entire body.

He absorbed her shudder then let her absorb his. Their flesh seemed to ripple with the aftershock. He collapsed against her, rolling onto his side, then his back, and took Maggie with him, supporting the length of her against him.

She smiled down at him, her teeth flashing briefly before the curtain of her hair blocked the light from below. "Tell me about Beryl," she said huskily.

He blinked, surprised. "You do pick your moments."

Maggie nudged his nose with hers. "Tell me," she said.

Connor shifted so Maggie could slide onto her side against him. He liked the way she kept one leg over his, liked the proprietary air. "I met Beryl in Denver," he told her. "Almost two years ago. She was working in her mother's dress shop."

"And since you needed a dress . . ."

"And since I was walking by the shop on my way to the saloon I happened to see her through the window. I thought she was pretty."

"She's beautiful."

"All right. She *is* beautiful." He noticed that Maggie's expression didn't change. It didn't matter to her that he thought Beryl was beautiful. It was a fact—more simply, an act of nature. "I courted her, brought her and her mother out to the Double H, and—"

"You brought her mother here?" Maggie asked incredulously. "I never knew that."

"You never wanted to hear before, remember?"

Maggie's fingers had been drumming lightly on his chest. They stilled for a moment as she realized there had been times when he wanted to explain. "Go on."

"I was being gallant," he said. "And respectable. Grace came along as Beryl's chaperone."

"Are you saying that you and Beryl never—"

He put a finger across her lips. "No," he said. "I'm not saying that. I wish I could."

It was what she had expected, exactly what she had always thought, but it was still difficult to hear. "You didn't know me then."

"That's right. I didn't even know someone like you existed."

Maggie placed her hand over his heart. "Do you always know the right thing to say?" she asked. She kissed him lightly on the mouth. The kiss lingered a moment.

Connor pulled a piece of straw from her hair as she leaned away again. "Almost never," he said.

She smiled. "What happened then?"

"At Beryl's suggestion I invited Rushton here for the wedding and she ended up marrying him." There was no bitterness in his voice; saying the words without it was a new experience for Connor.

"She fell in love with him," Maggie said softly. "And neither of you could believe it."

"We *refused* to believe it, I think. I know I did. I couldn't accept her choosing my father over me. My pride was battered. I beat his down as well."

"He was still willing to marry her on any terms."

Connor nodded. "But the seed had been planted. He never believed she married him for love."

"She was angry at him for that," Maggie said. "Angry at you both. She became what you expected her to be. Vain. Shallow."

One of his brows rose. His glance was skeptical. "Let's say that she emphasized those traits," he said dryly. "They were certainly there."

"Perhaps," Maggie said. "She's also very clever."

Clever, Connor thought. Yes, it was the right word to describe Beryl. Unlike Maggie. He simply smiled at her, listening.

"She tried to make Rushton understand," she went on. "Tried to make him prove he felt something for her by making him jealous."

"He *was* jealous."

"But he never really let her know that. And she couldn't find any way to tell him how she felt. Then you married me and her dilemma became even more complicated. She couldn't make him jealous if you seemed totally unavailable. If Rushton knew you loved me, *really* loved me, then he could be certain you wouldn't take an interest in Beryl. You had to seem available. She doubled her efforts to get back at both of you."

"I know," he said. "I was there. Through all of it."

Maggie plucked a piece of straw from the mound and traced Connor's lower lip with one end. "Your pride's not stung again, is it, realizing she never wanted you at all?"

His pride *was* stung. "I think she wanted me a little bit," he said, his tone sulky.

Maggie laughed. "I'll scratch her eyes out," she said fiercely, growling playfully as she nuzzled Connor's neck.

He was forced to laugh at himself. That was the secret of Maggie's real healing, he thought. "I believe you would."

"Of course." She laid her head in the curve of his shoulder. "When I saw you with her here in the stable, I almost did."

Connor remembered the coldness in Maggie's eyes on that occasion, the emptiness that had made her expression bleak. "I hurt you. I'm sorry."

"No," she said. "I hurt me. I didn't trust you and that's what hurt me. It frightened me when you left this morning and we hadn't talked about it, even more so when I realized it was Rushton that Beryl truly wanted, and how misplaced my anger was. If anything had happened to you . . ." She didn't finish. She couldn't.

Connor stroked her hair, his fingers sifting through the silky strands. "I was going to make you leave," he said quietly. "And it occurred to me that Beryl might help me drive you out. You were right not to trust me completely. God, Maggie, I want to make you happy."

"That's not your job," she whispered, tears gathering in her eyes. "In fact, the pursuit of happiness is one of *my* inalienable rights." She lifted her head so he could see her face. "I'm happy now," she said. "With you. With Meredith."

"You should be a doctor," he said. "Not a rancher's wife. If I leased some land to Rennie for the railroad we would have the money—"

"I wouldn't go back east without you," she said. "I won't go anywhere without you."

"Then I'll go with you while you study."

"Oh, Connor." She framed his face with her hands. "What a beautiful gesture."

It *was* a gesture, he realized, because they didn't have the money and Maggie didn't have an acceptance from any medical school. "I mean it, Maggie," was all he could say.

"I know you do."

He had to be satisfied with that. Connor turned on his side and fingered the edge of Maggie's chemise. He traced the swell of her breasts. "My mother told my father to leave the Double H," he told her.

It was difficult to think with his hand moving slowly over her skin. "You believe Rushton, then?"

"I have to, don't I? When I realized that I was prepared to do the very same thing to you, it all seemed clear. He said she never once asked him if he wanted to go."

"You've never really asked me," Maggie said. Her breath caught as the heel of his hand passed over her nipple. "But, no, I don't want to go . . . not without you." Her breast seemed to swell in the cup of his hand, stretching the material of her chemise. "Did you ever . . . mmm . . . tell Beryl about the . . . mmmm . . . brothel?"

He liked the way she hummed her pleasure. "No," he said. "She told me you did." He lowered his head as he tugged at her chemise. Her breast was bared. He covered it with his mouth, sucking gently.

"I wonder—" Fire shot through her limbs, tugged at her loins, and brought her hips arching against him. "—how she knew."

Connor had more important things on his mind. He didn't try to respond. In a little while Maggie forgot anything but whispering Connor's name.

By turns they were demanding. By turns they surrendered. They shared kisses, traded caresses. "Your mouth," he said. "Here." And then he drew her down. "Touch me," she said. "There?" he asked. His fingers stroked. "Yes," she whispered. "Just there . . . oh, and there."

Her skin was warm and soft. The hay shifted under them as they moved. Kittens peeked from behind a mound then disappeared again. He raised her chemise to her hips. She opened to him. "Like that?" he asked. She nodded, watching him. "Just . . . like that."

Pleasure drawn so tightly had to snap. Maggie's breath came shallowly, her skin flushed. Connor's heart hammered. Their bodies were faintly damp when they finally parted.

She drew one finger back and forth along his arm as he held her to him. "I like being tumbled," she said.

"I thought you might."

She fell asleep smiling.

*   *   *

Fifteen days came and went before Beryl pronounced Rushton well enough to leave. Over the course of his recovery she had attended to all his needs, eschewing help from every quarter. Watching her come and go, even Dancer was impressed.

Beryl smiled more easily, not a calculated arrangement of her mouth but openly, with genuine amusement that brightened the pale blue of her eyes. Rushton's gaze was most often wondering, like a man struck by good fortune so suddenly he could not quite comprehend it. He saw Connor laughing with Maggie, and knew they were both pleased and amused by the way his eyes followed Beryl as she moved through a room, or stared at her vanishing point the moment she left. The remoteness disappeared from his dark eyes, the lines in his face eased, and once again the resemblance between father and son was striking.

Rushton read a great deal during his confinement. He grumbled there was not much a wounded man could do in bed. His wife took pleasure in showing him otherwise.

Maggie was pleased to see Rushton and Connor talking together, trading ideas about the ranch, about the railroad, about . . . women. Overhearing them on the subject of the latter, she smiled to herself and kept silent. Sometimes it was good to be such a mystery to her husband. Later, she told Beryl what she'd heard and they laughed together until their sides ached.

It was within minutes of their planned departure that Rushton motioned Beryl to step inside their bedroom and shut the door. Packed trunks and valises littered the floor as Beryl stepped carefully around and over them to reach her husband. He was standing by the bedside table, a book in one hand, a letter in the other.

"What have you got there?" she asked.

He handed her the letter. "I was getting ready to return this book to Connor's study. I've never had a chance to read it. That fell out when I was leafing through the pages. You can see it's addressed to Maggie."

She glanced at the letter. "It's from a medical college."

"Read on," he said. "It's dated last April. It must have been slipped into the book then and forgotten. The book was probably stored at her sister's until we brought it out. I'm sure Connor's never seen that letter."

Beryl placed a finger on Rushton's lips. "Let me read," she said, her eyes skimming the contents. Taken aback, she read more slowly the second time:

It is a great pleasure to accept your application to the Philadelphia Medical College for Women. In examining more than one hundred and fifty applications, the admissions board agrees that yours is particularly outstanding. We welcome the opportunity to meet with you and discuss your curriculum and boarding arrangements.

The letter went on, praising Maggie's accomplishments and commitment in having chosen medicine as a profession. Beryl's eyes kept returning to the very first sentence.

"Maggie was accepted," she said softly, raising her face to Rushton. "She turned *them* down, not the other way around."

"It looks that way," he said.

"Who knows about this?"

Rushton shook his head. "I think we do. She's let everyone believe just the opposite, including Connor."

"What should we do?"

"Go on letting everyone believe it, I suppose. It's Maggie's affair. She had her reasons." One of them was napping in a crib in the next room. Rushton took the letter from Beryl, folded it, and slipped it back into the leather bound copy of *Gray's Anatomy,* just the way he found it. "She's had more than her share of interference in her life. Her father . . . me . . . ."

"Me," Beryl said regretfully. She took the book back from him. "Let me think about this."

"Beryl. I don't want—"

She placed one hand on his shoulder, raised herself on tiptoe, and kissed him on the cheek. "Trust me this time, Rush," she said. "I won't interfere. Just the opposite, in fact."

He studied her face. Her eyes were clear and so was Rushton's conscience. "All right." He kissed her lightly on the mouth. "I'm going to tell Connor we're ready to have the wagon loaded." He glanced around the room. "Is this everything?"

Beryl's glance followed her husband's. She nodded, satisfied. "Everything." When Rushton left, Beryl kicked the black leather bag back under the bed.

* * *

Standing on the lip of the porch, Maggie watched Connor say goodbye to his father. Tears gathered in her eyes and she blinked them back at first, then simply let them fall. One of them dripped on Meredith's cheek.

"Let me take her before she drowns," Dancer said.

Maggie gave him a watery smile and handed over Meredith. "I didn't expect to cry," she said.

Dancer snorted, bouncing Meredith lightly in his arms. "Don't know how you expected anything less. Look at 'em. It weren't so long ago that one'd say black and the other white just as a matter of principle." He grinned widely, one side of his scarred face puckering. "Now they disagree 'cause they enjoy it."

As Dancer spoke, Maggie saw Rushton lean down from the wagon and extend his hand to Connor. It was grasped firmly, held, and given up reluctantly. Connor stepped back from the wagon. Maggie could see the emotion in his eyes mirrored in his father's.

Rushton glanced at the house and said roughly, "Where's Beryl?"

The front door opened. "I'm coming," she said, hurrying across the porch. She stopped beside Maggie and held out *Gray's Anatomy*. "I didn't have time to put this away," she said. "Rushton was looking through it last." Her voice dropped to a whisper and her pale blue eyes were earnest. "You may want to think about the bookmark you left in there. Connor would want to know, but it's your decision." Without waiting for recognition or a reply, Beryl thrust the book in Maggie's hands, hugged her hard, then tripped lightly down the steps. Connor helped her into the wagon.

Beryl secured her bonnet, fastening the lavender ribbon beside her cheek. She waved to Meredith, smiled farewell to Dancer, and had something to say to each of the hired hands. Her gaze drifted to the porch where Maggie stood clutching the book. She kept her eyes on Maggie, but her words were for Connor. "If she loves you as well as you love her, I'd say you got what you deserved."

Glancing at his wife, Connor grinned. He took the steps to the porch in a single leap and came to stand beside Maggie. He put one arm around her and pulled her close. "If she loves me half as much, I'd say I still got the better of the bargain."

Embarrassed, Maggie leaned into Connor and merely smiled to herself.

Rushton picked up the reins. "This is it," he said. He looked around again at the trunks, bags, and supplies in the back of the wagon. "Or is it? Beryl? Where's that black case you couldn't let out of your sight on the way here?"

Beryl fiddled with her bonnet ribbon, making adjustments where none was required. "What, dear?"

"That black case," Rushton repeated. "The one that looked like a physician's bag. I think you kept your brushes and combs in it."

"Oh, that thing. Don't worry about it, Rush. I left it for Maggie." She spared a glance for Maggie and Connor on the porch. They were simply staring at her blankly. "I left it under the bed in the guest room," she told them. Beryl took the reins from Rushton's hands and gave them a snap. The team started forward.

The sky was clear. Sunlight had burned off the early morning mist and shone brightly in the valley. The wagon rolled past the stable, the corral, and took the path that followed the stream. No one at the house moved until it was out of sight. Gradually the hired hands drifted back to their work, Luke and Ben to the horses, Buck and Patrick to the cattle. Dancer kept Meredith with him and headed for the kitchen. Connor and Maggie stood together, feeling the tug of separation as a loneliness in their hearts.

"I didn't think I'd miss them," Connor told her, giving Maggie's shoulders a slight squeeze. "Do you remember the day they got here? God, I wanted to run for cover."

"You'll get your chance. It's only a matter of time before Jay Mac and Mama descend on us. They'll probably bring Skye. Then Michael and Ethan and Madison will want to visit . . . and Rennie and Jarret."

Just thinking about it made Connor want to seek out a retreat. "I suppose the best cover is with Mary Francis at the convent."

Maggie laughed.

"What's that that Beryl gave you?"

"Gray's Anatomy," she said. "It's one of my books I left with Michael. She or Rushton were looking at it. I'll put it away." She kept it close to her side, her heart pounding a little erratically. She would tell Connor about the medical college one day, but not now, not when he would have to move heaven and earth to make her dream come true. "Let's go in."

Connor nodded. He waited by the door to the study as Maggie shelved the book. They headed down the hallway again. A few steps on the other side of the bedroom that Rushton and Beryl had used, he stopped. Maggie paused, looking sideways at him.

"What is it?" she asked. Connor's brows were drawn, his dark eyes vaguely unfocused as he looked right past her, deep in thought. "Connor?"

Tugging on Maggie's sleeve, he backtracked to the open doorway. "Do you remember what my father asked Beryl just before they left?"

Maggie was struck by the urgency in his voice. It was completely at odds with what he was discussing. "He asked if she had all her belongings."

"That's right," he said quickly and prompted her again. "And he was looking for . . ."

"Beryl's combs and brushes."

"No!"

"Well, he was looking for the bag they were in."

"That's right!"

"Do I win something?" she asked, bewildered.

Connor's face cleared. He burst out laughing, picked Maggie up, and spun her into the room. "If I'm right, you've won all the money in the kitty." He set her down, steadied her, and dropped to his knees beside the bed. Thrusting his arm beneath the frame, Connor felt around. Suddenly his hand touched what he was looking for, what he was hoping to find. He drew it out slowly, watching Maggie all the while. "All twelve thousand dollars," he said, pulling out the bag.

Amazement stole her breath as Connor opened the black valise. Memories that had only vaguely teased her rushed to consciousness. "Oh, my God," she whispered hoarsely, dropping to her knees. Even her voice was suddenly familiar, the aching whisper of someone who needed help desperately and had depended on this visitor to provide it. Quite without thinking, Maggie touched her throat. "It's like you said before," she told him, "I thought you were a doctor."

He nodded, watching her closely. Her expression was distant as memory drew her backward in time.

"You gave me whiskey," she said slowly. "I thought it was for medicinal purposes."

He vaguely remembered saying something like that. "I wanted you to relax." His breath came easier when he saw her smile was wistful, not accusing.

"I was very relaxed . . . very . . ." Her voice trailed off, then she added on a somber note, "I wanted you."

Connor waited as Maggie let silence stretch between them.

"Afterward I was afraid . . . I was ashamed."

"Maggie," he said gently.

"No. It's all right." Her face cleared as she looked at him directly. "I don't feel that way anymore. But then . . . you have to understand I didn't know what I was doing afterward."

"What are you talking about?"

"That," she said, pointing to the bag. "I never looked inside it. I needed somewhere to hide my nightshift after I got dressed. I stuffed it in there and ran out of Mrs. Hall's with your case. When I got home I threw my clothes and the nightshift in the fire and pushed the bag under my bed, out of sight. The next morning I didn't remember anything about it. Never once, in all this time, did I really believe I took your money."

Maggie's green eyes were filled with regret. "I'm so sorry," she said. "I've never . . . I'm so sorry."

Connor picked up the bag and turned it over. Bundles of paper bills dropped like stones to the floor. He picked up one, untied it, and tossed the money in the air. It burst like a roman candle over their heads then fluttered toward them. When Maggie reached out to catch one, it was her hand that was caught. She was pulled slowly, inexorably toward Connor.

"I'm not," he said.

There was nothing remote about the distinct gleam in his eye.

Epilogue

May 1884

The auditorium was crowded with family—most of it, it seemed, by the same family. That was certainly Connor's point of view when he glanced over the first three rows before he sat down. He picked out Schyler's beacon of red hair immediately as she craned her neck to see the stage and his ears caught Mary Francis's bright laughter. Michael was sitting next to Ethan, her arm curved under his. Beside them, Madison teased her little brother with the end of her pigtails. Rennie and Jarret sat together, separating their young twin daughters on either side. The girls were peeking around their parents, giggling as they communicated with glances and gestures. Rushton was there and Beryl was beside him. He held his three-year-old son in his lap while Beryl surreptitiously fed the boy small pieces of a cookie. John MacKenzie Worth was glancing at his pocket watch, then at the stage, then at his wife. He looked as if he might be about to grumble about the late start of the ceremony, but then his wife touched his hand and smiled gently at him. Anything he was about to say was simply swallowed.

Connor took his seat beside Dancer Tubbs. The prospector was wearing a new suit and a shirt so white he complained it would near blind him before the day was out. Meredith climbed from Dancer's lap onto her father's. Connor helped her straighten her dress.

"Will it be soon?" she asked in a whisper loud enough for two-thirds of the guests to hear.

"Soon," he said, pressing his forehead against hers.

Almost immediately there was a stirring in the crowd as the Dean of the Philadelphia Medical College walked on stage and took his place behind the podium. Silence settled as anticipation held the audience still. Madison stopped teasing her brother, the twins ceased giggling, Beryl put the cookie away, Meredith sat primly, and even Jay Mac Worth was properly subdued.

"Ladies and gentlemen, honored guests . . . it is with great pride that I present the graduating class of 1884."

It was no light, polite applause that attended this announcement. As the curtains swept open and the twenty-three women on the stage were revealed, the auditorium thundered with the crowd's approval.

Looking out from her place on the stage, it seemed to Maggie that most of the thunder came from the first three rows. She saw them all in a single glance: her mother and father, all the Marys, Jarret, Ethan, the nieces and nephews, Rushton, Beryl, Dancer, Meredith . . . then Connor. He held her glance as he applauded her and she was honored by what she saw in his eyes: fierce admiration for her accomplishment.

She wanted to go to him. She wanted to leave the stage and go to him, let him take her in his arms and hold her.

As if from a great distance she heard her name being called. She thought when she stood she would fall, that her legs couldn't support her. Connor would, though. Mentally she reached for him and the answer was there as he leaned toward her. She stood slowly, hesitated, looked to him again. His smile pushed her forward as she walked across the stage and took her place at the podium.

Dr. Mary Margaret Holiday unfolded her notes and began her valedictory speech.

"Come to bed," Connor said, watching his wife with some amusement. "It's been a long day. Or do you want to sleep with that instead?"

A little guiltily, Maggie laid her diploma down. "It's going to take some getting used to," she said, "but I'm not prepared to sleep with it." She turned back the table lamps so only a flicker of light remained and climbed into bed beside Connor, nestling next him. Her hair lay like fiery silk against the pillow. "Sometimes I despaired of this day ever coming," she said quietly. "This afternoon I thought I never wanted it to end. But now, with you here, I'm glad it has." She rubbed her cheek against his chest, stroking his arm idly. "You've given me so much . . . left so much behind . . ." She turned, lifting her face to see him better. She touched his jaw with her fingertip, brushed it along the strongly carved line. "You've weathered four years in the east pretty well, but I'm recommending the Colorado cure."

"The entire state?" he asked, one brow kicking up.

"All the Double H," she said. "Space and silence . . . Meredith doesn't even remember."

"Do you think she'll like it there?"

They had been away four years while Maggie went to school. Connor had left the ranch in Luke's capable hands. Dancer gave up prospecting and stayed on as a cook. Ben and Patrick and Buck remained loyal to their boss in his long absence. There were a few more hands Luke had hired that Connor didn't even know. Leasing the back quarter of the property to Northeast Rail had made the ranch busier than ever. Cattle drives were shorter, civilization closer, but the valley was largely untouched. Maggie had no fears of how their daughter would respond to the breadth of the sky and the lay of the land. "She's every inch her father's daughter. She'll love it."

She said it with such conviction that Connor was forced to believe her. "Did you hear her this afternoon?" he asked. "She was so excited."

"Everyone heard her," Maggie said dryly. "At least I think she was the only child there who interrupted my speech with, 'Is Mama ever going to stop talking?' "

Connor squeezed Maggie's shoulders, chuckling. "You've never been accused of talking too much before."

She had to smile. "Everyone important in my life was there."

"Jay Mac was beaming. You would have thought the entire thing was his idea."

"I'm sure it was . . . in *his* mind." She began stroking his arm again. "It doesn't bother you?"

He shook his head. "I know the truth."

So did Maggie. Connor Holiday had made his magnificent gesture a reality. His long-lost poker winnings bankrolled her education and their home in Philadelphia for the duration of her studies. He argued with her objections until she tripped over herself and mentioned the acceptance she had turned down a year earlier. After that he just ignored her. He knew it was what she wanted and in the end she admitted it to both of them. "Rushton will be sorry to see you go."

"He'll have to find someone else to manage his Philadelphia steel mills."

She tapped him lightly on the arm. "He'll miss you for more than that."

"I know," Connor said after a moment. "It will take some getting used to. I've become accustomed to this arrangement . . . the closeness."

Maggie knew he wasn't merely speaking of geography. She slid one arm across his chest. "You heard him today at the reception—they'll visit us."

Connor kissed the crown of her head. She couldn't see his wicked smile. "Do you realize we'll have to add more rooms to the ranch house?" he asked.

She became very still. "Why is that?" she asked, carefully neutral.

"Because if everyone who said they'd visit, does, we'll be sleeping under the stars ourselves."

She relaxed. "You can't imagine how much I'd like that."

"Hmmm," he said, kissing her again. "I'd like that, too." The pressure of his mouth changed slightly as the kiss lingered, then deepened. "But we should probably still add a room," he whispered against her lips. "For the baby."

Maggie's eyes opened. "Meredith's not a—" She stared at him more intently, saw the hint of laughter in the shape of his mouth and the warmth of his eyes. "How long have you known?"

"A few days."

"I was going to surprise you."

"I'm surprised," he said agreeably. He rolled Maggie onto her back.

Her arms looped loosely around his neck, her fingers threading through the dark hair at his nape. His eyes darkened, touching her with their unwavering intensity. "Love me," she said softly.

He touched her nose with his, his lips a moment away. "Shhh," he whispered. "I don't want a chatterbox."